Mystic Vows

Susan Stitely

PublishAmerica
Baltimore

© 2006 by Susan Stitely.

All rights reserved. No part of this book may be reproduced, stored in a retrieval system or transmitted in any form or by any means without the prior written permission of the publishers, except by a reviewer who may quote brief passages in a review to be printed in a newspaper, magazine or journal.

This is a work of fiction. Names, characters, corporations, institutions, organizations, events or locales in this novel are either the product of the author's imagination or, if real, used fictitiously. Any resemblance to actual persons (living or dead) is entirely coincidental.

First printing

At the specific preference of the author, PublishAmerica allowed this work to remain exactly as the author intended, verbatim, without editorial input.

ISBN: 1-4241-5613-0
PUBLISHED BY PUBLISHAMERICA, LLLP
www.publishamerica.com
Baltimore

Printed in the United States of America

*Dedicated to the Memory of Lost Loved Ones…
Through Cherished Memories They Remain Faraway,
but Forever Within Our Hearts.*

Many past loved ones have influenced my life and continue to dwell in the depths of my mind and the core of my being…until we meet again—God Speed!

And in Honor of my Loving Husband…to have and to hold in this life and the next, as genuine soul mates beyond the Hands of Time.

And to my beautiful daughters…always follow your Hearts and may your Hopes and Dreams surpass a lifetime, for you have surpassed mine.

Acknowledgments

A very special thanks goes out to Stephanie D. Hauserman, Christina M. Heck, Sandy L. Gill, and Charlotte Welsh for offering their time and skills.

An enormous thanks to family and friends– Ruthann & James, Diana & Donald, Jim, Jimmy, Sondra, Patti & Andy, Bobby, Sammi, David, Ricky, Justice, Bobbi Jo, Barbara, Sylvia, Barb & Tony, Janice, and Jody.

And finally, thank you to all the Dedicated Associates at Wal-Mart #5470 & 2230.

Thank you all for many Words of Encouragement and creating a huge Support Structure!

Prologue
Costa Rica—1789

Edmond paced ferociously back and fourth outside his wife's room. His emotions ran high as his gut twisted and knotted in all directions. He hung his head in despair and buried his face within his hands. He knew all to well that this would be her final hour. There was no longer any hope for recovery and they'd soon part for all eternity. Their family hung on by a thread and he remained powerless to prevent the chain of events that led to their bitter demise. Their sons were with her now and he could only imagine what they were discussing behind closed doors. He warned them not to upset her any further and not to, under any circumstances, become hostile with one another in her presence.

Edmond allowed his mind to drift to fonder times, nearly a lifetime ago. He recalled his youthful and wilder days. He never instigated a battle he could not finish or win. He became a fierce adversary in the arena and overpowered his opponents as he overshadowed his merciful heart, for had a pure soul and could not knowingly inflict pain and suffering upon the weak and defenseless. His mother had orchestrated a benefit crusade for charity when he was twenty-two. The campaign consisted of a series of popular events including jousting, archery tournaments, riding and hand-to-hand combat.

Edmond prevailed in every round. He was untouchable in jousting and proved himself as an expert marksman and rider. Before the hand-to-hand combat, his father took him aside.

"The victor of tonight's combat challenge will win Count Consuelo's daughter's hand in marriage; make your mother and I proud, son."

Edmond could not believe his ears as the words echoed throughout his mind; he wondered if this was his chance to win the fair maiden. He never witnessed her beauty first-hand, for few men upheld that privilege. He left his father with his thoughts in disarray. He went for a stroll to clear his mind and crossed paths with a young peasant woman just down the street from the arena. He could not avert his gaze as she sauntered exquisitely.

Edmond never saw such beauty. He suddenly felt undeniable desire and passion for this young woman. Edmond closed his eyes, convinced he simply imagined the young woman who captivated his eyes and stole his heart. When Edmond opened his eyes, the young woman struggled with a rogue who meant to take her innocence. He raced to the rescue and decimated her adversary. Before Edmond could subdue the rogue, the man ran off cowardly. Edmond helped the young woman to her feet.

"Are you all right, my Lady?" he asked, and then apologized for the savage behavior of some men.

The young woman remained silent but felt extremely grateful and silently vowed to reward his heroism. She rendered Edmond speechless as he gazed into the most beautiful green eyes ever bestowed upon him. Suddenly, the contest meant nothing to Edmond as he held her enchanting gaze.

"I promise to bequeath justice if this rogue attempts to show his face again!" Edmond's mercy was his only weakness, that is, until his gaze fell upon her. He silently vowed to court the most beautiful woman in the land—the young woman standing before him. He left hesitantly struggling to uncover the best way to approach his father. One day he would become Lord Edmond Costello. Along with the title came great responsibilities and duties. It was nearly impossible for him to marry a commoner, but he did not care. He knew fate would conquer all. Edmond stopped abruptly, realizing he did not get the beauty's name and quickly returned to the scene of the transgression, but felt disappointment when he learned she already left. He strolled away with a heavy heart and prepared for the challenge.

Edmond entered the combat circle, closed his eyes briefly and then noticed Angelina seated on his right flank next to her father. He narrowed his eyes and thought he could see a glimmer of despair upon her face, even at this distance. Angelina is the beloved daughter of the powerful and revered Count Byron Consuelo. Financially, they would make the perfect match. Angelina was everything he ever dreamed about, and so much more. She had skin of porcelain, a sleek and curvy bodice with long mocha wavy hair. She remained cloaked in innocence throughout her childhood and now, at the tender age of sixteen, every heir in the land sought to claim her as his own. Angelina had also been his dream, but now he had another dream and she had striking green eyes that sparkled in the afternoon sunlight.

For a moment, Edmond forgot where he was. He reeled from his thoughts as his opponent, Lord Devlin Cordoba, entered the combat circle with a thunderous applause. They were the finalists left to compete for the beautiful Angelina. Edmond briefly thought about throwing the fight but his pride would not allow it, for he never lost a battle and was not prepared to stand down now. They began to fight valiantly, blow after blow. Edmond thought Devlin fought courageously. Edmond wielded his sword and sent Devlin plummeting to the ground. Devlin quickly returned to his feet after a brief moment. He regained his bearings as they encircled one another. The two men conveyed their determination through steadfast eyes. Edmond turned from Devlin and focused his attention beyond the crowd.

His blood began to boil when he detected the rogue from earlier. He refused to forsake his vow and took a step towards the crowd, for his thoughts no longer lied with the challenge or the prize at hand. Devlin seized the moment and gave Edmond a ferocious blow to the back of the head. The blow forced Edmond to the ground but he quickly leapt to his feet. His head ached and his vision blurred but he was still able to locate the rogue.

He quickly left the confines of the ring and forced his way through the crowd. Everyone gazed at him in awe, as he ran with intent. Edmond tackled the rogue to the ground, continued to beat the man senseless, and stood up triumphed. He smiled, completely pleased with himself. He told the crowd what he witnessed earlier that day and they applauded his heroism. Edmond was well aware that he broke the rules of engagement and bowed honorably as he gracefully renounced the challenge, naming Lord Devlin Cordoba the victor.

He glanced over at Count Consuelo and the prizewinning Lady and found complete shock upon their faces, especially on Angelina's. Edmond watched, as she appeared to become faint, "Probably from all the excitement," he whispered. He immediately left to find his true prize, his mystery damsel. He searched for three painstaking hours with no prevail. She appeared to vanish from the kingdom without a trace.

Edmond returned home with a heavy heart, for he was certain his father would forgive his actions with the mysterious beauty by his side. He hoped his father would understand why he chose this path—while forsaking another. He drew in a deep breath and held his head high as he entered the great room. Edmond nearly gasped when he saw his father standing beside Count Consuelo. He could not fathom the meaning.

"We are glad you could join us son," his father proclaimed.

Edmond remained silent as he assessed the situation.

"I come to you under extraordinary circumstances," Byron said. Byron gazed upon Edmond with sheer delight. "You, Edmond Costello, have won the challenge today!"

Edmond shook his head and reminded the Count that he broke the rules of engagement by leaving the combat ring.

Byron waved his hand aside, completely dismissing that fact. "In my mind, you are the rightful man for my daughter's hand," he nearly demanded. Before Edmond could reply, Byron motioned for his silence. Edmond, completely taken off guard, obeyed the Count's wishes. The great room fell silent before Byron began, as he met Edmonds gaze and gave an earnest smile.

"My daughter approached me tonight with a terrifying confession and described an incredible tale of heroism wrought with danger. It has come to my attention that Angelina sought out a day of adventure and freedom before her betrothal. She dressed as a peasant woman and, with no thoughts of the consequences, left the safety of the palace. A rogue seized her with intent to harm, as a hero raced to her rescue. You were that hero today, Edmond. You rescued my daughter from an unruly rogue and you kept the vow you made to her, even when faced with defeat. I would be proud to call you son!"

Edmond stared at Count Consuelo with wide eyes, "What about Lord Cordoba?"

"I will handle Lord Cordoba and smooth all political ties."

Edmond wondered if this was a dream, for it nearly sounded too good to be true. During his bewilderment, Angelina stepped into the room. Edmond knew it was unmistakable as he gazed into those familiar green eyes. He never fully understood why she chose to confess and vowed whatever he had done to do again ten times over. He recalled becoming deeply lost within her eyes each night. They shared a passion that many dream of but rarely find. He remembered how proud he felt the day they became Lord and Lady Costello.

The announcement echoed throughout the entire land for all to hear. Angelina held many mysteries within her grasp. He never judged or questioned her actions; he merely loved her more for them. Later, a grander force bestowed two heirs upon them. Enrico was first born and then Antonio followed making their family complete, but the years that followed were hell on earth.

"Mother wished to speak to Enrico in private," Edmond heard a voice whisper. Edmond's eyes moistened as Antonio reeled him from his thoughts. Antonio touched his arm as they both felt the inevitable drawing near.

Edmond nearly gazed at his son with contempt but quickly averted his eyes, for this was neither the time nor the place for malevolent thoughts. Edmond could not help but wonder where he failed as a father.

The family slowly decayed from an evil he could not comprehend and he watched helplessly as their world turned upside down. He thought how peaceful life once was and vowed to cherish the fonder memories. Edmond wondered if Enrico could handle the truth and carry the family burden. Their futures now rested in his son's hands.

Edmond knew his eldest son was more like Angelina. Enrico may have his suntan complexion and jet-black hair but possesses her munificent heart. Her blood coursed through his veins. Enrico inherited her breathtaking green eyes and her naturally generous spirit. His heart told him if anyone could save them from their servitude, it was Enrico. He realized, when the boys were still young, that Enrico and Antonio were as different as night-and-day.

Enrico upheld a pure soul while Antonio's soul remained tarnished. Antonio became a disgrace and Edmond knew his heart maintained hatred and jealously towards his brother. Antonio made it very clear that he loathed Enrico in every way. The only virtuous quality Antonio possessed in his blackened soul was patience. His patience knew no bounds and Edmond believed this made Antonio even more dangerous. Edmond closed his eyes and returned his thoughts to Enrico.

Enrico's heart knew no bounds and still could not find true happiness as Edmond wished for him. The same kind of happiness he has found with Angelina. Enrico did come close once, Edmond recalled, as his expression grew dim. He could not bring himself to relive that terrible nightmare—not again. Now, there was no chance for Enrico to find contentment unless he could destroy the mystical realm about to imprison them. Enrico's world was about to change forever, shattering at his feet that would take an eternity to piece together again. Edmond's heart sank as he felt Angelina slip away. A few moments later, Enrico exited her room pale and stupefied. Edmond knew Enrico finally fully understood the magnitude of his birthright. Enrico alone would bear the mysterious legacy and Edmond knew he would do it honorably.

Chapter 1
The First Encounter

    Hannah walked Bandit down Cold Springs Lane, as she did most days like this, and allowed her mind to wander. Bandit is a brown and white German Shepard mix with black paws, adopted from the local animal shelter. He was four months old when they brought him home on May 12, 1990. As Hannah thought back, she recalled how furious her father became when she ran into the house as Bandit trailed behind. He stated that he was not a dog lover and never would be. To him, dogs were bothersome creatures that demanded too much attention and upkeep. Her mother worried about her though and thought a puppy was just the answer, for Hannah spent most of her days, back then, locked up in her bedroom with her nose in a book. Eventually, her father caved in and Bandit nestled into their family nicely.

    Hannah had to move her beloved pet outside six months ago and they forbade her to bring him back into the house because her nephew was allergic to canine dander. Hannah recalled the sadness in Bandit's eyes the first night she left him outside all alone. Many times, she felt Bandit was her only friend and could not withstand the loneliness that crept into her soul late at night, for Bandit always nestled at the foot of the bed. Not only is Bandit a friend, he has also been her soul confidant and a good listener these past two years. She told Bandit about her day as he cocked his head to one side, wagged his tail and nuzzled her leg, as though he understood. She told him about her hopes and dreams. Even in school, Hannah has always been a loner, for she does not have many friends. Hannah is an unpretentious girl from a large family with one older brother, one older sister and one younger sister.

    She was born and raised in the small Pennsylvania town of Greenville. Throughout Hannah's childhood, most of her friends have been boys and she always received a cold shoulder from female classmates. Hannah came to think that she was not good enough for them and began to believe they were actually better than she was. It took years for Hannah to realize they were actually jealous of her. Apparently, she drew attention away from them. She could not fathom why the girls were jealous of her. Only one of her male friends was available, but not desirable. Many had the reputation as rebellious. However, she did enjoy the company of two of her classmates.

One is her best friend, Austin, who has a girlfriend in a neighboring school district. The other is a boy who lives down the road, but his family despises hers. Hannah shuddered at the thought. She is from a rather dysfunctional family. Her oldest sister, Jenna, had a baby as a teenager, married Clayton Campbell and all three reside at home. Her brother, Jacob, joined the Navy in 1990 and left for Germany after completing basic training. Hannah's younger sister, Kayla, is always preoccupied with friends, for she is extremely popular and well liked in school. Someone in the household is always on the go and they rarely share a family moment. Hannah relishes the private moments when she ventures out for an after school walk, alone, with Bandit.

Her mind continues to drift, as she turns and strolls back down the rarely driven road. Hannah dreams of adventure somewhere else, anywhere other than Greenville. Greenville is a small rural community with a population of eighty. Therefore, she is a dreamer of far off lands and unspoken adventure, with danger lurking around each corner. Hannah would give anything for a forbidden lusty rendezvous, for she is a romantic fool. Something within the far reaches of her soul suggests there is more to life than this humble existence. She longs for sultry night walks along the beach or finding herself entwined in a love triangle between two dashing adversaries dueling to preserve her honor and win her affections. Her heart pound uncontrollably as the duel ends and the victor takes her into his overpowering arms. Something always reels her from her thoughts and she sighs, "Until next time!"

She also dreams of being outspoken, beautiful and venturesome. Austin had called her beautiful once. It is a memory she will carry forever. After they had finished analyzing his relationship, he nudged up against her and said, 'You're the funniest and most beautiful girl I know.' She had smiled and said, 'With one exception.' She hardly thought of herself as being beautiful. She is barely eighteen. Hannah is slender with long blond hair, which she absolutely despises. She wishes she had thick curly hair, like Kayla. Her breasts developed earlier than those of her female classmates. She has a perfect hourglass figure and men whistle when she passes by. Still, beauty is not a word in her vocabulary because self-esteem is something she has to work on.

Hannah woke up for school to the sound of the alarm clock pounding in her head. She did not get any sleep, for she spent most of the evening dreaming—again. "Another wonderful night and another horrible day," she whispered. Hannah heard her sisters begin to bicker down the hall.

"Step aside, I need the mirror!" Jenna screamed at Kayla.

Then she heard Caylob, her nephew, wake up and begin to wail for his morning breakfast. Hannah knew there was no use fighting for the bathroom, for it had already imprisoned two intruders. She always thought of captivating ways like this to help inspire her mornings. Hannah made due with a small mirror in her bedroom and did the best she could with her long straight hair. She ended up pulling it back into a ponytail, making her appear much younger then eighteen. She trudged downstairs and found her mother, Rebecca, feeding Caylob in the kitchen.

"You better grab a bite to eat before the bus comes," Rebecca exclaimed.

Hannah obeyed as usual and went to the front porch to await the bus. She waved to her father, Brian, and Clayton as they left for work. Brian is head sawyer at Greens Lumber Mill and Clayton is a lumber grader there. Clayton is determined to save up enough money to purchase a small house for his family after Jenna graduates from high school this year. Hannah respects Clayton because he is responsible and remains dedicated to his family. Sometimes she felt he deserved better.

The last two trickled down from the woodwork moments later. Hannah smiled to herself, rather amused by her antics. Jenna came out all dolled up with big hair, tight clothes and a layer of make up upon her face. Kayla apparently lost the battle in the upstairs dungeon, for she looked rather plain. Hannah thought she looked prettier though and flashed a warm smile. Although they never discussed it, Hannah wondered if Kayla felt the same as she did. *Surely, Kayla must feel there is more to life, something more exciting.*

Hannah narrowed her eyes and saw their bus approaching. She grinned and whispered, "Once again the warden closes in to take us to prison." Neither of her sisters commented about the remark so she assumed they did not hear her. The Greenville High School sits two miles down the road, which meant a short bus ride. It did not give Hannah enough time to finish exploring an exotic escapade and the bus arrived just as she reached a juicy part. After arriving, her sisters went their separate ways and Hannah stood, once again, at her locker. She smiled warmly when she noticed Austin waiting nearby. *He must have waited for at least ten minutes.* Austin's friends surrounded him and Hannah noticed as they watched him curiously.

Austin kept glancing over his shoulder and knew his friends could not fathom why. He caught a glimpse of Hannah out of the corner of his eye. He immediately left the group and walked over to her with a sparkle in his eye.

"How was your night?"

She flashed him a grin, "It was fine, just fine," she replied, as the bell rang. Austin watched Hannah turn and just like that, she was out of sight. Hannah said that things were fine, but Austin did not believe her. He thought he heard sadness in her voice. In that instance, he promised to love her forever. If there were a remote chance of being with her, he would break it off with his current relationship.

After the bell, Hannah went straight to homeroom. Most of her school days are devoted to daydreaming. Hannah is a good student and received straight A's since the Fourth grade. She repeated the Fourth grade and since then has felt the need to prove herself. During second period, she overheard some female classmates talking about a female Senior removed from school premises during first period for fighting. They whispered amongst themselves and stole glances back at her. Hannah instantly realized they were speaking of Jenna. Things like this did not make it easy for her. Even though Hannah got straight A's, the teachers never saw her as anything but Jenna Campbell's younger sister. Jenna upheld one of the worst reputations in school and maintained a D average, while keeping up with her rebellious and promiscuous ways. To make things worse, she is married with a baby. This was not the proper behavior of a typical mother and the teachers ate it up. Hannah sighed to herself, for she knew it would not be a pleasant evening at home.

Austin joined her for lunch and smiled as he sat down. These are the moments she cherished the most at school. Today was exceptional because they did not discuss *her*. The name never came up and Hannah felt rather pleased with that. The remainder of the day flew by quickly. Before long, the bus dropped her and Kayla off at home and they could hear the chaos coming from the house.

Hannah quickly flashed Kayla an annoyed look; "I'm taking Bandit for a walk!" Kayla understood and nodded, "Don't worry; I'll take care of it!"

Hannah found herself alone, once again, with her only friend. Best of all, it was quiet and easy to become lost in thought. It was like visiting heaven for a while during this breezy fall afternoon. Fall was her favorite season because it was not hot or cold. Things were tranquil, at least, until she heard a vehicle approaching in her direction. She pulled Bandit off the road, as the car raced by. Hannah flinched. *Slow down*, she screamed within her mind. She has never been outspoken, even at times like this. She always gritted her teeth and took what life threw at her. She then heard the car stop and turn around. The car approached slowly this time around, as it crested the hill. It was a new shiny black Corvette. Normally she would not be interested, but Jacob had wanted a Corvette since he was sixteen. She remembered how he used to keep calendars of Corvettes in his bedroom and always referred to the Corvette as the greatest American muscle car.

Hannah felt a little nervous as the vehicle paused briefly and then pulled up along side her. She gave Bandit the command to sit and he obeyed. The window rolled down slowly and inside she noticed two men in their mid twenties. She could not fathom what they wanted but managed a sincere smile and asked, "Do you need directions?" She thought the driver whispered, "I think I just found heaven." The car moved forward slowly and parked along the shoulder. The driver stepped out and now stood directly in front of her. He was tall with broad shoulders and jet-black hair, slightly curly in the back.

The stranger adorned black jeans and a buttoned up long sleeve black shirt. He chose to leave a few buttons undone, revealing part of his muscular chest. His shirt appeared to hug his biceps. Hannah made no immediate observations of his eyes, for he wore mirrored black shades. He stared for a while and then removed his sunglasses. *Oh God*, she nearly murmured. She instantly became lost in his eyes for a few moments, maybe longer. She lost all concept of time now.

His eyes were the deepest emerald green. His gaze finally captured hers and for a split second, she felt unknown longing and desire. Reality of who she was came rushing back. Hannah's thoughts began to jumble and she finally concluded that he knew nothing of her background. With a smile, Hannah decided to seize the moment, for she always dreamed of being someone else and now had the perfect opportunity to truly become another. She turned up the charm and flashed a warm seductive smile. The stranger instantly returned her smile.

First appearances can be deceiving, but he sensed there was more to this blazing beauty than what meets the eye. He spoke in a strong soft tone and explained that he is from out of town.

"Out of the country to be exact!" he quickly noted, and then explained that he was in town visiting distant relatives. He instantly became intrigued with the young woman standing before him and decided to go to great lengths until he acquired her name. Only in his wildest dreams did he imagine ever meeting someone so beautiful and so innocent. He secretly began to desire her the first moment their eyes met. He would not allow himself to deter, even though he fully understood the magnitude of her identity. He crossed his arms over his broad chest, incoherently protecting himself, as he threw caution to the wind.

As they talked, Hannah stunned herself when she became a colorful, spontaneous woman. She no longer felt like a girl and even blushed when she caught herself flirting. Hannah knew this type of behavior was completely out of character for someone with her personality. Something inside her longed for attention from the stranger standing before her. An unknown force urged her to close the gap between them. She quickly dismissed the voice inside her head and secretly fell head over heals. His accent became sensual bliss to her ears. Hannah could barely contain herself and felt her cheeks strain with each smile, for they were not accustomed to such activity. She pondered her thoughts for a moment and wondered if he could sense the impact he had over her. He conveyed his status with each word he spoke.

"My colleagues are holding a social gathering tonight in my honor at their Hacienda."

Hannah nearly gasped. *He must be of Spanish origin.* Her eyes drifted to his chest and her cheeks flushed. She silently marveled at the way he pronounced the word, *hacienda.*

Hannah immediately began to daydream about his exotic countryside; away in a day and forever lost to the only life she has ever known. Reality came rushing back as he lightly touched her arm with his hand. He knew that she drifted away in her mind and allowed her a brief moment, but only a moment. He flashed a smile and invited her to attend tonight as his special guest.

She smiled and mused, "I am sorry Sir, for I don't even know your name!" Her heart and mind conflicted with one another. Her heart silently yearned to accept the invitation while her mind rejected.

"I'll tell you mine if you tell me yours," he murmured.

He offered his hand and Hannah reluctantly declined the offer.

"My name is Enrico, my Lady."

Enrico captivated her with his distinguished and confident demeanor. Talking to him was like taking a step back in time. Hannah desperately wished she could converse with him in his native tongue. She drew in a deep breath and exhaled slowly, "Sir, my name is Savannah," she replied, as the sunlight danced across her deceitful eyes.

He took her delicate fingers into his and pressed his warm wet lips against her dainty hand. Hannah felt feverish and her heart beat wildly, as he tilted his chin and met her gaze with his brilliant emerald eyes.

"It is a pleasure to make your acquaintance, Savannah," he spoke softly and slowly, allowing the name to roll off his tongue. "So, now we are no longer strangers," he said, and once again asked for her presence tonight as his special guest.

She reveled at his accent, and interest. Without giving it another thought, she agreed.

"Then I will pick you up at your Haci…your home," he stammered.

"You may pick me up right here, Enrico."

"As you wish, my Lady. I shall have to leave you for now, until tonight then," he said, in a confident tone.

Hannah's heart began to race, for evening allowed her a far better chance to consider such a proposition. Before departing, Enrico leaned down and patted her dog. "*Hello Bandit,*" Hannah thought he whispered. She dismissed the thought immediately for it would have been impossible for him to know Bandit's name, for she did not recall saying it in his presence. Enrico stood and gazed into her baby blue eyes.

"Does eight O'clock sound alright, my Lady?"

"Eight O'clock sounds fine."

Enrico told her to dress casual, then, as quickly as he drove into her life, she watched him drive away. All of a sudden, she felt as though she was in a different league—his league. Hannah was all beside herself and wondered if she daydreamed their encounter. She sighed and speculated whether he would even show up tonight. Although Hannah could not say for certain, something in his tantalizing eyes told her he would return. The only thing she felt certain of was she would return to find out, one way or another.

Hannah decided she had no more time to reflect on the matter and needed to return home to prepare. She strolled into the backyard and tied up Bandit. She leaned down, gave him a hug and planted a kiss upon his head. "This is just between us boy."

Bandit nudged her leg with his cold wet nose. Hannah took the notion as an approval and it warmed her heart. As Hannah stood, she heard shouting coming from behind and then heard the back door slam. She turned and noticed Jenna standing on the porch crying. She glanced over her shoulder and saw her father's car approaching. *Oh, if they were only aware of the whirlwind about to encircle them.*

Rebecca opened up the back door with piercing eyes. "Hannah, come inside!"

Hannah did as instructed, foreseeing an unfavorable outcome. She noticed how exhausted her mother looked. Her parents and Clayton would want to speak to Jenna outside, in private.

"Mom, she called me white trash. What was I supposed to do, walk by saying that's cool?" Jenna tried to explain.

Once inside, Hannah looked at Kayla with a hopeless expression, "So what did I miss?" she asked, not really meaning it as a question.

Kayla did not respond, but rolled her eyes instead. Kayla's expression was priceless. The drama is almost unbearable for Hannah. She quietly marched upstairs on a secret mission. As usual, no one seemed to notice her grand escape. *If only tonight could be this easy.* She quickly concluded that disappearing tonight should be effortless, for she dreamt about it nearly every night but never had a reason to go through with it, until now.

Although Hannah is eighteen, she is still a Junior in High School and her parents continue to keep her under lock and key to prevent her from making the same mistakes as Jenna. Hannah knew tonight would make the difference between fantasy and reality. She still held onto the notion that Enrico may not show up. She quickly dismissed the thought reminding herself that he would be there. Hannah glanced at the clock and saw it was almost six-thirty. She quickly made her way down the hall and slipped into Jenna's room. She was mindful not to disturb Caylob, asleep in his crib, and quietly raided Jenna's closet.

Jenna accumulated a large selection of mature sexy clothing. Hannah managed to find a suitable ensemble and then helped herself to some make up. When Hannah finished, she went back to her room to pack the items and conjured up an excuse for leaving. After tempers died down, she approached her mother.

"Mom, I have something to ask you," Hannah said, with a spark of delight in her tone.

Rebecca looked at her intently with questioning eyes. This was rather unusual, for Hannah never spoke to her about anything these days. Hannah explained she met one of her female classmates, Kirsten, along the road while walking Bandit.

"We have so much in common and she asked if I could sleep over tonight. May I?"

Rebecca's eyes widened, as she wondered if Hannah finally found her first female friend. Under normal circumstances, she would ask a million questions. But the dispute she just encountered left her feeling exhausted. Rebecca quickly noticed a duffle bag in the corner of the hallway. She eyed up Hannah and simply said, "Have fun; I see you already packed an overnight bag."

Hannah smiled and seized the bag as she embraced self-determination. Rebecca could not remember the last time she saw Hannah so excited about something and then recalled Hannah had the same facial expression the day they adopted Bandit, nearly two years ago. Rebecca sighed knowing her younger daughters deserved more attention than her days allowed. She heard Caylob begin to cry upstairs and did not give Hannah another thought.

Chapter 2
The Ring of Eternity

Hannah walked down the street grinning in self-satisfaction. She knew it would be easy, although she hated to deceive her mother. She also believed no one would miss her in the household tonight. Hannah glanced at her watch and noticed it was nearly seven O'clock. She still had an hour to change and make herself presentable. Surprisingly, she remained calm considering what was about to happen. Hannah paused for a brief moment. *What is about to happen?* She did not consider what the evening held in store for them, especially now that it spilled over into the morning light.

Hannah felt a cold chill as she stood in the same place where she encountered Enrico earlier. Her thoughts stilled as loud noises surrounded her. Her heart pounded rhythmically to the sounds as she felt her breath slip away. A moment later, her mind quieted and she continued walking. *It's only cold feet!* She shrugged those feelings away as she approached a worn ATV trail that lead to an abandoned strip site. She reached her destination and the time has come to unleash her alter ego, Savannah.

Hannah knew she would not have to follow the trail far, just out of site from the road. She set her bag down and shuddered, for this was the first walk she took alone since Bandit came into her life. A piece of her felt as though she betrayed his loyalty. She pushed the thought aside and tried not to think about it again. Hannah refused to feel guilty because for once, she decided to do something for herself for a change—even if she did not know exactly what that entailed yet. Hannah knew she would have to hurry before it became dark. She positioned a small mirror on a branch, removed her shoes and socks and then slipped off her jeans. Hannah quickly glanced around. She had the strangest notion that someone watched her, as she stood there half-naked.

Impossible. Hannah smiled as though there were eyes upon her, for Savannah was not modest by any means.

She slid the pantyhose up each leg and around her waist. She pulled up a black mini skirt that hugged each curve. It was five, maybe six inches to short in her opinion.

"You only live once, right?" she asked aloud.

"Right!" she replied.

It amused her to answer her own question. Hannah fidgeted in her bag, removed a pair of black high-heeled stilettos and slipped them on her feet. She never wore stilettos before and nearly lost her footing. She laughed, as she caught her balance, and imagined falling into Enrico's massive arms. It was a seductive thought on her behalf. She took out a small jewelry box and carefully removed a delicate gold anklet. She clasped it around her right ankle. Hannah was now pleased with the bottom half.

She pulled off her cotton T-shirt and folded it neatly in the bag. She removed a white silky long sleeved shirt that adorned a long layer of ruffles at the end of each sleeve. The shirt was slightly longer in the back and stopped just above the naval in the front. It accentuated her breasts with a few buttons up the front. She wished for a full view of herself but made do with the small mirror. *Beggars should not be choosey.* Hannah ran a brush through her long blonde silky hair but was not pleased and decided to pull it up in a bun, which looked rather classy. It was time for the rest of her jewelry. She rummaged through the bag but the matching necklace and earrings she packed were not there. Hannah sighed as she realized they sat upon her dresser.

Hannah was ready for make up and recalled her mother's words, 'When it comes to make up, less is more.' She completed the look with a light powder finish, sparkling jade eye shadow, mascara and a hint of rouge upon her lips. She checked her watch and drew in a deep breath. Enrico should arrive in ten minutes. The timing was truly perfect. Hannah decided not to wear her watch because she wanted to lose all concept of time tonight. She tossed it into the bag, along with the remainder of her belongings, and zippered it closed. She picked it up and began walking back towards the road. Before she rounded the final bend, she noticed a black limousine parked on the shoulder of the road.

She gasped, "Is that for me?" Hannah paused, knowing this was the final moment to turn and walk away. She realized how fast the chain of events occurred that led up to where she stood. Her knees felt weak as her heart pounded uncontrollably. *What am I walking towards?* The reality of the situation remained an unknown. Her thoughts became an array of mixed emotions. She could not decide whether she walked towards an adventure, a fantasy, or the stranger. After careful consideration, Hannah convinced herself that she walked towards all three. With that decided, she flashed a warm inviting smile and stepped forwards to pursue the unknown. As she approached the limo, the driver stepped out and opened the rear door. He took her bag, placed it in the trunk and waited for her to step inside. Hannah glanced in the doorway but all she could see were black slacks.

She carefully climbed into the limo and immediately smiled at Enrico as their eyes met. She positioned herself beside him and allowed her knee to rest against his. Enrico returned her smile and flinched. He then flashed a smile twice as big feeling rather pleased, for he noticed she did not adorn any jewelry. With that knowledge, he leaned down and pulled out a small box, draped in metallic emerald gift-wrap, tied with a black silken ribbon. Enrico held it delicately as though it may break within his strong hands. He sat silently for a moment staring at it intimately and then handed it to Savannah, along with his heart. His heart told him that he made the right decision. Hannah accepted the gift with a sincere smile.

"Enrico, you shouldn't have."

Enrico knew damn well he should not, but temptation got the best of him.

Hannah carefully removed the gift-wrap and held a jewelry box. She opened it and gasped as she stole a quick glance at Enrico. She noticed he looked rather pleased. In her hand, she held a beautiful matching emerald necklace, earrings and a ring. The ring adorned a brilliant emerald with a cluster of diamonds surrounding it. Hannah thought it was too much, undecided whether or not to accept such a gift. After a moment of contemplating, she made a decision.

"They're beautiful Enrico, thank you, but I couldn't possibly accept such a gift."

Hannah leaned in and gave him a thank you hug. It became obvious that Enrico expected such a reaction, as he returned her embrace warmly.

"Your welcome," he whispered, and then kissed the nape of her neck.

Hannah blushed as tingles ran down her spine.

"May I put them on you?"

"Yes you may."

Hannah turned and Enrico clasped the necklace around her neck. As she turned to face him, he slipped the ring upon her finger. It was a perfect fit. He left her put on the earrings and as she finished, he took her hands into his and whispered, "I hope you like them, for you wear them well."

Before she could answer, he leaned back and became comfortable. Then, with his index finger, gave a come-hither gesture. For once, she wanted to obey and slid into his warm inviting arms. If he was trying to seduce her, it was working. In that moment, the girl everyone knew was lost to the world as she became Savannah. She could not say how far they traveled or the location of the hacienda and she did not care, for that was irrelevant. There were greater proposals at hand.

Enrico had a million thoughts racing through his mind. He had to be careful and patient. He decided to play it cool and follow wherever she led him and then, where her experiences lacked, he would assume the lead. He knew she did not understand the significance of accepting the emerald ring, but she would learn the consequences in time. Enrico could not help feeling there was more to this voluptuous young vixen then anticipated. Seeing her and being with her took every ounce of his being to keep from taking what is rightfully his and making love to her right here, right now. He felt her tremble and heard her whimper as he slipped his hand inside her blouse and caressed her warm firm breast. This was all the pleasure he would allow himself—a mere crumb before the feast. He gently kissed her neck.

"We're here," he whispered, as he removed his hand from her blouse.

Hannah adjusted her blouse. "Where is here?"

Enrico heard concern in her voice and replied quickly, "At the Hacienda."

The car stopped briefly but then continued and Hannah noticed a massive gate as they passed through.

"Enrico, am I dressed appropriately?"

Concern now escalated into fear and Enrico answered honestly.

"No woman has ever looked more exquisite."

He hoped to calm her nerves. He knew it was merely fear of the unknown and that she would become familiar with her surroundings soon enough. She realized how vague he remained about their whereabouts and concluded that it created additional intrigue and mystery this way. The car stopped and moments later the driver opened Enrico's door. He stepped out and helped her to her feet. Hannah nearly gasped aloud, as she viewed the front of the *hacienda*. It was a mansion, even larger if that was possible.

"Are you nervous?" he asked, and then gently squeezed her hand in an attempt to reassure that everything would be fine.

Hannah remained silent as they walked up a stairwell that opened to a grand balcony. Positioned in the center of the balcony was a set of double doors.

"Are you ready?" he asked, as he led her towards the entrance but then paused and added, "Wait here for a moment."

Hannah did as instructed and Enrico strolled over to the door attendant. Enrico whispered softly as the door attendant stole a glance at her with wide eyes. Enrico walked back, took her hand, bowed and then kissed it ever so gently.

"The time has come," he stated, as he led her to the grand entrance.

Time for what? Hannah had no time to reconcile her thoughts. Enrico grasped her hand firmly.

"Do not panic," he whispered, as they passed through the formal entryway to the sound of their arrival announcement.

"Lord and Lady Costello," Hannah heard the door attendant bellow. Nothing could have prepared her for this.

"What," she nearly cried, but it was too late. She watched as their audience rose and gave them a thunderous applause and then raised their Champaign glasses to toast their arrival. Enrico gazed into her eyes and found confusion deep within.

"Only for tonight," he whispered, and then smiled.

Hannah thought he added, "*And for all eternity.*" They walked down the grand stairwell and stepped onto the Ballroom floor. Enrico turned to meet her blue eyes and discovered she desperately searched for answers as he held her gaze. Tonight would last forever in his mind, for it was the first night he held his Lady Costello.

"Will you dance with me?"

Just then, the Troubadour began to play a Spanish ballade. Hannah heard the music begin as Enrico closed the distance between them. He held her tightly assuming the lead. She pressed her chin against his cheek.

"I can't dance to this music."

"Yes you can. Feel the music and allow me to lead you."

They began to dance rather erotically as he secretly attempted to seduce her. Enrico turned and twirled her; it was the most sensual and erotic experience she ever encountered. Hannah closed her eyes and began to feel the music within her soul and the steps magically came to her. Slowly at first, but then they were mystically sweeping across the hardwood floor. Enrico paused and tilted his chin down as she tilted hers up. His mouth fell inches from her full moist lips. He could nearly taste her now. They stood there facing one another as her right shoulder lingered below his right shoulder. His left hand held her right hand firmly. Simultaneously, their free hands felt for the others right chest. Their gaze remained steadfast, held captive by the others eyes and heartbeat. They became frozen in time, for neither one could move a muscle. Enrico wanted her immediately and every instinct asked what he waited for.

They slowly encircled one another in sync to each beat of their hearts. Hannah felt his pulse quicken as seconds turned into minutes. Enrico could not hold out any longer. He remained a gentleman and sent her into a spin. When Hannah returned to him, her back rested against his chest briefly before he spun her around and slid his knee between her thighs. Enrico dipped her as he rocked back and fourth to the rhythm of the music. Hannah began to breathe heavily and for a moment, she felt as though her feet never touched the floor. All of her senses were completely in tune to him as the music ended. Neither one realized that their audience now encircled them. Those seated, now stood to give them a standing ovation. Enrico began to perspire and his black hair glistened under the fluorescent lighting. He leaned down, took her face into his strong hands and kissed her lips, both forceful and tender. There tongues did the dancing now.

When they finished, he kissed her hand and said, "I do not wish to stay long." Everything happened so quickly that Hannah had no time to collect her thoughts, nor did she want to. She knew she would remain forever lost in the moment. Only one thought lingered within her mind. *What did Lord and Lady Costello mean?*

Enrico released her from her thoughts. "We should mingle for awhile and pay our respects to our host and hostess."

With that said, they were in amongst the crowd. They were at the peak of formalities. Enrico handled all introductions, as each man kissed Hannah's hand briefly. Nobody lingered for long, for they knew she was with him and he kept a watchful eye upon her. Enrico remained protective as though she was a delicate possession.

After paying their respects, they left the ballroom and made their way upstairs. Hannah wondered where they headed, as they walked hand-in-hand. His thumb caressed her knuckles—sending tingles up her arm. They came to a long hallway.

"Not much farther," he whispered, and then came to a halt in front of a beautifully detailed Oak door.

The door appeared to be more than a century old. Hannah knew they reached his bedchamber when he opened the door. She stood inside and gazed at the most beautiful series of rooms she ever encountered. Hannah turned when Enrico locked the door.

"So we won't be disturbed, my Lady," he whispered, and then walked into the next room with a massive fireplace. Enrico lit a fire and took exceptional care to tend to every detail. He dimmed the lights and called out, "Savannah, come and sit." He knew that it was wrong to call her by this name, but tonight was their night. Right or wrong, it was their night to shine, for they may never have this moment again.

Hannah glanced about the room and felt as though she stepped back into the early eighteenth century. She walked over to the armoire and slid her fingers across the wood grain. Even the tall bedposts were hand carved and intricately detailed in every way. She stood in front of a large mirror and viewed her reflection. Hannah noticed how small she appeared within her surroundings. She felt like a single rose bud about to blossom in a vast botanical garden. Each piece of furniture seemed eccentric. She realized that each piece made its way from generation upon generation. Hannah nearly felt out of place and wondered where she fit into the equation. She wandered into the next room and appeared lost in thought.

Enrico reached out his strong arm and touched her hand, releasing her from her thoughts. He instantly smiled and patted the seat next to him. She sat down, adjusted her skirt and slipped off her heels. They snuggled and watched the shadows dance about the room. The red-hot ambers that fell beneath the hearth mesmerized her. Enrico slowly stood, stoked the fire and added another log.

"Would you like to get more comfortable? You will find suitable attire in…"

But before he could finish, Hannah shushed him with her finger. "That would please me; would that please you, my Lord?"

The surprised look on his face told her that he understood when she stepped into the next room. Enrico hoped she would pass the final test as he waited with anticipation.

Hannah found a sexy little negligee prominently displayed in the wardrobe. It was black, long, lacy and extremely revealing. "Suitable for the great Lady Costello," she whispered—still not comprehending the meaning. She could not understand and did not wish to understand, for it felt so natural to be here with him in such a manner to suggest she was his one and only Lady. Enrico is still a stranger to her, but Hannah felt like she already spent a lifetime by his side. She pondered over her thoughts as she undressed. This would typically be an awkward situation and yet, she felt relaxed. She wondered if this was a natural reaction to—*To what?* Hannah could not decide if she felt comfortable due to falling in love or mere feelings of lust.

The answer came to her swiftly. She was in love and tonight, well tonight, would unfold itself.

Hannah reached for the negligee and then paused, as something else caught her eye. An emerald majestic silken robe hung beside the wardrobe. She ran her fingers over the luxurious fabric and felt electricity. Hannah felt an even deeper connection to Enrico as she slipped the robe over her bare shoulders. She stepped back in front of the mirror and viewed her reflection. The robe called out to her.

"Lady Costello," it whispered.

For a moment, Hannah merely thought she imagined the little voice within her mind. She could not shake the feeling that she truly became another. Hannah simply shook her head in denial, knowing things like that are impossible.

She turned to venture back and suddenly froze a few feet from the door. She raised her brow and gazed at a portrait hanging above the doorway. The woman in the portrait had remarkably high cheekbones and stunning emerald eyes. Her hair was long, dark and wavy and she had a fair complexion. Her chin rested upon her hand and she appeared to gaze directly at Hannah. Hannah gasped and slid her fingers over her ring, for the woman in the portrait adorned the same ring. Hannah instantly realized that she gazed at a portrait of Enrico's mother. The woman smiled mysteriously, but Hannah saw sadness within her eyes. Hannah took a few moments to reconcile her thoughts.

Enrico waited rather impatiently in his bedchamber. The massive walls closed in around him as guilt and betrayal crept into his soul hindering his intentions. Enrico fully understood the extent of his sinful pleasures. Tonight was not proceeding as expected. Something about Savannah complicated his duty. Lust was one thing, but his heart felt alive and began to fill with warmth and devotion. He could not explain his feelings. He became flustered as if he were in love. *Impossible.* His thoughts became unmistakable as his soul filled with an overwhelming presence he had not felt in years. Enrico could no longer deny his heart and hoped he misinterpreted her identity. He fell for the Lady in question and smiled as he admitted it to himself. The force that bound them was unmistakable. He unexpectedly fell in love with Savannah. Enrico paused to the sound of knocking upon the door. He opened the door and gasped as his father stood there, appearing agitated.

Edmond stormed into the room, "Enrico, this is an outrage," he proclaimed.

Enrico coaxed his father into the hallway, closed the door and turned to meet his father's hostility head on. "Father, I know what I am doing. Things are under control; please do not interfere."

Edmond's lips quivered as his hands began to shake. Every ounce of his soul told him that Enrico was a far better man than this. "You announced her as your Lady Costello and she bears the family crest. I am no fool."

Enrico maintained his composure as his blood began to boil. "Father, I am in control!"

Edmond paced the floor, stopped mid stride and met Enrico's deceitful gaze. "Search your soul Enrico and I believe you will find what I see. I have never had the privilege of watching two spellbound souls in search of one another, until tonight. This union can not take place."

Enrico averted his eyes towards the doorway. He did feel as his father described but he refused to admit the truth. Edmond swiftly interrupted his thoughts.

"Vow you will send her home, Tonight."

Enrico managed to find the strength and courage to meet his fathers demanding gaze with certainty and honesty. "I will accept the consequences of my actions and I will do so with honor."

"Enrico, I know you far to well. Look me in the eye and tell me you are willing to risk your future, our future, for this young woman."

Enrico searched his heart and looked his father square in the eye. "Yes I am."

Edmond knew there was nothing more he could say. "Then my Son, you have become a fool. You should do your duty and move on."

Enrico did not wish to argue with his Father any further. "I appreciate your concern Father, but this is my Decision."

Edmond hung his head knowing damn well Enrico deserved to find happiness and his gut twisted with turmoil.

"Tell me Enrico, why does she spark your fancy? She must be of great importance for you to risk so much."

Enrico remained silent.

Edmond walked away murmuring, "This is inconceivable and unforgivable. You can not keep her son."

Enrico watched his father leave with a heavy heart. He knew Savannah would determine her own destiny and their fate now rested upon her shoulders. Enrico placed his back against the wall and brought his hands to his face. *What am I doing?* He could not move and could not think clearly. He reminded himself that he could not—would not—change his mind. Enrico went back inside and relocked the door. "No more disturbances," he whispered.

His heart beat wildly, uncertain of what lied ahead. Savannah's identity will be uncovered—tonight. He felt certain of that. His passions run deep. Enrico knew he could not withstand another heartache. Enrico alone knew what his mother conveyed upon her deathbed. His father remained oblivious to the entire truth regarding the family legacy. He thought back to his mother's final moments. He recalled the sadness her eyes conveyed when she squeezed his hand with every ounce of strength she had left.

"Come closer, Enrico," she whispered.

Enrico moved in next to her as his heart began to ache.

"Only you can destroy the destructive path which bestowed itself upon our family. You possess the power to prevail and put an end to the madness. I can only assist you so far. I am about to tell you something I have never told anyone before, not even your father, so listen carefully. This will all end when you seek out the *luz del dia.* I alone can soften the nightmare and you alone can abolish it." She took out a ring and handed it to him. "This is the Ring of Eternity. Search your heart and you will understand the truth and discover the pure and honorable path."

Enrico strained to listen, as her voice softened to a bare whisper.

"When I am gone, you will take my place as…"

Enrico felt his heart skip a beat as she left his world forever. He found himself contemplating her final words. It was not until much later when he fully understood. Enrico reeled from his thoughts when he felt eyes upon him and turned to meet Savannah's gaze.

He came face-to-face with his destiny and she wore a robe—his robe. He nearly hung his head in disappointment, certain that the robe concealed the black negligee. His heart sank. The true Lady Costello would have entered the room as bare as the day she entered the world. Enrico instantly realized she was not the *luz del dia.* He could not explain what came over him. Enrico decided to abide by his duties and send her home. He stepped forwards as Hannah threw herself into his arms and kissed him passionately. Enrico knew the choice she made. All traces of guilt escalated during this sacred moment.

The beautiful buxom still managed to enthrall his senses. He needed to be certain of her identity before making any rash and premature decisions. He untied the robe and it descended upon the floor. His Savannah stood there like an angel peering at him seductively—Warm, soft and bare. She slowly drew her hand and touched it briefly to her head, allowing her long hair to flow gracefully around her bodice. Enrico felt a fire burning within his soul as he swept her off her feet and carried her to the bed—his bed.

"You are so beautiful, my Lady," he whispered, as he laid her down benevolently. He quickly began to disrobe, for Savannah was the true Lady Costello. Enrico could no longer deny the inevitable.

"Don't hurt me," she whispered, and then added, "I've never been with a man before, my Lord."

He looked into the most innocent and sensual blue eyes ever bestowed upon him.

"I know and I promise to never hurt you as long as I have a breath left in my soul."

With that said, Enrico began to lightly caress her bodice. He enticed her soul and lured her heart to him. He barely touched her flesh, sending Hannah ablaze. She arched her back and felt compelled to part her knees, welcoming him into her sacred domain. Enrico hesitated—conflicted between pleasure, honor and pain. Hannah read his eyes and closed the distance between them. She spoke to his soul and rendered him speechless as he heard each word. He wondered how this was possible and laced his fingers around hers, allowing himself to become undone. Enrico entered her soul, slowly at first, as she whimpered beneath him.

"I will never hurt you Savannah," he whispered and than engulfed her mouth with his, as he surged deep into her soul, repeatedly.

She heard him whispering things that held no logic. Hannah thought she heard him say, *"I will see that you return home."* Home—She did not wish to return home; she wanted to stay with him forever. She quickly dismissed the thought. Hannah knew she was not hearing correctly or thinking clearly. Enrico was making love to her and she to him. They met every sexual expectation. Hannah grasped his buttocks when she felt her soul explode with ecstasy, as she cried out. She motioned her hips to press against his. Enrico began to slow down, ever so gently.

"Shall I pleasure you again, my Lady?"

She let out a whimper and he took it as a yes. He cupped her breast and began to suckle upon her nipple. He removed himself from her soul and pleasured her until she exploded again. She fidgeted beneath him as he met her gaze. Hannah noticed his hair glistened as it did downstairs. He made his way back to her mouth and plunged his tongue deep inside as he invaded her soul once more. Enrico cried out as he felt his soul deny honor and relinquish all duties. When the thrusting ceased, he met her gaze and professed his undying love.

"I love you too Enrico!"

The night swiftly passed as they dreaded the approaching sunrise. They fell asleep in one another's arms.

Enrico tossed and turned all night. He envisioned Savannah fleeing from him. Each time he attempted to get close, she refused him passage into her soul. Wherever she ran, he followed. Enrico escaped the nightmare and sat upright in a cold sweat. He turned and gazed at Savannah still asleep by his side. He quietly lied back, wrapped his arms around her and watched her breathe. He silently wondered if they would ever have this moment again. He could not bear the thought of a single night without her. He needed her in his heart, in his soul and in his bed. Enrico knew he was the first and he vowed to be the last.

Hannah felt Enrico's arms around her. She felt the passion radiating from his body and most of all, she felt safe and secure. She just experienced a rather daunting dream but dismissed the nightmare, feeling certain Enrico would never stray far from her side. She tilted her brow as he cupped her chin with his fingers and drew her full moist lips to his. He kissed her tenderly, tasting her sweetness. Enrico slid his thigh over her hip and fully took advantage of the final hours left beneath the moonlight. For in the morning, he will awaken to Daylight.

The ascending sunrise helped coax them out of bed. Hannah suddenly felt empty inside and pressed her face to his chest, "I don't want to leave you Enrico."

He ran his fingers through her silken hair, "I know, I don't want you to leave either."

Hannah tilted her chin to meet his gaze. She stared into his emerald eyes trying to invade his thoughts. Enrico rested both hands upon her shoulders.

"I make you—here and now—a solemn vow. I vow to send for you when the time comes. For now, you must return home."

Hannah felt the power in his touch, heard the sincerity in his voice and knew he'd never violate such a sacred vow. Before Hannah knew it, the limo dropped her off where it had picked her up.

"I will send for you…I Promise," Enrico hollered, as the limo drove away.

Hannah walked home staring at the promise of his return adorned upon her finger. Her heart shattered, for even a single day apart would feel like an eternity. She ran her fingers across the emerald and whispered, "It's the same shade as his remarkable eyes. Far away, but forever in my heart."

Chapter 3
The Situation at Hand

Returning home to a normal life was far more difficult than Hannah imagined. They shared but a single night, but the memories would last a lifetime. The only concept that she embraced was his promise. Therefore, she would wait for him to wander back into her life. Her family noticed a difference in her that weekend. Hannah felt relieved when her mother did not ask about Friday evening. Kayla entered her bedroom Sunday night and closed the door.

"So, how was Friday night?"

Hannah flinched and gave a little smirk. Before she could explain, Kayla confessed that Kirsten is a friend of hers.

"Hannah, I talked to Kirsten on the phone for over an hour Friday night!"

Hannah's eyes widened. Kayla promised not to mention this to their mother if Hannah could enlighten her with a juicy story. Hannah broke down and told Kayla about the mysterious stranger. She spoke of the limo, the social gathering and their dance together. Hannah purposely left out all other details.

Kayla flashed a look of total disbelief. Hannah immediately held out her hand and showed Kayla the emerald ring.

"Oh my...It's beautiful Hannah!"

Hannah quickly became aware of her sister's loyalty and wondered why she did not notice it before. She explained that Enrico vowed to send for her at the appropriate time.

Kayla knelt down and pleaded, "Hannah, you must take me with you. Please, I wish to leave this one horse town. I too dream of another life."

Kayla looked so desperate and lost, Hannah simply replied, "Yes, I will make it happen." She completely understood Kayla's feelings—all to well. Kayla leapt to her feet, threw her arms around Hannah and then ventured towards the door and stopped mid stride.

"You weren't his escort, were you?"

"No, of course not!"

"Of course not Hannah, forget I asked."

Hannah thought about Friday night and replayed the same scenes repeatedly within her mind. She barely slept the entire weekend.

Austin noticed a complete transformation, both inside and out, in Hannah Monday morning. She spoke softly and adapted a carefree approach to life. He could not deny the sparkle within her eyes. He became lost in thought during second period study hall. He could not fathom what brought about the change in a mere weekend. He instantly noticed that she left her hair hang down for once. Nevertheless, one thing remained certain, he liked it and loved her even more. He made plans to break it off with his current relationship. Lately, each time he looked at her, he saw Hannah staring back at him. He could not get Hannah out of his mind. Hannah pierced his thoughts each night. He envisioned waking up to her smiling face each morning. Somehow, some way, he vowed to make Hannah his.

Austin focused so much of his attention on Hannah that it just dawned on him that Colby did not call all weekend. Colby has been his best friend since grade school and called most every night. Austin made a mental note that Colby was absent from school today. This confused Austin, for Colby would definitely skip a Friday but never a Monday. Austin needed to get in touch with him. He had left his favorite ball cap over at Colby's house this past Friday. He wanted nothing more than to have it returned. That particular cap was special to him in its own unique way. He has held on to it since he was three. It took him years to grow into it, for the cap belonged to his father and remained his prize possession.

Austin held few memories of his father. He recalled how young he was when his father passed away. His mother told many stories throughout the years and Austin always wished he had the opportunity to get to know him, the man that gave him life. Austin knew he would have made a great father when the time came. He would have been involved in every one of their activities. Most of all, he secretly desired a son. He wished for a miniature version of himself to carry on the family name. He quickly reeled from his thoughts, for they became too painful. He returned his focus towards Hannah. Austin secretly loved her ever since grade school.

Hannah noticed everyone noticing her. Her actions and words were unlike her. She behaved as though she'd never step foot in the Greenville High School again and marveled at the thought of it. There was only one person she'd miss and he genuinely enjoyed her company when she was just plain ordinary Hannah. She vowed never to forget Austin and their lunch dates. With each passing day, Hannah remained just as optimistic as the day before. One night, Hannah sat in her bedroom gazing out the window as the sky released its splendor of snow and realized that days have turned into weeks and weeks have turned into months. The cold reality of truth placed its grip upon her and she began to sob uncontrollably. Three months have passed and it became clear that Enrico would not send for her—his Lady Costello.

These forsaken thoughts severed through her heart like a dagger that pierces its victim after the climax of a battle. However, it was not a battle that inflicted her wounds; it was an enchanted evening shared between two lovers soon forgotten. The tears fell like rain when she recalled Kayla's question. 'You weren't his escort, were you?' echoed throughout her mind. "No," she cried, but came to the realization that was all she had been to him, his escort for the evening. 'Only for tonight,' she recalled him say. He used her and the pain would forever remain unbearable. Hannah wondered how she could be so blind. All the signs were there, right in front of her nose. His emerald eyes blindsided all rhyme and reason. She closed her eyes in an attempt to rid Enrico from her mind, but not from her heart.

Rebecca watched helplessly as Hannah reverted into her old self. Hannah became withdrawn and distant once again. Rebecca secretly hoped it was just the classic case of wintertime blues, for the snow made it nearly impossible for Hannah to walk Bandit everyday. She hoped Hannah would come out of her shell as spring approached. Jenna needed her attention for now. Jenna would likely graduate in a few months and leave the nest. She knew her oldest daughter overcame great lengths to make it this far.

Jenna's worst enemy has always been herself. Rebecca never believed Jenna deserved the lack of respect she received from the faculty after becoming pregnant last year. Still, Jenna only aggravated the situation by failing to overcome their expectations. Graduating this year would be a triumphed victory for Jenna. Rebecca vowed to give her the best graduation party ever, even if Jenna could not attend the graduation ceremony. Rebecca did not dwell upon the reasons, for she could not change the past now.

A month later, Hannah stopped feeling sorry for herself. She knew no matter what or how she felt, the world would continue to revolve with or without her. Any man that would use her was not worth anymore of her time.

Her mind agreed, while her heart remained silently unconvinced with no response. She continued to grow closer to Austin over the next couple of weeks. She began to feel love and admiration towards him. Hannah remained silent for fear her emotions emerged from the rebound. Austin deserved much better than that. Today the Planning Committee announced the date for the Snowball Dance.

"Are you going to the dance?" Austin asked Hannah, during their lunch date.

"I'm not sure," she replied, and then added, "How about you?"

Austin thought for a moment, concealing his true reply, and met her baby blue eyes. "My girlfriend has to baby-sit."

Hannah perked up, for she knew an opportunity when presented with one. Austin managed to spark more than just her curiosity. "We could go together as friends," she boldly stated.

"That sounds like a plan."

"It's set then; we'll meet up at the dance Friday night."

The Snowball Dance was the only thing on Hannah's mind. Her mother made her a beautiful mauve satin dress on Wednesday. Rebecca is an excellent tailor and takes pride in her god given talent. Friday night approached more rapidly than Hannah realized. Kayla curled Hannah's hair and applied her makeup. Hannah looked beautiful.

Kayla took her hand. "If it is a new dream you wish for, I wish it too," she whispered, acknowledging they would not be leaving town together.

"Thank you," Hannah whispered. She appreciated Kayla's approval and understanding. Kayla was now more like her best friend and confidant rather than her sister. Hannah allowed a tear to escape her eye and Kayla wiped it away.

"You look wonderful tonight."

"So do you Kayla."

Hannah hugged Kayla and they ran downstairs as Brian started the car. Rebecca met them at the kitchen door with her camera.

"You both look lovely this evening. Have a wonderful time," she told them, as she snapped a few pictures.

Kayla posed for several pictures before climbing into the car. Brian dropped his daughters off at the main entrance and waited until they entered. Kayla's friends instantly met her as she entered the building. Kayla did not mind leaving Hannah. Something told her Hannah would be just fine. After all, she was there to meet Austin.

Austin stood in the hallway watching the students as they arrived. He did not want to miss her grand entrance. He was early and spent some time with friends. Austin's eyes widened when Hannah walked though the doors, for she was the most beautiful woman he ever laid eyes upon and he felt his heart skip a beat. Her long blonde hair, baby blue eyes, full lips, curvy bodice and blossomed breasts were mere icing on the cake. He cherished everything about her, even the little things. The way she twirled a strand of hair when she became nervous was always a complete turn on. He treasured her completely. She could do no wrong in his eyes. He admired her spirited personality most of all. He was immediately by her side.

"I have a table waiting for us," he whispered, as his hand guided the small of her back.

Hannah felt eyes upon them as they stepped into the cafeteria. His circle of friends watched from a distance with inquiring eyes, as Austin led her to their table.

Kyle took Austin aside, "Austin, what are you doing?"

Austin was not alarmed and smiled cunningly. Kyle released him and returned to their table to address the group.

"Has anyone heard from Colby?"

Everyone simply shrugged.

"I can't believe he would up and move without telling any of us," Austin replied, and then added, "If anyone hears from him, tell him I want my cap back." Austin quickly composed himself, for he was not there to discuss Colby or socialize with his buddies. He gave Kyle the gesture to move the group further down the table. Kyle got the hint and slid the group down, giving Austin the privacy he desired. Austin and Hannah sat and talked half the night, as the music became a whimsical backdrop. He gazed at her from across the table, searching for courage. Hannah wondered if he would ever ask her to dance. Finally, Austin rose, walked behind her and extended his hand, "Would you like to dance?"

Hannah's favorite slow song began to play.

"I thought you would never ask."

Hannah accepted his hand and felt her soul take flight. Austin led her to the dance floor, wrapped his arms around her waist and pulled her close. His embrace sparked her fancy and their friendship escalated, as Hannah imagined standing along a beach. Her hair and lacy skirt blew in the wind as Austin slowly approached. He leaned in and kissed her passionately as the sun set across the horizon. *Can my soul learn to trust another man?* Hannah felt delirious as her heart yearned to love again.

They danced in slow circles as she draped her arms around his neck and rested her cheek upon his shoulder. He tightened his embrace and cradled her with his affections. Anyone watching knew there was magic in the air. Kayla glanced over her shoulder, pleased with what she found. She had not seen Hannah this happy in months and it warmed her heart. Austin tilted his chin and gazed at her full moist lips. He was about to plunge into unknown territory and was unable to foresee an outcome, as he wondered where her feelings truly lied. Hannah boldly met his eyes and seized the moment. She cupped the base of his neck and drew his mouth to hers. They kissed passionately, engulfing one another.

Austin felt a tap upon his shoulder but did not care and refused to stop until he was fully satisfied. Hannah saw a chaperone glaring at them with disapproving eyes as she opened hers and realized it was Mrs. Gillus, the Home Economics teacher.

"You only get one warning."

They each managed a smile and returned to their table. Austin held her hand as they sat side-by-side. He knew her true feelings and now possessed the courage to follow through with his intentions. "I have something to tell you in private," he whispered. They went into the hallway and rounded the corner towards the stage entrance. Austin's heart beat rapidly as he rested his hands upon her waist. "I just wanted to let you know that I broke it off with my previous relationship. I have loved you since grade school. Will you be my girlfriend, Hannah Marie Brockwell?"

Hannah instantly threw her arms around him. Those words were music to her ears. "Yes, of course I will," she cried.

They shared another private tender kiss. They snuck onto the stage and spent the remainder of the evening slow dancing in the dark. They listened to the music and felt one another's heartbeat. Their sense of touch became keen as they explored the first stage of their budding relationship.

"Can I drive you and Kayla home?" he whispered.

Hannah accepted with a warm hug and sealed the offer with a kiss. They left the stage feeling as though it was their special place. This is where they shared their first unofficial date. Hannah found Kayla and instructed her to call their parents to inform them they have a ride home. Kayla called and told their father they would be home shortly. Austin and Hannah continued to hold hands the entire way to the car. It was a cool crisp night and Austin offered Hannah his coat. Hannah instantly accepted and slid the warmth of the fabric over her bare shoulders, secretly attempting to replace an old memory. *Far away but forever in my heart.* Hannah shuddered and quickly dismissed the thought.

Austin felt Hannah shiver and quickened his pace. He unlocked the doors, opened Hannah's door and turned the heater on high. Austin felt sheer delight, as he became attentive. He felt like a peasant who just won over a fair maiden. With one touch of his hand, he held an angel. A mile down the road, Austin reached for her hand and then hesitated. He did not notice it before but she adorned a rather expensive emerald ring, surrounded by diamonds, upon her *left* ring finger.

He wondered how he missed it earlier. He thought the ring was costume jewelry at first, but it did not match the dress. He then recalled seeing it that Monday he noticed a difference in her and again last week during their lunch date. He could not shake the feeling that she concealed something of importance. The only sparkly item she adorned troubled him tremendously. He escaped his thoughts when Hannah touched his hand.

"We're almost there; it's the second house past Cold Springs Road." Hannah suddenly felt a chill. It was the first time she spoke the name of the road since that cold disheartening night. She quickly suppressed those feelings and refused to acknowledge the abandonment that began to overwhelm her soul. Kayla announced their arrival, knowing Hannah became lost in thought. Hannah jumped and gazed into Austin's eyes.

"Take your time saying goodnight. I will tell Mom and Dad about the wonderful evening," Kayla whispered.

Austin did not acknowledge Kayla and returned Hannah's gaze, "Where were you just now?"

Hannah flinched, "I will always cherish our first dance," she said soothingly.

Austin smiled, as he took hold of her wrist and turned her hand over. His smile faded, "This is a rather unique ring. May I ask where you acquired it?" he asked gently, concealing all concern in his voice. *And whom you acquired it from.*

Hannah was lost for words as panic began to set in. She withdrew her hand, "It was a gift and now I can't take it off. I've tried everything imaginable."

Austin heard fear in her voice. Another thought rushed into his mind like a freight train. *Hannah never said the ring was a gift from her parents.* He closed his eyes, took a deep breath and looked her directly in the eyes. He felt compelled to ask the one question that now weighed upon his mind. "Hannah, who was the gift Fr…" but before he could finish, the porch light flickered.

Rebecca stood in the doorway. "Hannah, it's getting late."

"I have to go Austin. Call me tomorrow." Hannah stepped out of the car and waved goodbye as Austin disappeared into the night.

Rebecca greeted her at the door. "How was your evening with your new boa?"

Hannah blushed slightly, "I'll tell you all about it Mom!"

Austin left with unanswered questions. The night had been magical, but he could not shake the feeling that someone else lurked in the distant shadows. He refused to go home right away. Instead, he drove down to Hawk River to dwell upon his thoughts. He found a familiar rock formation, took his usual seat and gazed at the glassy water beneath the stars above. The night remained clear and vivid as the moon shined brightly. Lately, he came here to think about Hannah. Tonight was no exception, for he did not like the words that echoed within his mind. *'It was a gift and now I can't take it off.'* He shook his head and began to analyze every word. Hannah never said the ring was a gift from her parents, and if it was, then she should not feel the need to remove it from her hand and she would wear it proudly. He decided her parents did not give her that ring. First, she adorned it on the wrong finger and second, they could not afford such a ring. It looked like a family heirloom. He did not think any family in town could afford a ring of that magnitude. Austin knew this to be true, for his mother worked at a ritzy jewelry store up town.

She specialized in heirloom pieces and conducted appraisals for collectors and insurance companies. He decided to draw a sketch of the ring tomorrow and have his mother investigate. This eased his psyche, but not much. He loved Hannah for so many years and finally held her tonight as he always dreamed. One thing remained certain, "That damn ring could ruin everything," he whispered, and then closed his eyes. His heart told him so. Austin clenched his fists and made Hannah a sacred vow. "I vow to accept and love you no matter what secrets lie dormant in the past. If anyone, past or present, tries to get in our way, they will answer to me." He felt a chill soar through his bones when the crisp cool air began to blow around him. Austin grew weary and knew he would not find slumber until he spoke to his mother in the morning. He drove home and crawled into bed, deeply disturbed in thought.

Hannah rose early to take Bandit for a walk. She wanted to tell him about last night. They walked down Old Church Hollow, in the opposite direction of Cold Springs Road. Bandit seemed excited to hear about her new boa. She dropped to her knees and rubbed Bandit's ear, "I think you will like Austin!"

she whispered. She then glanced at her watch, jumped up and decided to head home. Hannah desperately tried to remove the ring as they turned around. "Why can't I take it off?" she cried. It both troubled and intrigued her at the same time. "I shall have to try again later Bandit," she proclaimed. Hannah thought about asking Kayla for assistance. For now, she hurried home to await Austin's call.

Austin rose early. He wiped the sleep from his eyes. He did not fall asleep until the wee hours in the morning. He drew a sketch of the ring and trudged downstairs. Austin found his mother, Janice, packing her lunch in the kitchen. "Mother, I have an assignment due on Monday and I think it's right up your alley."

Janice raised her brow, "What's that Austin?"

He handed her the sketch and then described it in detail. He explained that each student received a sketch of something significant. "The assignment is to research the object and write a report on the findings."

Janice observed the sketch carefully. "I shall have to do some research on it at work today. May I keep the sketch?"

Austin handed her the sketch and she wrote down some notes in the margin.

"I can't make any promises but I think I can help you with your assignment." She paused and stared at the sketch intently. Her silence conveyed more than mere interest. "It looks oddly familiar to me," she finally confessed.

Austin smiled knowing his mother would not disappoint him. "Thanks Mom!"

"Don't thank me yet. I expect you to write your own report."

Austin chuckled, but his amusement only ran skin deep.

"So, what are you up to today?" she asked, then zipped the cooler closed.

"I'm thinking of taking my new girlfriend for a horse ride." Austin paused, and then added, "If she's allowed."

Janice picked up her cooler and met his gaze, "I bet she's lovely."

Austin flushed, "Her name is Hannah, Hannah Brockwell."

Janice smiled warmly, for she has heard of the family, and Jenna's antics. She sighed, knowing gossip spreads quickly within their small rural community. One person's tribulations can quickly become the topic of discussion and ridicule. Their family has faced that firing squad once. "I have to go to work now, but I will retrieve that information for you. We'll talk more about this tonight."

Austin looked at his watch and saw it was seven O'clock. He decided it was too early to call Hannah just yet but would call in a couple of hours after he rested upon the couch.

It was now a quarter to eight. Hannah had no idea when Austin planned to call. Kayla hung out in Hannah's bedroom all morning, since Hannah returned from her walk. The two sisters tried to remove Hannah's mysterious ring. They attempted to use cooking oil and petroleum jelly. Kayla tugged on the ring with all her might but it simply would not slip off. In fact, "It never even tried to move," Kayla pointed out. "Have you tried flipping it around with the emerald facing palm side up?"

"No!" Hannah cried and instantly tried. Again, the ring would not budge.

Kayla backed up a bit with a grim expression, "Hannah, I don't think that's an ordinary ring!"

Hannah's eyes widened and began to moisten, as her hand trembled. "Please don't say that Kayla, you're scaring me."

Kayla collected her thoughts, "Who put the ring on your finger—you or Enrico?"

Hannah could not fathom where Kayla headed with such a question. "Enrico Did!"

Kayla sat down and briefly glanced around the room trying to find the right way to convey her thoughts. "Hannah, what if Enrico is the only one who can remove the ring, since he put it on? I know this is difficult, but what is the last thing he said to you?"

Hannah took her time and replied honestly. "He promised to send for me when the time comes."

Kayla gasped, as the answer lingered right in front of her nose. "Hannah, if Enrico is the only one that can remove the ring from your finger, then the ring is his property. Technically, you now belong to him." Kayla stared at the emerald ring permanently attached to Hannah's finger. The ring encircled not just any finger but the ring finger, which signifies a promise. *A promise of his return!* It all made perfect sense now.

Hannah became speechless. She could not utter a sound. Her mind became an array of frantic thoughts.

Kayla felt Hannah's anxiety and took her hand, "Hannah, I think this is his way of saying you belong to him until he chooses otherwise."

Hannah remained silent for a moment and began to whisper the bitter truth. "When we first arrived at the hacienda, the door attendant announced us as Lord and Lady Costello."

Kayla gasped and clasped a firm hand over her mouth, attempting to remain silent.

"Enrico was very protective of me. It all makes sense to me now, if that's remotely possible."

Kayla kept quiet and attempted to read Hannah's thoughts. They sat together in silence. Hannah broke the silence, speaking in a bare whisper now, and explained what happened after the social gathering. Kayla was not the least bit surprised and this disturbed Hannah tremendously.

"I knew you were out all night Hannah! I believe Enrico still intends to send for you, even after all these months."

Hannah shook her head, "But I am in love with Austin. Enrico is too late, for I choose to be with Austin now." Hannah turned as their mother called out.

"Hannah, telephone!"

"We will figure this out...together," Kayla whispered, as Hannah approached the doorway. They exchanged a brief look and simultaneously swore to secrecy.

Kayla remained in Hannah's room and wondered how Hannah managed to get herself into such a predicament. She wondered if Enrico bestowed a curse down upon Hannah. At first, she thought Enrico merely existed in Hannah's mind. But the emerald ring, which permanently attached itself to Hannah's finger, made a believer out of her. She worried about Hannah's safety. Kayla has never believed in unknown and supernatural forces before; but then, none were ever presented until now.

She could not deny the tangible evidence that forewarned the future. Enrico truly is a mysterious man. *If he even is a man.* She quivered at the thought of it and wondered what power he must possess over Hannah. Kayla knew Hannah to be a shy and quiet girl who never drew attention her way. Hannah is down-to-earth and a prominent student. *This mysterious stranger misled and abandoned Hannah, yet still manages to claim her as his own.* Kayla wondered if she knew Hannah at all and what other secrets she might disclose.

Hannah ran downstairs and picked up the phone.

"Good morning Hannah!"

Hannah instantly felt feverish, "Good morning Austin."

"Would you like to go horseback riding with me today?"

Without thought, Hannah cupped the phone and yelled, "Mom, may I go riding with Austin today?"

Rebecca entered the room holding Caylob, "I suppose that would be alright."

"Thanks mom!" Hannah uncapped the phone, "Austin, what time will you pick me up?"

"I'll pick you up at eleven. I'll see you then, bye."

Hannah hung up the phone. Her heart filled with anticipation, for she never rode a horse before. This eased her mind and she did not give Enrico another thought. Kayla walked into the kitchen and poured a glass of water.

"Mom, what should I wear to ride horses?"

Rebecca laughed, "Preferably old clothes."

Hannah started to race off.

"Oh Hannah…come back here for a minute." Hannah returned to the kitchen as Rebecca seized her gaze and asked earnestly, "You really like this boy…don't you?"

Hannah blushed, "Yes, yes I do."

Rebecca held her gaze, "Is he the one who gave you that emerald ring?"

Kayla nearly choked on her gulp of water and managed to hold her tongue.

Hannah managed to speak, "Yes, is…isn't it pretty," she stammered.

Rather amusingly, Rebecca added, "Honey, I think you're wearing it on the wrong hand; don't you think?"

Hannah managed to shrug, playing innocent. Rebecca handed Caylob to Kayla, walked around the table and hugged Hannah.

"Go get ready and wear your beautiful ring on any finger you like."

Hannah ran upstairs. *Another successful escape.*

Caylob fell asleep in Kayla's arms, so she took him upstairs to his crib. Rebecca wondered what she should prepare for lunch. Brian and Clayton worked a half-day today and she knew they would be starved when they walked through the door around twelve-thirty. Jenna would stroll in shortly after that from her weekend job. She laughed to herself. *Hannah and Kayla are special daughters, both unique in their own ways.*

Both are bright prominent students. Both are still young, innocent and naïve. Rebecca held no concerns for her youngest daughter and Hannah remains sweet, sincere and eager to please. She often wondered how hard this past year has been on them. They deserved a lot more of her time—and attention. Rebecca considered returning to her old job at the bank now that Jenna graduated and is about to leave the nest. She wanted to do something special for them in the meantime. Rebecca began to thumb through the newspaper. She came across a particular ad that caught her eye.

The article read:

Dark Horse Advertising Inc., a Reputable advertising firm, seeks beautiful young woman ages 17-18 to model latest fashion. Selected models will receive a substantial allowance. Length of work consists of two weeks beginning December 8th in beautiful Nicaragua. All expenses paid and no experience necessary. Models will pose for various retail ads and promotional advertisements. Models may keep copies of all photos for future portfolios. Do not miss this once in a lifetime opportunity. See application on C-4.

Rebecca wasted no time and cut the ad out, along with the application. This was a perfect opportunity for her daughters. Kayla is beautiful with long dark wavy hair and she always adored Hannah's long blonde shimmering hair. Both girls have perfect complexions and are tall and slender with hourglass figures. They are delightful and well endowed. Rebecca made up her mind. This would be their Christmas present. *Any agency would be blind not to select my daughters.* They needed an adventure for a change. She noticed they seemed to reconcile their differences and now spent a lot of time together. They could consider the trip a vacation together with benefits. She scanned over the application. Rebecca needed to submit photos and measurements. She had to hurry, for the application deadline was in a week.

Austin picked Hannah up at eleven-thirty.
"Are you Hungary?" Austin asked, as she sat down in the front seat.
Hannah thought for a moment and realized she forgot to grab a bite to eat. "Actually I am Austin."
Austin smiled, "Glad to hear that."
Hannah began to laugh. "What are you planning?"
Austin thought about how much he loved her laugh. He chuckled and said, "You'll see." He drove down to Hawk River and parked in a small pull off. "We're here," he announced. Austin got out and opened the door for her. Hannah never saw the river up close and personal before and instantly became excited. Austin opened the trunk, removed a picnic basket and a small cooler.
"You're taking me on a picnic," she gasped. No one ever took her on a picnic before and she nearly wept out of joy and surprise.
Austin heard instant gratification in her tone and it warmed his heart. "I

thought we would eat first before going riding." Austin handed her the picnic basket and took her hand into his. They strolled, hand-in-hand, down a little path that led to a series of large boulders along the waters edge.

"It's breathtaking," Hannah proclaimed.

Austin was quite pleased with himself. This is where he dreamed of taking her on their first official date. They sat the basket and cooler down. Austin opened the basket and removed a thin red and white-checkered blanket. He unfolded the blanket and laid it down flat. Austin dropped to his knees and smoothed out the corners. He set two paper plates and cups upon the blanket. "It's nothing fancy, but it'll do," he said humbly.

"I think its wonderful Austin. Thank you."

They sat down and got comfortable. Austin carefully removed two Tupperware containers and a bag of potato chips. One container held sandwiches, while the other held two slices of Janice's homemade apple pie. They sat and ate under a brilliant blue sky nestled quietly in the shade of an enormous Sycamore tree.

Hannah noticed how deceiving the river appeared. One section looked like a sheet of glass, calm and tranquil, while the next section became wild and unruly. White tipped rapids coursed throughout the river and then became calm. Hannah suddenly felt like the river. Her appearance remained calm on the exterior while unknown forces surged deep beneath the surface that penetrated her soul. Hannah began to notice how green the trees and water looked. She allowed her mind to drift. Ironically, everything appeared to be green and Hannah's eyes quickly scanned their surroundings. She observed the trees, the river, her ring and *his* eyes. *No! Not now, not ever.* Enrico seemed to have a grip over her psyche. Hannah suddenly felt watchful eyes upon them.

Austin watched her questionably, trying to read her thoughts. He did not like what lurked within her eyes. He reached out and touched her arm, "What are you thinking about," he asked apprehensively.

At that second, all she could manage was a smile. Once her mind cleared, she held his hand and rested her palm upon his cheek, to reassure him that things were fine. "It is such a lovely day for a picnic, it is so beautiful here. Thank you for sharing this place with me."

Austin felt her hand tremble as she touched him. He decided to ask no more, not today. They tidied up and held each other as they stared up at the clouds. Hannah felt safe and secure wrapped up in his arms.

She began to tickle his sides and then underarms. They laughed and wrestled playfully upon the blanket. Austin rolled Hannah over gaining the vantage point, but she quickly broke free and ended up straddling him. She flashed him a seductive look and then leaned down for a kiss. He never knew a girl to be so bold. Hannah was vibrant, colorful and full of zest. Austin loved being with her, for she made life interesting and fun. He knew there would never be a dull moment in their relationship and he looked forwards to a promising future. He instantly returned her kiss. An undeniable passion coursed through his veins. They settled down and caught their breath. Austin leapt to his feet and helped Hannah to hers. He threw the blanket over his shoulder, gathered up their belongings, and walked hand-in-hand back to the car.

"So, where do you ride horses around here?"

"My house!"

"You have Horses?"

"Yeah, I have two of them."

Hannah never expected Austin to be the kind of man to have horses. He had a gentle touch outside of school. She noticed he was different during school hours for he talked tough and demanded respect, especially from his buddies. She loved him even more after seeing his softer side.

They drove over to his house. Austin heard the phone ringing as he stepped out of the vehicle. "Phone, be back in a second," he hollered, and ran towards the house. He darted into the living room and picked up the phone, "Hello," he said. There was a brief moment of silence. Then, Austin heard a harsh spoken tone that sent chills down his spine.

"Take the girl home. I will say this only once. The next time I have to repeat myself, it will be the last thing you ever hear. I promise you that." The voice paused, and then added, "If you think you can steal her heart away with a mere dance and a picnic, you are gravely mistaken. I have the power to take her away from you for all eternity. She bears my mark upon her. Consider yourself warned, so keep your distance."

Austin heard the line go dead. He stood there with the phone in his hand staring at it in disbelief.

What the Hell was that? His thoughts took over. *Was I just threatened? By whom?* Austin decided if this man wanted a fight, he would give him one. Nevertheless, to play it safe, he thought they should remain in the house for the time being. He needed time to put things into perspective. He would be damned if he let anyone come between them, not now. He wondered if they would be safe in the house. Apparently, this man knew where they were and observed them on their picnic together. He also knew about the dance they shared. Austin thought very carefully about the caller's words. *'I have the power to take her away from you for all eternity. She bears my mark upon her.'* Austin knew he must think rationally. He is not sacred for himself but he is afraid for Hannah. Earlier, he saw fear within her eyes—even if it was for a brief moment. He managed to calm his nerves and stepped outside. Austin decided not to tell Hannah about the phone call. He did not wish to see that fear within her eyes again, for he had enough fear for them both.

"Hannah," he said, speaking as soothingly as possible.

She looked into his eyes as he focused on her brow. He could never lie to those baby blue eyes.

"My Mother is having car troubles and I have to pick her up. I am sorry, but I'll have to cut our date short. I promise to make it up to you."

Hannah managed a pretentious smile, "Don't worry about it Austin," she said, concealing all disappointment in her voice.

He forced himself to smile. "Let's get you home then."

Hannah walked over for a hug and a kiss. As much as Austin wanted to, he did not embrace her in return. She could not fathom why and tried not to acknowledge that it bothered her but deep down, it did. Austin's heart shattered. The thought of running away with her crossed his mind. He wanted to protect her from this lunatic, who ever he is. She never mentioned another man before. He wanted so much to take her into his arms and demand the truth, but he feared the unknown. He instinctively drove her home instead.

Enrico sat behind his desk, knowing they will be reunited again. Every inch of his body longed for her touch. It remained inevitable, for she will remain his for all eternity. Enrico felt devastated and anger controlled his thoughts. "No mere boy will ever get in my way. Austin will never know Savannah as I do. He will never touch her or feel her in his arms ever again," he snarled aloud. Enrico stood and approached the wall. He drew his fist back and released a whirlwind of emotions bottled up far to long.

"Easy brother," a voice said from behind.

Enrico closed his eyes knowing Antonio lounged in the doorway.

"What has you so enraged, Enrico?"

Enrico remained silent and rested his head against the wall trying to control his rage.

"She must be a great beauty to have you all worked up like this."

Enrico clenched his fists, "Antonio, I'm not in the mood for your antics," he warned.

"I must meet this blazing beauty for myself. Who is she?" Antonio refused to take his eyes off Enrico, for Enrico could turn quickly and possessed a deadly blow.

"Damn it Antonio. I'm not in the mood."

Antonio flinched and knew he overstayed his welcome. He left his brother's room and closed the door.

Antonio never knew Enrico to curse. He wondered what woman could cause so much turmoil for his brother. Enrico behaved rather strangely for months now. A devious expression overshadowed Antonio's face, for he would soon find out. The bait has already been set—complete with hook, line and sinker. He would be patient and wait for the woman in question to venture to him. Enrico always got everything as a child and for once, Antonio would make him share. Any woman that could drive Enrico into a wild frenzy was a woman worth meeting—a woman worth taming. He knew Enrico would never forgive him for such a malicious act. If the two brothers were to share a bed with the same woman, it would cause war between them. Antonio stood outside Enrico's room with crossed arms and a devious smile, for he had everyone right where he wanted them. He vowed to seize the only opportunity ever presented to him.

Austin dropped Hannah off and rushed home as fear and rage coursed through his veins. He ran into his bedroom and grabbed his father's handgun. He loaded the 9mm, carried it outside and concealed the gun in his vehicle under the driver side seat. He knew it would be a long afternoon awaiting his mother and decided to venture out for a walk to ponder his thoughts. There was no denying that the man on the phone meant serious business. *She bears my mark upon her.* Austin felt lightheaded, for he now knew who gave Hannah the emerald ring. The truth overwhelmed him. *Does Hannah belong to another?* Austin had no answer to his own question. Hannah expressed feelings for him and clearly wanted a relationship with him. "Why does she still wear the other man's ring?" he asked aloud. Austin recalled her explanation about not being able to remove the ring from her finger. Nothing made sense to him. The man on the phone expressed dire hatred towards him. Austin shuddered, as he imagined Hannah giving herself intimately to another.

He hung his head and returned home knowing his mother would pull into the driveway at any moment. He rounded the bend and noticed her SUV already parked in the driveway. Austin ran into the house and found her in the kitchen preparing supper.

"I have Great news Austin! I was able to find that information you needed." Janice felt pleased when she handed Austin a manila folder.

Austin did not hesitate. He took the folder and retreated to his room, "Thanks mom!" he yelled. He abruptly came to a halt and glanced around the doorframe, "If the phone rings, it's for me and I'll answer it," he cried.

"Okay, I'll call for you when supper is ready."

Austin turned on the light, closed the door and opened the manila folder—completely unaware of what lied within. His hands began to tremble and part of him did not want to uncover the truth.

Inside the folder, he found several pages from the Internet. The pages came from a family hierarchy vault located in Costa Rica. *Costa Rica*. The pages spoke of a wealthy family whose lineage dated back to the early seventeenth century. The pages moved forward to 1789. The article read:

Lord Edmond Costello ruled The Kingdom from 1748-1789. During this time, Costa Rica was a prominent region unsurpassed with vast riches. Lord Edmond Costello wed the daughter of the revered Count Byron Consuelo in 1747. The marriage between Lord Edmond Costello and Angelina Consuelo sparked a feud between Costa Rica and Nicaragua. Lord Devlin Cordoba ruled Nicaragua during this rigid period. Angelina Consuelo bequeathed two sons upon Edmond. Enrico Costello, first born and heir to the Empire, and Antonio Costello were raised to uphold duty and honor. Edmond oversaw the political reign concerning Costa Rica for forty-one years.

Lord Costello and Lord Cordoba unleashed their mighty armies in one final ferocious battle. Both Empires crumbled to the ground in 1789, known as The Great Tragedy. The Costello family vanished without a trace. There is still much to reveal regarding the events leading up to The Great Tragedy. Historians discovered an emerald diamond ring among the ruins, shortly after the battle ceased. The ring was a family heirloom belonging to Angelina Consuelo. The ring has been nicknamed the Ring of Eternity. It had been the greatest possession of the Consuelo Dynasty.

The Ring of Eternity disappeared in 1789 mysteriously, shortly after its discovery. It remains speculated that thieves broke into the vaults and stole the ring. Many believe the Ring of Eternity holds mystical and extraordinary powers. Angelina Consuelo was the last known person to bear the family crest. Therefore, Historians conclude that the family perished in the fire and the intensity of the flames engulfed their corpses. Historians never assigned a value to The Ring of Eternity. It remains a priceless artifact.

The next page contains the last known photo of The Ring of Eternity, sketched in 1789.

Austin drew in a deep breath and turned the page. He gasped and began to breathe heavily, for there was a picture of Hannah's ring. "How can this be?" Many questions arose within his thoughts but he had no logical explanations. He felt an overwhelming sensation that Hannah did not fully understand either. Austin knew he would have to break down and ask. He did not wish to alarm Hannah in any way, for she already danced around the truth. Austin did not want to back her into a corner, but he knew the man on the phone would not give up. A tingle raced down Austin's spine as he wondered how far the man would pursue the matter. All Austin cares about is Hannah's safety—nothing else matters.

"Austin, Suppers ready."

He closed the folder and walked into the kitchen.

Janice noticed how pale Austin appeared, "Are you feeling alright?"

Austin managed to shrug his shoulders, for so much weighed upon his mind. "Mom, what are the chances of ever seeing the Ring of Eternity?"

Janice found amusement in the question. "If you saw that ring, it would be a cheap imitation."

They sat down and ate their supper in silence. Her words offered no comfort.

Chapter 4
The Opportunity of a Lifetime

It has been two weeks since the mysterious phone call and Austin did not receive any further calls. Then again, they did not venture out on any other dates either. Austin continued to keep a safe distance. He only saw Hannah during school hours and conversed with her on the phone, sometimes late into the evening. He longed for her touch and for her kisses. The situation infuriated him. He desperately wanted to spend time alone with her, for today was the last day of school before their three-week break for the Christmas holiday. Austin decided to make the best out of the day. His determination persevered over all rhyme and reason. He met Hannah at her locker and gazed into those baby blue eyes. Austin placed his hands upon her shoulders, pressed her back against the wall and kissed her passionately. He did not care who witnessed the forbidden rendezvous.

"Let's leave before lunch," he whispered. "I have a doctor's appointment, which I will cancel, and you can go home sick."

Hannah smiled, "It just might work," she returned. She paused for a moment and declared, "It's a date."

They secretly made their plans during second period study hall. She'd go to the nurse before fourth period and pretend to be ill. Hannah would then pretend to call home and proceed to tell the nurse that her brother-in-law, Clayton, would pick her up. Austin's mother had a new SUV with dark tinted windows. Their plan was absolutely fool proof.

Austin picked Hannah up as planned. The nurse watched Hannah exit the main entrance and step into the vehicle. Hannah managed to contain her arousal, as she walked towards Austin. "Austin, you are a genius," she cried, after closing the door.

Austin took her right hand and bestowed a kiss upon it, "I'm going to take you somewhere that nobody knows about," he whispered.

Hannah's heart began to overflow, for part of her wondered where his feelings lied these past two weeks. "How long did you have this planned?"

"For a week now."

They drove half an hour outside of town to an old abandoned brick home.

"It isn't much but no one will suspect we're here." His mind hoped that no one suspected their whereabouts. He lowered his gaze to the Ring of Eternity. It no longer bothered him—It down right frightened him now.

Hannah caught him lingering and remained on guard.

"May I see it Hannah," he asked, pretending to act curious.

Hannah reluctantly held her hand out to him.

Austin wrapped his fingers around it and gave a little tug. She spoke the truth, for the ring did not budge an inch. He tried to slide it back-and-forth and from side-to-side. He drew half a grin, "That's stuck alright. By the way, who did you say gave that to you?" he asked casually.

Hannah flashed him an earnest look, knowing damn well she did not say. After a brief awkward moment, Hannah smiled warmly, "Let's go inside."

Austin quickly agreed. He had no idea how this would turn out, but he worked hard on it all week. He grabbed a flashlight from the backseat and instructed her to wait there for him. He took two steps and quickly changed his mind. He was not about to let her out of his sight for a second. "Come here, Baby," he whispered gently, and removed a long sleeve shirt from the backseat.

Austin gently rolled the shirt and carefully placed it over her eyes. He used the sleeves to tie the make shift blindfold behind her head. Hannah instantly became amused and asked no questions, for she trusted him completely. He took her hand and led the way. Austin led her to the porch and helped her up each step. He opened the door as his heart raced frantically. He locked the door after they entered. Hannah jumped a little when she heard the click of the lock and her heart beat wildly now. Austin returned to her side and took her hand once again. He felt her trembling. He could not see her eyes, but her expression revealed all. He tenderly kissed her brow.

"I'll be right back," he whispered and then walked away.

Hannah could hear his footsteps as the floorboards creaked beneath him. She wondered what surprises awaited her. He returned and led her through another doorway. Austin stood behind her and removed the blindfold.

Hannah could not believe her eyes. She stood there stunned, as candles illuminated the room—providing a warm soft sensual glow. Austin pulled out the couch and decorated it beautifully with an afghan and an array of throw pillows. Austin turned on the stereo to soft rock. He stepped over to the bed and sat down, quite pleased with himself. Hannah approached him slowly, fell to her knees, placed her head against his chest and threw her arms around his waist. She held on for dear life. She knew this was not the proper time nor place. Austin went to so much trouble preparing for this afternoon. Many unknowns raced through her mind. Hannah realized if she wanted a future with Austin, there could be no secrets between them. The time came to make peace with the past and the forsaken emerald ring that now entraps her.

Austin stared down at her with sympathetic eyes, for this is exactly what he expected. He massaged her shoulders with his strong hands trying to soothe her soul. "I love you Hannah, no matter what," he whispered.

Hannah shook her head. She could only imagine what Austin must be thinking. She did not wish to deceive him any further. Enrico would remain part of her past and now, he attempted to invade the present. Hannah knew she must tell Austin the truth so he can decide their future. She gazed up at him with moist eyes, "You mean so much to me. I do not want to lose you Austin, not ever. I love you," she said honestly.

He felt her tremble in his arms. Austin saw past her tears and looked deep into her soul, "Hannah, nothing you could ever say or do would make me love you any less."

Austin watched as Hannah stood and became aloof but he refused to give up so easily. He reached out and grasped her delicate wrist wheeling her against his chest. Hannah melted into the curves of his arms. She nestled against his strong chest and tender heart. Austin was everything she ever dreamed of—and so much more. She did not attempt to fight him as she sat there vulnerable upon his knee. Hannah drew her dainty hands to his shoulders and placed an arms length between them. Enrico's image slowly crept into her mind as she thought about kissing Austin. She shook her head and Austin saw panic within her eyes.

"Hannah, talk to me," he nearly demanded.

Hannah could not dodge the truth any longer, for she no longer had the strength. Hannah quickly averted her eyes and whispered, "Austin I fear we can never be together completely; he won't let us."

Austin tilted her chin to meet his gaze, "We can let him interfere or we can fight him," he stated, and then closed the gap between them.

Hannah wanted one last kiss from him before she bared her soul. She laced her fingers behind his head and engulfed his mouth forcefully. He returned the gesture and lied back pulling her on top of him. They moved gracefully, completely coordinated with one another. Hannah wrapped her leg around his and propped her cheek upon one hand, as she lied across his chest.

"You don't understand Austin. I can't possibly fight him." She watched him flinch, but kept talking. "I freeze and I feel like I can't breathe whenever I'm in his presence. I see images in my mind and I hear his thoughts as he reads mine. It scares me when I'm at his mercy."

Austin began to stiffen beneath her. Hannah was certain he would roll her aside and leave, never to glance back. Instead, Austin ran a hand down her spine, "Who is he?"

Hannah drew in a deep breath and released it slowly. "His name is Lord Enrico Costello," she managed to whisper.

"What," Austin cried, and then rolled Hannah over and leapt to his feet. He began to pace the floor relentlessly. The name Costello ripped through his mind. He tried to comprehend the situation, but did not know where to begin.

Hannah knew her worst nightmare was afoot, for Austin would surely abandon her.

Austin regained clarity and met her gaze, "Did he give...did he place that ring on your finger?" he stammered.

"Yes!"

The radio shut off and the room fell eerily silent—Silent enough to hear a pin drop. The silence seemed to last forever. Austin felt the need to choose his words carefully. He walked over to where Hannah sat, caressed her arms with his fingertips and knelt before her. He prepared his heart to accept the entire truth. "Hannah, you must tell me everything," he whispered grimly.

Hannah sighed and dared to meet his gaze. "A stranger approached in a Corvette and asked me to attend a social gathering in his honor." Hannah quickly averted her eyes and barely spoke above a whisper. "I now regret that I ever went." Hannah wanted to crawl into a corner and hide, as the world began to cave in around her. She began to sob for fear of losing him.

Austin made a fist as he wrapped her up in all his love, "Did he hurt you?" he asked tenderly.

She shook her head, "Austin, you misunderstand. Enrico was a complete gentleman, but now he pursues me to no end. He calls most every night and expresses dire hatred towards you. I feel his eyes upon us everywhere we go. We cannot escape him and I fear for your safety. I cannot run from him;

Enrico said he would send for me when the time comes." Hannah embraced him, "Austin, you can still walk away from this nightmare."

Austin could not believe his ears. Hannah is willing to confront this man alone to protect him. He stepped back and met her gaze, "Do you love me?" he asked earnestly.

Hannah needed no time to think, "Yes," she replied.

He smiled devilishly, "Then I cannot walk away, for we are in this together and we shall confront him together," he whispered, as he took her hand in reassurance.

Hannah withdrew her hand quickly, "I can't…we can't possibly confront him," she stammered.

Austin read her eyes as the undeniable truth flooded his heart. He fully understood the magnitude of their brief relationship. Hannah could not resist Enrico and could not possibly face him again. Austin thought carefully, for Enrico is not an ordinary man. He wondered if Enrico was even human. Enrico remained an extraordinary being with exceptional powers. Austin came to loathe Enrico's relentless presence. He grasped the fact that Enrico maintained his power over Hannah.

Austin wondered how he could protect her from something he did not fully understand. It remained unclear if victory was even attainable. Their future remains uncertain, but Austin refused to admit defeat under any circumstance. He vowed to fight for her until the bitter end. He realized fear of the unknown always leads to defeat. The unknown was now crystal clear and he decided to use this newfound knowledge to his advantage. It became clear that Enrico could sense her every move. It remained the only reasonable scenario. He is certain this is how Enrico knew about the dance, their picnic and her whereabouts. Austin closed his eyes as he felt certain Enrico knew where she was at this very moment—And who accompanied her. He could not turn back the hands of time; Hannah is with him now and he would not change that for anything in the world. He knew they must take advantage of the time they have together. Austin sat down beside her and captured her gaze, "I love you Hannah. We will conquer this battle together and only together, can we prevail!" Something in the pit of his soul told him so.

Hannah knew she found her soul mate, as she looked deep within his eyes. Her destiny sat right before her. She desperately wished she'd realized it sooner. Neither one knew what Enrico was capable of if he found out they were together now. Austin rose and sauntered across the room to retrieve the manila folder. He stopped mid-stride, unable to discuss Enrico any further.

Instead, he carried the burden concerning the Ring of Eternity alone. He returned to Hannah's side and allowed his body to speak for him. Every ounce of his soul told him they might never have this chance again. Desperate times call for desperate measures and Austin let go of all inhibitions. They lied upon the bed and united as one body, one mind, and one soul.

The next morning, as Hannah dressed, she heard her mother calling.
"Hannah, Kayla, come downstairs?"
Kayla met Hannah in the hallway, "Do you know what this is about?"
Hannah shrugged her shoulders, "I have no idea."
The two sisters trudged downstairs expecting the worst. They were astonished to find their mother elated. Rebecca greeted them with a warm inviting smile.
"I have something extraordinary to tell you; come into the living room!"
They followed, seated themselves and watched Rebecca with curios eyes. Rebecca could not quit smiling.
"I submitted applications for the two of you to take part in a modeling program and your applications were both selected," she nearly cried.
Kayla immediately jumped in excitement, "Where are we going and when do we leave?" she asked eagerly.
"You leave in three hours and you will be in Nicaragua for two weeks."
"Merry Christmas," Brian added.
"Nicaragua," Kayla shouted.
It became obvious that Kayla was on cloud nine. Hannah, however, did not share Kayla's enthusiasm. She thought about it and concluded that it was just what the doctor ordered. She needed time to herself, away from Enrico's prying eyes. She would miss Austin terribly, but thought the trip was best in the long run. It felt good to know she would return in time to spend Christmas with her family and Austin. "Mom, Dad, I don't know what to say, but thank you," Hannah said, meaning it with all her heart.
Rebecca smiled, "You are very welcome," she said, and hugged both girls.
Kayla grabbed Hannah's arm, coaxing her upstairs. "You better get packed and then call Austin, for we don't have much time."
Hannah and Kayla packed their luggage, mindful not to forget any necessities. Brian gathered the luggage and sat it on the front porch. *I'd swear they packed enough for a year.* Rebecca went over the details regarding the trip with Kayla while Hannah called Austin.

* * *

Austin finished his morning ride as the outside ringer began to ring. He reluctantly went inside to answer the phone. Austin took caution as he picked up the receiver and brought it to his ear, "Hello," he said forcefully. Austin sighed with relief when he heard Hannah say, "Austin, it's me." He greeted her affectionately, "Hi Baby, how are you?"

"I have something to tell you, but I don't have much time."

Austin listened intently as Hannah spoke about a modeling campaign she and Kayla were about to embark on.

"Mom submitted applications for us. Austin, our applications were selected; isn't that wonderful?" Before Austin could answer, Hannah explained further. "It's a Christmas present from our parents and we'll be out of town for two weeks."

Austin suddenly realized she would be a lot safer out of town for the next couple of weeks, away from Enrico. He gripped the phone tight, "Hannah, that's wonderful. Have a great time; I'll miss you."

"I'll miss you too honey; I'll call you from the airport."

Austin panicked, "Airport! Hannah wait; don't hang up. What airport?" he cried, as the dial tone echoed in his ear. He hung up the phone and immediately called her back. He desperately needed more information. The phone rang four times and Austin heard the answering machine say, "You have reached 555-1952. We are unable to take your call right now, but if you leave your name, number and a brief message, we'll return your call as soon as possible." Austin hung up the phone after leaving Hannah a message to call back before departing. He needed to know where their travels would take them. He'd try again in a few moments. Austin walked into the kitchen to get a glass of orange juice. The phone began to ring, as he poured the juice. He raced to the phone, assuming Hannah was returning his message. Austin answered the phone with a warm and tender, "Hello!"

Austin did not hear Hannah's voice. He heard a familiar cold harsh tone instead.

"You disobeyed my wishes and now I have no choice. I told you I had the power to take her away from you."

The line immediately fell dead. He instantly called Hannah and Rebecca answered the phone. "Is Hannah their?" he asked impatiently.

"I'm sorry Austin, but their limousine just picked them up. I'm sure Hannah will call as soon as possible," Rebecca explained.

Austin felt his world begin to shatter, as his knees gave out and he plummeted to the floor. *What have I done?* He unintentionally helped seal her fate and felt he handed Hannah over to Enrico on a sliver platter. He recalled Hannah's words. *'I'll call you from the airport.'* Austin felt a shred a hope. He could still prevent her from proceeding. He desperately needed to know the planes destination. All Austin could do was hope and pray for the best as he awaited her call.

Hannah and Kayla enjoyed their limo ride. They traveled for about three hours before arriving at the airport. The girls stepped out of the limo and stood before a sign that read: *Welcome to Sangria Airlines.* They were at the Pittsburgh International Airport. Kayla glanced down at their departing tickets for Managua, Nicaragua, she held tightly in her hand. The driver took care of their luggage as a woman, wearing a rather professional business suit, approached them.

"Hello, my name is Allison and I'm the Representative Director. I need to check your names off the manifest and collect all departing tickets," she said with a bright smile, and then added, "I wouldn't want to leave anyone behind."

Kayla grasped the tickets even tighter. Holding them made the trip feel more realistic. She reluctantly handed them over and Allison shook both their hands as they introduced themselves.

Allison directed them to security and offered directions to terminal B, flight 807. "Stand by the large banner; you can't miss it."

They stood in the security line. Kayla politely nudged Hannah on the shoulder and pointed to a sign informing each passenger to empty their pockets and remove all jewelry upon entering the security scanners. Hannah's eyes widened but knew there was nothing she could do and shrugged her shoulders. She stepped up to security and explained that her finger swelled and she could not remove her ring. The security guard motioned her through the security scanner and waved her off to the side. The detector beeped and another security guard waved a security wand up and down her body in a slow sweeping motion. The wand beeped only when it encountered the ring. They motioned her to proceed. Kayla awaited her on the other side. They exchanged a glance of trepidation as they tackled the first step of their adventure.

They made their way through the airport without any difficulties and stood beneath a large banner that read: *Dark Horse Advertising Inc. Welcomes all Seasonal Models.* Other girls quickly joined them. Hannah made a mental note that each girl present adorned longhair. Hannah checked her cell phone reception only to discover there was no service. She sighed, certain that she checked the coverage area before leaving. Hannah had to call Austin as promised. She tapped Kayla on the arm.

"I'm going to find a payphone; I'll return shortly."

Kayla waved her off, as Hannah looked frantically for a payphone. She noticed one just down from the terminal. She found a souvenir shop and purchased a twenty-minute phone card. The flight would not depart for another forty minutes. She quickly made her way back to the payphone. Hannah dialed Austin's number and sighed with disgust as the automated voice hissed in her ear.

"There are ten remaining units available for this call."

Apparently, Hannah forfeited the first ten units because she chose to utilize a payphone. She rested her brow against the phone. The phone rang twice and Austin immediately answered.

"Hello," Austin whispered.

Hannah jumped, "Hi Austin, I'm at the airport and we're awaiting our flight to Nicaragua," she said. Hannah placed a hand over her ear, "I can barely hear you Austin; you're breaking up." Hannah could not understand what Austin attempted to tell her, but the tone of his voice told her it was important. "Han…, d…t get…the pl…," is all she heard. The remaining ten units expired in no time flat and the call immediately disconnected. Hannah looked at the phone, "I will call again once we arrive in Managua," she whispered. Hannah smiled and thought about Managua. She anticipated basking in the warm sunlight. She hung up and returned to the terminal. Hannah found Kayla, who already began to make new friends.

Austin hung up the phone realizing Hannah did not comprehend his warning. He cringed in despair. Hannah was in grave danger and he remained powerless to prevent the inevitable. He knew Hannah unsuspectingly embarked on a collision course venturing directly into Enrico's path. Austin felt the gravest notion that this entire escapade was a ploy to entrap her.

He suddenly wished he heeded Enrico's warning. It was too late now, for Hannah was gone. "I should have showed her the manila folder," he nearly screamed. He felt certain if Hannah knew all available information regarding the Ring of Eternity, she would be safe wrapped in his protecting arms. Austin felt responsible and hung his head in shame, for he would never forgive himself for withholding information.

* * *

    Hannah counted nearly fifty girls. She found little amusement in the idle chitchat and gossip that now surrounded her. Kayla seemed to relish her popularity. Hannah was just happy to get the hell out of Greenville for a while. She is optimistic for Kayla, for modeling is right up Kayla's alley. Allison instructed all the girls to push together as photographers took photos and news media personnel interviewed her. Boarding procedures commenced shortly later. They'd arrive in Managua via three private jets. Hannah grabbed Kayla's arm as gates one, two and three boarding lights illuminated, for she wished them to stay together. Allison broke the girls up into groups. Hannah and Kayla gathered in-group three and stood at gate three. Hannah thought the entire process was rather chaotic, for girls ran in all directions. Allison quickly returned order within the groups.
    Hannah and Kayla boarded their jet. Hannah sighed in relief, for there was no seating arrangement. She sat beside Kayla and noticed the flight attendant counting heads.
    "I have fifteen passengers," she called to Allison, who stood outside the plane.
    They were in route before long. Hannah slept most of the flight—politely choosing to avoid their newfound comrades. Kayla gently woke her as they approached the Managua International Airport.
    "How long was I asleep?" Hannah asked, and then rubbed the sleep from her eyes.
    "Four hours."
    Hannah gazed out the window and noticed the coastline. "Isn't it beautiful?" she asked Kayla, nudging her arm.
    Kayla leaned over and agreed, "Look how blue the water is."
    Hannah's eyes moistened. For once, she perceived the world in many shades other than green. All passengers prepared for landing by placing all trays in an upright position and fastening their seatbelts. The captain maintained a smooth landing.
    Allison greeted them once again when they exited the plane. There were three limousines awaiting their arrival. The girls separated into groups of five. Allison assigned Kayla to limo one while Hannah awaited limo three.
    "Where do we venture next?" Hannah asked Allison.
    Allison smiled vibrantly, "You'll see," she replied.
    The limo ride lasted two and a half hours. Hannah remained motionless and speechless the entire ride as she gazed out the window. She noticed how

beautiful the countryside appeared. It nearly astounded her when a huge lake came into view. Hannah pressed her face against the tinted glass as she noticed an island in the middle of the lake. Hannah gasped when a castle, nestled in the center of the island, became noticeably visible. *Is that where we're heading?* The limo came to a halt shortly later. The chauffeur opened the door and Hannah exited quickly, filled with anticipation.

She saw Allison standing by a large dock and noticed a ferry just behind her. The group gathered before her.

Allison explained that they were the final group and the ferry would return in thirty minutes. "Upon departure, you will form a single line and begin check in procedures," she explained, and then added, "This is the final leg of your journey but your adventure has just begun and many doors of opportunity await each and every one of you."

The group waited patiently. Hannah's mind filled with a million thoughts. She checked her cell phone reception to discover there was still no service. Hannah began to loathe cell phones and glanced at her watch. It was nearly seven-thirty. *That can't be right, it's still daylight.* It dawned on her there was a one-hour time difference. It was actually six-thirty in Nicaragua. Hannah adjusted her watch as the ferry prepared to dock.

The group boarded the ferry wondering what surprises the castle held in store for them.

"What is this place called?" Hannah asked Allison.

"You are about to step onto hallowed ground. The castle is known as the Castillo de Isla and was once home to…"

"We're docking," someone cried.

Allison realized they were not interested in learning the history of the castle and sighed. She rounded up the group and prepared the final manifest.

Hannah left Allison and thought about how ordinary her day started—twelve and a half hours ago. She felt they covered more territory in half a day than many experience in a lifetime. Hannah became grateful and promised to cherish the memories she would soon experience with Kayla. She made a mental note of how beautiful the lake looked and burned a picture into her memory that would last an entire lifetime. The group stood behind the yellow line as the ferry docked.

Hannah departed the ferry and stood before the enormous castle. She noticed how worn the masonry appeared and felt the castle was strong enough to withstand the hands of time. Invasive ivy transcended the main wall making it visually impossible to determine where the castle ends and the botanical gardens begin. There was no mote surrounding the castle as childhood fairytales often depict, for the lake became its mote. Hannah gazed at the west wing with a peculiar expression.

The west façade of the castle appeared dark and grim with overcastted shadows. Hannah stood on the walkway, which led to the botanical gardens, and gazed up at the sky. The sun was about to set in the west and she understood that the east-facing façade should be overcastted, not the westward side. Hannah glanced at her own shadow, which faced east. The castle's shadow reflected in the opposite direction and she could not fathom why. The castle appeared uncanny, but Hannah quickly dismissed these thoughts, for the Castillo de Isla made the hacienda look like a bungalow. The windows are twice the height of Hannah and the windowsills appeared four feet thick. Hannah imagined how warm and cozy it would feel to curl up with a good book and several throw pillows. She decided to do just that, if their demanding schedules allowed free time. Hannah doubted they would spend much time in their rooms. She knew they would be extremely busy. The door attendant opened the door for them as they entered the castle. They all walked into the main lobby completely in awe. Allison instructed them to wait a moment while she oversaw last minute check in procedures.

Chapter 5
The Castillo de Isla

Antonio sat behind the Registration desk and was on the verge of a splitting headache. He greeted forty young women but none turned out to be the one he desperately searched for and his mind grew vex. He felt insipid and his patience began to run thin, for there was nothing special about any of these girls. He found each girl to be vain and obnoxious. The idle chitchat, the gossip and the giggling were more than he could bear.

Allison appeared in the doorway and announced the final group of five.

Antonio closed his eyes and replied harshly, "Proceed."

He began to speculate whether or not the young woman in question was even present. Antonio forced a smile as the next group approached the desk. "Sign your name on the next available line." He glanced at the back of the line and the final young woman enthralled his senses. She was tall and slender with long blonde hair. Antonio thought she had the body of a goddess—One that Enrico would graciously lie down and offer his own life to protect.

Hannah observed the entire room. The man seated behind the desk appeared intrigued. She noticed that his shirt was partially unbuttoned revealing his upper chest. She watched as the group, one-by-one, signed their names. Hannah scanned her thoughts. *This man seems familiar*. She could not determine his height, but his broad shoulders told her he was tall. She noted his muscular physique. Hannah felt no physical attraction towards this man whatsoever. Part of her actually detested him. She could not fathom why though. It was clear she never met the man before. Hannah is generally a very good judge of character. Enrico has been her only downfall. Something in her gut told her to beware of the man seated before her.

Antonio instantly noticed she was unlike the others. They were chatty and giggly while she remained poised and sophisticated—more like a woman. The first four girls signed their names and he saw nothing that captured his gaze. Antonio motioned for the door attendant to close and lock the door, as the final woman approached the desk. He stood up from his chair to show respect for the blonde beauty. "Sign your name please," he instructed, and then pointed to the base of the form.

Hannah bent down and attempted to sign her name, but the paper kept sliding across the table. She tilted her chin, glanced up at her host and managed a pretentious smile. Hannah felt slightly embarrassed and politely drew her left hand and held the paper, firmly in place, to keep it from sliding. Without even thinking, she signed *Savannah*. Antonio's eyes widened with delight.

His search was over, for she came to him as predicted and she adorned the Ring of Eternity—The crest of the Costello legacy. "I am pleased to make your acquaintance, Savannah," he whispered.

Hannah flinched and glanced down at her signature. She quickly realized what happened and politely walked around the desk to exit where the others had, but found the door locked. She turned abruptly to find the man staring at her intently with crossed arms. Again, she noted his height, broad shoulders, muscular physique, dark brown wavy hair and gray eyes. He looked familiar but Hannah could not place her finger when or where she might have seen him before. Antonio encircled her once, ogling seductively down upon her. Each time he took a step closer, she took a step backwards. Antonio mused with delight.

Before Hannah understood what was happening, he backed her into a corner. "I wish to join the others," she demanded firmly.

Antonio smiled devilishly, "Allow me to introduce myself," he hissed, and then reached for her hand. "I am Lord Antonio Costello and I am delighted to make your acquaintance, my Lady." Antonio then kissed her hand tenderly.

"What," she cried. She knew any attempt to run was futile, for he already took firm grasp of her wrists and held her steadfast.

"It would give me immense pleasure if you would accompany me upstairs," he whispered sternly. He whirled her around so her back rested against his chest as he crossed her arms. He continued to keep a firm grip around her delicate wrists.

Hannah tried to fight his strength with no prevail and his power overwhelmed her senses. She withdrew resistance and he slightly loosened his grip.

"Isn't that better, my Dear," he whispered in her ear, and then added, "I think we'll get along marvelously," and kissed her cheek.

Hannah closed her eyes and felt a cold chill run down her spine.

"If you refuse to walk, I will be forced to carry you."

Hannah walked forwards and allowed him to lead from behind, for she did not wish to be carried. She secretly conserved her energy. They walked down a long corridor, which opened up to a stairwell. "This is hardly necessary," she whispered, and then added, "You already proved resistance is futile."

Antonio grinned, "That we agree upon." He allowed her to walk beside him. One hand kept a firm grip around her waist while the other kept hold of her wrists.

They reached the top step and Hannah turned to face her abductor.

"Are you Enrico's brother?"

"Yes," he replied sharply.

She paused and whispered, "Why are you doing this?"

Antonio heard fear in her voice and replied in a warm soothing tone, "Shhhh...we're almost there."

They continued to saunter and Antonio pressed her back to his chest once again as they approached an elaborate Cherry stained door. He continued to grasp her wrists with one hand and opened the door with the other. He released her and instantly locked the door, once inside.

"So we won't be disturbed, my Lady."

Hannah nearly panicked as those words echoed throughout her mind. Antonio crossed the room and chilled a rather expensive bottle of Chablis.

"Would you like a thirst-quencher, my Lady?"

Hannah immediately declined. Antonio sat the bottle aside and removed a rather intricately carved wooden box from the armoire. Hannah noted the armoire resembled the one at the Hacienda. She kept a fearful, yet watchful, eye upon him. She watched as he removed two clasped platinum bracelets and a watch from the box.

He placed the watch upon his wrist and turned to Hannah with the bracelets in his hand, "Put these on," he instructed.

Hannah glared at him with uncompromising eyes, "If you think I'm placing those things on my wrists after being stuck with a ring on my finger, you are gravely mistaken."

Her words amused Antonio. He smiled and crossed his arms over his broad chest. "We can do this the easy way or the hard way; the choice is yours," he murmured, as his smile faded.

Hannah became aloof, ignoring him completely.

"Savannah," he whispered tenderly.

Hannah still refused to acknowledge him.

"Savannah, look at me," he demanded.

Hannah met his gaze with unwavering eyes as Antonio pleaded with her.

"I don't want to hurt you, but I am prepared to use force…if necessary!"

Hannah found herself in a difficult situation. She thought about the request and attempted to rationale the reasoning, feeling certain there were strings attached. "I will not take them from your hand, but you may lay them upon the armoire," she decided, after careful consideration.

Antonio did as instructed and moved away. "I promise not to touch you; I will wait for you to come to me," he whispered, and then bowed.

"I will never come to you." Hannah paused for a moment and approached the armoire slowly. She reluctantly picked up the bracelets, examined them closely and, one by one, clasped them over her wrists. Antonio showed instant gratification as he relentlessly declared victory. Hannah immediately attempted to remove the bracelets with no prevail, as sheer panic overshadowed her heart.

Antonio unbuttoned his silken shirt and revealed his entire chest. He walked over to the bed, piled up a few pillows and rested back upon them. He lounged and appeared rather comfortable, while Hannah felt like leaping out of her skin. Her flesh began to crawl as fear filled her soul. He straightened one leg upon the bed and allowed the other to dangle off the edge.

Antonio patted the space between his legs, "Come and sit," he whispered.

"I don't think so," Hannah returned firmly. There was no hesitation in her response as she began to back away.

Antonio's smile widened, "Savannah, you do not yet understand the magnitude of your bracelets; allow me to demonstrate." He glanced at his watch and pressed the second hand twice.

Hannah jumped in pain at that exact moment, but refused to give him the satisfaction of crying aloud. The bracelets unleashed a pulsating shock that truly hurt. She fought vigorously to remove them once again but soon realized it was futile and fought back the tears. She met Antonio's icy gaze as he, once again, motioned her to come and sit.

Antonio gazed into her beseeching eyes and nearly gave in to her silent plea. He refocused quickly, "That was the absolute lowest setting; you bring this upon yourself, Savannah. Do not fight me," he whispered gently, but forcefully and once again patted the space between his legs.

Hannah sauntered towards the bed. Her legs stiffened as his gray eyes beckoned her to come hither. She closed her eyes briefly but was unable to silence the voice embedded within her mind. *'I will wait for you to come to me,'* the voice continued to hiss. She stopped dead in her tracks—realizing Antonio was the devil incarnate. Her hands trembled while her heart spoke defiance, but her mind submitted and forced her legs to continue on their journey—A journey that led to the devil himself.

Hannah approached the bed, turned and sat where Antonio instructed. He instantly pulled her close and swung his leg up. She now sat motionless between his thighs. Hannah tried to remain calm in an upright position, but Antonio slowly forced her back against his bare chest and held her there. He could feel her tremble in his powerful arms and loosened his grip. He felt certain she would not try anything foolish now.

Antonio began to caress her shoulders as her body quit trembling. He knew how easy it would be to take her now, but patience had always been one of his strongest virtues. He held his watch out and pressed the first hand twice.

"No," Hannah screamed. She turned and pressed her cheek against his chest.

"Shhhh," Antonio whispered, as he embraced her. He pointed at the ascended bedposts, "Do you see those small antennas?"

Hannah turned, gazed up and nodded.

"Those are your boundary points; as long as you do not leave the bed, you'll remain safe." Antonio tilted his chin and kissed her brow, "Sleep time, my Lady; I know you must be exhausted after your long journey."

Hannah felt his cold icy breath upon her flesh and fell unconscious where she lied. Antonio smiled, for he knew damn well Enrico must be worried sick about his precious Savannah.

Enrico emerged from deep sleep in a cold sweat. His gut twisted and knotted. His head pounded and his wrists throbbed with an ache he could not explain. He scanned his thoughts and for once, he could not locate her. He felt uneasy as his eyes became fierce. He no longer had control. Enrico paced the floor vigorously, back and forth. He heard a knock upon the door and turned,

MYSTIC VOWS

"Enter," he shouted fiercely. Jeano, his most trusted servant, colleague, and friend, entered the room rather alarmed.

"What troubles you, my Lord," Jeano asked, after assessing the situation.

"Nothing!" Enrico shamed himself, for he knew Jeano meant no harm. Jeano served his father loyally. He possessed special skills even Enrico did not fully understand. Jeano remains Enrico's soul confidant and has been like a second father to him. Enrico met Jeano's questioning gaze with crossed arms.

"I have lost control Jeano; why have I lost control?"

Jeano flinched knowing the only way Enrico would no longer possess control is for someone powerful enough to assume control. He carefully chose his words and spoke gently. "When did you notice the change?"

Enrico closed his eyes, "In the middle of the night," he stated, and then added, "Jeano, I felt her pain and anguish."

Jeano quickly searched his thoughts but found no answers. He could not find any words of comfort, so he remained silent. Enrico tried to control his fear with no prevail. He vowed to discover the truth. For the first time in his existence, he felt powerless.

Antonio awoke from sleep feeling his brother's torment. He smiled, completely pleased with himself. Savannah still lied upon his chest. He carefully pressed the first and second hands on his timepiece once and the bracelets slid off her dainty wrists. He carefully unbuttoned a single button upon her blouse. He slid his hand and cupped her warm firm breast. He reveled with delight, but knew today was not the day. *Patience.*

Hannah began to squirm in her sleep and snuggled closer against him. Antonio's eyes searched for answers but found none. Hannah became lost in the moment as she dreamed. She began to caress his leg at first, beginning at the knee and ending at his thigh with long smooth strokes. "Does that fancy you, my Lord," she said, barely above a whisper. Antonio's eyes widened now, for she completely caught him off guard. He could not, did not want to understand, for he rather enjoyed the moment. His loins began to ache for her.

No woman has ever unleashed such passion within him before—with a single touch. Antonio began to understand what came over Enrico. New thoughts rushed into his mind. He now decided to raise the stakes. Hannah rolled off his chest and onto her back. Antonio quickly straddled her. She drew her knees up and hugged his hips. He ripped the buttons from her blouse and caressed her nipples tenderly at first and then with raw passion. She moaned beneath him as he swooned in and kissed her full moist lips. Her kiss exhilarated his senses. Every ounce of her body beckoned for him but he wanted to leave her begging for more. When he finished kissing her, she whispered, "Enter my soul, Enrico," and squeezed her thighs around him.

Antonio leapt to his feet and collected his thoughts. *How could I be so naïve?* He clenched his fists in rage. "I should have known you would continue to mull over my brother."

Antonio cursed Enrico to no end. He felt more than just anger, for his pride had just taken a bullet and left a gaping wound. His icy gaze returned to Hannah. She sat there staring at him with confused eyes. She quickly covered herself after realizing her blouse was torn. Hannah wondered how her blouse ripped and why Antonio exhibited anger towards her. She recalled having a wonderful dream about Enrico. A dream about…and her thoughts came to a screeching halt as she speculated what happened.

"You are full of surprises, my Lady," Antonio hissed, after regaining clarity over his thoughts.

Hannah averted her gaze, "May I please join the others now?" she begged.

Antonio tilted her chin to meet his stern eyes, "For two weeks you belong to me and only me."

Hannah drew up her knees, crossed her arms and buried her brow, incoherently protecting herself.

Kayla kept busy, jumping from one photo shoot to another. She did not expect modeling to be so difficult—Or demanding. The photographers took one hundred and twelve photographs this morning alone. They photographed each girl separately, one-by-one. Hannah's predicament remained oblivious to Kayla. Kayla loved modeling and hoped Hannah enjoyed it just as much. She looked forwards to her next session this afternoon. It was to be held outside, down by the lake. Kayla did not anticipate parading around in a skimpy bikini, but she did find one of the photographers rather sexy though. The cook prepared for the first meal period. Kayla belonged to the first group. They ate at eleven-thirty. She assumed Hannah belonged to the second group and ate at twelve-thirty. It felt strange not to see Hannah in the past sixteen hours. She hoped their paths would soon cross.

Hannah sat at Antonio's desk in the study, which connected to his bedchamber. Her hair dripped wet, as she waited for lunch. The waiter stood outside the door and knocked twice. Antonio ran from the lavatory and opened the door. The waiter wheeled a food cart inside and briskly left. Antonio brought two silver trays into the study and placed them upon the table before her. He returned to the cart and brought back two additional trays.

"I didn't know what you preferred so I had cook prepare a little of everything."

Antonio's hair also dripped wet as he sat down. Hannah remained unresponsive.

Antonio reached across the table and took her hand, "Things could be a lot worse," he insisted.

She immediately withdrew her hand and gazed at the dinner trays. If opportunity knocked, she vowed to seize the moment—secretly wishing there was a knife under one of the dinner trays.

Antonio lifted the trays one-by-one. Hannah held her breath with each motion of his hand. The first tray offered boneless chicken breast in duck sauce with a side of wild greens. Hannah saw no knife. The second tray offered a lobster tail and shrimp scampi with a buttery garlic sauce. Hannah saw no knife. The third platter offered an array of fresh fruits including strawberries, grapes, honeydew and a banana with a side of yogurt. Again, she saw no knife. The fourth tray offered succulent glazed ham with a baked potato and a side of sour cream and chives. Hannah remained steadfast as she observed a carving knife. The food was far from her mind, even though her stomach told her to enjoy.

"Antonio, I'm parched; I'll partake in some wine now," she whispered, never taking her eyes off the knife. She remained in a trance as it called out to her.

Hannah could not focus her attention on anything else. Antonio smiled as he stood and retreated to the bedchamber where the wine sat, still chilled from the previous night. Hannah heard the bottle open as she leapt to her feet and seized the knife. She felt triumphed victory as her senses began to soar. She stood beyond the doorway as Antonio poured the glasses. He finished and carried the glasses towards the study. His senses tuned into her every move and foreseen her intentions. He sat the glasses down and stepped through the doorframe. Hannah attacked with a ferocious might. She managed to slash his arm but he overpowered her and quickly took control of the situation. Antonio restrained her in the chair and observed his flesh wound.

"My dear, did you really think it would be that simple?" he mocked, and then added, "You do not yet understand your calling, but you will…in time."

Hannah did not understand. She recalled the complexity of the shadows upon the castle and concluded that Antonio controlled both wings, but dwelled in one. Her heart ached when she realized she walked right into Antonio's hands. Shadows soon became a secret fear. Hannah could still not fathom why she dreamt about Enrico. She was with Austin now, but the dream cast a shadow of doubt within her soul. Hannah watched as Antonio clenched his fists.

"You would be wise not to mull over my brother, Dearest. You belong to me now." His expression became fierce, but then softened, "You should eat something; you'll need your strength," he whispered. He leaned down, closed the gap between them and kissed her brow.

Hannah observed both sides to Antonio. He could manage to be tender and compassionate, yet firm and powerful. She feared both traits. Hannah managed to eat a few bites with trembling hands, as Antonio remained a raging river with moments of tranquility.

Kayla finished eating lunch and desperately wished to find Hannah. *Hannah must be around here somewhere.* Finally, she asked Allison if she knew Hannah's whereabouts. Allison checked the manifest and insisted that no woman present signed that name. Kayla tensed.

"May I see the manifest?"

Allison reluctantly handed the manifest over.

Kayla scanned through the names and saw *Savannah* at the base of the list. Kayla sighed with relief, for she understood that Hannah inadvertently signed *Savannah*. Her mind eased and her body felt limber again. "Where is Savannah?"

Allison looked at her with questioning eyes, "Savannah belongs to group two and is scheduled for back-to-back photo shoots after lunch."

Kayla returned the manifest and walked away feeling at ease.

Antonio answered another knock at the door and then returned to the study with three garment bags and locked the door. Hannah heard a commotion arise from the bedchamber. Antonio removed an ensemble from the first garment bag and handed it to her. "You are to model a new winter line." He then sat in the corner and peered at her seductively from a distance.

Hannah removed her robe, a section at a time, and dressed as discreetly as possible. She sported a pair of low-rise jeans, a formfitting sweater striped in earth tones with a solid black tee underneath, black heeled boots and a twill cap. Antonio instructed her to pull her hair up. The ensemble came complete with accessories, including the bracelets from earlier. Antonio removed a classy khaki trench coat from the second garment bag. Hannah slid her arms inside and over her shoulders. She looked great on the outside, but her heart concealed all emotions beneath her exterior. Hannah no longer heard noises arising from the bedchamber.

Antonio stood and unlocked the study door. The bedroom now looked like a photo set. Hannah observed props, winter backgrounds and a variety of cameras. Antonio picked up a camera and focused the lens.

"Strike a pose, my Dear."

Hannah glared at him, "I assume you're a photographer now," she returned condescendingly.

Antonio tilted his chin and raised his brow as he twisted his lip into half a smile, "Photography is a hobby of mine," he simply stated.

Hannah posed in front of a snow capped mountain scene. She could not bring herself to smile, not even once. Antonio snapped nearly a hundred pictures. She soon grew tired and no longer wanted the camera in her face. Antonio ordered her to remove her coat. She obeyed and the session continued.

"Savannah, can you remove the sweater and strike a girls gone wild pose?"

Hannah started to enjoy the entire process and figured she would rather have Antonio take her picture than anything else.

She unbuttoned her sweater and removed its tie back. Hannah tossed the sweater aside and placed the tie back around her neck. Antonio turned on the fans as she removed the cap and allowed her hair to flow gracefully. She placed her thumbs in the front pockets and rested her hands. She shifted her weight to the right foot and angled her hips. She slightly bent the left knee and pointed her boot inward towards the camera. The stance and hands were complete. She quickly focused on her eyes. She tilted her chin and gazed directly into the camera. Hannah slightly drew open her full lips.

Antonio gasped, for she nearly took his breath away. He intended to use this photograph to his advantage. Suddenly, he could not wait to wrap up the session. He snapped another fifty shots, just for the hell of it.

"You are absolutely gorgeous; the camera loves you," he murmured, and then added, "I think I'm in love with you," as he took her hand into his.

Hannah withdrew her hand, "There is another garment bag; I'll change and come back," she said coldly. She attempted to drag out the photo shoot, for this was better than the alternatives. She stepped into the study and unzipped the remaining bag. It surprised her to find the bag empty. "Antonio, is this some kind of sick joke?" she cried

Antonio tilted his chin as he place the camera down and met her questioning gaze. He closed the door to formalities and decided tonight was the night to make Savannah his. They had but twelve days left and he vowed to make them count.

Hannah stormed back into the bedroom and threw the empty garment bag at his feet. "I demand to join the others," she screamed. She raced to the door and found it unlocked. She ran down the hall as corridors veered in all directions. Her heart raced wildly as she tasted sweet freedom.

Antonio stood and smiled. He knew damn well this wing of the castle remained sealed off from all others. "Let the games begin," he announced. He tuned into her whereabouts the second she raced through the doorway. He summoned a crew to reorganize the room, "I need the job complete in one hour," he demanded.

Antonio stepped into the hallway and turned left. Hannah turned right, but he decided to cut her off at the pass. The corridors deceptively entwined to form a vast labyrinth. He alone knew how to unlock the mystery. Enrico too became confused in the complexity of the corridors on several occasions. Every possible direction leads to the focal point. Antonio remained the only being who understood this. Hannah raced frantically. Every new corridor resembled the last. Antonio decided it was time to make his intentions known.

"Savannah," he called out seductively, allowing her name to roll off his tongue. "It is time to meet your destiny; search your soul and I know you will feel it too."

Hannah cowered in a dark corner remaining perfectly still. She hoped to remain unnoticed as he passed by.

"Come Savannah...you can not hide forever," he coaxed, toying with her now.

Hannah closed her eyes and drifted away in her mind, but every fantasy led to him. He was inside her mind and now lingered in the shadows of her soul. Fear consumed her emotional state. For once, she wished Enrico were by her side to protect her. Antonio honed in on her position, raced around the corner, and stood before her with crossed arms.

"My brother is not by your side; he abandoned you once and he abandons you now."

Hannah shook her head ferociously. Her mind told her that Antonio spoke the truth, but her heart denied the accusations. Antonio succeeded; he skewed her emotional state. He leaned down to pick her up with no prevail. She fought with every ounce of strength left and ran down another corridor.

Antonio maintained his composure. "We can do this the easy way or the hard way; the choice is yours," he cried. Antonio remained still and waited in silence.

Hannah made one last attempt to unlock the mystery of the labyrinth with no prevail. She rested her back against the wall and drew her hands to her face. Hannah desperately tried to keep it together as Antonio tormented her with clear visions of his intentions. Hannah opened her heart and fought back the only way she could think of. Antonio now saw visions of Hannah and Enrico within his mind. Hannah made certain that he knew she seduced Enrico. She overheard him cursing Enrico and quickly honed in on his position. She began to back away.

Antonio clenched his fists, "You will pay for that, my Dear," he shouted ferociously. He ran rampant now and held nothing back.

Hannah ducked around the corner and listened intently, but no longer heard footsteps. She suddenly felt eyes upon her and cringed as she turned slowly. She met his icy steadfast gaze. Antonio flung her over his shoulder, as though she were a rag doll. He carried her, kicking and screaming, all the way to his room. He tossed her upon the bed, pressed the first hand on his watch twice and locked the door, one last time.

Kayla's photographer took more than enough photos. She never grew tired of the constant attention. She posed as minutes turned into hours, hours turned into days and days turned into weeks. It was time to depart the magical castle where all dreams are possible. This place would forever remain in her mind. She glanced out the window and saw the black limousines begin to line up. She packed all her belongings along with her photos. She decided to keep them separate, at the last minute, to ensure proper handling. Kayla did not have the chance to view the photos and decided to flip through them on the long journey home. Kayla wished she could remain in Managua forever. She took one last glance at her surroundings before calling the bellhop.

* * *

Hannah also began to pack. Antonio refused to keep his hands to himself as she did so.

"Do you need any help?" he whispered.

Hannah did not respond and she refused to look at him. Every ounce of her being loathed him in every way as she wished him dead. She spent two weeks, a Christmas present from her parents, in a single room—with him. She barely slept and she barely ate. Hannah felt completely drained and was literally exhausted. Her heart ached from disgrace. Antonio also felt exhausted, but he knew he would recover just fine. He felt like a brand new man. Hannah placed the bag upon the floor.

"Unlock the door; I have to leave," she whispered.

Before unlocking the door, Antonio sat her down upon his bed one last time. He took her face into his hands and made a solemn vow, "If you tell anyone about our time together, I vow to hunt down your entire family, Austin and my own flesh and blood," he warned, and then added, "Do I make myself clear?"

"Perfectly," she replied coldly.

He kissed her tenderly. Hannah jumped to her feet.

"If opportunity opens another door, I will seize it," he called, as she reentered freedom. Antonio secretly slipped her photo packet inside the luggage bag, setting his plan in motion. He smiled coldly and called for the bellhop.

Hannah understood all to well what he meant. She ran downstairs and never glanced back. She vowed to put this nightmare behind her. Hannah's breathing increased as she realized many lives rested upon her silence. She saw Kayla waiting at the base of the stairs and greeted her with a pretentious smile. Hannah was glad to find Kayla unharmed. Kayla too smiled warmly with bright eyes.

"Wasn't this trip hectic and exciting at the same time?"

Hannah simply nodded. Kayla was still overwhelmed with the magnitude of the trip and did not notice any changes in Hannah. This stunned Hannah, given her present state. The girls shared a limo to the Managua airport. Hannah slept the entire two and a half hours but refused to allow herself to drift to deeply in fear of having a nightmare and causing a scene. Kayla woke her gently upon arrival.

Hannah had no difficulties during the security check at the airport. However, the terminal check was a different story. Hannah was taken aside as an interpreter explained that her passport was stamped *Business*, but the Business Stamp remained blank.

"We are terribly sorry, but until this matter can be resolved, we'll have to deny you access to this flight," the interpreter explained, as politely as possible.

Hannah waited for a later flight until her paperwork was in order. She watched Kayla board the flight in despair. *What else can possibly go wrong?*

Chapter 6
A Sacred Vow

The interpreter returned several hours later.

"Miss Brockwell, the Managua International Airport apologizes for any inconveniences. It turns out that Dark Horse Advertising Inc. applied their stamp to an incorrect page. Your jet will be ready in a few moments. Again, we apologize for any inconveniences this mix-up may have caused. The Managua International Airport is offering free flight tickets to Nicaragua..."

"No thank you; that won't be necessary."

Hannah flashed a genuine smile as the interpreter turned and walked away. She wondered if she would make it home in time for Christmas and teetered on the verge of an emotional breakdown. Hannah did not wish to return to this cursed country. She pushed her emotions deep within her heart and locked them there. *I just want to go home, is that too much to ask for?*

"Miss Brockwell," the receptionist whispered.

Hannah glanced up and noticed the boarding light. There was no one else in line. *Some privacy at last.* A twisted smirk crept across her lips as she sauntered down the tunnel and boarded the jet. To her astonishment, the jet was top notch and equipped with every luxury. It had both living and sleeping quarters and a lavatory with double sinks. *I'll wash up first and then Enrico...Enrico! Why can't I get him out of my mind...and heart?* She felt confused and closer to him then ever. She could not shake the feeling that...

"The Managua International Airport hopes this will compensate for your delay, Miss Brockwell!" The captain spoke fluently as he shook her hand. "There is one other passenger on board; if you'll take a seat, we can proceed momentarily."

Hannah took a seat upon the couch and melted into the contours of the armrest. Her heart stilled and her mind became lucid. Surprisingly, she felt nothing. Ten minutes later, they were in route. She began to relax. *Finally. If I ever lay eyes on another Costello...*

"Miss," a voice whispered from behind. "Would you like a glass of Champaign?"

Thank God, a flight attendant. "That sounds nice," she replied, to weak to turn around. She held out her hand for a glass, but received a warm suntan hand instead. Hannah jumped to her feet and dared to meet the stranger's eyes. She came face-to-face with Enrico's emerald gaze. She could not decide whether to run or embrace him. *What is he doing here?* She shielded all thoughts from his questioning eyes. She forced a translucent smile but could not prevent her lower lip from quivering. Hannah read his expression and instantly realized he did not buy her deceptive illusion.

Enrico read her eyes and questioned her actions. He needed to see, with his own eyes, that she was all right and discover whom she spent the past two weeks with. Enrico felt both relief and torment when he sensed her presence this morning as complete control returned to him. Nothing could ever keep him from his Savannah, so he came as quickly as possible. He did not like the appearance of her physical condition. *She looks as though she hasn't slept in days.* He reached for her but she did not welcome his embrace. He flinched when he saw fear within her eyes. Enrico executed caution now, for he had given no reasons for her to fear him.

Hannah thought her eyes deceived her, so she quietly lied upon the couch and closed her eyes. *This is just a figment of my imagination. I'll take a nap and he'll be gone.* Enrico could not fathom her exhaustion. She appeared weak and malnourished to his keen eyes. He wondered when she last ate a decent meal. Enrico leaned down, slid a hand beneath her, picked her up and carried her to the sleeping quarters in the next room.

He covered her legs with a blanket and noticed she adorned a long sleeve sweater. *Who wears a sweater in Nicaragua?* Enrico dismissed the thought feeling certain she prepared for the cold weather awaiting her back home upon arrival. She obviously was in dire need of sleep and Enrico gave attention to her every need. He turned to leave as Hannah opened her eyes. Her eyes widened. *It wasn't a dream! He's actually here.* Hannah fought a lump in her throat and whispered, "Please stay with me Enrico." *What...what am I thinking?*

Enrico stopped dead in his tracks. He turned and slowly approached the bed. He sat down as she made room for him. "Savannah," he whispered gravely, and then added, "I want...I need answers; please talk to me." He reached for her delicate hand, drew it to his lips and kissed it as he laced his fingers between hers. Enrico refused to shelter his true feelings. "This is tearing my heart apart," he confessed. "I love you, body, mind, heart and soul."

He averted his eyes for a moment and noticed a purplish bruise on her tiny wrist just above the sweater line. Enrico quickly went to investigate, but Hannah immediately withdrew her hand and shook her head. He obeyed the request, for now. His heart told him she left wounded. He bit his tongue and controlled his rage. Enrico got comfortable beside her. His body longed for her touch, but he knew this was neither the time nor place. Hannah used every bit of remaining strength to climb atop Enrico and kiss him passionately. He quickly returned her kiss.

She could no longer bear the thought of Antonio's kiss lingering upon her lips. Part of her resisted the urge while her soul took flight and seized the moment. Hannah felt exhausted and could not comprehend her emotions as she melted into the curves of his body. Her cheek nestled into the curve of his neck, her palm rested upon his firm chest and her knee draped over his thigh. She fell asleep and remained lost to the world for the next few hours.

Enrico tried talking to her and asked numerous questions, but she fell deep asleep and would remain asleep for some time. He gently slipped out from under her. "First order of business," he whispered. He knelt beside the bed with the utmost of honorable intentions and examined the bruise upon her wrist. He took her hand and kissed it tenderly as he rolled up her sleeve. Shock overwhelmed him. He saw fresh bruises up and down her arm and her wrist looked slightly burned. He quickly observed the other arm to find it equally bruised.

"What did this man...this Rogue...do to you?" he asked, with no response. Disgust, anger and rage overwhelmed his soul. Only one word lingered in his thoughts—*Revenge.* He vowed to seek revenge upon this monster. He then recalled a technique Jeano often utilized. Jeano once said, 'If you clear your mind and focus all your energies towards a focal point, such as another, you can gain passage into their soul.' Enrico tried this technique with no prevail. He suddenly wished Jeano were there.

Enrico paced back-and-forth, as they headed for Pittsburgh. He found her carry on bag still lying in the living quarters. He picked it up, sat it upon the couch and opened it. He discovered a manila envelope lying on top. He carefully opened the folder and removed many photographs of Savannah, mostly in long pants and long sleeves. *These are professional photos.* There was something about them, for she did not smile. Enrico clenched his fists as his keen eyes viewed one particular photo. Hannah's eyes appeared seductive and alluring. Enrico wondered who took the photos and whom Savannah peered at seductively. Enrico knew what had to be done, for he desperately needed answers.

Hannah woke six hours later and was surprised at how rested she felt. She learned that they stopped to refuel. The pilot informed her that Enrico entered the airport briefly to attend to business.

"Which airport are we at?" she asked intuitively.

"Pittsburgh International, my Lady."

Hannah questioned his last remark and seized her window of opportunity. She walked off the plane and out of Enrico's life. She refused to allow Enrico to discover the truth about Antonio. Enrico meant too much to her to risk such a dark revelation. She would not—and could not—allow Enrico to choose between Antonio and herself. Selfishly, Hannah wanted all the revenge to herself. She had no clue how she would make it home, for she took nothing with her. She entered the airport and found the nearest payphone. She immediately called Austin collect as her heart pounded uncontrollably.

Austin pounced on the phone after it began to ring. It was early morning and Janice still slumbered in her room. "Hello," he said eagerly. The line remained silent. "Hello," he repeated.

"Austin it's me, Hannah."

"Where are you?"

"I'm at Pittsburgh International; there was a delay in Managua."

Austin listened as Hannah explained that the second jet belonged to Enrico and that she walked off while he attended to business. He remained silent controlling his thoughts.

"Austin, I need your help; I'm trapped with no luggage and no money. I just want to return home to you and my family. If I get back on that jet, I fear I never will."

"Do not return to the jet," Austin returned instantly, and then added, "I will come for you; I'll be there in two hours."

"I'll be waiting at the main entrance; I love you!" she whispered.

Austin cringed as he heard a tear in her voice. "I love you too, Hannah," he said, and slammed down the phone. Austin quickly wrote a note for his mother and grabbed a road map. He vowed to kill Enrico if he dared to lay a single hand upon her—no regrets and no remorse.

Enrico sought out Derrick, a life long colleague. He hoped Derrick could offer some answers. Derrick worked security at the airport and owed Enrico a favor. Enrico stood motionless outside the main security parameter. Derrick instantly noticed him and ventured over quickly.

"To what do I owe the honor, my Lord?"

Enrico stared at his old friend grimly, "I need answers to questions I believe you can assist with."

Derrick read Enrico's eyes and saw the importance in the request. His eyes revealed a level of determination Derrick never witnessed before. Derrick began to question Enrico's motives. "What is it you need to know?"

Enrico sharpened his gaze. "Two weeks ago a group of young women boarded private jets destined for Managua. Who authorized and compensated the arrangement of those jets?"

Derrick flinched, "I will need some time," he insisted.

Enrico disagreed, "You have five minutes," he stated, and meant every word.

Derrick raced to his computer and overrode the security code attaining access to the financial records. He scrolled down to December 8 and noticed an entry for three private jets chartered from Sangria Airlines. Dark Horse Advertising Inc. authorized the transaction. Derrick could find no personal name assigned to the corporate account. He returned to Enrico with the findings.

Enrico clenched his fists. "So the coward hides behind a corporate name."

Derrick wore an expression of puzzlement upon his face. Enrico instantly sensed something was wrong. Without hesitation, he left Derrick and ran back to the jet. He ran through the living quarters and into the sleeping quarters. The pilot came in and stood behind him.

"I'm sorry my lord but she left, probably when I was making my checkpoint rounds."

Enrico became enraged. *Whey would she run from me?* Enrico needed her and he loved her, but right now, all he thought about was claiming his revenge upon the rogue that harmed her. Revenge overwhelmed his rationale and he vowed to succeed. He left the jet and reentered the airport.

Hannah remained inconspicuous in the ladies restroom. She pretended to fuss with her hair each time a woman entered. Her stomach rumbled but she had no money for a bite to eat. A woman entered and observed her curiously. Hannah could not fathom why the woman continued to stare.

The woman approached, "Honey, no man is worth that," she conveyed solemnly, pointing at Hannah's bruises.

Hannah cringed and remained silent, for no words came to mind.

"Honey, do you need help?"

Hannah shook her head and the woman reluctantly walked away. Hannah stood there motionless, finally hitting rock bottom. She suddenly wanted the world to leave her alone and envisioned a secluded forest perched high upon a mountaintop.

Enrico searched for Savannah with no prevail. He felt he had no other choice and approached Derrick. "There is a young woman, a reported runaway, somewhere in the airport. She has long blonde hair and is five foot seven inches. We must locate her," Enrico demanded.

Derrick did not question Enrico and immediately alerted security and followed through with the intercom announcement. "Miss Savannah Brockwell, please report to Terminal A, Gate Three. Miss Savannah Brockwell, please report to Terminal A, Gate Three."

Enrico quickly scanned his thoughts.

Hannah began to panic. She quickly tucked her long hair inside her sweater. She felt Enrico closing in on her whereabouts and quickly glanced at her watch. Austin should arrive in thirty minutes at the main entrance. She looked around and felt helpless. Hannah closed her eyes and desperately wished Enrico would simply leave her alone. She knew they would search the restrooms and turned to leave. Hannah jumped and stared at the woman from earlier.

"Honey, I believe you should let someone help you," the woman stated.

Hannah felt trapped, "Is anyone out in the concourse?" she asked abruptly.

The woman glanced around the doorframe and shook her head. Hannah ran out and straight into Enrico's arms. He held her steadfast, mindful not to hurt her, and thanked the woman for her help.

The woman smiled, "Take care Honey, and allow your loved ones to help you," she said, and then walked away.

Hannah met Enrico's gaze with contempt. "What did you tell her?"

"Simply that you were a runaway and attempted to run back into the arms of the man who inflicted these bruises upon you," he explained, and then whispered, "Escape is not an option."

Hannah gasped and wondered how much he knew. Enrico kissed her cheek affectionately. Security surrounded them before Hannah realized what was happening. She found herself trapped with no place to run.

Derrick handed Enrico a pair of handcuffs lined with foam padding. Enrico hated to add insult to injury, but he would not risk losing her again. The rogue that abducted her may return. He only thought about her safety and upheld the utmost desire to protect her. He silently promised to release her in the custody of her family. Ten armed security officers escorted them through the concourse. Hannah quickly retracted a previous thought, for she now hit rock bottom. She watched helplessly as spectators stared at them and briskly stopped to face her abductor.

"Please do not parade me through the airport like this; I deserve better."

Enrico felt her despair and removed his jacket. He draped it over the cuffs and now Hannah appeared to carry the jacket.

"We no longer need your services, gentlemen," he stated.

Security immediately left their side.

"Does that please you, my Lady?"

Hannah shook her head, "Releasing me will please me," she whispered.

Enrico sighed, knowing her request was out of the question, "This is for your own protection," he returned.

They now stood at the main entrance.

Enrico embraced her tenderly and added, "You left me no choice."

Hannah stood on her tiptoes and glanced over his shoulder. She caught a glimpse of Austin's car across the parking lot. She noticed that security spread throughout the room and they continued to keep a watchful eye upon them.

Enrico felt Austin's presence and grimaced. *This boy will not take her home; I will reunite Savannah with her family.* He stepped back when her thoughts lingered elsewhere. Hannah observed a woman approaching the revolving door. The woman struggled with a large rolling luggage bag and a small child. Hannah found a small window of opportunity. The luggage bag became stuck in the revolving door, leaving a gap just wide enough for Hannah to slip through.

She darted, knowing Enrico became lost in thought. Hannah slipped through the door with ease. Enrico and Security exited the airport through the security entrance. Hannah ran with all her might, as Enrico followed. She glanced around but no longer saw Austin's vehicle and began to wonder if she ever did, as Enrico closed in on her. Hannah felt like she could no longer breathe and fell to her knees. She glanced up and saw a bus swiftly approaching. Her heart stilled, when her eyes closed, and welcomed death head on.

Enrico forced her out of harms way and then lazed atop her upon the asphalt. "Are you hurt?" he asked frantically.

Hannah shook her head, as her eyes moistened. Enrico picked her up and sat her atop the nearest vehicle. He took her face into his hands and his heart melted, but he still could not get the photo out of his mind. Security stood nearby and he silently motioned them to stand alert. He felt Austin's presence overwhelm his senses, as Hannah glanced over his shoulder and met the boy's gaze. Austin used hand gestures to convey his plans. Hannah blinked several times to alert she understood. She returned her focus to Enrico and pushed him back a step, placing an arms length between them.

"Lets walk and talk."

Enrico removed one cuff from her wrist as Security spread throughout the parking lot. Hannah smiled, completely taking the gesture as trust. Enrico took her hand and slid her off the car. He continued to hold her hand. Many thoughts raced through her mind. Hannah watched Austin secretly park the vehicle a dozen cars down and continued to lead Enrico in that direction. Hannah abruptly paused, as she heard security sirens. Security vehicles rapidly approached from all directions. She watched helplessly as Security began to close in around Austin's vehicle. Enrico stood still, while Hannah continued to walk, but the handcuff tugged at her wrist. She turned, only to realize Enrico attached himself to her.

"I want the truth," he demanded softly.

Hannah lost all rhyme and reason, "You can't handle the truth," she cried.

Enrico allowed his rage to get the best of him. He pointed at Austin's vehicle, "Seize the boy; under no circumstance is he to leave the airport," he demanded.

"No," Hannah screamed.

Enrico walked to his limousine and Hannah had no choice but to follow.

Austin watched the approaching security guards. He realized something went wrong when Hannah appeared to struggle with a man. Hannah now followed the man into a limousine. Security cleared a path and the limousine proceeded to exit the airport parking lot towards the freeway ramp. Austin floored the accelerator as a security guard jumped out of his way. Austin maneuvered the vehicle in and out of parking lots in an attempt to elude security. He watched helplessly as the limousine drove out of sight. Security sirens surrounded him and he had nowhere else to turn.

He glanced up at the freeway. The SUV had the clearance to maneuver the curb. He sat there for a moment and second-guessed his chances, as three security vehicles closed in around him. He slammed the SUV into four-wheel drive and left the parking lot. The vehicle plowed through the snow and climbed up the embankment effortlessly. Austin floored the accelerator as he approached the freeway, "Thank god it's not rush hour," he cried, hoping for the best. Three vehicles swerved to miss him.

Austin cruised around ninety-five miles per hour in search of the black limousine. His gut knotted as an overwhelming feeling stabbed at his heart. Suddenly he felt he traveled in the wrong direction. He slammed on the breaks and nearly caused a pile up. Austin crossed three lanes of traffic, jumped the median strip and now traveled westbound. He was determined and refused to give up without a fight. He returned to the airport. His gut told him that Enrico would not venture far from his jet. He knew which terminal the jet resided at and quickly found it. He watched from above as the black limousine came into view.

Enrico reached for Savannah, but she became aloof.

"I only wish to return home," she whispered.

Then and there, Enrico realized he could not force his hand against his beloved Savannah. He knew she needed time to confess on her own terms. He began to feel guilty and wished they could replay the situation at hand. He removed the cuffs and kissed her cheek. She did not meet his gaze. *The boy did make it this far.* As frustrating as the situation was, Enrico came to accept their devotion for one another. *Austin also cares for her safety.* This doubles safety measures, for Hannah will always be in the presence of one or the other.

He reluctantly opened the door and stepped out of the vehicle. He held his head high and made an honorable decision, "Go, he's waiting for you," he whispered and then pointed to Austin standing atop the embankment. Enrico closed the door and gave the chauffeur explicit instructions.

Hannah began to breathe heavily. She did not understand why Enrico released her, but she would forever remain indebted to him. She hung her head and began to sob uncontrollably. She quickly fought back the tears and focused on Austin.

Austin watched a man exit the vehicle, speak to the driver and stand at the base of the boarding platform. The black limo proceeded around and approached him slowly, as the man watched. Austin's heart beat wildly. The limo stopped on the shoulder as Hannah jumped out and embraced him. They fell to their knees and kissed one another passionately. Hannah felt Enrico's anguish but pushed those thoughts aside and focused on the man holding her affectionately. Hannah longed for his loving embrace.

Enrico smiled briefly, for Austin proved himself capable of being prepared for anything, but his smile quickly faded. Enrico watched from afar, as the love of his life embraced another. His heart became heavy as they drove out of sight. He knew he'd hold his *luz del dia* again—It was their destiny.

Hannah dreaded to return home. She desperately needed time alone, to reflect on the past, present and what the future holds. Austin remained silent the entire ride home and for that she was grateful. Hannah caught him glancing at her and still she said nothing. All Hannah wanted to do was sleep, so she reclined her seat and slept. Austin wanted to ask what she has been through but sensed she did not wish to talk about it just yet. Someday he hoped she would come to him and divulge the secrets of the past two weeks. Part of him though, did not ever want to know.

Enrico paced back and forth in the jet. The pilot came in with grim news.
"I caught a glimpse of a man leaving the plane but I did not get a clear view of him."
Enrico glanced around and realized Savannah's luggage was still on board and quickly opened it and discovered the manila folder was gone. He had plans to return to Nicaragua for answers, but his plans abruptly changed. There were answers to discover elsewhere.

Hannah's family was thrilled for her to be home, for they will celebrate Christmas tomorrow. She had to lie about the entire trip. For her it was far from magical, unlike the stories Kayla reminisced about. Rebecca hoped Hannah's lost luggage would turn up soon. She wanted to see her daughter's professional photographs. Austin would not be joining them for Christmas dinner, for it would be too awkward. He understood, as long as she was home where she belonged. He left her house feeling relieved. Though she did not thank him for picking her up today, he knew she appreciated it. He saw it in her eyes and felt it in her embrace. She needed time, and he would give her all the time in the world.

Hannah slept all night, but it was not a peaceful sleep. She remained restless and kept seeing a dark alluring man venturing closer and closer to her, until she awakened in a cold sweat.

"Hannah," she heard her mother calling. "Come help with dinner Honey."

Hannah dressed quickly, thankful it was wintertime, and wore a turtleneck. She slowly walked downstairs and helped Rebecca in the kitchen preparing and baking Christmas dinner. Later, her mother walked into the living room to announce that dinner would be ready in about forty minutes. Kayla set the table with grace, for two weeks in front of a camera instilled a new classiness about her in everything she does now. Rebecca turned when she heard a knock upon the door.

"That must be the courier from the airport!"

She left the kitchen and walked down the hallway to the front door. Hannah and Kayla listened quietly as Rebecca shrilled and cried, "Oh, how wonderful. The man from the airport is here with Hannah's luggage!"

"We've been expecting you; this is awfully nice of the airport to deliver like this, especially on Christmas day." Rebecca thought for a moment as he stared at her in bewilderment. He turned to leave, but Rebecca stopped him saying, "Surely you traveled far and it is Christmas after all; if you don't have to leave right away, would you stay for dinner?" She felt bad that he had to work on Christmas day to deliver her daughter's luggage and it was the least she could do.

"That's not necessary Madame, I do not wish to impose," the stranger replied.

"Nonsense," Rebecca insisted, and then added, "I won't take no for an answer."

He followed Rebecca into the house.

"May I take your Jacket?" she asked, and then added, "Where are my manners. My name is Rebecca Brockwell, I'm Hannah's mother." She reached her hand out and the stranger gladly accepted.

"My name is Enrico Costello. It's an honor to make your acquaintance Mrs. Brockwell."

Rebecca blushed a little saying, "The pleasure is all mine, and please call me Rebecca."

She took him into the living room and made the introductions.

Hannah and Kayla remained in the kitchen in disbelief.

"Is that Enrico?" Kayla asked questionably, and then added, "Who was the other man, for he looked familiar?"

Hannah nodded to the first question and simply shrugged off the second, as she averted her eyes. Both brothers visited her today and Enrico was about to partake in Christmas dinner with them.

"He shouldn't be here," Kayla whispered.

Hannah felt dizzy and whispered, "What is he doing here and what can he want?"

This put her family in jeopardy but she could not cause a scene, not here.

"Hannah," Rebecca called.

Hannah's heart sank, she felt like she could truly lose conciousness.

Kayla gave her a nudge and whispered, "You have to go."

Hannah walked into the living room and desperately tried not to meet his gaze.

"Hannah, this is Enrico Costello from the airport and he has returned your luggage!"

Enrico sat upon the couch and instantly stood to take her hand. He drew her hand to his lips and said, "It is a pleasure to make your acquaintance Miss Hannah Brockwell," knowing she would forever remain his Savannah.

Hannah felt feverish and she suddenly longed for his touch.

Instantly aware that all eyes were on them, he released her hand and said with a chuckle, "I always wanted to do that."

Hannah's parents were instantly amused.

"This will be one of the most interesting Christmas's the family has ever spent," Rebecca proclaimed.

Enrico remained courteous and charming—a true gentleman. When he decided to show up at her home, he did not know what to expect. He did not wish to impose but he secretly desired an invite, for now he could spend Christmas with her, make certain she is all right and determine where her feelings truly lie.

He noticed she wore a turtleneck and a long sleeved sweater. *Undoubtedly to conceal the bruises.* Enrico closed his eyes for a brief moment. She looked beautiful today. He wanted to rush by her side, take her in his arms and just hold her. Enrico was there for information, so he sat back as the family divulged all thoughts on the subject. "You said that you expected me," Enrico questioned.

Rebecca chuckled, "A gentleman from Dark Horse Advertising Inc. heard of Hannah's misfortune and delivered her photographs this morning and informed us a courier from the airport would arrive shortly," she explained.

Enrico thought about her words and secretly clenched his fists. The rogue dared to steal a visit with her at home. He desperately needed answers but refused to force his hand again. He had to remain calm, no matter what the circumstance.

Another place had been set for Enrico at the table, ironically beside Hannah. The family trickled out of the room one by one until only they remained.

Enrico rushed to her side and whispered, "Please tell me if you are alright." He grasped her arm, "Who visited you this morning?"

"Dinner time," Rebecca called from the kitchen.

A million thoughts raced through his mind now. They walked into the kitchen together and sat down. Succulent ham, homemade stuffing, mashed potatoes and gravy lied upon the table. Rebecca and Kayla added green bean casserole, cranberry sauce, freshly baked rolls, and pumpkin pie to the table and then took their seats. They all bowed and Enrico grimaced at the notion, but followed suit as Brian said grace.

"Dear Heavenly Father…thank you for this bountiful feast you have provided. Watch over our mortal souls and feed us with the bread of life. Protect this family, for we remain faithful servants and forever at your mercy, Amen."

There was a moment of silence and then Brian added, "Lord…please watch over our daughter and keep her in your good graces…and if the time comes…please welcome her into the kingdom of Heaven, for she is a daughter of us both. Amen…and all God's children said…Amen. Let us take a moment in prayer."

Hannah and Enrico snapped their heads up and stared at Brian with immense curiosity. His head was still down—Lost in silent prayer. The entire table was like that. Enrico dared to meet Hannah's gaze. He found a million questions lurking behind her baby blue eyes. Enrico shrugged and bowed his head once again. No one at the table seemed to notice her father's last comments. The silence, to Hannah, felt eerie, unnerving, and lasted ten minutes or so. Then, as if nothing happened, they raised their heads and began to eat. Hannah did not know what to feel but if no one else felt uneasy about the situation, she decided not give it another thought.

Enrico's appetite escaped him when he thought how selfish he was to keep her with him. His world flipped upside down the moment she walked into it. Her parents were kind and deserving people and obviously cherished her. Out of respect, he still ate a moderate helping of food and found it delicious. He could not remember when he last had a home cooked meal, so he stopped thinking about it and focused on the most beautiful and vibrant young women seated next to him. She belonged to him—heart, body, mind, and soul. Her family would have to wait, for he was not about to let her go now.

During dinner, Hannah and Enrico kept reaching for the same helpings and their hands brushed against one another's. He caught her blushing briefly and caressed her calf with his foot. She did not push him away. He felt her love and devotion within the pit of his soul and instantly realized she still loved him. He wished so much to change the past as guilt and betrayal crept into his soul. He felt responsible and therefore vowed to make it right.

After dinner, the family retreated to the living room and glanced at Hannah's photographs. Rebecca opened the manila folder while Enrico noted a change in Hannah's expression. He immediately sensed her conflicts. He could not take his eyes off her as he sat across the room, while the family gapped at the photos. Hannah remained distant and was quick to flash a false pretentious smile. When asked a question, Hannah answered quick and brusque. She became aloof, speaking only when necessary. Enrico knew she was uncomfortable and needed to get out of the house for a while and was clearly not ready to discuss the past two weeks. Enrico stood and announced his pending departure.

"I have a long journey ahead and I must be going. I thank you immensely for the generous hospitality."

Rebecca wanted him to stay longer but Enrico declined the offer. He began to feel shameful for intruding on their Holiday. There was only one thing left for him to do. He had a Christmas present for Savannah and desired privacy.

Enrico grinned as an alibi came to his lips. "Ms. Brockwell, would you be kind enough to accompany me to the limo? I have a sister back home and need help choosing between three gifts I've selected."

Hannah wished to decline, as Rebecca gladly accepted the honor for her.

"Hannah has exquisite taste and helped the other gentleman for an hour selecting a present for his niece."

"Is that so." Enrico could not take his eyes off her now.

Hannah gasped and reluctantly followed Enrico to the limo. He opened the door for her and embraced her warmly. She completely submitted to his persistency.

"It's not what you think Enrico; a man from the agency returned my photos…that's all."

He gazed at her for a moment and forced her back. "What did you discuss with this man…For an Hour?"

Hannah quickly averted her moist eyes.

"Savannah, look at me."

Hannah met his gaze as he took her hand.

"The man removed the photos from my jet; I feared he may come here and that's why I came. I also have a gift for you and it comes from the heart. I promise never to force you into a corner again. I may ask, but I will never force my hand. Please forgive me."

Hannah's eyes widened as Enrico rendered her speechless.

"I love you and I will never rest until I uncover the truth."

Hannah felt his words were sincere, but shook her head. "Then you will never find peace." There was so much she wanted and needed to tell him. She knew he was the only one who would fully understand but too many lives rested on her silence, including his. There was nothing left to say so she exited the limo and walked to the edge of the porch. The sun glistened off the snow so she shielded her eyes and noticed Austin's car approaching.

Enrico sat back and closed the door. He gazed at Hannah through the tinted glass. She appeared dark and smoky but he could still see the tears glistening upon her cheeks. *I love you more than life itself.* He could no longer control his rage. He broke a Champaign glass and held a piece of glass within his palm. He clenched his fist until blood ran from his hand. "On my blood, I vow to avenge her honor and forsake all others until I succeed." He felt Savannah's fear and heard her silent cry for help. Enrico knew the rogue would return for her and he'd be waiting to proclaim his vengeance. This rogue forced Enrico's hand against Savannah and he would pay dearly—with his life. Enrico watched Savannah with a heavy heart as they parted ways.

Austin spent most of the day contemplating and decided he needed to see Hannah on the holiest of days. He wished to hold her and profess his undying love. Austin felt a disturbing presence he could not shake as he drove down Cold Spring's Road. His skin became cold and clammy as his palms began to sweat. He heard shouting within his mind and his vision grew dark. The episode lasted a few minutes before warmth returned to his body and silence eased his mind. His vision returned as he gripped the steering wheel and swerved to miss an animal along the road.

Austin slowed his breathing and forced a twisted smile. *At least I didn't kill Rudolph.* He managed to find amusement in the situation. Austin blamed the episode on lack of sleep. He lied awake all night worrying about Hannah—anticipating Enrico's next move. The love and devotion he felt towards Hannah now consumed every thought. He hoped to surprise Hannah and lift her spirits.

Austin pulled up to the stop sign and felt his skin begin to crawl. A limo pulled out of the driveway and not just any limo, but the same limo from yesterday. Austin still had no answers for the madness that occurred at the airport. He could not begin to understand the chain of events that led to her shackles, the airport incident and her release. His mind grew frantic with uncertainties. The only thing he is certain of right now is that Enrico visited Hannah today. He lowered his brow and shook his head. He pulled the car off the road to clarify his thoughts before proceeding.

Then and there, Austin decided they should leave their small rural community for the big city skyline. He hoped that Enrico would have difficulty locating them in a big city. He believed it was the only rational solution to their dilemma. Pittsburgh was completely out of the question because it held too many painful memories. In fact, Austin refused to reside near any airport, for good reasons. He hated big cities though.

He was born and raised a country boy his entire nineteen years. He knew it would be a huge sacrifice but in the end, Hannah was completely worth it. He also felt his mother would not understand. She raised Austin as a single parent and he remained her only child. Austin had always been her little man and he did not wish to abandon her. He hoped, in time, she would come to accept the union and be happy for them. Austin decided to wait until after their high school graduation in a few months to ask Hannah for her hand in marriage.

He pulled the vehicle back onto the road and proceeded through the intersection. Hannah stood outside in the bitter cold without a coat upon her bodice. Austin pulled into the driveway, leapt from the car and offered Hannah his coat after feeling her shiver. He noticed her eyes moistened at the gesture, but then wondered if they moistened before hand. "Was that Enrico?" he nearly demanded.

Hannah merely nodded, for no words came to her lips. Austin hung his head and embraced her, certain of his decision now. Hannah led Austin inside and her family greeted him warmly.

Chapter 7
Unconditional Love

Hannah and Austin returned to school a few days later and their usual lunch dates commenced. Hannah fell into a state of depression, undecided which way to turn. She felt pulled in every direction. At times, she felt incapable of breathing. Her mind said one thing, while her heart felt another. The winter seemed to last forever. She sighed with each passing day as winter slowly turned into spring.

Rebecca entered Hannah's bedroom with a warm smile, "Jacob sent you a letter and it arrived today," she whispered.

Hannah's face illuminated as she took the letter from her mother's hand. Rebecca felt certain if anyone could pull Hannah out of her funk, it was Jacob. Rebecca left the room with a hopeful heart.

Hannah tore the envelope opened and then paused. She glanced at the envelope and discovered the letter was postmarked from Germany. Hannah hung her head. Jacob's tour of duty was nearly up and she hoped he was back in the States. She unfolded the letter carefully.

It Read:

My Dearest Sunshine,

I know I do not write as often as I should. Germany is a fascinating place and they keep me busy with drills. My tour of duty is nearly complete and I hope to make it home in time for your graduation. Mom tells me that you may be Valedictorian of your class. I always knew you would succeed. You have become a bright and intelligent young woman. Whenever things get rough over here, I imagine your warm smile. I've missed seeing you these past four years. I know you took it hard when I chose to leave and I am sorry for that. I think that is why it took me so long to write. I felt guilty then and I feel guilty now. We will see one another soon; I promise you that. Until then, keep up the hard work and keep me in your prayers and thoughts, for you remain forever in mine. You will always be my Sunshine.

 Love,
 Jacob

  Hannah held the letter close to her heart, refolded it and tucked it away in a special place. She caught herself smiling and could not stop. Jacob always managed to enlighten her spirits. She no longer felt despair, as hope and admiration filled her heart. Hannah and Jacob shared a special bond throughout childhood. When he left, Hannah felt she lost her best friend and carried that burden with her. Bandit replaced his friendship and helped ease the transition, but Bandit never fully fulfilled the emptiness Jacob left behind. Hannah embraced the news of Jacob's pending return. She felt certain Jacob would like Austin. Hannah's senses felt rejuvenated when she returned to school the following day.

  Austin instantly noted the change in her demeanor. He knew she still encased dark secrets within her soul, but he felt the love of his life return to him. Hannah could not wait to graduate. This eased Austin's mind. He did not know how she would react to the proposed move, but he'd cross that bridge when the time came. Graduation was only three months away. He sat in second period study hall when the school nurse approached him.

  "Austin," she whispered, "Can you step into the hall for a moment."

  Austin rose and wondered what he could have done.

  The nurse led him out into the hall and turned. She placed a hand upon his shoulder. "I'm sorry to tell you this, but your Aunt passed away this morning." Austin became confused, for his mother was an only child.

  "Your mother has given permission for you to leave and she'll be waiting at home for you."

  Austin left the school in bewilderment.

  He reached his vehicle and paused, "Do I have an Aunt I never knew about?" No answer came to mind, as he drove home and met his mother in the kitchen. Janice gazed at him intently. Austin saw fear within her eyes. "Mom, I don't have an aunt," he whispered. He did not wish to upset her, but he did not want to beat around the bush either.

"Your father had a younger sister, Grace. She passed away this morning. I don't expect you to attend the funeral service, but I thought you should know."

Austin raged inside. Knowing his Aunt Grace would have been a way of knowing his father, for they grew up together. He wondered how his mother could keep such a secret from him for all these years. "I wish to attend; when is the service being held?"

Janice closed her eyes, "The viewing is tomorrow night and the funeral service will commence the following morning at eleven O'clock," she whispered.

"Are you going?"

"I will accompany you," she returned, and then walked away.

Austin felt his mother concealed more than she revealed but he could not place his finger upon the deception. He was lost to the world for the remainder of the day, deeply disturbed in thought. He barely slept that night, but still woke feeling refreshed. Austin spent the day down at Hawk River. That evening, Janice and Austin dressed in black and drove to the viewing.

"Who will be there?" he asked, breaking the silence.

Janice merely shrugged. They could not find a parking place and had to park down the street from the funeral parlor. They stepped out of the vehicle and Janice clenched his hand. They sauntered up the street and entered the building, hand-in-hand. Austin did not recognize anyone present. He noticed a frail elderly woman standing in the corner—alone. They approached the casket, paid their respects and slowly walked away. Austin felt a hand upon his shoulder. He turned slowly and gazed into the eyes of the frail old woman from the corner.

"It is so nice to finally meet my grandson," she whispered, and then embraced him.

Austin and Janice both froze.

The woman stepped back and eyed Austin up and down. "You are the spitting image of your grandfather," she announced with a warm heartfelt smile.

Austin instantly smiled, for no one had ever said that to him before. He stole a glance at his mother.

Janice flashed a false pretentious smile, for she felt faint. "Austin, this is your Grandmother, June Desmin."

Austin's eyes widened. June coaxed Austin into the next room. Austin knew it was against his mother's best wishes but he followed anyways. Again, he wondered what she concealed from him.

June handed Austin an envelope, "Don't blame your mother, for she is a nonbeliever. Austin, inside this envelope is your birthright. It belonged to your father, but he declined to accept it and now it belongs to you. I hope you will accept it and use it wisely," she explained. June embraced him one last time, and then added, "You truly are a spitting image of your Grandfather." With that said, she walked away.

Austin slipped the envelope into his blazer and returned to his mother's side. He noticed how pale she looked. "Are you alright?" he asked sympathetically.

Janice shook her head and they immediately left. Austin drove home, for Janice felt incapable of driving.

"How come I never met Dad's family?"

Janice could not look at him, but replied, "Your Father and your Grandmother had a falling out and he made me promise that you would never meet her until the time was right. I don't think it is the right time Austin. I feel as though I betrayed your father's wishes today. I won't be attending the funeral service tomorrow morning out of respect for your father. I hope you understand."

Austin frowned and agreed, but he did not understand. "Then I will not attend the service either," he whispered. Austin could not fathom his mother's silence for all these years. He thought about Hannah and wondered if all women were naturally talented at concealing secrets. He chose not to judge Hannah and refused to judge his mother now. He had two special women in his life and he loved them both. Secretly he wondered what the envelope concealed and realized that the human soul was capable of concealing anything the soul bearer felt necessary. He felt certain he would never reveal the secrets concealed within the envelope.

Austin raced to his room upon arrival and recalled his grandmother's words. *'This is your birthright.'* He opened the envelope and glanced at legal forms and documents. Attached to the first form was a single key. He read the form carefully, not fully understanding the legal terms. His signature was required at the bottom and he needed his birth certificate, social security card and a valid form of identification. Austin held the key up and gazed at it curiously. *What secrets do you unlock?*

The form gave an address and Austin knew it was at least a day's drive in each direction. He decided to take a couple days off school for bereavement. He thought about asking Hannah to join him, but felt the need to make the journey alone. Austin grabbed a road map and found the quickest route possible. He placed the key on a chain and wore it around his neck for safekeeping. He had no idea what he was getting himself into and did not care. He went to bed early, anticipating an early morning.

He waited until Janice left for work and wrote a note explaining he would return home for supper the following evening. Austin dressed formal and sported the same blazer from yesterday. He stood in front of the mirror convinced the look was both professional and distinguished. He sighed, contemplating whether to attend his Aunt's funeral service without his mother's knowledge. He did not have all the facts regarding his Father's family and curiosity consumed all rhyme and reason.

He finally decided to detour from his initial plans and postponed the trip for an hour. He got into his car and held the key in his hand. The key would have to wait for he had unfinished business to attend to. He slipped the chain, along with the key, down his dress shirt and slammed the gearshift into drive. He suddenly understood why Hannah chose to embark on her own adventure. Although her outcome remained dark and uncertain, Austin hoped this outcome would shed some light on his present situation. He left to seek out unchartered territory.

He arrived at the funeral parlor to discover an empty parking lot. He noticed June standing in front gazing at him warmly. He stepped out of the vehicle and approached her slowly. "Where is everyone?" he asked softly.

Her gaze became complex, "Austin, the service was over an hour ago. Didn't your mother inform you of the time?"

Austin secretly clenched his fist within the front blazer pocket. His mother had lied to him and he could not fathom why.

June wrapped her arm around his, "I so wanted to venture to the cemetery to see my daughter's final resting place...but alas, I have no means of transportation. When one reaches my age, it is hard to obtain a drivers license."

Austin looked down upon her with sympathetic eyes, "I'll take you, Grandma," he whispered.

June's eyes moistened and she embraced him most affectionately. "You are kind and passionate like your father and his father before him. I have been blessed with a wonderful husband, son and grandson."

Austin did not want to let her go, not ever. He now treasured three women in his life.

Austin helped her to the car. He felt certain June's fragile old eyes had seen a thing or two in their time and there was much to learn from the woman seated next to him. They fell silent as Austin drove to the cemetery. Austin wondered why no other relative offered to drive her. His heart ached, for he recalled his Grandmother standing—alone—in the corner at the viewing while the room stood packed. He felt certain that no one comforted her there last night. The family even abandoned her today and left her standing in front of the funeral parlor—alone, once again. He parked the car where she instructed. June reached across the front seat and rested her fragile withered hand upon his.

"Say that word again, for I have waited so long for you to call me Grandma," she whispered.

Austin held her hand tightly. "I love you Grandma," he returned with moist eyes.

She placed her palm upon his cheek, "I will never grow tired of those words. I held you as an infant, warm and soft, and cradled you in my arms," she whispered, and then added, "You have your Grandfather's eyes."

They sat in the car gazing at one another with loving eyes. Austin felt certain that an eternity passed them by. He needed a million answers, but could not recall a single question. He stepped out of the vehicle and carefully offered a helping hand. June appreciated the gesture and gladly accepted. They slowly walked down a small path to a row of hedges and came across a single tombstone. Austin could smell the freshly unearthed soil.

"Wait here a moment," she whispered, "I would like to say goodbye in private."

Austin tightened his grip and then released her. He remained where he stood, deeply lost in thought. His thoughts were in disarray. He began to map out her life within his mind. She obviously became an outcast to the family and he could not fathom why. She was the most kind and sincere woman he ever had the privilege of meeting and she still had one family member who adored her. She returned with moist eyes.

"I am feeling tired and would like to return home," she whispered softly. "You may drop me off at the bus station next to the funeral parlor."

"Nonsense Grandma. I will take you home." Austin refused to take no for an answer.

June gladly accepted as Austin helped her into the car. She gave him directions and he turned onto a dirt road. The driveway was unpaved and they finally reached a small shack. The home was in dire need of repairs. He noted that the roof needed replaced and half the siding was missing in the front. She invited him inside for a glass of lemonade. Austin could not refuse and followed her inside. The key around his neck would just have to wait, for there was a greater situation at hand. Austin noted that the support beams on the front porch were close to collapsing.

His heart felt heavy and every ounce of his soul wanted to make things right. He noted how clean the home was as he followed her into the kitchen. June did not have much but she obviously treasured what she did have. He gazed upon her with questioning eyes as she lit a candle.

"This is for my daughter," she whispered, and then set the candle upon the table.

June departed to the next room and Austin investigated a pit in his gut. He stepped over to the light switch and flipped it up. Nothing happened. He walked over to the faucet and turned it on. Again, nothing happened.

The pit in his gut felt nauseous. He clenched his fists and wondered how anyone could allow this woman to live in poverty. Austin took a seat at the table and managed to smile as June entered the room. She carried two cans of lemonade and retrieved two glasses from the cupboard.

"I apologize that I don't have any ice at the moment."

Austin opened the cans and poured them into the glasses. It was the sweetest lemonade he ever tasted, for June offered it out of kindness. Unconditional Love became the sweetness that quenched his thirst. June sat down and rested her brow in her fragile hands.

"I hate to rush you off, but I am tired and need some rest."

Austin understood and left his Grandmother's home with a heavy heart. He promised to stop in on his way home as he stood under the sagging porch roof. He returned to his vehicle and drove away, staring into the rearview mirror.

Austin noticed a beautiful home for sale just outside of town. He stared at the craftsmanship and hard work that went into building the house, for this was the type of home his Grandmother deserved. Austin drove for the remainder of the day and finally reached his destination at ten O'clock. The bank was closed for the evening and Austin found a cheap motel to spend the night. The motel was less than desirable but it felt like a mansion when compared to his Grandmother's home. Austin's eyes moistened when he felt her love and admiration towards him, as he slowly drifted asleep. He awoke the next morning with a knot in his gut, but could not place a finger on the cause. He dressed in the same clothes from the day before and waited for the bank to open.

He parked out front and his palms began to sweat as he held the envelope tightly. He held his head high and ventured inside. The bank was sophisticated and appeared elaborate, unlike the small hometown banks he was accustomed to. He approached two men sitting behind the front desk and introduced himself. The gentlemen announced his arrival and led Austin into a side office. Austin handed over the envelope, his birth certificate, social security card and his driver's license. The manager checked the information and led Austin into the back vault to the safety deposit box. He removed the box, placed it upon the table and closed the door. Austin stood motionless and could not think clearly. He approached the box and slid his fingers across the keyhole. He gripped the key tightly, unprepared for what he may uncover.

Austin slipped the key inside, turned it gently and opened the lid. He found numerous papers inside written in a foreign language. Austin could not read a single word. He sifted through the pile, came across an old photograph of a beautiful young woman and realized it was his Grandmother. He held the photograph to his chest and closed his eyes, knowing there was so much he did not understand. He carefully removed the papers and left the room. He approached the front desk and handed over the papers. "Can you tell me what these are?" he asked the woman standing behind the counter.

She smiled warmly, "Certainly Sir," she said, and then took the papers. She glanced at them and her eyes widened, "Sir, I can have this ready for you in a couple of hours," she stated.

Austin gazed at her questionably, "I will return at Eleven O'clock," he stated and then walked away.

Austin returned to his vehicle and stopped as he eyed up a small diner just down the block. His stomach rumbled, so he sauntered down the street to grab a bite to eat. He ordered a glass of lemonade and the breakfast special. The lemonade tasted good, but not as good as yesterday. He pondered his thoughts. "What secrets lie within the documents?" The waitress overheard him and eyed him up questionably. Austin averted his eyes and ate his breakfast. He finished and glanced at his watch. It was a quarter to eleven. He ventured back to the bank, sat in the waiting area and glanced at magazines.

"Mr. Desmin," a voice called from behind.

Austin sat the magazine down, stood and turned as the Branch Manager extended his hand.

"My name is Mr. Gladstone and I handled all the necessary paperwork. If you'll follow me, I'll make this as painless as possible and get you on your way."

Austin shook Mr. Gladstone's hand and followed him into another office.

Mr. Gladstone closed the door and both men seated themselves. Austin began to tense anxiously. He leaned back and prepared for anything.

"Mr. Desmin, you are a very wealthy man. The papers contained account numbers from old stocks and bonds. I took the liberties of electronically wiring the funds into one of our new accounts. Here is your starting balance, your ATM cards and a book of starter checks. A box of checks should arrive in one to two weeks. I used the mailing address presented on your driver's license."

Austin remained silent and reached for the figures. Austin's eyes widened, for it was beyond a substantial amount. His heart overflowed. "Are we finished?" he asked anxiously.

Mr. Gladstone nodded and rose. Austin grabbed his belongings and darted for the door.

"Is there any further information you desire in regards to the nature of the documents," Mr. Gladstone hollered, but it was too late. Austin already exited the front door. Mr. Gladstone shrugged his shoulders. "It really is an interesting turn of events."

Austin raced to his vehicle and drove for the remainder of the day. He arrived at his Grandmother's lane at six-thirty with an overflowing heart. He planned to purchase the beautiful home he saw yesterday afternoon for her. He slowly drove up the lane as his heart leapt from his chest. He parked the car and ran towards the house. Austin immediately noticed the collapsed porch roof. "Grandma," he shouted and ran around the debris.

He heard a faint sound and saw her arm exposed from the rubble. His heart skipped a beat as he raced to her side. He removed boards and tiles without thought. Many pieces were too great for him to remove, but Austin felt the strength of eight grown men. He moaned and groaned as he pulled off huge sections at a time. He finally pulled her pale limp body from the rubble. He immediately removed his blazer and propped it under her head, trying to make her as comfortable as possible.

June squeezed his hand, "Such a good Grandson," she whispered, "You returned as promised."

Austin held her hand and gazed into her eyes. His eyes moistened as he felt her spirit slip away. "Can somebody help us," he shouted. Her breathing became slow and shallow. "Please, I need help," he cried, as tears streamed down his cheeks. He felt helpless, for he knew she did not have a telephone. He tilted his chin and kissed her brow tenderly, "I love you Grandma; more... more than words can convey," he stammered, fighting the lump in his throat.

She managed a smile and then closed her eyes. Austin embraced her lifeless body. He could not help but wonder why they reunited only to become separated. No words could express the pain and sorrow he felt. Austin would give every cent he has for her return.

Harold Baker walked his dog along School House Hollow Road when he heard a cry for help. He honed in on the caller's position and raced up the lane. He rounded the bend and saw a young man embracing an elderly woman. His eyes moistened at the sight. He grabbed his cell phone and immediately dialed 911. He noticed the collapsed roof and derived a conclusion. The ambulance arrived within fifteen minutes. The paramedics had to pry Austin away from her lifeless body. They knew the young man was in shock and placed a warm blanket around him. Austin saw one paramedic carrying a black body bag. Austin threw the blanket upon the ground.

"No, you can't," he shouted, and then whispered, "She has lived in the dark for far too long."

The coroner felt Austin's desperation and obliged his wishes. Austin watched in agony as his Grandmother left him, bound for the mortuary.

He could not find slumber all night long. He paced around his Grandmother's home. He glanced at old photographs and captured a glimpse into her life. He wandered into the living room and noticed a picture of a baby prominently displayed upon the mantel. He instantly recognized the baby, for his mother had the same picture. In that instance, Austin knew he lived in June's heart for all these years. He came close to changing her life, giving her everything she rightfully deserved, and wished he could turn back the hands of time. He rested upon the couch feeling nothing but sadness and regrets.

The next morning, he found himself at the same funeral parlor. He spared no expense and gave her a funeral fit for an angel. He placed the obituary in the local newspaper and surrounding communities. He did not know whom to call, for he knew nothing about the family. Austin only hoped that family members would read her obituary and venture in to pay their last respects. Austin had the entire funeral parlor decorated with red roses. He refused to conform to traditional style, for his Grandmother was not an ordinary woman. He stood at the casket and waited for several hours. She appeared so peaceful and lifelike. It felt like she would sit up at any moment with open arms. Their brief time together changed Austin's view of life and death. He vowed to never take Hannah for granted and cherish every moment God wished to bestow upon them.

The funeral director approached him slowly, "Mr. Desmin, I do not think anyone plans to attend," he whispered. "It is getting late and I will have to close up shortly."

Austin met his gaze with steadfast eyes, "One more hour," he pleaded.

The funeral director agreed and walked away with a heavy heart, for he had witnessed many funerals but this one choked him up inside.

Austin heard the front door and turned. He rounded the bend and met his mother's gaze.

She embraced him, "Oh Austin, I am so sorry that this happened," she whispered. Austin returned her embrace.

"Someone wanted to see you."

Austin glanced behind Janice and noticed Hannah standing in the entryway. They raced towards each other and met in the middle of the room. Austin was glad to see her and feel her in his arms. He realized that this was his family now. He took Hannah by the hand and introduced her to his Grandmother. Hannah thought she was a lovely woman. Austin placed a large black and white portrait next to the casket of June as a young woman. The funeral director entered the room and Austin knew it was time to leave.

He privately approached the casket. "Goodnight Grandma, I'll see you in the morning," he whispered, and then rejoined the others.

They stayed at a local hotel for the night. Janice did not question Austin's decision to share a room with Hannah. Austin needed to tell Hannah so many things, but could not utter a word. His eyes moistened and Hannah embraced him warmly. Hannah wished she could make all his sorrow vanish. She comforted him during his time of need and Austin loved her even more. The funeral service was scheduled to begin at Ten O'clock the following morning. Austin and Hannah were the first ones to arrive and then Janice followed shortly. Austin backed up the service until Eleven O'clock, in hopes of last minute arrivals, but no one came. He stood and slowly approached the Pastor with a heavy heart, "You may proceed," he whispered.

The Pastor held a lovely service and at the end, they all rose and sang…Amazing Grace.

Chapter 8
An Unexpected Visitor

    Austin came to accept the turn of events that occurred over the past three months. He felt a void in his heart that only Hannah could fulfill. June came into his life and he'd be forever grateful for the time they shared, no matter how brief. Austin did not want to make the same mistakes twice. He wanted Hannah to be his wife and he wished to cherish her and care for her until death parts them. Austin refused to waste any further precious time, for he learned first hand that, the quality of time outweighs the quantity of time. He decided to propose after their graduation ceremony next week and continued to conceal the secrets regarding his birthright until he received answers. Austin recalled his Grandmother's words. *'Use it wisely'*. He intended to do just that. He vowed to give Hannah the life she deserved and use his given birthright to decimate Enrico and the cursed *Ring of Eternity*.

    Hannah could not wait to graduate. She held on to the hope that Jacob would return in time. She planned to attend the last day of school. It was the last day she'd feel like a prisoner and secretly embarked on a personal mission. Hannah chose not to participate in Senior skip day, as Austin did. She wanted Austin to have a day with his friends, for she would have him for the rest of her life. She also felt, as Valedictorian of her class, she should set an example for the following generation of Seniors. Besides, she needed information. Hannah stood in the restroom fussing with her hair during Lunch period when she heard several teachers approach and quietly entered the janitor's closet. Hannah desperately wanted answers before carrying out a hidden agenda. She listened quietly for an opportunity to present itself. She heard Mrs. Walker, Ms. Cardigan and Mrs. Bartaro enter the room. Mrs. Walker teaches English, Ms. Cardigan teaches World History and Mrs. Bartaro teaches Physical Education.

The group obviously needed a quiet place to conduct their gossip.

"Can you believe our Valedictorian this year is Hannah Brockwell?" Mrs. Walker asked, and then added, "Tammy Lynn Johnson would have been a more ideal candidate considering her parents are prominent and influential citizens within the community."

"It isn't fair that Tammy has to settle for Salutatorian," Ms. Cardigan stated bluntly.

Mrs. Bartaro leaned forwards and reapplied her lipstick, "Hannah will never amount to anything just like Jenna Campbell never did and I never cared much for Kayla either."

"You have to wonder what kind of role models those Brockwell girls had during their upbringing," Mrs. Walker said, adding her final two cents.

"None of the girls ever seemed to fit in very well," Mrs. Bartaro whispered.

"Thank the good Lord above that we only have to deal with one more of those girls," Ms. Cardigan said, finalizing the conversation.

They left moments later.

Hannah emerged from the closet with her teeth clenched, "What more did they want?" Jenna did not have the opportunity to attend her graduation ceremony. That was her punishment for fighting with Mrs. Walker's daughter. The teachers blackballed her that year. Hannah finally realized Jenna never stood a chance against the hypocritical School Board. Then and there, she swore sweet vengeance. She decided to make the school pay for belittling her sisters and questioning her upbringing. Hannah felt they behaved cowardly for speaking such words behind her family's back. Hannah was certain if she looked up hypocrite in the dictionary, their faces would be portrayed. She left the restroom to plan her last solemn mission before saying goodbye to Greenville—forever.

Hannah kept her plans to herself. Neither Austin nor Kayla knew what was in store. She spent the last three days determined to ensure the Ceremony would go off without a hitch, while her family prepared for her graduation party. Rebecca orchestrated a family get together sparing no expense. Hannah's grandparents, aunts and uncles were all due to arrive at any moment. Rebecca expected a full house. There were not enough tickets for everyone to attend and Hannah sighed with relief. Her grandparents would prepare the cookout while Brian, Rebecca, Jenna, Clayton, Colby and Kayla attended the Ceremony. Austin offered his remaining tickets to her, but she declined the offer. Hannah smiled warmly when Rebecca handed her a card from Jacob. Hannah immediately opened it.

The Card Read:

My Baby Sister
When I was big, you were small
I watched you walk and take your falls
You've come so far, so now reach for the stars
Stand before the group, straight and tall
Stand with pride, honor and most of all
Imaging me standing in the back,
As you toss… your Graduation cap
I'm proud of you Sunshine, Happy Graduation
I hope it's everything you wish
Love, Jacob

Hannah closed her eyes knowing she'd cherish the card forever. A letter slipped out of the envelope and she opened it immediately.

The letter read:

My Dearest Sunshine,

I am terribly sorry, but I was not granted an early leave and I am unable to attend your Graduation Ceremony. I so wanted to be a part of your special day. I hope to see you soon. Until then, keep your chin up and keep me within your prayers.
Love,
Jacob

Hannah decided to follow Jacob's advice. She stayed up half the night preparing and perfecting her Valedictorian speech. She barely slept a wink.

She rose early the next morning, tuned into the local radio station, and listened to the local forecast. *Perfect—Still rain as previously predicted.* She smiled knowing the Ceremony would take place indoors. She overheard Clayton in the hallway and wanted advice. Hannah grabbed his arm, coaxed him into her bedroom and closed the door.

"Clayton, I need help and you are the only one I can turn to."

Clayton quickly read her eyes, searching for answers, "Are you in trouble?"

"No, nothing like that."

She quickly explained what she overheard last week.

Clayton became infuriated when she finished. "Your parents are good people, Jenna and I have succeeded in life, Kayla will graduate next year with honors and you are the Valedictorian for crying out loud." He shook his head unable to comprehend the allegations. He said the last thing that came to mind, "This isn't right."

Hannah quickly agreed and asked him to help carry out her plans. He instantly nodded and smiled deviously when she finished explaining.

"You will be Jenna's all time hero if you succeed," he added.

They prepared together.

"Hannah, time to go," Rebecca cried from the base of the stairs, "You don't want to be late."

Hannah flashed Clayton a grin, "Mom, I'm not ready yet; I need a few more minutes," she cried, beginning phase one of her plan.

Clayton calmly stepped into the hallway, "Go ahead without us; I'll bring her out to the school," he shouted, "And don't forget to save me a seat in the first row."

"Alright Clayton...Thanks!" Rebecca grabbed her camera and several rolls of film, "I believe we have enough," she questioned Brian.

Brian nodded and then they quickly left to ensure good floor seats. Jenna, Kayla and Colby left moments later. Hannah and Clayton quickly went over their checklist. They felt certain everything was in order and decided to leave. Clayton extended his arm and blocked the doorway.

"This will be the best Ceremony Greenville High School has ever known," he exclaimed.

Hannah smiled nervously, as Clayton lowered his arm and proceeded into the hallway.

Clayton turned and met Hannah's uneasy gaze. "My gut tells me you are going to do just fine. Jenna will be proud."

Hannah smiled and followed him downstairs. Clayton made it to the school in record time. Hannah stepped out of the vehicle and found the strength and determination to follow through. She gazed at the bricks that imprisoned her for so long. Only Austin remained the light at the end of the darkness that now entrapped her. *Let the games begin...Savannah.* She walked into the School Auditorium with her head held high. She marched right past her teachers and joined her classmates back stage. The curtain opened on queue.

Hannah quickly scanned the audience and found her family in the front row. Rebecca already snapped several pictures. Clayton held Colby as promised and Hannah saw Janice seated beside him. She sighed in relief as everything went as planned. She saw Jenna questioning the bag that sat at Clayton's feet. Hannah watched as Clayton dismissed it with a wave of his hand. The auditorium fell silent as Principal Charles Thomas stepped up to the podium.

"On behalf of the Greenville Junior/Senior High School, I would like to welcome you as I present the Graduating Class of 1994."

The auditorium filled with a thunderous applause.

"The Board of Directors will hear from our honorable and distinguished guest speakers, the Salutatorian will present her speech, Diplomas will be handed out and last but not least, we will hear from our Valedictorian."

Hannah cringed, for the Valedictorian never spoke last before. The decision to proceed was made for her and she refused to stand down now. Hannah despised the entire Ceremony. She felt somewhat grateful to speak last. She vowed to give them a grand finale. The guest speakers spoke for an hour. Tammy Lynn Johnson spoke for half an hour. Diplomas were next on the agenda. Austin sat a few seats down from Hannah and felt her frustration, as the Board of Directors blackballed her. He secretly wished to make them pay, for Hannah deserved better. The sheer mention of her name reeled him from his thoughts.

"Miss Hannah Marie Brockwell," Principal Thomas announced.

Her family stood, offering a standing ovation. Hannah respectfully approached the podium and accepted her diploma with a pretentious smile. She stood tall and proud, shook Principal Thomas's hand and then returned to her seat. She glanced at Austin and flashed him a devious smile. Austin instantly knew something was up, but he could not fathom what.

"Mr. Austin Cole Desmin."

Austin jumped and realized it was his turn. He stood and approached the podium.

Janice and Hannah's family rose and gave him a standing ovation, as he accepted his diploma. Austin shook Principal Thomas's hand and proceeded back to his seat. He gazed at Hannah as he passed by, rehearsing his proposal. Love, fear and sadness radiated from her gaze. He presumed two of the three emotions. *Love for me—Fear of Enrico—Sadness over...* His mind drew a blank as he dwelled upon his thoughts.

Receiving of diplomas took another hour. Finally, Principal Thomas announced, "It gives me great pleasure to introduce this years Valedictorian...Miss Hannah Marie Brockwell."

Hannah rose and took her rightful place at the podium. She laid a few notes aside, removed the microphone from its holder and stepped in front of the podium. "I would like to thank the faculty here at the Greenville High School, for their words of encouragement and wisdom throughout the years have been priceless. I would especially like to thank my wonderful parents. If not for them, I would not be standing before you today as Valedictorian. This is truly an honor."

Hannah glanced at Clayton, who already began to hand out umbrellas to their family. He even handed one to Janice, who looked at him questionably. Hannah continued speaking profoundly and her voice did not waver, as she stood tall and proud. "Each and everyone of us will pursue vast opportunities, love, and far greater adventures then those experienced within the confines of these walls. We stand before you today as brave men and women about to embark on life's grandest journey—The journey of faith, courage, and strength. The Faith...to believe in ourselves and uphold veracity. The Courage...to walk the roads less traveled. And the Strength...to overcome life's most difficult decisions when faced with a fork in the road."

Hannah paused briefly, struggling to breathe. Her words overwhelmed her senses, as she spoke from the heart. But she refused to give in to her own emotions. Austin eyed her up curiously and prepared to race to the rescue. He eased back in his seat and waited impatiently, as Hannah overcame her struggles.

Hannah immediately wrapped up her speech. "I only have two words to describe how I feel but first, I would like to express my deepest gratitude." She fumbled for a pack of cigarettes and lit up. She hated the idea of smoking, but it would serve her purpose for now. Hannah tore off her graduation gown revealing a black mini skirt. She turned from the audience and they read *Kiss It* stitched across each cheek. Just then, the sprinklers began to shower the audience.

Hannah's family opened up their umbrellas. Hannah never felt such liberation in her life. The Ceremony turned into pandemonium. The audience flocked to the exits in all directions. Hannah remained on the stage completely dripping wet and felt glorious victory. Her gaze fell upon the back of the room. She closed her eyes and imagined Jacob standing there. She opened her eyes and stared at Jacob, as he stood there dripping wet and

applauding her actions. She smiled, for he obviously approved.
Kayla ran on stage, "How could you keep something like this from me?" she demanded, and then burst into pure laughter.
Enrico walked outside and chuckled. He knew damn well that smoke from a single cigarette would not activate the sprinkler system. He felt her desires and made the impossible possible. He'd keep this secret to himself, for this was her moment to shine in the rain. He glanced up towards heaven, waved his hand aside and added irony to the magic. He walked across the parking lot, feeling Savannah's presence stronger then ever, as her soul returned to him—completely. He stepped into the limo and gave the driver explicit instructions.
Hannah searched for Jacob again, but he was nowhere in sight. She felt certain she imagined him standing there. Kayla grabbed her arm and they joined their family.
Rebecca scolded at first and then hugged her, "I'm sure you had your reasons."
Hannah smiled at her warmly. Clayton congratulated her on both accounts. They walked outside and Hannah embraced the irony. The heavens were a mixture of cobalt and azure—stretched as far as the eye could see. The sun glistened in the afternoon sky. It had not rained as predicted, although it did rain inside. It was a remarkably beautiful day and Hannah's mind knew fate was on her side, while her heart suspected an outside force.
Austin joined up with them, "Baby, when it rains, it pours," he chuckled.
They all returned to the Brockwell home to celebrate, as Austin ventured home to change first.
Ruth, Hannah's grandmother, finished decorating the graduation cake. She heard all about Hannah's escapade and rolled her eyes, while beaming a smile.
Ruth glanced at Rebecca, "I believe she gets it from you," she stated, and then added, "You too had a wild streak in your younger days."
Jenna walked into the kitchen now, for she could not miss such an opportunity. "Grandma, tell us about our mother's wild streak," she encouraged.
Rebecca's eyes widened, "Mother, I don't believe this is neither the time nor the place for stories."
"Nonsense," Ruth replied. She sat down as Jenna and Kayla huddled around her feet.
Hannah walked upstairs to change, for victory felt refreshingly cool.
She entered her bedroom and closed the door knowing Austin and Janice

would arrive shortly. She suddenly felt eyes upon her. She stood motionless for a moment, dripping water upon the carpeting. Hannah did not feel a cold chill run down her spine. Instead, she felt a warm sensation trickle up her back. She instantly felt Enrico's presence closing in and turned slowly. Enrico embraced her and briefly pressed his lips to hers.

Hannah placed an arms length between them, "Does anyone know you are here?"

Enrico smiled warmly and shook his head.

"How did you get in?"

"A magician never reveals his secrets, my Lady."

Hannah took a small step forwards, clutched his shirt and rested her brow against his firm chest. "You have to stop doing this," she whispered.

"Stop doing what, my Lady?"

Hannah froze for a minute deeply lost in thought. *Do I want Enrico to quit pursuing me or to stop invoking such passions and longing within my soul?* Hannah felt her heart skip a beat and closed her eyes, for she had no answer.

Enrico heard her thoughts and caressed her arms with his powerful hands.

Hannah knew she must remain strong, like Savannah did earlier. She tilted her chin and dared to meet his mesmerizing emerald gaze, "You must leave...Now," she managed. *Don't go.* Her heart yearned for him to stay but she held her stance and remained firm.

Enrico obeyed her request. "Until we meet again," he whispered, and then kissed her hand slowly and tenderly. He took a step back, "I brought you a graduation present," he whispered, and then vanished before her eyes.

Hannah lunged forwards, but he was gone. "Far away, but forever in my heart," she whispered. Hannah shook her head and wondered if she merely imagined the encounter. She sat upon the bed, gazed at the promise adorned upon her finger and questioned the decision to close all doors to her heart. One day that door would swing open, but to whom? Again, she had no answer.

Hannah changed her clothes and ventured downstairs into the kitchen.

"And that is the last time your mother ever snuck out of the house."

Rebecca's face turned red. "Okay girls, that is quite enough." She glanced out the window, "Hannah, Austin and Janice just pulled in," she cried. She turned and realized Hannah stood behind her.

Hannah smiled.

"Honey, are you feeling well...you look a little pale?"

Hannah averted her eyes, "Mom, I'm fine."

Rebecca greeted their guests at the door, "Everyone is here; come on in."

Hannah flashed a pretentious smile. *Not everyone is here.* Her thoughts lied with Jacob now. She missed her older brother. He played an important role in her life. He always knew how to make her feel better about situations. Jacob always managed to see past the thunderclouds and reveal the sunshine.

Austin immediately took Hannah aside. "I must speak to you...in private."

Hannah read his eyes and saw the importance in his request. "My uncle is in my room but the living room is unoccupied." She led Austin into the living room and sat down.

Austin stood and began to pace the floor. He rehearsed the proposal speech a hundred times and still felt nervous. His heart teetered on a limb as he knelt down and took her hand. "I love you Hannah Marie..."

Jenna raced into the living room, "There's a limo outside," she cried.

Hannah jumped up and firmly held Austin's hand. Everyone immediately ran outside. Hannah held her breath when the chauffeur opened the back door. Austin gripped Hannah's hand. It felt like an eternity passed before Jacob stepped out. Hannah immediately withdrew her hand, raced over to Jacob and threw her arms around him. The entire family was now present.

Jacob gazed into Hannah's big blue eyes, "What's wrong Sunshine; what is it?" he whispered. Jacob always felt a special connection to his younger sister.

"I just can't believe you are here."

"I couldn't miss your graduation. Did you get the card I sent you?"

Hannah nodded with moist eyes. "In your last letter, you wrote that you were denied leave," she questioned.

"I'll explain later."

"Let's eat," Ruth announced.

They ventured inside and everyone carried a plate to the outside patio. Hannah could not take her eyes off Jacob. She stood behind him and rubbed her hand upon his head, "It's so short."

The family laughed. Hannah still felt a special connection to Jacob, even after four years. They laughed and joked just like old times.

"How did you manage your leave?" she finally asked.

Jacob smiled warmly, "My guardian angel," he simply stated.

Hannah raised her brow.

Jacob laughed, "Well, that's what I call him." The family did not understand, so Jacob started from the beginning. "A man arrived on the base last night, via private jet. He discussed things with the Admiral and the next thing I knew, I was granted leave and we boarded his jet. We landed in Pittsburgh and here I am."

Austin gasped, "Who was this man?" he asked carefully.

"He identified himself as Hannah's courier and a friend of the family."

Austin seized Hannah's arm, "We must talk," he whispered.

Hannah met his eyes, "Not now Austin!"

The family ate and played a game of cards. Jacob, Jenna, Hannah and Kayla each passed cards back and fourth beneath the table.

Rebecca and Brian laughed, "Just like old times," they stated.

Jacob and Austin discovered they had a lot in common. For the first time, Austin felt a sense of family. Hannah and Austin's graduation party was a total success.

The family left one-by-one. Ruth was the last one to leave. Hannah embraced her grandmother warmly, uncertain when she'd see her again. The immediate family remained, and yet, the household felt empty. Hannah stole a private moment with Jacob.

"What's on your mind Sunshine?"

Hannah stared at the floor and fidgeted with a strand of hair before meeting his hazel eyes. "You stated that you and Enrico boarded the plane together. Was he present today?"

Jacob read his sister like the cover of a book, "Yes he was," he whispered, "Hannah, he loves you and he is a good man. I don't have much time, for I must return home in the morning."

Hannah embraced him warmly, "Jacob, you are home. Your four years of service are up; you told me yourself in a letter I received last week."

Jacob shook his head, "Let's just enjoy the evening," he said and coaxed her downstairs.

They joined their family in the living room. Hannah sat back and watched how Jacob interacted with the family. He seemed distant and desired her attention above all others. He always knew how to make her feel special. Brian and Rebecca retired upstairs first and Kayla followed shortly after.

Hannah gazed into Jacob's hazel eyes and embraced him, "Jacob, please don't leave tomorrow," she pleaded.

Jacob forced her back a step. He feared Hannah became too attached and he did not wish to cause her further undo pain. "I must return in the morning," he said forcefully and gave no further explanation.

Hannah became confused; Jacob meant the world to her but she felt the brush of his cold shoulder. Hannah quickly dismissed the thought, for she refused to let anything ruin their evening. She was glad he made it back for her special day and vowed to cherish the time they spent together. They stayed up all night reminiscing about their childhood.

The next morning, while Jacob prepared his departure, Hannah thought about Jacob's statement. *'He loves you and he is a good man,'* echoed within her mind, as she wondered what Enrico discussed with him during their flight from Germany. Jacob crept into the room and sat beside Hannah upon the sofa.

"Good morning Sunshine; how are you holding up?"

There were so many things that Hannah needed to tell him, but she chose to remain silent.

Brian and Rebecca stepped into the room.

"Jacob, your limo just arrived," Rebecca whispered.

Jacob stood, saluted and embraced them affectionately. He quickly left the room and darted upstairs to say good-bye to Kayla. Hannah felt a knot in her gut. Something bad was about to happen, but she could not fathom what. Hannah waited on the porch and stared at the limo. She wondered if Enrico sat inside watching her. Suddenly the back door opened and Hannah approached slowly.

She came face to face with Enrico's emerald eyes. She felt sympathy and sadness radiating from his gaze. She turned when Jacob exited the front door and rushed to his side. "Don't go Jacob; I sense something bad is about to happen."

Jacob smiled warmly, "Do not feel sad for me…I will see you on the other side," he whispered in her ear, before turning abruptly and entering the limo.

Hannah stepped off the porch step as Jacob shook Enrico's hand. She heard Enrico whisper, "Are you ready?" Hannah froze. *Ready for what?* Then, without warning, the door slammed shut and they drove away. Hannah stood in the driveway and called out to her brother, but it was too late. She closed her eyes when they drove out of sight, as Enrico spoke to her heart.

"Jacob loves you and he wished to see you," he whispered within her mind.

Hannah ran inside and retired to her bedroom. She cried herself to sleep, unable to find contentment.

Jacob and Enrico drove to the Pittsburgh airport and boarded Enrico's private jet, bound for Germany. They landed at the naval base twelve hours later.

Jacob shook Enrico's hand one last time, "Take care of her, Enrico," he said and then turned to walk away.

Enrico stopped him. "May I ask why you call her Sunshine?"

Jacob returned and smiled warmly. "The family returned from our great grandfather's funeral feeling pretty glum and we all sat down in the living room. Hannah raced into the room and announced, 'While you were away, Pappy Isaac called!' She was four years old. She handed our mother the telephone and ran upstairs humming a tune that only our great grandfather knew, 'Something's got a hold of me.' Hannah never had the opportunity to meet Pappy Isaac. The room fell silent for a moment and then everyone began to smile. Hannah, single handedly, brightened the entire room; so naturally, I have called her Sunshine ever since."

Ironically, Enrico knew all to well and understood Jacob's reply. He watched Jacob leave with a heavy heart and hoped Savannah would understand that he only had the best of intentions. He granted Jacob precious time with his Sunshine. Enrico smiled warmly.

That night, Brian and Rebecca received a phone call from Jacob's naval base. Rebecca screamed and clung to Brian. She fell to her knees and sobbed uncontrollably. Hannah and Kayla raced downstairs.

"What is it Mom; what's wrong," Kayla pressed.

Hannah took a step back and placed a hand over her mouth. Rebecca reached out, grasped them and pulled them to the floor.

"There...there's been an accident," she stammered through the tears.

All three embraced one another nestled beside the kitchen table. Rebecca placed a hand over her mouth, searching for words of comfort, but found none. Brian hung up the phone, knelt down and embraced his family.

"There's been an accident and your brother passed away," he managed.

Hannah immediately stood, "No...No, Jacob can't be dead," she screamed, as tears formed in her vacant eyes and overflowed down her cheeks.

"When?" Kayla demanded softly.

Brian wiped the tears from his sorrow stricken eyes, "The admiral said yesterday morning, but he must have read the report wrong. We all know Jacob was here with us." Hannah shook her head violently and ran upstairs to be alone.

She ran into her room and slammed the door. Hannah threw herself upon the bed and buried her head in a pillow. She sobbed uncontrollably. Nothing made sense to her. She refused to believe he was gone forever. She sobbed until there were no tears left. She sat up and glanced around the room as her heart ached. Hannah suddenly froze and closed her eyes. She heard Jacob whispering to her heart and placed a hand over her mouth as tears of joy streamed down her cheeks. She removed her hand, slowly caressed her cheek and smiled. She felt Jacob's hand brush her cheek as he whispered to her heart.

"Don't cry Sunshine; I will see you on the other side."

Hannah felt Jacob's presence vanish. "Don't go Jacob," she whispered, but his presence no longer lingered in the air. Something in his words stilled the sadness that lingered in her heart and calmed the storm that raged within her mind. She wiped away the tears resting high on her cheekbones. *Enrico knows more than he lets on.*

She lied upon the bed and recalled past events. *Enrico picked Jacob up and brought him to us. Jacob, himself, told me not to feel sad for him and just know he said, 'I'll see you on the other side.'* Hannah's thoughts became random. She smiled warmly through fresh tears and put the final pieces together. Jacob did pass yesterday morning. Enrico sensed her desires and somehow—someway—granted them one last visit together. Hannah approached the window and looked up towards heaven. "I'll see you on the other side," she whispered.

She refused to believe Jacob was gone forever. He'd forever live within her heart. Something told her nothing was—as it seemed. Her heart filled with hope as the sun beamed its rays down upon her brightly. Enrico managed to cross through the depths of mortality to make her dreams come true. She closed her eyes and made a silent sacred vow, for she knew what must be done. She'd forever remain indebted to Enrico for this selfless act. Hannah did not comprehend how, but she understood why. *Because he loves me.*

Jacob had a military burial and laid to rest in their quaint little town at Mossburg Cemetery. Hannah ventured to his final resting place a week later. She went in search of answers and hoped to invoke Jacob's spirit in the still of the night. If Enrico could grant them a visit from beyond the grave then Hannah felt certain Jacob could speak to her heart once again. She slipped out of the house undetected, unaware that Austin silently lurked in the shadows.

Austin watched from afar, as Hannah strolled down the street at Eleven O'clock. *Where is she going?* He knew Hannah was taking Jacob's death hard and planned a midnight rendezvous to offer further condolences and help ease the pain. Dismay overshadowed his heart as he followed her to the local cemetery. He quickly searched his own soul, as an unanswered question lingered within his mind. Two tragic accidents separated them from a loved one and he felt certain Enrico was behind the malicious acts. He needed to get Hannah as far away from Enrico as possible, *and Savannah too. Damn Enrico to Hell.* He silently vowed vengeance in Jacob and June's honor. Austin felt a cold chill when he realized he stood close to his father's grave. He shivered and closed his memory to the past. He refused to relive ancient memories and remained focused on Hannah's private torment. He watched from afar, as Hannah wore her heart on her sleeve.

Hannah ventured to Jacob's grave, which rested beside her paternal grandparents and maternal grandfather. She carried but a single red rose and placed it atop the tombstone that read:

> *In Loving Memory*
> *Jacob Lee Brockwell*
> *Loving Son and Devoted Brother*
> *1972-1994*

Hannah's eyes moistened. "Jacob, I need to know what you meant the last time we spoke to one another. Please help me understand. I'm so lost and confused without you. I...I refuse to believe..." but Hannah fell silent and smiled warmly as Jacob spoke to her heart.

"Don't cry for me Sunshine, I'll see you on the other side. Enrico will make certain of that...he promised."

"What?" Hannah screamed and jumped to her feet. "Jacob, don't go." She glanced around the cemetery and found both Austin and Enrico watching her from opposite ends of the cemetery.

"Go to him, he loves you!"

Hannah closed her eyes and whispered, "Tell me what to do Jacob, who do I run too?" Hannah heard no reply, for only she could make that decision.

The battle lines were clearly drawn and one opponent would fall on his sword consisting of broken dreams and empty promises. She professed her love, at one point or another, to them both. She glanced, inconspicuously, back and fourth between them. The last thing she wanted was for them to see one another. Hannah gazed at her soul mate, a handsome and loving man with copper hair and a generous spirit, whom she loved with all her heart. Savannah gazed at Enrico, a mysterious stranger with tantalizing green eyes, full of passion that enthralled her senses. Hannah envisioned growing old

MYSTIC VOWS

with Austin. Savannah envisioned… but the canvas within her mind drew a blank. Hannah wondered what that meant.

When her mind fell silent, fog rolled in all around her. She could not make out any tombstones and stumbled into one. A dark image appeared in the distance. She froze in her tracks as it approached slowly, as if in slow motion. She noticed black fabric swaying in the breeze. She fixated her eyes on the object and realized it was Antonio dressed all in black. His shirt fluttered in the breeze, revealing his entire chest. Hannah remained motionless unable to move, as her breathing increased.

Austin stumbled about, frantically trying to locate Hannah. He began to panic as he heard a voice hiss, "S-a-v-a-n-n-a-h." He stumbled into a tree and fumbled for a branch. He ravaged at the tree like a wild animal until a limb snapped off. He used the stick as a blind man would use a walking cane. He was now able to move freely through the cemetery. He lost his bearings and did not know which direction to head. The fog was thick and damp. *Damn you to Hell Enrico.*

Enrico sensed Savannah's fears and frantically searched for her. For once, he felt relieved Austin was there. The fog penetrated his soul and he sensed pure evil lurking everywhere. He closed his eyes and focused on Savannah's whereabouts with no prevail. He could not locate her and felt powerless. The unnamed rogue assumed control once again. He shouted for Savannah, but she did not answer.

Hannah continued to stare into Antonio's gray vacant eyes. She opened her mouth to answer Enrico but the shallow fog consumed every breath. The fog clung to her, continuing to render her immobile. Antonio appeared to glide whimsically through the cemetery. He reached her and stood an arms length away. Hannah's knees felt weak but they did not give out from beneath her. Antonio crossed his arms and stared down upon her.

"Did you find the answer you were looking for, my Dear? Allow me to make this heart-wrenching decision for you."

Hannah did not respond—could not respond. Antonio reached out and took her hand, forcing her to open her mind—and her heart—to Enrico.

Enrico hit his knees as he stood in the rouges bedchamber at the Castillo de Isla. He eyes fixated on Savannah with a shadowy figure—and she was caressing his leg with a long slow sweeping motion. He gasped as he watched the figure ravage at her blouse as she whimpered beneath him. He quickly slammed the door to the vision. He shook his head, for he did not want to believe such an escapade took place. *Is this the truth she conceals?*

Antonio released Hannah and renounced all control back to Enrico. He turned and walked away as the fog lifted. Hannah fell to her knees and began shaking. *What just happened?* She looked up, emotionally shaken, as Enrico towered above her with scornful eyes.

Enrico could not break free from the vision. His heart denied the accusation, but his mind remained skeptical. Hannah reached for him but he took a step backwards. She wanted—needed—to show him the reasons behind the false vision but could not. Hannah was afraid she'd reveal Antonio's identity—unable to conceal his face behind a shadowy mask. Enrico searched for answers as he held her gaze. The magnitude of the vision forced him to keep an arms length between them and rendered him speechless. For the first time since their encounter, Hannah felt disgrace and shame radiating from his gaze. He turned and left when Hannah broke eye contact, as Austin emerged from the shadows.

Hannah embraced Austin; thankful he was unharmed. She could not help but to think about Enrico. She wondered how much he saw—or believed. Her heart told her that he would uncover the truth underlying the vision. Her heart maintained confidence while her mind remained skeptical.

Chapter 9
Spirits That Lie Within

A week passed since that dreadful night in the cemetery. Hannah no longer felt grief-stricken over Jacob's passing. She felt numb and possessed a greater sense of awareness. She realized how fragile life—and love—actually is. She refused to acknowledge Antonio's antics and focused on Jacob's final words. She wished to show Enrico the same courtesy that he bestowed unto her, for he took it upon himself to grant her one final visit with Jacob. Jacob would forever remain close to her heart and continue to live in the shadows of her mind—and spiritually within the present. Hannah thought twice about running downstairs and announcing that Jacob contacted her.

She decided not to, after careful consideration. She worried that the family would not think it amusing a second time. Therefore, she kept the revelation to herself and focused on Enrico. She refused to cause him any further pain. "He must never find out about Antonio's betrayal." Hannah felt a chill creep up her spine, for it was the first time she had spoken *his* name aloud since leaving Nicaragua. Her eyes moistened and she quickly fought back the tears.

The family remained on edge all week. Hannah felt an emotional high and did not want to appear insensitive. She felt a calmness she could not begin to explain. Her heart felt at peace, while her mind refused to believe Jacob was gone. Hannah quickly noticed a change in her father's demeanor. Brian dealt with his son's death the best way he knew how. He began taking extra shifts at work and became distant and withdrawn. Hannah seemed to be the only one who understood. He left early and came home late. She did not judge his actions.

Hannah continued to replay Jacob's words over-and-over again within her mind and smiled each time. *I know you're not dead. I can hear you talking to me late at night.* Days became short and weeks seemed non-existent. Before she realized it, a month had passed and the family settled back into their usual routine. Rebecca took Hannah and Kayla shopping for the day and returned home with take out for lunch. The family enjoyed a movie that very afternoon.

Austin arrived shortly after the movie ended. Hannah embraced him at the door wearing a huge smile upon her face. They spent every waking moment together. He gazed into her baby blue eyes, "How about that horse ride I promised you?"

Hannah needed no time to think and ran off to grab a pair of jeans. "Mom, Austin and I are going riding," she hollered.

"Alright, have fun."

Hannah took Austin's hand and laced her fingers between his. The Ring of Eternity grazed his fingers and he desperately wanted to ask if Enrico's presence would daunt their date, but did not. He did not wish to discuss Enrico. He knew the time approached when they'd have to face reality head on, but not tonight. They arrived at Austin's home around 4:00 PM. Hannah caught him glancing at his watch.

"Are you in a hurry?"

"I have a surprise for you." Austin stepped out of the vehicle and opened her door. If all went well, he planned to propose tonight. Austin felt a chill and his body grew numb. He suddenly wondered if Enrico purposely caused their private torment merely to delay the proposal at hand. *If that bastard inflicted these wounds, he'll pay dearly.*

Hannah released Austin from his thoughts, as she placed her hands upon his hips and stepped in for a tender kiss. This impromptu action was unexpected but he seized the moment, for this is exactly where he wished the evening to proceed. Austin led her to the barn and saddled two horses. One was a majestic brown mare with a blonde mane, both tame and gentle. The other was a painted stubborn stud with a black mane, both wild and unruly. Hannah fell in love with both horses instantly. She introduced herself to the mare and stroked her neck.

"Hi there, my name is *Savannah*."

Austin immediately raised a brow. Hannah did not acknowledge her falter. He quickly dismissed the notion and pretended not to notice. He felt he had to win her heart again; it was an overwhelming feeling he hid deep down.

"Austin, what are their names?"

He patted the mare, "This is Susie and this big boy is Jasper," he said, and then patted the stud.

Hannah approached Jasper while Austin held his breath.

"Hi there Jasper, I'm Hannah," she whispered.

Austin sighed with relief, for Hannah was not lost to him completely. He instantly realized that Enrico did not overpower her entire soul. Hannah reached out to pet Jasper with her left hand but the horse lunged forwards and snorted.

Hannah immediately retreated while Austin quieted Jasper's spirit. Hannah stared into Jasper's eyes and saw fear radiating from his chestnut gaze. She quickly looked down upon her ring and nearly fainted, for animals do not lie. For the first time, the ring upon her finger felt evil and unnerving. She felt certain that Jasper sensed something very wrong. She frantically tried to remove the cursed ring with no prevail. Austin rushed to her side as tears streamed down her cheeks.

"Why can't I take this cursed thing off?" she screamed helplessly.

Austin embraced her affectionately and thought about the manila folder, but could not bring himself to reveal the horror behind the truth. "Hannah, if you ever want to talk about things, I am here for you. No matter what."

Hannah immediately thought about Antonio, but could not bring herself to discuss those frightful two weeks. The lovers embraced as each continued to conceal their deepest unspoken secrets.

Austin managed to calm both Hannah and Jasper's fears. Jasper munched on an apple while he helped Hannah upon Susie and they started out slowly. He explained basic commands using the rains.

"If you want Susie to turn right, hold the reins to the right and vice versa for left."

Hannah felt like a natural before long. They trotted through a bridal trail that led to a field where Hannah noticed a tent nestled beneath a large oak tree. Austin built a campfire and they roasted marshmallows over an open flame. Hannah could faintly hear a trickling brook off in the distance. Her mental clarity became sharp as she indulged in pure sweetness simmered to perfection. She also felt eyes upon them but remained silent. *Not now...not here.*

Austin approached Hannah slowly with craving eyes. He had not yet begun to indulge his sweet tooth. She felt his desires and longed for his touch. So many factors came between them lately and she wanted to wipe the slate clean. She met him halfway and engulfed his mouth. Austin rolled Hannah over on a blanket upon the grass. His chest caressed her breasts as his hands cradled her face and then slid down her thighs. Their passionate kiss soon spilled over into the tent. Austin held the love of his life and yet wondered where her heart truly lied—and whom it desired. *Hannah, please come back to me!* He felt Hannah return to him completely and smiled tenderly as he wrapped his arms around her silken bodice—warm and inviting.

Hannah secretly fought a silent conflict within her mind. Hannah wanted Austin in every sense while Savannah attempted to suppress the urges. In the end, Hannah prevailed and embraced her destiny. Austin seized the moment as Hannah fully accepted his intentions. Her hair smelled of lavender and her hands felt like velvet as they explored his flesh. His wandering hands slid down her thighs and found a blossoming rose. The Thorns of Passion penetrated her heart, welcoming unbridled cravings while forsaking eternal desires. Their bodies entwined to form one heart and one soul within the Garden of Eden. They gazed at the full moon overhead and counted the stars one-by-one, as they illuminated the night sky.

Hannah no longer felt eyes upon them but did feel dire hatred radiating from above and closed her eyes briefly. The night was clear and vivid, but the peace and tranquility did not last long. Hannah began to feel an overwhelming sense of disapproval. The stars slowly disappeared as thunderclouds rolled in overhead. She felt a cool chill in the air. Austin also felt it and held her hand tightly. The field became dark and eerie. The clouds began to emit a light rain shower, as Hannah sensed *his* anger and resentment.

Hannah quickly embraced those feelings. She grabbed Austin's arm and coaxed him out of the tent. She began to dance and laugh in the rain. Austin stood there and watched her curiously. Hannah was bound-and-determined to put the past behind them. The thunder began to rumble louder as Hannah secretly renounced the destiny chosen for her. For once, she did not have a care in the world. Austin began to feel nervous.

"We should venture back before the lightening sets in," he finally announced.

"If you insist," she mumbled. Hannah froze and her eyes blackened.

Austin could feel her hatred as Hannah ran towards the tent, gazed up at the dark sky and glanced about the field. She shook her fist. "You will not win; do you hear me. I will not play your games," she screamed into the darkness. A bolt of lightening struck the oak tree, sending a limb crashing down upon the tent and setting the tree ablaze. Hannah jumped and became frightened as the tree burned.

She instantly wished she had not invoked Antonio like that. She felt his presence looming over them from above and it forced her to her knees. Austin felt her fear and wanted to rush to her side, but the lightening spooked the horses. He chased down Susie, leapt upon her back and galloped after Jasper. Hannah remained frozen and watched the rain extinguish the blazing tree. "Please leave them be; I didn't mean it," she whispered. She felt a hand upon her shoulder and screamed. Hannah turned swiftly and met Enrico's emerald gaze. Enrico stared at her intently. He felt her anguish and reached for her hand. Hannah quickly declined the offer.

"Please leave Enrico," she nearly demanded.

He shook his head and tried to communicate to her heart, but she quickly slammed that door in his face. He attempted to penetrate the fortress with no prevail.

Hannah revealed true courage, for she attempted to face the rogue alone. She looked overhead and noticed that the thunderclouds moved on. She no longer felt Antonio's presence and sighed in relief. Hannah returned her gaze to Enrico and felt the love radiating from his steadfast eyes. Her courage suddenly melted into fear and her eyes moistened. She learned first hand that life is fragile. She could not bear the thought of a loved one facing Antonio's wrath simply out of defiance.

"What was I thinking?"

Enrico embraced her, but Hannah did not return his embrace.

"Please Enrico, I wish to be alone," she pleaded.

Enrico still could not fathom her silence but did not press the issue as promised. He bowed and kissed her hand tenderly, "As you wish, my Lady," he whispered, and then walked away with a heavy heart. "This rogue has power over her," he whispered. Enrico clenched his fists in rage as this new revelation surfaced. His Savannah nearly played into the rogue's hands tonight, for the rogue penetrated her thoughts and she provoked the situation. Savannah would never escape his sights again until he discovered the rogue's identity. He felt her turmoil as the Thorns of Passion shattered his heart.

Austin returned riding Jasper and holding Susie's reins. "Hannah, time to leave," he stated sternly.

Hannah flashed him a sympathetic look and his heart melted. He felt uncertain whether or not the moisture upon her cheeks was tears or raindrops.

She climbed atop Susie, "Let's go home," she whispered.

They trotted down the path that led back to Austin's house. Austin immediately put the horses in the barn, removed their riding gear and closed their stalls. He turned and embraced Hannah affectionately, "What happened up there, Sweetheart?"

Hannah felt him tremble and quickly flashed a false pretentious smile, "Let's get out of these wet clothes; I really must be getting home."

Austin nodded and led her into the house. He handed her a pair of jeans and a sweatshirt. "I'm sure they'll be baggy on you, but they're warm and dry."

Hannah smiled warmly and closed the bathroom door.

Hannah changed slowly and wore the clothes Austin chose for her. She secretly replaced an old, but vivid memory. Austin managed to ease her mind in so many ways. She wished there was a safe way of letting him know that, but could not think of any. She selflessly kept her thoughts hidden from the world—including Austin. Hannah could not help but wonder why Antonio made his presence known tonight. *Why now...after all this time?* She dismissed her own thoughts, for Antonio was not a man of rhyme and reason.

Austin gently tapped upon the door, "Are you finished?" he asked tenderly.

Hannah stepped out and engulfed his mouth. Her mind told her to flee to ensure his safety, but Hannah could never run from her soul mate—or true love. Austin ensured her once that they were in this together and they would end it side-by-side. She clung to his promise. "It's late Austin and I must return home."

Austin drove her home, no questions asked, but his heart beckoned for her to stay.

Hannah stepped into the house and Rebecca met her at the top of the stairs. "How was your ride?"

Hannah smiled.

Rebecca gazed at her questionably, "What are you wearing?"

Hannah met her gaze with astonishment. "Austin and I got caught in the thunderstorm."

Rebecca's gaze grew complex, "What thunderstorm?"

"Didn't you hear it mom; there was lightening and everything."

Rebecca shrugged, "We didn't get a thunderstorm here," she stated, and then added, "I'm glad you're alright; Goodnight Hannah."

"Goodnight Mom."

Rebecca retired to her bedroom and closed the door. Hannah also retired to her bedroom after realizing it was Eleven O'clock. She was too tired to put pajamas on and crawled into bed wearing Austin's clothes. They were big, but extremely comfortable. Hannah fought sleep and recalled the events of the evening. She began to tremble, certain they would hear from Antonio again. But when and where remained a mystery? Hannah finally allowed herself to drift asleep.

The entire family woke at two in the morning when the phone began to ring relentlessly.

Brian entered the hallway first, "Who in the world can that be?"

Hannah shrugged and followed him downstairs. Brian picked up the phone, "Hello," he muttered cordially. He repeated himself and quickly hung up.

"Who is it?" Rebecca cried from the top step.

"There was no one there!"

Kayla shrugged and returned to her bedroom. Brian and Hannah reached the hallway when the phone rang again.

"Brian, just let it ring. The neighbor's lights are still on and I can see kids wandering around downstairs. I'm willing to bet they're crank calls," Rebecca hollered, standing in front of the hallway window.

Brian sighed, "All this fuss over a crank call." He shook his head, paused for a moment and returned to the kitchen. Brian glanced at the caller ID box, "Caller Id says Unavailable, but they may have their number blocked," he informed Hannah. They left the kitchen and retreated upstairs when the phone rang a third time. "Damn it; I have to get up for work in a couple of hours," Brian murmured.

Hannah felt her father's agitation. "Go to bed Dad; I can handle these little punks and then I'll turn the ringer off for the rest of the night." Hannah returned to the kitchen and picked up the receiver as Brian marched upstairs. She held the phone to her ear, "Okay, the game is over; don't call again or I'll be forced to call your parents," she stated sternly. Hannah heard a chuckle on the other end. "Who the hell is this?"

"The game has only just begun, my Dear," Antonio hissed.

Hannah gasped and slammed the receiver down. The phone rang again within seconds. She slowly picked it up and drew it to her ear.

"I wish to see you again Savannah; I have a hunger that only you can fulfill and a heated desire only you can extinguish."

Hannah froze for a moment and slowly hung up the receiver. She immediately turned the ringer off and sat at the kitchen table alone in the darkness. She watched the red ringer light illuminate nearly fifty times before the calls ceased and her mind fell silent. Hannah placed her brow upon the table and cradled her head with crossed arms. She felt certain that the worst was yet to come. *'The game has only just begun,'* echoed throughout her mind. Fresh tears moistened her eyes as she raised her head. Hannah knew what she must do. She had to leave Greenville, never to return. It was the only way she could ensure the safety of her loved ones. Hannah reaffirmed that she would not leave without Austin. Austin remained unaware of Antonio and she intended to keep it that way. She wandered outside for some fresh air in hopes to bring clarity to her mind and still her aching heart.

Austin woke at three o'clock to the sound of the telephone. He sat up and wiped the sleep from his eyes. He trudged into the living room and picked up the receiver, "Hello," he said, still half asleep.

"Take the girl and leave town, for if you don't, I will," an old familiar voice hissed, and then hung up.

Austin felt wide-awake now. He slammed the receiver down and immediately called Hannah. Austin could no longer deny that something happened up in the field while he chased after the horses. He left the phone ring numerous times, but no one answered. He hung up and tried again with no prevail.

He grabbed his keys and felt the need to check in on her, knowing damn well Enrico certainly called his beloved Savannah. He reached her house and noticed the back porch light turn off. He parked at the local video store just down the road to remain inconspicuous. Austin sauntered down the street, quietly ducked around the side of the house and noticed a silhouette sitting upon the porch swing in the pale moonlight. He realized it was Hannah moments later and immediately rushed to her side.

Hannah jumped, "Austin, what...what are you doing here?" she stammered, half in shock.

Austin remained silent and sat down beside her. Hannah gazed into his deep auburn eyes and saw contempt. She averted her eyes, turned and leaned into his open arms. She drew her knees up and rested her bare feet upon the swing. He cupped his fingers over her chin, tilted her brow and kissed her full moist lips passionately. They gazed into one another's eyes. Hannah closed her eyes and released the tension that weighed upon her chest.

"Austin, let's leave town together. I love you and want us to be together, but not here in Greenville."

Austin sighed with relief, "That is exactly what I was about to say," he whispered, and then reached for her hand.

Hannah placed her bare feet upon the porch and stood. She gazed at Austin sensing the bitter truth. Antonio also called Austin tonight. They remained silent for a moment, attempting to penetrate one another's thoughts.

Austin broke the silence. "Why do you wish us to leave?" he asked softly, hoping for a truthful response, but prepared for a dishonest reply.

Hannah closed her eyes and penetrated his thoughts, "So *he* can not find us," she whispered.

Austin's eyes widened, for he knew she spoke the truth. "Enrico called me tonight," he stated.

Hannah jumped and reeled around, "Enrico!"

Austin nodded gravely, "It was the same voice as before."

Hannah's eyes widened to this new revelation, for she was completely unaware that Antonio continued to harass Austin like this. She paced back and fourth across the porch deeply lost in thought. *He thinks its Enrico.*

Austin will continue to remain safe, for he believes Enrico called tonight. Hannah decided to use this newfound information to her advantage. She could now keep Austin at bay where Antonio was concerned; for Austin had no reason to believe another man was involved. She shook her head and began to massage her temples. Hannah felt uncertain if she could knowingly withhold the truth about Enrico and Antonio. She recalled Jacob's words, *'He loves you and he is a good man.' Enrico is a good man!*

Hannah felt Enrico deserved better than to be named a vile monster. Antonio is the monster that haunts her late at night. She knew Enrico was a kind and passionate man. Hannah sighed as her eyes moistened and drew the only plausible conclusion. She had no choice but to leave her skeletons in the closet and allow Enrico to remain the martyr. This was for their safety and her peace of mind. Her mind and heart conflicted.

Austin observed her actions in bewilderment. He knew Hannah was conflicted and did not wish to disturb her. He sat upon the porch swing silently and recalled her words, *'So he can not find us.'* Enrico demanded that he leave town with Hannah, but Hannah desired them to escape Enrico by leaving town. The two responses coincided with one another. He refused to hand over Hannah on a silver platter—not again. Many questions arose within his soul. Enrico clearly wanted Hannah to leave town with or without him. He wondered now if it was the right thing to do, but he refused to risk the outcome of disobeying Enrico twice. Enrico abducted her once and Austin refused to allow that to happen again.

Hannah reeled him from his thoughts as she lightly touched his arm. Austin tilted his chin and met her baby blue eyes.

"Let's try and get some sleep upon the sofa," she whispered, "We can determine all necessary arrangements in the morning."

Austin followed her into the house and they fell asleep upon the sofa in one another's arms and woke to the morning light in the same manner.

Chapter 10
Too Close for Comfort

The following Sunday, Austin and Hannah attended church service in town and talked to their Pastor afterwards with no prevail. Their Pastor refused to join them in holy matrimony due to their ages. They left the church with heavy hearts. Austin returned home, grabbed a phone book and began to call other local Pastors, but each conversation ended the same. Each Pastor had concerns about their ages and sensed they were on the run from something. Austin decided to try one last time.

The following Sunday, they waited outside for Sunday service to let out at the Church of God, just outside of town. Austin led Hannah up to the pastor and shook his hand. They overheard a woman call him, Pastor Bob. Pastor Bob instantly realized the couple wanted to discuss something important in private. He led them through the church and into one of the backrooms. Hannah glanced around the room, for she now paid close attention to her surroundings. It was a Sunday school room. Hannah saw religious coloring books, puzzles and games scattered about on the bookshelves.

Pastor Bob met Austin's gaze, "What's on your young minds?" he asked in a calm tone.

Austin cleared his throat. "We are in search of a Pastor to join us in Holy matrimony."

Pastor Bob glanced back and fourth between them and questioned their motives. They looked young to his old fragile eyes, "When is the date?" he asked apprehensively.

Austin held his gaze and his voice did not waver. "As soon as possible, next week preferably."

Pastor Bob gave the same spew he gave to all young couples. He explained that marriage was a commitment for life and was not something they should rush into. "You still have your entire lives ahead of you for such a big decision," he explained. He drew his attention towards Hannah when he finished his spew. "Is this really what you want Miss?"

Hannah wasted no time with her reply, "Yes, it is what we both want," she nearly cried.

Pastor Bob rubbed his temples and realized he could not change their minds. They appeared overly anxious and he questioned their motives. He tried hard to be persuasive with no prevail. "There is the matter of a marriage license and blood tests," he stated, rather pleased.

Austin's eyes gleamed with a flicker of hope as he handed the pastor a folder, which contained their marriage license and test results. Austin and Hannah obtained the marriage license from the local courthouse. Hannah quickly averted her eyes so Pastor Bob would not discover her inner conflicts.

Pastor Bob instantly noticed her noncommittal actions. "May I see the ring?" he asked, after Hannah sparked his curiosity.

Hannah hesitated for a moment and reluctantly held out her hand. Pastor Bob seemed intrigued at first and then became aware of what his eyes gazed upon and he felt his heart skip a beat. He remained silent as he approached the door.

"I am sorry, but I can not give you the kind of services you seek," he remarked, as he opened the door.

Austin stepped forwards, "May I ask why not?"

Pastor Bob remained silent, as he felt a little guilty. The young man before him certainly loved Hannah. He knew Austin deserved more answers but he felt a cold familiar presence and he knew the good lord himself could not help them now. They could not escape the one solemn promise that bound them, only the ring upon her finger held the secrets. "I must ask you both to leave, now," he demanded.

Austin recognized Pastor Bob's agitation so he collected his folder and shook the Pastor's hand. "Thank you for your time," he mumbled, and then walked out the door. Hannah went to follow but Pastor Bob stopped her and flashed a sympathetic look, "Good luck Savannah," he whispered. Hannah stood dead in her tracks. Her eyes desperately searched for answers as Austin took her hand and forced her departure.

Hannah was all beside herself. *He knows...but how?* She felt dazed and confused. She wondered if Pastor Bob was one of Enrico's colleagues. She kept her thoughts to herself. Hannah did not wish to cause Austin any further turmoil. She knew Austin merely wanted to do the right thing by her, for he wished to make her his wife. Hannah became worried. If Pastor Bob were one of Enrico's colleagues, Enrico would soon discover they wished to wed. She was not sure how Enrico would react to such a revelation. She reflected upon her thoughts as Austin drove them home.

Pastor Bob began to lock up the church. He tidied up, cleared the pews of hymnbooks and began to work on next week's sermon. It was moments like this when he wondered why he even bothered. He remembered his reasoning, "Keep the faith," he whispered. His thoughts were with Hannah now. He knew her soul became lost in the shadows of her own...

Pastor Bob returned from his thoughts as he suddenly felt eyes upon him. He quickly turned and met Enrico's cold gaze radiating from the back of the ministry. Under normal circumstances, he'd demand to know how the perpetrator gained access, but these were not normal circumstances and he already knew the answer. Pastor Bob fumbled for words. "Lord Costello, to what honors us with your presence?" he managed.

Enrico remained silent as he slowly walked up the aisle and stood at the Alter. "You speak as though someone else accompanies you in this desolate place.

"You are in the house of the lord," Pastor Bob returned cautiously, for he did not condone Enrico's blasphemy.

Enrico stared at Roberto with cold isolated eyes. "Your so called Lord remains silent and absent. You are now in the presence of your only Lord," he shouted fiercely.

Roberto's heart ached for Enrico's soul for Enrico has been lost for so many years. He wondered if Enrico would fully understand the magnitude of his own destiny—and *hers*.

Enrico regained his bearings as he composed himself. "Pastor, you have been visited by the Lady Costello, have you not?"

Roberto took a double take, for he never heard Enrico call him pastor before and this revelation rendered him speechless, for Enrico had lost his eternal faith. Many times he had tried to bring Enrico around with no prevail. "That is correct," Roberto replied.

Enrico felt weak, but he refused to sit down—not here. "She wishes to wed then...I presume," he returned coldly.

Roberto nodded and Enrico could no longer control his temper, but he managed to bury his rage deep down.

"Let go of your hatred and release all *fears.*"

"Never!"

"Only then can you accept him back into your heart and become free once again. It is the only way Enrico." Roberto tried one last time to save Enrico's soul.

"Let him back into…why would I ever accept…do not speak these words again in my presence. Do I make myself clear?" he demanded. Enrico could not think clearly as he publicly renounced his eternal faith in the most holiest of places.

"Perfectly."

Enrico said the only thing left to say, "I've done my duties and I have abided by my destiny. And for what, to have the only woman I have ever truly loved—the woman I have vowed to forsake all others for—to run from me and find another lover. Not just any lover, but her soul mate. There is a greater Devine intervention upon us now and I will never forget nor will I ever forgive for this betrayal."

The room fell silent and Roberto broke the silence as he cleared his throat. "So, you still believe in Devine power?" he asked questionably.

Enrico's eyes turned black as coal. "I never denied the existence, merely the presence or lack of…I should say." Enrico suddenly felt a calm clarity overwhelm him, as though he were free from some terrible burden. *Had I just announced my faith?* He pushed the thought aside. "Roberto, I come to you not as my colleague and friend but as my Pastor. Why is he working against me?"

Roberto did a double take; Enrico has never referred to him as *his* Pastor before.

Roberto was nearly lost for words, especially when Enrico hit his knees and began to pray. Roberto gave him a few moments of silence. When Enrico finished, he rose and met Roberto's gaze.

"Did you find what you were looking for?" Robert asked, still in shock.

Enrico dismally shook his head as Roberto placed his hands upon his shoulders.

"Instead of asking why, maybe you should ask who. I feel there is a diabolical intervention at hand here, not Devine. Remember his teachings, my Son. God vanquished Adam and Eve from the Garden of Eden out of love, not anger. In time, they realized the errors of their ways and returned to his doorstep. I believe Han...Savannah will find her way back to you in time—it is her destiny."

Enrico found some comfort in these words, but not much. He turned to leave and heard, "God be with you, Enrico." He closed his eyes still unsure if his faith returned, for there were still so many unanswered questions.

Austin and Hannah felt discouraged but not defeated. They agreed to leave anyways and call to inform their families that they eloped. Their hearts already united and they felt it unnecessary to sign a dotted line to make it appear official. They had no idea where they would go or what they would do, but felt that love would see them through the challenges that awaited them. Austin desperately wanted to leave Enrico in the rear view mirror and had the means to accomplish the task. He still planned to propose properly, but wanted everything to be perfect. Austin continued to conceal his inheritance from Hannah. He knew that wealth corrupts and vowed material possessions would never come between them. They made plans to leave less than a week away.

Hannah continued to replay Pastor Bob's words within her mind and wasted no time. She raced around the house and gathered up her most treasured belongings that night. Jacob's letter and card were the first things packed. Hannah hid her activities from the rest of the family. She kept to herself for three days deeply lost in thought, uncertain where Enrico's intentions lied. She refused to allow Enrico to persuade her heart in the opposite direction, for her decision was final.

Hannah woke on July 22, fully prepared to leave the following night. Kayla watched Hannah walk into the hallway completely aglow and instantly knew something was up.

"Where are you going?"

"Why do you ask?"

Kayla chuckled, "If you want to hide your suitcases under your bed, make sure the comforter hangs to the floor to conceal them."

Hannah smiled, "Thanks for the heads up."

Kayla took Hannah's hand, "I know you and Austin are planning to elope, Good luck." Kayla tilted her chin and turned to walk away, "I trust your decision, Hannah," she whispered.

Rebecca was in the kitchen making blueberry pancakes. "Hannah, can you come in here?" she hollered.

Hannah approached the kitchen with a heavy heart. Hannah loved her mother very much and knew leaving like this was unconceivable, but she had no choice in the matter. The fewer people that knew the better off everyone remained.

Hannah walked into the kitchen and took a seat, just as Rebecca placed a bag upon the table.

"I got an interesting phone call last night," Rebecca said with a grin.

Hannah took caution, for she had no idea where the conversation led.

Rebecca smiled warmly; she did not wish to make Hannah squirm too much. "You got a phone call from Dick's Travel trailers last night before you got home. Therefore, I took a message for you. It seems the salesman will have the paperwork ready tomorrow morning," she explained.

Hannah did not know what to say.

Rebecca extended her hand, "Honey, you are nineteen and have graduated and I can no longer make your decisions for you. If you and Austin are planning a trip, you should follow your heart and go for it. It sounds adventurous and since I have no idea where you are planning to venture, I took the liberties of getting you an atlas and a paper map of every state. A small camper like that can be taken anywhere!"

Hannah's eyes widened. She raced around the table and hugged Rebecca, "Thanks Mom," she cried. *Thank God I have her blessings.*

Rebecca returned her daughter's embrace, "When are you planning to leave?" she asked, as her eyes began to moisten.

Hannah did not have the heart to tell her mother that they planned to skip out of town the following evening without so much as a goodbye, "In a couple of weeks." Hannah quickly averted her eyes, and then added, "I know it sounds soon but we wanted to travel during the summer months."

Rebecca laughed, "Feel free to leave sooner if you like, I am very excited for you." Hannah could hardly believe her mothers enthusiasm. She could not wait to call Austin and invite him over to look at maps with them. At least, until her father walked through the back door with an unexpected guest. Brian finished changing the break pads on Rebecca's car and took it for a spin around the block.

Brian walked through the door, "Look who I found walking down Cold Spring Road after his car broke down!" he announced, as he and Enrico walked through the back door.

Rebecca warmly greeted Enrico's entrance. Hannah's smile quickly faded.

Brian grabbed the phone and the phonebook, "I can recommend a couple of mechanics to save you a buck or two, Enrico!" he exclaimed, and handed the phone over.

Enrico thought the world of Brian and appreciated the offer. Money was not an option to Enrico but he was not about to let that known, "That would be great, Sir."

"Please, call me Brian."

Hannah stood there motionless, uncertain where the conversation led. She wanted to run, but did not know whether to run from him or to him. There was no mistaken the love she felt in her heart, but she was undecided in her head between love and lust. Enrico now became the forbidden apple in the Garden of Eden. She devoted herself to Austin now, but a part of her would always need—and desire—Enrico.

Enrico accepted the phone and called a tow truck to take the Corvette to a local garage. He then called the garage to let them know the vehicle would arrive shortly. The man in the service department took the telephone number where he could reach Enrico incase of unforeseen complications. Enrico apologized to Hannah's family for any inconveniences and thanked them for their hospitality. He remained a perfect gentleman and was pleased at how smoothly things went. He secretly desired to get Savannah alone in hopes of winning her heart once again.

Rebecca just finished making some pancakes, "Are you hungry, Enrico?"

Enrico flashed a grin, "I don't wish to impose."

"Nonsense!" Brian stated.

Enrico sensed Hannah's emotions; he sensed longing and distance from her. He knew her feet and mind wanted to flee as far away as possible while her heart kept her firmly planted in her seat. This knowledge put him at ease.

Rebecca handed Enrico a plate of pancakes, "Feel free to stay as long as you like. What brings you to our neck of the woods, anyways?"

"I'm on vacation; since my last visit here, I fell in love with this town and its surroundings, so here I am," Enrico replied, and then reached for the Maple syrup.

Rebecca was instantly intrigued, "Where are you staying?"

"I saw a charming bed and breakfast just down the road, but now I'll have to see how much my car is going to cost; I may have to settle for a cheap motel outside of town," he explained.

Hannah gave a little chuckle. Enrico was smooth; she'd give him that. She now knew exactly where the conversation led.

"I can not allow that," Rebecca exclaimed, "You will stay here and that's final."

Enrico did not argue and accepted the more than appreciative offer. Brian was instantly thrilled to have another man in the house. He needed some male bonding since Clayton moved out.

Hannah felt her gut twist into a knot as Enrico eyed up the maps lying upon the table.

"Are you planning a trip?"

Rebecca stepped right in to brag up Hannah, "I brought these maps home for Hannah; her fiancé, Austin, is planning to travel with Hannah for awhile and we're very excited for them," she explained, and then gave Hannah a little hug.

Enrico raised a brow and grinned deviously. He already foreseen the upcoming trip and was there to persuade her heart in a different direction and was determined to succeed. His deep emerald eyes pierced hers. Hannah thought he could peer into her soul and desperately tried to conceal the longing she felt for him with no prevail.

Kayla watched in silence unsure if she should help Hannah escape his grasp or help Enrico pave a path back into Hannah's heart. Kayla noticed the attraction once again between them and longed to find a love that powerful. *Enrico refuses to give up.* She wondered if Hannah truly wanted him to give up. She raised her brow when Hannah captured his gaze with burning desires.

Hannah caught Kayla staring and lowered her gaze. "Mom, I'm taking Bandit for a walk," she announced, and then added, "Want to come along Kayla?"

Enrico instantly rose, "May I join you," he asked, and quickly added, "I really need to get a few things out of my car before the tow truck arrives."

Hannah grinned, "If you like…come on Kayla."

Kayla thought for a moment, "I'll take a short walk with you," she murmured.

Hannah grabbed Bandit's leash and walked out the door. Kayla and Enrico immediately followed, one more pleased then the other. Bandit showed his affections as he nuzzled Hannah's leg as she untied him. Bandit ran directly to Enrico. Enrico knelt and began to play with the dog affectionately.

"You don't have to leash him. I'm certain he will not runaway."

Hannah did not acknowledge his statement and attached the leash, as her hand brushed against Enrico's for a split second. *God, even Bandit enjoys his company. Don't look at his eyes—his moist lips—his...* Hannah immediately halted her thoughts and noticed Enrico flush. She turned and quickly walked away. It took all her will power to turn her back on those emerald eyes. Kayla shrugged her shoulders as Enrico followed.

Hannah started chuckling, "So, what do you think is wrong with your corvette?" she asked cynically.

Enrico glared at the ground and refused to acknowledge her antics. Hannah suddenly realized Kayla's favorite TV program was about to start. She knew it was selfish of her to drag Kayla along and began to feel guilty. "Kayla, you don't have to come along if you don't want to."

Kayla grinned, "Are you sure?"

Hannah nodded, as Kayla turned and ran back towards the house.

Savannah's thoughtfulness touched Enrico. He enjoyed watching her with her family. He began to realize that Savannah held many different passions within her heart and guilt crept into his soul for wanting to consume all of them. Enrico imagined taking her into his arms, throwing her to the ground and making love to her. He desperately needed to hear her whimper beneath him as he straddled her curvy bodice. He ran his hands over her ample breasts and down her stomach past her navel to her thighs. He could hear her whispering his name.

"Enrico," Hannah said, as she placed a hand upon his arm.

He seized her, drew her to his chest and held her firmly. Hannah let her guard down for split second and engulfed his mouth. The forbidden act ended as quickly as it began.

"I'm sorry," she gasped, and then stepped back. Hannah did not understand what came over her.

Enrico placed his palms upon her shoulders, "You never have to apologize to me Savannah, not ever," he proclaimed.

Hannah shook her head, "I do need to apologize, Enrico, for I was wrong, this is all wrong," she cried, and then added, "We need to return; I do not trust..." but Hannah abruptly ended her thoughts. She became embarrassed and felt as though she betrayed Austin's love. She knelt down and patted Bandit to assure him all was fine. Hannah stood, gently turned Bandit around and sauntered towards the house.

Enrico knew, without any shadow of doubt, that Savannah still loved him. He felt her body beckoning for more. He finished her thoughts knowing she did not trust herself in his presence. He called to her but she never glanced back.

"Savannah, please stop," he cried.

Hannah stopped but did not turn to meet his gaze. He continued towards the vehicle and retrieved an overnight bag.

Hannah glanced over her shoulder. The sun glistened off the hood of the Corvette. She shielded her eyes from the suns glare with her hand and allowed her eyes to drift as Enrico ran. Hannah saw his straining biceps mold to his white T-shirt. She squinted her eyes as the sun beamed down upon them. She watched as impure thoughts flooded into her mind. For once, Savannah watched as the love of her life ran in the opposite direction. This realization made her gasp. Enrico could choose, at any time, to walk away from her and never glance back. Hannah wondered for the first time why he chose to stay nearby and not continue with his life. *What does he have to gain by standing by me when I profess my love to another?* Hannah sighed when an answer crept into her mind. *Because he loves me! I L...*

"Let's go home," he announced.

Hannah raised her brow, "Don't you ever give up?"

Enrico smiled and took her hand, "I'll never give up on you, my Lady," he replied, and then drew her hand to his moist lips.

All her instincts wanted to give him much more than a mere hand. Hannah blushed and immediately withdrew the offer. Enrico nearly succeeded, but Hannah remained firm, took his hand and pulled him towards the house. "Come on Romeo," she chuckled.

Bandit led the way as they returned home. Enrico slipped his hand around her waist and pulled her close. This act was both tasteful and appreciated. Enrico always managed to make her feel comfortable and safe when she needed it the most. They reached the house and Hannah placed Bandit back in his run.

Enrico followed her into the house. The family spent the entire day lounging around and talking. Hannah needed to call Austin, but did not know what to say. She decided to play it safe and say nothing at all. The garage called to say Enrico's vehicle would take about a week. The transmission needed replaced and the parts were on order. Nightfall approached swiftly. Kayla helped Hannah pull out the sofa bed and make it cozy. Enrico retired to the bathroom to change and later strolled into the living room sporting navy blue cotton sleep pants and a clean white cotton T-shirt, which Hannah thought was a little to small.

Rebecca entered the room, "Enrico, you may hear the phone ring in the middle of the night. They're prank calls from the neighbor kids so try to ignore it. Hannah handles all calls in the middle of the night," she explained, and then added, "I've had the number changed…twice."

Enrico looked at Hannah grimly. Hannah averted her eyes in every direction except towards him, for she could not bear to see the questions that lurked within his eyes. Enrico sensed her discomfort.

"Hannah, Kayla, let Enrico get some sleep; I'm sure he had an exhausting day," she whispered, and then motioned the girls upstairs.

They obeyed and followed her upstairs.

Enrico stood at the doorway and reached for Hannah's hand after Rebecca and Kayla passed by. Hannah walked slowly and Enrico tugged at her arm as she stood on the first step. He squeezed her fingers before releasing them. Hannah rather enjoyed the attention and the gesture. The family turned in for the night. Kayla spent the night in Hannah's room. Both girls looked at each other and grinned.

"Goodnight Enrico," they cried slowly.

Enrico closed his eyes, "Goodnight, my Lady," he whispered. He smiled, believing Savannah loved to drive him wild. Enrico lounged back and stared at the ceiling, knowing Hannah hovered above him like an angel, as pending duties chiseled at his heart. Fear, Anger, and Doubt became his secret prison. Hannah remained the only ray of hope. He knew if he listened hard enough, he could hear her heartbeat. He became restless and could not sleep. He tossed and turned until he finally drifted asleep to the beat of her heart. It was rhythmic and soothing. He slept peacefully for a few hours.

Enrico woke abruptly when he felt Savannah's pulse quicken as the phone rang. He heard footsteps upon the stairs as the phone continued to ring relentlessly. Enrico remembered Rebecca say, *'Hannah handles all calls in the middle of the night.'* He pretended to sleep as Hannah tiptoed past him and darted into the kitchen. She hesitated before picking up the receiver.

"Good evening Savannah, I trust you slept well," Antonio presumed, and then added, "I have missed you greatly."

Hannah wanted to scream but kept her emotions in check, "Do not call here again, please leave me alone once and for all," she pleaded.

Antonio chuckled; he was rather intrigued to get her all flustered like this. Savannah typically remained calm, but her behavior tonight was unlike her. "My best regards to your family," he remarked gravely.

"I swear, if you come near them, I will kill you myself," she threatened, attempting to keep her voice low.

"My dear sweet Savannah, the great Lady Costello should not say such seductive and alluring things, for it makes me want you even more."

Her hands trembled as she pressed the phone tight against her ear, "Go to Hell."

"Savannah...we can do this the easy way or the..."

Hannah immediately slammed the receiver down and shed a tear. Knowing he'd never give her a moments peace. "Why won't he quit tormenting me?" She fought a lump in her throat as another tear glistened upon her rosy cheek. Her thoughts became random but focused on Enrico. He slept in the next room and yet seemed a million miles away. Hannah was incapable of allowing him access into her soul and it pained her greatly. She needed to break free from her family and Enrico to maintain a safe course. *Far away, but forever in my heart.* Distant feelings resurfaced that she could not drown. The tides of change were upon her as she drifted out to sea—barely staying afloat upon the *Sea of Intrigue.* Hannah turned and froze dead in her tracks, as Enrico stood in the doorway with crossed arms.

His eyes darkened dangerously. "Who made the call?" he demanded softly. His eyes did not waver as he held her gaze for some time. Every ounce of his being demanded the truth while his heart secretly protested.

Hannah masked her inner turmoil with deceptive calmness and forced a pretentious smile. "Its nothing, go back to sleep before we wake everyone up," she whispered. Hannah tried to slip past him, but he remained steadfast. Her eyes glistened with fresh tears now. Enrico reached for her, but she did not accept his embrace and staggered backwards.

"Stop running from me. Share with me your darkest fears, for this is clearly not nothing!"

Hannah jumped as the phone began to ring behind her.

Every inch of Enrico's body tensed as he gently forced Hannah aside. He walked over to the phone and answered it. The mere thought of another man pursuing her made him lose control—and all mental clarity. He felt like crushing the phone with his bare hands and eliminating the problem at hand. He picked up the receiver and placed it to his ear, "Hello," he muttered. All he heard was silence. "I demand to know who this is!"

Hannah carefully pried the phone from his grip, "It's not what you think," she managed to whisper into the receiver.

"You disappoint me lover, for he can never fully satisfy you as I can; until we meet again," Antonio hissed and then hung up.

Hannah felt weak and dizzy. Everything that could go wrong did go wrong. Antonio now knows that Enrico is with her. She could not think clearly. The last thing Hannah needed was Enrico questioning her further. She tried to retreat upstairs, but Enrico still refused her passage.

He used his arm to block the doorway, "Savannah, I need some answers so I can make all this go away; why won't you let me help you?" He could not fathom her silence. Enrico remained silent as he waited for a reply.

Hannah said the only thing that came to mind, "You can't help me...nobody can help me."

Enrico became agitated each time Hannah dodged the truth. He gazed deep into her big blue moist eyes, "Name the man that pursues you in such a cowardly fashion; I can stand here all night, my Lady," he whispered. His gaze penetrated her thoughts, but all he found were defensive barriers. Enrico began to lose his patience. He wanted to seize her and kiss her mouth until she submitted and spoke the rogue's name. Instead, he leaned in and closed the gap between them to offer her comfort, "Will you lie with me awhile?"

Hannah gasped, "Not now and definitely not here."

He put his hands on her face and whispered, "When and where? I need you Savannah."

His plea astounded her. "My Lord, I don't think you should say such things for I am promised to another man," she reminded him.

He shook his head, "Austin is a mere boy," he growled. Enrico ran his finger across the Ring of Eternity, "You are promised to me and only to me." Enrico relaxed his hand over hers.

Hannah became intrigued. She never saw this side of him before. He behaved foolish, jealous and protective at the same time.

He drew her in close, "You can't deny the naked truth. Search your soul and you will find that we belong together...united as one."

She pressed against him and listened to the sound of their hearts beating in sync with one another.

He made one last final plea that came from the heart. "Leave with me now so we will never be parted again and I can protect you for all eternity."

Hannah swore she could touch his soul as he opened up to her. "I simply can't Enrico; there are too many factors involved."

He then allowed her passage to the next room. Hannah tiptoed back upstairs and never glanced back, for she could not refuse those eyes a second time.

Enrico heard the phone ring once more. He walked over to it, cursed it and brought it to his ear, "I am Lord Enrico Costello and the woman you pursue is the great Lady Savannah Costello; now, if you would be so bold to give me your name." The voice on the other end remained silent. *The coward hides behind silence.* "Call again and you shall face my raft; come face-to-face with my Lady and I will destroy you slowly," he hissed and slammed down the receiver.

Enrico needed more answers and felt he deserved the honest truth. Savannah refused him simple honesty and chose to keep her secrets locked within her impenetrable heart. His tactics remained useless. He only hoped someday she could trust him enough to let him in. His love remained unconditional and he chose to stand back to see if Savannah would return her love in the same manner. Enrico tossed and turned all night, wondering just how much Austin knew and understood.

Antonio threw the phone aside. Enrico was indeed with her, even after all his attempts to keep them apart. Coercion was no longer enough. She still chose to defy him and he declared retribution. Jeano remained the only person who could shed some light on the situation. Antonio summoned him immediately. He never cared for Jeano much but, during times like these, he had his uses. Jeano entered the room as Antonio paced the floor vigilantly.

"You summoned me."

Antonio met his questioning eyes, "Where is my brother?" he asked, and then added, "I have an important matter that needs discussed."

Jeano thought about the question, found no foul play in Antonio's request and answered honestly. "Lord Costello decided to take a vacation to America for an undetermined length of time. Do you wish to speak to him?"

Antonio thought for a moment, "No, the matter can await, but inform me immediately upon his return." He quickly motioned for Jeano to leave him.

Jeano left the room questioning Antonio's demeanor. Antonio appeared extremely agitated and damn near hostile. Jeano made it his business to find out why, especially since Enrico was involved. He chose to handle the dilemma delicately. There was no way he'd contact Enrico without fully understanding the situation. Enrico had his own situation at hand, for Savannah was about to take flight and devote herself to another. Jeano did not understand their relationship.

He remained skeptical whether or not they understood it. They loved each other, professed their love too one another and continued to hold back their true emotions. He understood Savannah's turmoil, but still could not decipher Enrico's distress—or rationale. Enrico veered from his duties but still chose to abandon her. Jeano could only speculate Enrico's motives. He completely overlooked Antonio's mysterious behavior, as he focused on Enrico.

Hannah woke early, but waited for Rebecca to get out of bed before she dared to venture downstairs. She barely slept a wink. Hannah felt certain Enrico did not sleep well either. Brian strolled downstairs and started the morning pot of coffee. He seemed quiet and distant to Hannah. Brian had weekends off and Sunday mornings were his favorite, but this morning he acted as though he were depressed.

"We won't be attending church services today," Rebecca whispered before Enrico entered the room.

Enrico smiled warmly and gladly accepted a cup of coffee.

"Do you prefer sugar or cream?" Rebecca politely asked, as she poured cream into her own cup.

"I prefer mine sweet."

Hannah handed Enrico the sugar bowl and blushed, as their eyes connected. She read his gaze, understanding exactly what he preferred sweet. She quickly turned her head and glanced around the room. Brian appeared agitated and left to find solitude in front of the television. Hannah realized that the pre-game was about to begin. In Brian's eyes, Sundays were reserved for worship and then sports. Everyone else sat around the kitchen table, snacking on croissants, and chatting like old friends. Enrico noticed Hannah's vibrant smile as she laughed and it warmed his heart.

No one mentioned the numerous phone calls from last night and Enrico wondered how often the rogue called—especially since the family became accustomed to them. Enrico suddenly felt a pit in his stomach. A craving that only revenge could fulfill. The phone rang and Rebecca answered it.

"Hannah, Its Austin," she announced, and then spoke into the phone, "You must come over; I would like you to meet an old family friend."

Hannah nearly choked on her orange juice. She scrambled to her feet and raced for the phone, "I'll take it Mom!"

Enrico chuckled aloud, but silently cursed the boy. *This is the perfect opportunity to meet the boy...And claim Savannah once and for all!*

Hannah caught Enrico's devious smile and cringed. She did not know what to say. Hannah agonized while Enrico appeared rather amused. She grew irritated with his insensitivity. "Hi Austin, how is your morning?" she asked, and then slipped around the corner into the hallway for much needed privacy, for she did not want Enrico to listen in on their conversation.

"Whom does your mom want me to meet?"

Hannah paused, "No one important," she whispered, and then immediately began small talk.

Enrico seized the moment. It was time to make his presence known. He stood, casually walked into the kitchen and glanced at Savannah hiding in the corner. He grinned, "Rebecca, where should I freshen up at?" he asked rather loudly.

"One moment and I'll be right with you," she replied, as she dried the last breakfast dish and put it in the cupboard.

"Hannah," she cried.

Hannah nearly froze, but managed to muzzle the phone as best she could, "Yeah Mom."

"I did a load of towels last night, could you see if they're dry and hand a couple to Enrico? He would like to shower."

Hannah was all beside herself, "Austin, I'll be back in a second." She hesitantly placed the receiver upon the kitchen table and ran into the washroom.

Enrico was pleased but now had to encourage Rebecca to say his name once again while the phone lay in the open. "Where is the shower?" he asked cunningly.

Hannah returned carrying two towels.

"Hannah, can you show Enrico where the upstairs bathroom is?" she cried, not realizing Hannah now stood in the kitchen.

Hannah handed Enrico the towels politely, but truly wanted to throw them at him. "It's this way," she muttered.

"Take your time Enrico, we have plenty of water," Rebecca hollered, as they reached the stairwell.

Enrico began laughing aloud until Hannah flashed him a bleak expression. "You should really invite the boy over Savannah, for I'm dying to meet him," Enrico whispered. Hannah pointed to the bathroom as Enrico pressed her to his chest and whispered, "You're rather stunning when you're angry." Hannah broke free from his embrace and stormed back into the kitchen. She closed her eyes and tightened her grip around the phone, for she now had damage control to deal with.

Austin could not believe his ears. He felt certain this was not Hannah's doing. Enrico somehow managed to weasel his way into their home. The mere thought infuriated him.

"I'm back Austin, sorry about that," she whispered.

"Is that who I think it is?" he demanded.

Hannah answered carefully knowing she could no longer avoid the truth. "Yes," she stated. She watched as Rebecca and Brian headed outside.

"Kayla, your father and I are leaving with or without you. Hannah, we'll be back in time for lunch. Be a dear and entertain our guest!"

Kayla ran passed their mother and out the door.

"Mom wait, I'll go with you," Hannah nearly pleaded.

Rebecca glared at her, "You know we all can't fit in one vehicle and Enrico is in the shower. Invite Austin over and the three of you can hang out together…we'll be back soon."

Hannah watched them leave with a heavy heart.

For a moment, she completely forgot about Austin.

"Hannah…Hannah," Austin shouted into the receiver.

"I'm here," she whispered.

"I'll be there in ten minutes."

"No, I can handle the situation!"

Enrico ventured downstairs and watched Savannah curiously, as she began to squirm. He always hated to see her distressed, but know he rather relished the moment.

"Allow the boy to come over, my Lady; we'll have some fun together."

"No, Austin, that is not a good idea."

"I don't care, I'm coming over."

Hannah felt faint, "Austin, please don't," she cried, but it was too late. Austin was no longer on the line. She slammed down the phone, "Are you happy now," she screamed at Enrico.

He looked her square in the eye, "Completely, my Lady."

If looks could kill, Enrico would have dropped dead upon the kitchen floor.

"Does Austin also receive phone calls in the dead of night?" he asked flatly, "Or is he unaware that they exist?"

"That's none of your business," she snapped back.

"I make your safety and well being my business, for you are my Lady Costello," he said compassionately.

Hannah took a defensive approach. "If I could throw this ring at you right now, I would," she screamed, "But since I can't seem to remove it…I can't. Why is that Enrico? Who are you really and what dark secrets do you fail to disclose?"

They both turned their heads towards the driveway as a vehicle approached.

"Austin can't be here already," Hannah whispered. She drew in a deep breath and held it until Rebecca walked through the door and sighed with relief.

"I forgot my purse," Rebecca announced.

Hannah thought quickly and smiled deviously. "Mom, Enrico was just telling me that he needed to pick up a few personal items in town but was afraid to impose and cause you a second trip."

"Well, it's your lucky day Enrico. Come on," she said, and nudged his arm.

Hannah now expressed a mile wide grin as Enrico accepted—not having any choice in the matter.

Rebecca grabbed her purse and walked back to the car, "We'll be waiting Enrico."

Enrico walked over to Hannah, backed her into the corner and rested his strong hands upon her shoulders, "You are a clever little vixen," he whispered. He tilted his chin, moved in closer as he felt her go feverish in his arms and then brushed his lips to hers. They both reeled from their thoughts as the horn honked.

"Have fun, my Lord," she teased, as Enrico reluctantly walked out the door.

He watched hopelessly from the backseat as Brian pulled out of the driveway when Austin pulled in. Enrico watched the boy exit his vehicle and run into the house. He instantly balled his hands tensely and closed his eyes in dismay. Kayla reached her hand over and placed it upon his fist, offering comfort. She smiled a little as his hand relaxed. He appreciated the gesture, but it did not ease the tension. Kayla felt sorry for Enrico. She knew that he was hopelessly and madly in love with Hannah, for reasons she could not begin to comprehend. She thought about having her father drop them off at the ice cream parlor a mile down the road. They could walk home from there, but she did not want to interfere with the affairs of the heart. She sat silently in the back seat as Enrico became lost in vengeful thoughts. Secretly, he wanted to destroy the boy.

Austin entered the house, "Hannah," he shouted.

"I'm upstairs Austin."

He ran upstairs and entered her bedroom as Hannah finished rolling up a sleeping bag. He saw a stack of neatly folded blankets in the corner. Austin immediately saw red, "Did he sleep in here last night?" he demanded, "So help me God, if he…"

Hannah quickly interrupted. "It's not what you think…Kayla slept in here last night." She stood and embraced him. Austin welcomed her embrace, but his thoughts were elsewhere.

"Where is he?" Austin did not wait for a reply. He ran into the hallway and shouted, "Enrico!"

Hannah ran after him, "Austin, he isn't here. He went to town with my folks," she explained. "Mom forgot her purse and returned for it and I blackballed Enrico into going with them."

Part of Austin felt relieved while the other part felt cheated out of the opportunity to make his presence in Hannah's life known, once and for all. "We shall wait for their return," he affirmed.

Hannah wished to avoid such a confrontation all together, for both their egos ran full throttle. "Austin, I don't wish to sit around all day discussing Enrico…let's get out of here. I could stay over tonight and we can sign the papers for the camper tomorrow morning." Hannah leaned in and kissed Austin seductively.

Austin could not turn down such a proposal, "Let's get out of here then," he grinned. Enrico was far from his mind now.

Hannah returned to her knees. "Grab a suitcase!" She began to remove luggage bags from beneath the bed.

He searched her eyes for answers, but found none.

Hannah smirked, "We may need to leave quickly and this way I am ready. By the way, Mom gave us her blessings. I'm ready when you are." Hannah loved Austin very much and desperately wanted to put both Enrico and Antonio far behind them—each for different reasons.

Austin wasted no time; he grabbed three bags and ran downstairs. Austin placed the bags in his trunk before she made it to the bottom step. He grabbed the bags that Hannah carried and took off again. Hannah laughed aloud; his eagerness told her that he was more then ready. She left a note explaining she planned to stay over at Austin's tonight and would not return anytime soon. Hannah placed the note upon the table and turned to join Austin outside. She stopped, turned slowly and gazed at the bag of maps upon the table. She reached for them, "These may prove to come in handy," she whispered. Hannah left the only home she ever knew and walked towards the unknown with a heavy heart.

Austin realized that much must have happened in the past twenty-four hours. He wished he were there from the beginning when Enrico first revealed himself. He reached over and took Hannah's hand, "Are you Okay," he whispered, "He didn't hurt you in anyway…did he?"

Hannah hesitated for a moment, but did not dwell upon her thoughts for very long before answering, "No Austin, he remained a complete gentleman."

Austin raised his brow and closed is eyes, as though someone up above answered his prayers. "How long is he staying?"

Hannah shrugged her shoulders, "I'm not sure…maybe a week or two."

Austin gasped; he did not need to understand the reasoning behind the stay. He did not care how; he concerned himself with Enrico's motives. The same question looped repeatedly in his mind. *Why does Enrico go to such lengths?* Austin had no answers. "Hannah," he whispered, "I can not allow you to go back home, not to…"

Hannah rested her head upon his shoulder, "I know," she whispered. She already prepared herself for such a response. Part of her felt guilty. Hannah knew Enrico was an innocent in the misunderstanding, but she continued to let Austin believe they ran from him—failing to breathe a word about Antonio. Hannah reminded herself it was for their safety.

Chapter 11
Distant Shadows

The family returned from town in time for lunch. Enrico entered the house first only to discover Hannah's letter where the maps lay earlier that morning. He no longer felt her presence and quickly read the letter before Kayla entered the house carrying an armload of groceries.

"Hannah left...didn't she?"

Enrico nodded grimly and felt like destroying the letter.

"Will you walk Bandit with me when I am finished helping out here?" she asked, "I have some information you may find interesting."

Enrico's eyes widened, "I'd be obliged to accompany you." Enrico began to help so they could leave sooner.

Rebecca found amusement in Hannah's note and chuckled upon reading the final line. Kayla announced that she and Enrico would walk Bandit after the last of the groceries were put away.

Kayla grabbed the leash and Enrico followed her outside. He grinned briefly, for usually he led but lately he turned into a follower. Bandit was reluctant and refused to accept his leash. Kayla understood his confusion. Hannah was not there and he grew leery. Bandit did not want to leave his run when Kayla gently tugged upon the leash.

"Allow me," Enrico whispered, as he removed the leash from Kayla's grip. He dropped to his knees and began to whisper in Bandit's ear. Bandit perked up, wagged his tail and left the safety of his confines. "We're ready now," Enrico announced, as he stood and handed Kayla the leash.

Kayla's expression brightened, "What did you say to him?"

Enrico did not reply and merely smiled. Kayla thought his smile was to die for and felt feverish. She realized there was much to learn from the handsome man standing before her. She wondered exactly how much Hannah did—and did not—know.

They walked up Cold Springs Road. Kayla did not know where to begin, so she began to speak while Enrico hung on to every word. "I know Hannah is deeply and madly in love with you, Enrico. She's told me so…on several occasions."

Enrico raised his brow as he stopped her, "Why does she constantly run from me then?" he asked coldly.

Kayla could not offer any explanations, only theories as she continued. "Hannah has nightmares and I hear her cry late at night."

Enrico came to understand this on his own accord, "What do you know about the phone calls in the wee hours of the morning?"

Kayla held his determined gaze, "Dad answered them, when they first began, and then Hannah started venturing downstairs. I followed her one night and secretly picked up the phone in the living room. I hated to ease drop, mind you."

Enrico nodded and fully understood.

"I thought the voice belonged to you at first because the tone was similar to yours. The man was clearly no gentleman though. He kept referring to our trip to Nicaragua. He called her Savannah and the great Lady Costello. I'll never forget what he exclaimed before he hung up. He told her that she belonged to him and only him. If she ever spoke about him to anyone, he vowed to destroy everything she holds dear. Hannah slammed down the phone and began to cry. I wanted to rush over to her and demand what his intentions were, but I was afraid of doing more harm than good. I'm scared for my sister, Enrico. I'm certain you do not want to hear this, but maybe her decision to leave town is best for everyone. She runs from him, not you. I know she would choose to be with you if she could. I've watched her actions. Her body language speaks for itself. I'm not blind and neither are you. I see the way you two gaze at one another."

Enrico felt it was the perfect time to fish for more information since Kayla appeared to be honest with him. He looked into her eyes, unsure if he was willing to accept the truth, "Does she look at Austin the same way you see her looking at me?"

Kayla expected the question and answered honestly, "I've never seen her look at him the same way she looks at you," she insisted, as she placed a hand upon his arm.

Enrico looked at her with appreciative eyes, for he needed to hear that. He watched as Kayla became agitated and distant, "What's on your mind?"

Kayla fidgeted with her fingers and Enrico recalled Hannah did the same thing when she too became nervous. "May I ask you a question?" she asked timidly.

He nodded, but Kayla was not sure where to begin and remained silent for a moment.

"Why did you not return for Hannah nearly two years ago?" Kayla did not wait for a response and continued. "She waited patiently for months. You were all she ever talked about. In the end, Hannah believed she was just your escort for the evening. It became clear that the evening you shared was the most magical night she ever experienced. Yet, you remained absent. It truly broke her heart Enrico. Afterwards, she began to pursue her relationship with Austin, which quickly escalated. Why did you abandon her?"

Enrico closed his eyes for he did feel responsible for abandoning Savannah, but he still had to remain true to his duties. He felt conflicted those first few months. He desperately wanted to rush to her side, but his duties would not allow him the pleasure. He thought about her every single day. "How could she think she was my escort?"

Kayla flushed and confessed it was she who brought the subject up, "I'm so sorry Enrico; I did not know Hannah would take it to heart. Please forgive me," she cried.

"I do not blame you Kayla. I really need to speak to her alone. We have much to discuss," he explained, in hopes that Kayla would see things his way. Many new thoughts raced through his mind. *Kayla stated the voice was similar to mine.* He felt certain now that Hannah's fears began in Nicaragua.

He vowed to unmask the man behind the malicious plot. He began to understand that each ploy was a vicious attempt to entrap Savannah with intent to harm. The rogue conspired against him using Savannah as bait. *The rogue has the audacity to call her the great Lady Costello, completely understanding that she belongs to me.* Enrico wondered how the rogue concluded that fact. He made a fist, as the truth hit him like a ton of bricks. *The Ring of Eternity.* "Kayla, tell me about your trip," he nearly demanded.

"I'll tell you everything I know," she returned. Kayla spoke about the flight and explained how they were separated during the final leg of their journey. "Each group entered the castle separately and waited to register. There was a man, with physical similarities to you, sitting behind the registration desk that greeted us upon arrival. I remember he appeared to be agitated as though he waited impatiently for someone. We all stood in line and signed our names to the manifest. Wait…that was the same man that arrived Christmas morning with Hannah's photos…I thought he looked familiar!"

Enrico interrupted her, "What was this man's name?" he asked impatiently.

Kayla quickly scanned her memory, but the name never came to her, only a sound, "I believe his name began with an A…Anthony perhaps."

Enrico scanned his own memory, but held no recollection of meeting an Anthony. Enrico realized he must know the rogue, for the man remained silent on the phone out of fear of being recognized. Enrico began to understand that the rogue probably used an alias. He began to wonder just how far the two-week ordeal had gone. He shuddered at the thought as his heart turned fiercely aflame and he could no longer control his temper. "I want a description of the man," he demanded.

Kayla jumped, for she never saw Enrico this hostile before and answered quickly, "He had your complexion, dark brown wavy hair and gray eyes. His dress was similar to yours as well. He could have been your twin if he had green eyes and black hair," she explained.

"Was he as tall as me?" he snapped.

"I do not know; he was seated each time he greeted me," Kayla snapped back.

Enrico made a fist, walked to the nearest tree and punched it violently. He pictured the rogue standing before him. His thoughts consumed every action as he focused on one thought—*the rogue's blood.* He punched the tree until he could punch no longer. His hand swelled and his knuckles ran red with his own blood. Kayla screamed and begged him to stop, but Enrico did not hear her. His sleeve dripped with blood when he felt satisfied. Kayla ripped off her sweatshirt and wrapped it around his hand. Enrico paid no attention to her as he concentrated and pried into Savannah's innermost deepest thoughts.

He watched from afar, as Savannah tried to sign her name while holding the paper down with her left hand, exposing the Ring of Eternity. He watched as a dark figure loomed overhead, backing her into the corner. He watched her struggle with no prevail as the figure seized her and pressed her to his chest. Enrico dropped to his knees but never closed his eyes for a moment. He watched in horror as the rogue led her upstairs. Enrico recognized the stairwell of the Castillo de Isla. The castle sat across the Costa Rica border in hostile territory in the center of Lake Nicaragua. It was the residence of his mortal enemy, Lord Diego Cordoba. Enrico knew that he had no power there. He also realized that Kayla's description did not fit Lord Cordoba. The shadowy figure led Savannah into a room, released her and then locked the door.

Enrico heard Kayla pleading with him and became aware of his surroundings. He could no longer see into Savannah's mind, for that door slammed in his face. Enrico had never before experienced such an episode. He needed to consult with Jeano. He agonized over his visions, but focused more on what he did not witness. He felt confused and his hand hurt like hell. Enrico glanced down and saw his blood upon the ground. "What happened?" he asked, half stunned.

"What happened," Kayla screamed, "You tried to kill a tree; don't you remember anything?"

Enrico shook his head. She removed her belt and buckled it around the sweatshirt. She knew the method was crude but effective. Kayla's basic first aid training became second nature when she realized Enrico lost a lot of blood. She quickly turned to tie Bandit to a tree. She looked all around but Bandit was nowhere in sight. He ran off during the commotion.

Kayla knew Hannah would be upset but she did not have time to think about that now or time to chase after him. Enrico needed her attention. In the end, Kayla hoped Hannah would appreciate her decision. Enrico became lightheaded. Kayla instructed him to sit with his head between his knees. He appreciated her concern but knew it was completely unnecessary, for he would recover just fine. Enrico could not think clearly and desperately needed rest. He quickly fell asleep, knowing his strength would return to him upon waking.

Kayla grabbed her cell phone and immediately phoned her parents. Rebecca asked if Enrico needed an ambulance. Kayla did not think so but expressed that he did need a hospital. Brian and Rebecca wasted no time. They raced to Kayla's side and took Enrico to Mount Hawkins Medical Center. Enrico remained unconscious the entire way.

After examining Enrico, Dr. Madison determined he needed 102 stitches in his right hand. He told the family that Enrico's hand would heal nicely. However, Enrico did lose a lot of blood and was in dire need of a transfusion. A nurse drew a sample to determine Enrico's blood type. Ten minutes later the doctor returned with grim news and looked directly at Rebecca.

"Enrico has an extremely rare blood type that affects only 1% of the population; finding a donor on such short notice will require a miracle."

"What blood type does he have?"

"Type AB Rh-negative."

Rebecca sighed, "What a miraculous twist of fate." She did not attempt to conceal her enthusiasm as Dr. Madison narrowed his eyes and stared at her intently.

"Our daughter, Hannah, has that same blood type. She can be here in twenty minutes."

Dr. Madison prepared for Hannah's arrival, while Rebecca contacted her.

Hannah watched Austin answer the phone cautiously. "Hello." After a brief pause, he handed the phone to her. Hannah held it to her ear, uncertain what to expect.

"Hannah, don't ask any questions. We need you to come to the hospital right away."

"I'll leave immediately." Hannah turned and met Austin's questioning gaze. "Austin, I have to got to the hospital; Mom didn't go into any details except that I'm needed immediately," she said with a shrug, and then asked, "May I borrow your car?"

"Of course you can, but don't you want me to go with you?"

"I'm sure it's nothing major; I may be stuck there for a while and you need to pack yet."

He nodded, "You will come back here, won't you?" he asked suspiciously.

"That's the plan," she replied, and then kissed him goodbye.

Hannah grabbed his keys and left hastily. She had no clues to what transpired the call—or the dire urgency. She became lost in thought, while Austin wondered if this was another ploy by Enrico. Rebecca had initially called so he dismissed the thought and began to pack.

Dr. Madison addressed the family. "How did the accident happen?"

Kayla nearly panicked. She could not begin to explain the truth and she did not have a dishonest bone in her body. She managed to conjure up a believable tale. "Bandit ripped into his hand and then ran off." It was the only lie that came to mind.

Brian and Rebecca gasped, "Bandit has always been so gentle," they exclaimed.

Brian shook his head, "We can not worry about that now," he murmured, "Enrico is our main concern."

Rebecca nodded.

"Is the dog current on his shots?" Dr. Madison asked.

"Yes," Kayla answered immediately, knowing damn well Bandit was innocent. She vowed to let no harm come to him—come hell or high water.

Rebecca waited for Hannah outside the Emergency Room entrance. She watched impatiently as Austin's car approached the parking lot.

Chapter 12
Unbreakable Ties That Bind

Hannah parked and ran over to her mother. "Mom, what's wrong?"

Rebecca took Hannah's hand and led her inside. "There's been an accident; Kayla and Enrico went for a walk and Bandit ripped into Enrico's hand," she explained, and then added, "He needs 102 stitches and a blood transfusion; it turns out the two of you share the same rare blood type."

Hannah met Rebecca's gaze, "I'll help any way I can," she stated quickly, "Where do I go?"

A nurse took Hannah's arm, "Come with me," she stated, and then led Hannah towards the lab.

Hannah's thoughts became perplexed. *Bandit would not bite a soul, let alone the man I told him all about.* She knew it must be a mistake and the entire situation confused her. Hannah followed the nurse into a private room and was instructed to lie down.

"We need at least two pints…you may feel lightheaded."

Hannah rolled up her sleeve. "Take three if you need to."

The nurse raised her brow and narrowed her eyes. She gazed at Hannah intently, "I can take no more than two pints," she said admirably.

Dr. Madison peeked into the room. "We need those units immediately."

The nurse nodded and began. Kayla entered Hannah's room as the nurse inserted the IV and took Hannah's hand knowing she disliked needles.

"How is he?" Hannah asked with wide eyes.

"He's weak, but he'll be just fine once he receives this transfusion." Kayla saw fear and confusion upon Hannah's face as she held her hand.

"How did this happen? Bandit would not attack for any reason."

"I'll explain everything later."

The nurse finished taking two pints and smiled, "I'll take these units to Dr. Madison and check in on you in about fifteen minutes."

Another nurse came into the room five minutes later, "Miss Brockwell, I'm here to draw a second unit of blood."

Kayla stood to protest but Hannah quickly silenced her. Kayla understood that Hannah's emotions for Enrico penetrated beyond skin deep. She also understood that Hannah and Enrico would gladly offer their lives for one another. Kayla suspected that neither one knew the others true feelings. She wondered if they were actually destined for one another, as the nurse finished.

"Continue to lie down while I take this unit to Dr. Madison," she instructed, and then added, "Two pints is nearly to much for a young woman of your build; the procedure will only take a few minutes so try not to worry."

Hannah managed a smile as the room began to spin. She closed her eyes and entered a vortex of distant memories—and present desires.

Kayla looked at her sternly, "Hannah are you alright?"

Hannah simply nodded. Kayla watched her closely the next twenty minutes knowing damn well Hannah donated a risky three pints.

"Kayla," Hannah whispered softly, as she turned her cheek.

Kayla never took her gaze off Hannah, "What do you want?" she asked with a chuckle.

"Put one of these bandages on your arm," Hannah whispered.

Kayla became confused and raised her brow. "Why?"

"I want you to tell Enrico that you donated the blood."

Kayla could not fathom the request, "Whatever for?"

"I have my reasons," Hannah stated, not attempting to give any further explanation. Hannah's thoughts remained clouded as her heart pounded wildly.

Part of Kayla actually understood. "I'll cover for you this time, since you feel so strongly about the situation." She opened a bandage and placed it upon her arm.

"Thank you Kayla; please check on him for me."

Kayla reluctantly left the room and found Enrico three doors down. The room was empty and Enrico started to become alert. The color in Enrico's cheeks astonished Kayla. *He seemed so pale when we brought him in, even with his complexion.*

Enrico opened his eyes and vaguely noticed Kayla sitting before him. He felt disoriented and his vision out of focus. "So this is what it feels like," he whispered.

Kayla wanted to respond but remained silent knowing he was confused. She explained what happened instead. "You are in the hospital and just received a blood transfusion, so remain still and try to relax."

Enrico knew the transfusion was unnecessary but wished to thank the person who donated his or her own blood to him—a total stranger. Enrico could not sense Hannah but remained unalarmed. He knew he was still too weak from the ordeal.

"You gave us all a scare," she whispered.

He smiled as his vision became crystal clear. "I'm fine," he returned, and then asked, "Who was my donor?"

Kayla averted her eyes and danced around the truth.

Hannah stumbled down the hall and listened outside Enrico's door. She needed to see—with her own eyes—that he was all right. Before Kayla had the chance to admit the truth, Hannah collapsed in the doorway.

A nurse came running, "Miss, Miss, are you alright?" she cried.

Hannah's nurse overheard the commotion and came running, "Let's sit her down inside."

They seated Hannah on a chair just inside Enrico's room and grabbed smelling salts. Hannah instantly came face-to-face with Enrico's emerald eyes.

"Sir, you must lie back down," the nurse ordered, leading Enrico back to his bed.

Enrico wondered what just happened, as another nurse handed Hannah a cup of orange juice.

"Hannah, I just took two pints of blood from you, you…"

"You drew two pints…I also drew a pint."

Both nurses gazed at one another in bewilderment and then attended to Hannah's every need.

Enrico's eyes widened when he realized Savannah's blood coursed through his veins. Hannah instantly knew the secret was out. She did not know how he'd react, for her own heart soared on an emotional roller coaster.

The nurse eyed up her patients, "I expect you both to remain where you are for one hour until I return," she said sternly.

Neither one spoke, for different reasons, and merely nodded at her. They watched her leave, with heavy hearts. Enrico instantly returned his gaze to Savannah.

"Kayla, please leave us," he instructed, incapable of taking his eyes off Savannah.

Kayla quietly exited the room and closed the door.

"Savannah," he whispered.

Hannah did not respond. *Don't look into his eyes...*

"Savannah, please look at me," he pleaded.

Hannah dared to meet his gaze. *Oh God!* Her cheeks went aflame as she recalled every kiss—every touch. Her eyes moistened and a single tear escaped. She felt the need to protect him more than ever now, for she could not imagine life without him. Hannah could no longer deny the naked truth and nearly caved in to his unspoken desires, for the eyes never lie.

"You frightened me; are you alright?"

Enrico knew her heart still belonged to him as he rose and knelt before her.

Hannah rested her cheek upon his shoulder, "Don't ever leave me," she whispered.

He placed a hand upon her thigh, "I will never leave you, my Lady."

She glanced at his bandages remembering his stitches. "Does it hurt?" she asked sympathetically, and then reached out and caressed his hand.

"The only agony I feel is when we part. Your presence...rejuvenates my heart—your touch...rejuvenates my senses—and your passion...rejuvenates my soul. But, the truth will set you free." *Free from me.* Enrico pressed his moist lips to her cheek, even her tears tasted sweet. "Stay with me tonight."

His plea touched her heart. She stared at the wounds on his hand—and felt the wounds with his very soul. "As you wish, my Lord; I will stay by your side tonight," she whispered, as she became lost in his emerald eyes. Hannah stroked his dark hair and felt his heartbeat as they sat closely, in silence, for an hour.

Rebecca tiptoed into the room and found them sound asleep. She felt warm tingles as she nudged them awake. Hannah lifted her head off Enrico's shoulder and met her mother's smiling face. Enrico instantly felt uncomfortable, for Rebecca caught them in a vulnerable situation. He longed to have Savannah all to himself. He did not wish to share her with anyone, not even her own parents. Enrico refused to sit back and allow anyone to persuade her heart in a different direction. Rebecca's smile quickly faded.

"The doctors think the two of you should stay here tonight for observation and Brian and I agree. We will pick you both up first thing in the morning."

An orderly wheeled another bed into the room. Enrico thought it unnecessary as he smiled, for Hannah did not need a bed of her own since she was welcome in his. Rebecca handed Hannah a nightgown. Hannah nearly blushed but quickly kept her emotions in check. She still felt a little woozy as she drew a hand to her brow.

"Mom, please return Austin's car to him tonight; I'll call and let him know you're on your way," she said, and then handed over the keys.

Rebecca agreed and said, "Good night honey; you did a wonderful thing today and your father and I are very proud to have such a caring daughter." She leaned down, kissed Hannah's brow and left the room.

The nurse came in to check their vitals and handed Enrico a small cup containing two Vicadin, "I have to watch you take these," she said, and then poured a cup of ice water.

Enrico waved his hand aside, "I don't need any pain pills."

"They'll help you sleep honey; are you sure?"

Enrico flashed his bright emerald eyes knowing he wanted his mind clear tonight when speaking to Savannah.

She smiled warmly, "Press the call button if you change your mind."

The nurse walked out to the nurse's station and leaned over the desk, "Have you seen the young man in room 204? Now there's a fine example of a good foreign affair," she whispered, and then chuckled when her coworkers agreed.

Hannah did not feel comfortable changing in their shared restroom so she used the one down the hall. She pulled her pant legs up and slipped the nightgown over her clothes. She overheard the conversation at the nurse's station and wondered whether that kind of attention followed Enrico everywhere he went. *Women must throw themselves at him.* She could not help but wonder why he chose her—plain Jane Hannah Marie Brockwell. *He could have anyone.*

Enrico tried to become comfortable in bed. His mind kept drifting to his vision of Savannah and the dark figure at the Castillo de Isla. He quickly shook the image aside as he sat up and touched his feet to the floor. He felt good as new and smiled. He could feel Savannah's life giving blood coursing through his veins and became amazed with his newfound clarity. His senses picked up on every detail concerning Savannah. He felt one with her and could easily break into her thoughts now. But he was not about to do that again any time soon, for such powers frightened him.

Hannah walked into the room wearing a yellow knit nightgown. She felt dizzy from the long walk down the hallway. Her legs felt weak and gave out beneath her. Enrico lunged forwards and caught her.

"Are you all right Savannah?" he asked distressingly.

She remained motionless for a moment as he held her, "I'm fine," she whispered.

He helped her into bed and then sat down. Hannah glanced at his chest, which molded to the hospital gown. She tried to avoid further eye contact, for her eyes beckoned for much more. His chest sent her into a heated frenzy and she thought about caressing him through his pants. *He's not wearing any pants...Oh God...Don't look at his eyes.* She squeezed his hand and wondered if she would go to hell for such impure thoughts while promised to another. She could no longer deny her feelings towards Enrico. Her eyes widened.

"Did I hurt your hand?"

"Not at all, my Lady."

Hannah caressed his wounds, drew his hand to her mouth and planted a kiss upon the bandages. Enrico rested his thumb on her dimple and drew her mouth to his. Hannah moistened her lips and slightly drew open her mouth, as he cupped her chin. He continued to lure her in until he was inches from entry. He gazed deep into her eyes, as visions of the photo lurked into his mind. Without hesitation, he kissed her brow and returned to his bed.

Hannah gasped—expecting more. She suddenly felt jaded and attempted to mask the pain she felt within her heart. Just then, she remembered to call Austin. She wanted to use the payphone in the hallway but completely forgot. She simply did not have the strength to walk back down the hall. "Enrico," she said solemnly, "Can you remain silent while I make a phone call?"

Enrico remained silent for a moment. "As you wish," he murmured. He knew she was about to call *Austin.*

Hannah picked up the phone, "Please Enrico, no antics," she whispered, and then began to dial.

Enrico pretended to read a magazine as he listened intently.

Austin picked up the phone, "Hello," he said anxiously. "Where are you?"

Hannah explained that the hospital admitted a patient with the same rare blood type as her and needed a transfusion. Austin knew Rebecca placed Hannah on a possible donor list for such a situation. "I donated three pints and the doctors wish for me to stay overnight for observation because I continue to feel weak," she explained.

Austin wanted to be by her side. "May I come and sit with you?"

Hannah nearly panicked, "I'm afraid I wouldn't be much company and I'm ready for bed now," she returned.

"Alright sweetheart, get some rest and I'll see you in the morning," he whispered, "I love you Hannah and I'm proud of you!"

Hannah tightened her grip around the receiver. "Goodnight Austin and I love you too, more than words can say," she professed, and then hung up the phone.

Enrico felt his heart leap from his chest as he clenched his fists, "How touching," he murmured.

Hannah glared at him and noticed the door closed unexpectedly. She did not recall Enrico out of bed.

Enrico sat Indian style, "We have much to discuss Hannah; I have a few questions that need answers."

Hannah nearly gasped knowing this was the first time he called her by her true name. She dismissed the thought, realizing he must be upset from her previous conversation. Hannah felt she deserved such callous treatment, while Savannah continued to feel rejected. Still, she did not regret telling Austin that she loved him. "Okay, I'll answer what I can."

Enrico did not flinch, for he expected as much. "Why didn't you tell Austin I was the one in need of your blood…or that I am with you now?"

Hannah realized his gaze became intent and somewhat cold. "Why does it matter?" she snapped back.

Enrico refused to stand down and pushed forwards, "You said once that Austin knew about me, but how much does he actually know?" he nearly demanded.

Hannah became both intrigued and angry, "He knows that…" she began, but then grew silent and averted her eyes—unable to speak.

"He knows that you have intense feelings for me and that you've been denying your destiny; doesn't he." He penetrated her thoughts and began to relax a bit.

Hannah did not answer immediately. "Do you really want to discuss Austin?"

Enrico twisted his lips into half a smile, "No, I wish to discuss the Castillo de Isla," he whispered. His words pierced her inner most thoughts for a moment, but she quickly closed the door. For a second, he saw inside the room as she pleaded with the rogue. As quickly as the door opened, it closed on him once again. He knew it would be a long night, knowing Savannah would not be open and honest with him. Enrico still could not fathom why. He desperately wished to speak to Austin believing he could fill in some of the missing pieces—If Savannah confided in him.

Their nurse entered the room pushing a wheelchair. "Miss Brockwell, not all your paperwork is filled out and I'll need you out at the front desk if you don't mind. I'm sorry it's so late."

Hannah nearly leaped out of bed, glad to step aside from Enrico's firing squad, for she feared what he might uncover. "That sounds just fine."

The nurse looked at Enrico and flashed a flirtatious grin, "Don't worry Honey, I'll have her back in no time."

Enrico chuckled revealing a single dimple, "Take your time," he called out, as they left the room. Enrico jumped out of bed and grabbed the phone. He remembered Austin's telephone number from Savannah's caller ID. It was late and Enrico wondered if anyone would still be awake. He dialed the number and let the phone ring six times. He was about to give up when someone answered.

"Don't you ever get tired of calling; leave Hannah and I alone."

Enrico quickly heard a dial tone. He became mesmerized, realizing Austin also received calls late at night. Enrico knew it was time for Devlin to call.

Austin heard the phone ring twice and answered it as his blood began to boil. "What," he nearly screamed.

"Is this Austin?"

Austin fell silent. The voice sounded familiar but not identical. "Who's asking?" Austin held the phone firmly as he stepped outside.

"My name is Devlin Martinez and I'm calling in regards to Hannah."

"Who the hell are you?" *Hannah never spoke of a Devlin.* Austin waited impatiently for an answer, "Well," he demanded.

"I am Enrico's most trusted colleague and I call on his behalf tonight."

Austin's temper rose, "Any other time Enrico would call himself; what's so different about tonight?" Austin thought for a moment. This had to be the most meaningful conversation yet. He realized this call was different from the others and slightly calmed down.

"Enrico has information you may find interesting."

Austin cringed, "Hannah is soon to be my wife and I know all I need to," he replied bluntly.

Both parties remained silent for a moment.

"So you know of the events that took place at the Castillo de Isla then?" Devlin asked sarcastically.

Austin flinched not knowing what the statement meant. He knew it was Spanish but that was all and dared to ask, for Devlin obviously felt he knew something of great importance. "Go on," Austin murmured, admitting he was unaware of the events mentioned.

"Allow me to fill you in. The Castillo de Isla lies off the shores of Lake Nicaragua, where the photo shoot took place. A man who remains anonymous, the man that calls late at night, plotted against Hannah. I feel Enrico and you can both benefit by sharing information. This is why Enrico resides at the Brockwell house; he seeks the name of the man in question. Enrico will leave quietly after receiving the name. I am merely the messenger," Devlin explained.

Austin thought for a moment, "I do not wish to share information with Enrico or with you. I know who calls here late at night; it is Enrico himself. Surely you cannot deny that." Austin wondered if he believed his own words. This conversation sparked a shadow of doubt. He no longer knew who or what to believe.

"I assure you that Enrico does not harass his own Lady Costello. He merely seeks revenge upon the rogue who does," Devlin advised.

Austin remained unconvinced, "I wish an audience with Lord Costello; can you grant me that?"

"I cannot, but you will have an audience with me one day. You may reach me at 1-800-555-6706 if you change your mind," Devlin said, and then hung up.

Austin stared at the phone for a moment before writing the number down.

He trusted no one at this point, but did take the phone call seriously. *If Enrico sought revenge, why did he have one of his goons call?* It became clear to him that this was another ploy by Enrico to mystify his emotional state. He cursed Enrico for causing so much turmoil. Austin relaxed a bit knowing Hannah was safe and sound at the hospital. Tomorrow, they would put all this behind them, just as he promised. He refused to give Enrico—or Devlin—another thought. Enrico may be staying at the Brockwell house tonight, but Hannah was not with him. Austin loved her so much and vowed to protect her—forever and always. He attempted to fall back asleep with no prevail. He sensed something was about to happen and bolted upright in a cold sweat.

Enrico hoped Devlin got through to Austin. He sensed Austin was oblivious to the truth and hoped Devlin sparked enough curiosity for him to question Savannah. Enrico scanned his thoughts sensing Savannah was up to something. He quickly dressed and bolted towards the nurse's station. "I wish to check out," he nearly demanded, but then flashed a warm smile.

The nurse did not ask any questions and handed him the release forms. He signed his mark and sauntered down the hall. He rounded the corner and came to a halt when he saw Savannah awaiting the elevator. He grinned and ducked back around the corner, eyeing up the stairwell. Enrico raced down and jumped the last flight of stairs. He calmly sauntered out the main entrance and concealed himself around the corner, waiting patiently.

Chapter 13
An Undeniable Passion

 Hannah awaited the elevator. *Hurry up.* She hated to leave Enrico like this—again—but knew it was for his own protection. He would only ask more questions and she was not in the mood to fight with him any further. Hannah was uncertain where she'd stay for the remainder of the night, but felt confident enough to conjure up a plan of action. For the first time, Hannah felt like she controlled her own destiny. The elevator light illuminated and dinged as the door slid open. Hannah entered and realized how deserted the hospital appeared. She pressed floor 1 and the door closed. She strolled out the main entrance and glanced back, "Good Bye Enrico, my Lord…and my Love," she proclaimed aloud.

 She glanced around and started walking towards town, which was five blocks away. Hannah enjoyed the tranquility of the crisp night air. A full moon graced the night sky and illuminated the darkness. The stars shined bright overhead as she gazed up at heaven. She noticed a shooting star, let out a sigh of delight and quickly closed her eyes. Hannah secretly and silently made an enchanted wish. She found the shooting star had vanished upon opening her eyes. She continued to walk—*alone.*

 Enrico watched from a distance in amazement. She looked absolutely captivating in the moonlight and her blue eyes sparkled like sapphires. He desperately wanted to run over and take her into his strong arms. He overheard her goodbye as she called him—*her love.* Enrico wondered what other secrets he might uncover tonight as he lurked in the shadows. He decided to prepare for the unexpected, for there was magic in the night air. Several vehicles passed but the streets were rather deserted.

Enrico shuddered as he felt a cold chill race down his spine. He spotted a black limousine and became motionless as it pulled up to the curb, just one block from where Savannah stood. He could not move. Enrico stepped behind a shrub to conceal his identity. His heart raced frantically as he watched the limo questionably. The limo looked new and almost familiar. He did not take his gaze off Savannah now.

Hannah daydreamed, night dreamed, that is. Night dreaming was more suitable for such a spectacular evening. She looked ahead and stopped mid-stride. She saw the black limousine from her nightmares. Hannah hesitated for a moment and quickly performed an about-face. She traced her steps back to the previous curb as her heart beat wildly and fear overwhelmed her senses. She turned in a circle and desperately sought an alternate route.

She did not dare to walk down the dark alley and was on the verge of sheer panic. She watched in horror as the limousine began to approach. Hannah suddenly wished she stayed in the hospital with Enrico. For the first time in her life, Hannah decided to stand her ground and confront her worst fears. She remained firm, determined to find courage and strength in the depth of her soul. "You don't own me, not anymore," she whispered, as the limo pulled up along side her.

Hannah did not take any chances and took a few steps backwards, keeping a safe distance between the limo and herself.

The chauffeur stepped out and tipped his hat, "Lady Costello, his Lordship would like an audience with you at this time," he commanded, and then opened the back door.

Hannah's throat became dry, "Inform his lordship that I decline to give him the pleasure of my audience, not now and not ever," she returned coldly.

The chauffeur stepped forwards and extended his hand, "We can do this the easy way or the hard way," he announced.

Enrico overheard everything and leapt from behind the bushes. He instantly pulled Savannah out of harms way. Enrico stood between Savannah and the limo, "I demand an audience with your so called Lord," he screamed, as his blood began to boil.

The chauffeur pulled a pistol and cocked the hammer as Enrico attentively observed Savannah. Enrico turned with the speed of light, taking possession of the pistol. He tilted his chin and met the chauffeur with a deadly gaze.

The chauffeur came face-to-face with death defying green eyes and instantly knelt, "Lord Costello, I did not know it was you; please forgive me," he pleaded.

"Who is your master?" Enrico demanded, as a gunshot echoed throughout the crisp night air. Enrico lunged forwards, forcing Savannah to the ground and sheltering her body with his as the limo drove into the night. Enrico hovered above her, "Are you are alright?" he asked frantically.

"I'm fine," she whispered, "Thank you!"

He stood and helped Savannah to her feet. Hannah gasped when she saw the chauffeur dead along the curb.

"We should get out of here," Enrico said, as he took her hand and led her down the dark alley.

Hannah nearly unleashed her thoughts and trembled. W*hat would have happened if...* but quickly halted her thoughts.

Enrico stopped dead in his tracks and gently pushed her back against the wall. He held her shoulders firmly, "If what?" he asked tenderly.

Hannah looked at him with distant and vacant eyes. He closed his for a moment and pressed his lips to her brow and they continued walking. Enrico could not fathom why she chose to protect the rogue and was on the verge of loosing all control when he spotted a hotel just up ahead.

"We'll stay there for the remainder of the night," he said, as he pointed to the hotel. They ran when it began to rain. They passed valet parking and Enrico noticed the vacancy sign, as they calmly walked into the main lobby. Enrico approached the front desk clerk, still holding Savannah's hand, gently caressing her knuckles with his thumb.

"May I help you, Sir?" the desk attendant asked.

"I want your best room for the night," Enrico nearly demanded.

The attendant ran his finger down the register, "Ah, there is one vacancy available, the Honeymoon Suite."

"We'll take it!"

The attendant handed Enrico the register manifest. Enrico signed *Mr. Smith* and flashed a genuine smile.

The attendant did not raise a brow, for this was rather common. "Thank you Mr. Smith; what method of payment will you be using?"

"Cash," Enrico casually replied.

The attendant tallied the bill, "You may pay now or upon check out," he explained.

Enrico released Savannah's hand to remove his wallet from his back pocket. "I prefer to pay now."

"That will be $429.85."

Enrico removed five $100 bills, "Keep the change," he said, as the attendant handed him a room card.

"Thank you Mr. Smith," he returned, quite pleased, and then added, "Top floor, room 606. Have a pleasant evening."

Enrico turned to take Savannah's hand but found her nowhere in sight. He frantically searched for her, sensing her nearby, when he felt a tap upon the shoulder. He turned around and came face-to-face with the attendant.

"I believe the young Lady ventured into the lobby's shop; good evening again," he said, and then switched off the vacancy light.

Enrico ventured towards the shop. He watched Savannah for a few moments and returned to the lobby. Enrico approached the Concierge, "May I trouble you to help me with a surprise for the Lady accompanying me tonight…I'll make it worth your while."

The Concierge smiled, "Certainly Sir; what did you have in mind?"

Enrico explained and left the final arrangements to the Concierge. The Concierge assured him things would be in order in the appointed timeframe. Enrico wanted everything to flow smoothly, for this was the last chance to win Savannah completely. He felt confidant her heart belonged to him, but he had to win her mind. She kept herself aloof and protected her thoughts. She would not let him enter her private nightmare. He returned to the shop with a hopeful heart.

Hannah browsed the shop attentively. She saw many beautiful clothes that caught her eye. She especially adored a little black ensemble with a single green ribbon around the waistline. Hannah instantly fell in love with the dress but knew she would never have a reason to wear such an elaborate ensemble. The shop sold everything from hats to stilettos and everything in between. So much has happened in the past few hours. She tried to focus on happier times and allowed her mind to wander towards distant memories.

Hannah recalled a trip the family had taken to Lake Erie when she was a child. She remembered Brian and Jacob fishing along the shoreline while Rebecca, Jenna and Kayla played with her in the sand. It was not equivalent to the ocean but it remained forever beautiful within her mind. She supposed that was the reason for burning the picturesque Lake Nicaragua into her memory. Hannah wished she could remove the picture and has tried with no prevail. She shuddered and focused on the ocean.

The ocean remained her one untamed fantasy. She vowed to venture to the Atlantic coast someday if *he* would allow her such a simple pleasure. She shook the thought away and returned all her focus on the sand. She remembered how warm it felt between her toes as she frolicked along the waters edge. She recalled daydreaming about being a princess in a beautiful castle in another country awaiting the boy of her dreams. That was then and, now that she lived that nightmare, nothing in the world would make her return to such a horrific fairytale. Hannah still thought that the little black dress was suited for a princess. *I am no princess*, she reminded herself, as she placed the dress back on the rack. It was a silent chapter closed to the world—and her heart.

Enrico watched from afar, as she selected a dress and held it up to her bodice. He knew she would look remarkable in such a dress as he invaded her thoughts once again and vowed to make all her childish fantasies a reality. He shivered and recalled nearly loosing her tonight by an unforeseen force. Tonight was the proper time, if there was ever a moment, to turn back time. He proceeded forwards closing the gap and gently reeled her from her thoughts as he lightly touched her arm, "Savannah, lets retire upstairs," he whispered. Enrico handed her the room card as he led her to the elevator and ascended to the sixth floor. Hannah departed the elevator first, sauntered down the hall and briefly glanced out the window.

She gasped and gazed down at the black limousine from earlier. Only this time, Antonio stood along side it gazing up at her with contemptuous eyes. He placed a finger over his lips. Enrico saw her gasp and quickly ventured over. Hannah stepped in front of the window, placing her back to Antonio, as Enrico charged and tersely pushed her aside. He watched the back door close and felt like shattering the window, leaping towards retribution, but remained steadfast realizing it was unwise to leave his beloved Savannah alone.

Hannah rested her hand upon his waist, "He's waiting for us," she whispered. Enrico felt her hands tremble and spun her away from the window.

"This anonymous man is no longer my concern at this moment in time," he whispered.

Hannah unlocked the door and Enrico hurried her inside.

He rested his hands upon her shoulders forcing her to sit on the king sized bed. He knelt and gazed into her big blue eyes. Shadows cascaded over his emerald eyes and blanketed his heart, offering moderate protection. "Why do you protect him, my Lady?" he asked reluctantly.

Hannah winced, fully understanding the question. "My Lord, I do not protect him. I protect you; surely you see I do not flee from him in the same manner that I run from you…I do not love him," she attempted to explain. She prayed her words came out clearly, as she averted her gaze and began playing with her fingers.

Enrico accepted the explanation as he placed a hand upon her chin—forcing her to meet his gaze once again. "Do you trust me, my Lady?"

"Yes," she replied open heartedly.

"Do you love me?"

"Yes…God help me…I do."

Enrico's breathing increased. "Do you want me…my Lady?"

Hannah did not reply this time. She desperately wished he'd take her into his powerful arms. *Actions speak louder than words.* She quickly placed a hand to her temple and quieted her thoughts.

Enrico rose, "Come, we must get ready for I have a surprise waiting downstairs."

Hannah was not sure she could handle any more surprises tonight. She stood and glanced around the room, "So this is what a honeymoon suite looks like," she remarked. The room dictated formalities with the essence of romance. Hannah knew she had no other clothes to change into but still felt the need to shower—especially after Enrico threw her to the ground. She closed her eyes and recalled his powerful arms, which became a sinful pleasure she indulged in. She opened the lavatory door as Enrico called, "Savannah!" Hannah turned to meet his emerald gaze.

"I will have what I desire," he exclaimed seductively.

Hannah flushed and closed the door.

Enrico was pleased, considering the events at hand. He did desire Savannah and all her secrets. Enrico turned to a knock at the door, "Right on time," he whispered. He answered the door and the Concierge held out two garment bags. Enrico inspected them.

"Are they to your liking Sir?"

Enrico smiled appreciatively and thanked the Concierge. "Is everything in order?"

"Yes Mr. Smith; the lounge is ready as instructed."

Enrico tipped the man most generously. He carried Savannah's garment into the lavatory and hung it behind the door. He could see her naked silhouette through the etched glass doors. Enrico tapped lightly against the door, "I do not wish to rush you my Lady, but I too wish to shower," he said, remaining discreet.

Hannah froze, closed her eyes and could no longer deny the inevitable, "You may join me, if you like," she whispered softly. Enrico remained silent as Hannah watched his silhouette disrobe. Her heart beat wildly and her knees felt weak. She somehow managed to shock herself.

Hannah watched him approach and slowly opened the door—welcoming him into her private domain. He stood beneath the water as Hannah embraced him and engulfed his mouth with hers. His hair became saturated as he twirled her around, pressing her back against his muscular chest, and began nibbling upon her neck. He caressed her firm wet breast. She recalled his injured hand and felt the need to inspect his wounds. She turned and observed his hand and gasped, "Your hand, it's healed!"

He smiled and whispered, "I know."

Hannah finally realized he too disclosed secrets, only she remained uncertain if they were dark or not. Enrico pressed her back against the wall and lifted her as she squeezed her thighs around his hips. He kissed her so passionately that she could no longer deny him anything. She felt his extension between her legs and moaned, "My Lord, you're ready," as they both began to breathe heavily.

He gently placed her back down and gazed into her eyes, "Not yet my Lady, the night is still young."

Hannah did not question his motives. Her mother's voice echoed within her mind, *'Good things come to those who wait.'* Her heart ached as she realized half the night already passed. She helped him shower, imprinting every breathtaking image into her memory. He turned off the water and they stepped out together. Hannah noticed the garment bag as she dried off her bodice. Enrico thought she looked like a goddess before wrapping herself with the towel. He firmly grasped the towel and watched it float to the floor.

"You manage to invoke a rise in me, my Lady…with a single kiss."

"And you manage to shred every ounce of moral fiber…with a single glance."

Enrico wanted nothing more than to carry her to their bed. He watched as Hannah unzipped the garment bag, revealing the little black ensemble with a single green ribbon.

She could hardly believe her eyes, "Are we going somewhere?"

It pleased Enrico to see her smile in amazement. "The hotel lounge is all ours, my Lady!"

Hannah quickly glanced at her watch and saw it was only eight O'clock, "How can this be?" she asked and met his gaze.

Enrico smiled as he sensed a million questions arise in her mind. He pulled her to his chest and feathered his lips along her neck. He needed her to want him and left her body begging for more as he slipped out of the room.

Hannah instantly felt something mystical afoot. She did not question him—was incapable of questioning him. Hannah became lost in the magic that surrounded them. She remained in the lavatory while Enrico retreated to the bedroom. She picked up the dress and held it in her hands. She felt as though it was a forbidden object of desire. Hannah loved the feel of the fabric upon her bodice, for it hugged each curve. She used the blow dryer and left her long hair flow freely around her.

She found the same matching necklace and earring set along with a pair of stilettos at the bottom of the garment bag. Hannah observed her image in the mirror and for the first time in her life, she felt beautiful. She left the lavatory to show off the dress to Enrico. Hannah closed the door and came to a complete halt as Enrico stood before her wearing a black Armani suit and holding a single long stem red rose. He rendered her breathless.

Hannah desired him at that exact second. He strolled over and reached for her hand, "I am Lord Enrico Costello and I'll be your escort for the evening."

Hannah fell head over heels once again and wondered if it was all a dream. She never wanted to wake up, if it were a mere dream.

"Your every wish is my command," he whispered and drew her hand to his mouth, and then added, "Your every fantasy is my desire."

He kissed her hand tenderly. She vowed never to tire of this act. Enrico led her down the hall to the elevator. His thoughts raced uncontrollably, for the stakes were high and he needed to prevail. He could not protect her if she left with Austin. He feared loosing her forever. Enrico buried his feelings and refused to allow them to resurface again—not tonight. She chose to be here with him tonight and he wished to make her see that she made the right decision. Enrico vowed to be nothing but honest and sincere with the utmost honorable intentions. He wanted to give her the fairytale she rightfully deserved.

They made their way to the lounge. The room illuminated with the soft warm glow of candlelight, red roses adorned every table and music surrounded them. Enrico guided her to their table with his hand upon the small of her back. A lucrative bottle of champagne awaited them. Enrico poured two glasses while Hannah attempted to read the label. It was in French and she could not pronounce the words. Enrico caught her gazing at the bottle, "Nothing but the finest for my Lady Costello," he whispered.

Hannah loved the way Lady Costello rolled off his tongue and knew she would never tire of hearing those words. She glanced at her ring and fully understood its meaning. She belonged to him for the entire world to see. The music died down as a new song filled the air. They sipped their champagne, "Will you oblige your Lordship with a dance, my Lady?"

Hannah smiled and took his hand, "Anything my Lord desires," she returned seductively.

Enrico slipped a hand around her waist and held her hand to his chest. Hannah grew silent as Savannah embraced her destiny.

Chapter 14
Two Hearts to the Wind

Austin felt something in the air that materialized unnaturally. He noticed how time appeared to stand still. *This evening is taking forever.* His gut twisted with each passing minute. He swore he spoke to Hannah hours ago. He glanced at his watch and discovered it was only 8:42 PM. The night began to feel—Everlasting. Austin once again took out the manila folder. He felt positive everything would soon be but a distant memory. He could not help but to wonder if they could outrun the son of a man that existed more than two hundred years ago. Austin began to think all attempts to escape may be futile, but he refused to lose faith. He decided to acquire more information regarding the family's history, the Great Tragedy and the Ring of Eternity. *It may prove to be useful.* He fired up the computer and got online. He shuddered, feeling certain that something was very wrong.

Enrico turned Savannah slowly around on the hardwood floor. Once again, she felt as though her feet never touched the floor. The power of the song penetrated her soul, the power of his grip touched her heart and the power of his kiss unleashed an undeniable passion. Hannah felt complete. As Enrico danced with his true love, the rogue reached him at a deeper level. He found himself standing outside the rogue's bedchamber at the Castillo de Isla.

A raspy voice from the other side continued to mock him saying, 'You'll never know Savannah as I do, so completely, without secrets.' Enrico tried to shake the words from his thoughts but his mind quickly fused with his heart. He immediately retreated to the table as the song ended. He killed his existing glass of champagne and quickly poured another. He tried to silence the voice inside his head with no prevail.

Hannah watched helplessly from across the room, for Enrico suddenly felt a million miles away. She wondered what inflicted the change and dared not to ask. She joined him for another glass of champagne instead. She met his gaze and smiled. Enrico did not attempt to return a smile. He could hear her pleading with the rogue within his mind and the need to know the truth grew within his soul as it consumed every urge. Enrico felt more compelled then ever to uncover the truth, "We must return upstairs, now," he attempted to say soothingly, but spoke the words harshly.

Hannah stared at him for a moment and realized something was very wrong. She was not sure if they should venture upstairs together, giving his current state. Hannah drew the conclusion that she would never fear the man that inspired so much passion within her soul. She approached him and caressed his temples with her fingers. Enrico seized her hand tightly, relaxed his grip and then kissed her hand. He led her to the doorway, "We must retire upstairs," he whispered softly.

Hannah noticed the black limo outside their hallway window and realized that Antonio had his grip upon Enrico—attempting to avoid the inevitable. Hannah needed to release Enrico from Antonio's clutches and lure his soul back to her. She did not give a damn about Antonio's emotional state. She despised Antonio for his treacherous and manipulative ways. Antonio stood for all that is evil and destructive while Enrico stood for all that is pure and salutary. Hannah wondered how it was possible for them to be brothers. Antonio now toyed with Enrico's emotions and Hannah vowed to make him pay for such a malicious act. Hannah thought about running outside and ending the ordeal—once and for all. Realizing she'd merely walk into Antonio's trap, she refused to give him the satisfaction of playing along. Therefore, she stayed to help Enrico overcome the torment that inflicted him.

Antonio waited patiently outside. He felt certain she'd run out in her forbidden lover's defense. Antonio clenched his teeth as his hands balled tensely into fists and vowed to make Enrico pay dearly—for Savannah belonged to him. Enrico continued to undermine his strength and Antonio knew Enrico's passion did not run as deep as his own. Enrico would never be half the man that he was. Antonio vowed to destroy Enrico—once and for all—and he'd begin with the unattainable Savannah. Antonio stepped outside, gazed up and cursed the night sky. The sky lit up with shooting stars, creating a tantalizing crimson backdrop—the insignia of Passionate Desires. Antonio hit his knees, as he lost yet another battle. He vowed the next time he had Savannah within his clutches, he'd never allow her to leave and she'd never return home.

Enrico and Savannah made passionate love as if there were no tomorrow. Neither one knew what the future held for their forbidden lust as they allowed themselves to become undone. Savannah whimpered loudly and beckoned Enrico for more as he finally thrust the full length of his extension deep inside, until it reached her soul. He moaned with each thrust. Neither one held anything back as their souls united as one in a wild frenzy. Their clothes were scattered about upon the floor where they tore them off.

Their love making style was both tender and savage, just like their forbidden desires. Her unspoken secrets unlocked new passions and unleashed newfound ecstasy. New memories embedded their minds that would surpass a lifetime. They savored each moment and held each other completely. Each knew that the other was full of unopened surprises as they shook the bed and the entire world. They continued until they could barely breathe. Nearly every breath Savannah took was in erotic pleasure that she never knew existed. Enrico was pleased to see he pleasured her so much.

He slowed down, kissed her everywhere until she felt feverish and began to thrust again. He drank his fill, until the glass was empty, down to the last drop. When his thirst finally subsided, he escalated and drank the last drop. The glass was empty and he had more than his fair share—More than any one man deserved. He gazed into Savannah's eyes and found an angel gazing back at him. *This beautiful woman could have any man and yet...chooses me.* Enrico kissed her tenderly. He never wanted the night to end. For a moment, time stood still as they shook both heaven and earth in perfect rapture. They remained in each other's arms for the rest of the night.

Austin was up most of the night searching for information. He realized how early it was when he glanced at the clock when the phone rang. He answered quickly, suspecting who was on the line. It was the same cold voice as usual, only this time the voice sounded rather annoyed and angry.

"Where is your beloved Hannah?"

The question rendered Austin speechless.

"The information you seek will not be found under the Ring of Eternity, but can be retrieved under the Castillo de Isla. Once you find what you seek, take the Lady Costello and leave. For once I get hold of her, you will never get her back," the voice threatened, and then hung up.

Austin did not understand, so he ran to his computer to seek the answers regarding the new information. As he left the kitchen, something outside caught his eye. He stepped outside and discovered a picturesque night. The sky illuminated with shooting stars, stray bolts of lightening and what he determined to be a meteor shower. He wished Hannah were there to enjoy it with him. Austin never witnessed a meteor shower before and it was both inspiring and gut wrenching. He watched as brilliant rubies fell from the crimson sky. A new powerful feeling overwhelmed him; somehow, he lost his connection to Hannah. It was not as strong as before. He staggered back to his room feeling faint. He managed to find the strength to continue his search using the Castillo de Isla as the new keyword.

Enrico and Savannah woke before dawn. They tidied up and dressed in their clothes from the previous night. Hannah peered out the window and did not see Antonio anywhere in sight. She wondered what the headlines would say about the dead man found along the curb. Hannah knew they must return to the hospital. She could not bear the look of disappointment upon her mother's face if she were to discover the truth about them. She wanted to remain the *good daughter*. Hannah could not understand how Enrico possessed the capability of shredding all moral fibers with a single look. She closed her eyes as Austin's face crept into her mind. Enrico reeled her from her thoughts when he took her hand.

Hannah remembered his hand and briefly dismissed all thoughts of Austin. She quickly assessed the situation. "No one will understand your miraculous recovery; perhaps you should keep it under wraps," she commented, as he nodded gravely. *I cannot possibly expect them to understand... when I do not.*

Enrico reached out, grasped her arm and pulled her to his chest. He rested his chin upon her shoulder, "Last night will remain forever in my memory," he whispered.

They both felt the need to leave but neither one ventured towards the door.

Enrico spun Hannah around and locked her gaze. "Leave with me, my Lady."

Hannah's defensive instincts took control over her thoughts. She slowly shook her head and whispered, "My lord, I can't...please don't ask again."

He quickly read her thoughts and listened to her explanation and more importantly, he felt her disappointment. He fully understood she wanted to be with him but an unknown force kept her heart under lock and key. Hannah realized she made a terrible mistake. Her heart screamed in defense of the realization, for she loved Enrico in every aspect. Enrico loved her completely and vowed to continue to love her unconditionally, no matter what. The room remained silent as their eyes conveyed all thoughts to one another. They could hold an entire conversation without ever speaking a word.

Hannah released their intimate connection, "We should leave," she whispered.

Hand-in-hand, they sauntered towards the door—forcing themselves to place one foot in front of the other.

Austin realized morning crept upon him when sunlight peered through the window blinds. He stayed up all night bound-and-determined to find answers. Enrico maneuvered Austin's thoughts towards a new perspective. Austin wanted to shield and protect Hannah. He'd be ready for anything and knew further information would only help him do so more effectively. A yawn escaped his mouth as he wiped sleep from his eyes. Austin knew sleep was in order if he planned to leave town with Hannah before sundown. He glanced at his bags and then towards the monitor. He gasped, as his eyes fixated on the words: *Castillo de Isla*. He finally found what he searched all night for and the answers were right in front of his eyes. His mind jumped for joy as his heart remained silent. Austin felt like he was five years old, racing downstairs in search of his presents beneath the Christmas tree. He grasped the mouse firmly and began to read.

The article read:

The Castillo de Isla, known as the Island Castle, once dominated the shores of Lago de Nicaragua (Lake Nicaragua). The Castle featured two large wings. The family occupied the west wing while the east wing remained dedicated to Political Affairs and Social Gatherings. Vast botanical gardens surrounded the castle. The castle was home to the powerful and revered Lord Diego Cordoba, Lady Celeste Cordoba and their only child, Elissa Cordoba. Lord Cordoba wished to end a long overdue dispute and form an alliance with the Castillo de Maldito. The Castillo de Maldito has been nicknamed by locals over the years as The Castle of the Damned. The Castillo de Maldito was home to Lord Edmond Costello, Lady Angelina Costello and their two sons, Enrico and Antonio Costello. Enrico Costello was first born and heir to Costa Rica.

Lord Cordoba knew Enrico was unavailable for his daughters' hand in marriage and focused in on the younger brother, Antonio. Antonio under ranked Elissa, but the alliance was just as powerful. He presented his beautiful daughter at court and Lord Costello eagerly agreed. Lord Cordoba promised Elissa to Antonio on October 31, 1789. The first night after the union, the alliance shattered. Elissa Costello was discovered murdered in her bed with a single laceration across her throat.

Lord Cordoba blamed Antonio for the malicious and unforgivable act and the feud between the families swiftly escalated. Enrico relinquished his duties for a short period to defend his brother's honor. In doing so, Antonio assumed the throne and tried to overthrow Enrico. The two brothers clashed, destroying all blood ties. Angelina Costello pleaded with her sons, upon her deathbed, to reconcile and make amends. Reluctantly, they abided.

One week later, the mighty Costello and Cordoba armies were unleashed and ran rampant, causing chaos throughout the land. Both castles burned to the ground in one ferocious battle. The Castillo de Maldito bore the crest of the Costello dynasty, the Eternidad de Anillo (the Ring of Eternity). Angelina Costello adorned the Eternidad de Anillo proudly. It is said that Lady Costello drew strength from the ring and attempted to shelter her family with its power. Sadly, everyone involved perished and disappeared.

The remains from neither family nor army were uncovered. The events described have been called The Great Tragedy of 1789. A handful of family archives were discovered still intact under the Castillo de Maldito buried deep within the lower hierarchy vaults. The Great Tragedy still puzzles many scholars to date. Many scholars conclude that The Great Tragedy aspired over deceit and betrayal between brothers. Some believe Enrico and Elissa were involved and that Enrico murdered the new bride so Antonio could not have her. This then leaves some scholars to believe that Antonio tried to overthrow Enrico out of revenge for murdering his new bride.

These, however, are just speculations as the truth lies buried with the once great castles, along with their rulers. No bodies were discovered among the ruins. It has been determined that the intensity of the fire engulfed everything in its path including the royal families, servants and mountains of soldiers.

There have been many theories since many of the archives have been destroyed. The actual Ring of Eternity has never been seen again after its theft, shortly after its discovery. Some scholars conclude that one brother returned for it, more than likely Enrico Costello. A few questionable souls claim to have seen the Ring of Eternity throughout the years. No sighting has ever been fully confirmed. The Great Tragedy of 1789 remains the greatest tragedy known to Costa Rica and Nicaragua to date.

Austin thought about the article as new fears embedded within his mind. He read many theories and concluded that Enrico and Elissa were involved and Enrico murdered her so Antonio could never claim her as his own. Austin glanced back to the screen and reread, *Enrico relinquished his duties to defend Antonio's honor.* His eyes widened, "Of course he did…he knew damn well Antonio was innocent. Antonio sought revenge for the murder of his bride." It all made perfect sense to him now; for Enrico has called them both over the past two years with hollow threats. Austin realized his greatest fear. Would Enrico harm Hannah to keep her for himself? Austin made a silent vow and reached for the phone, for they would leave immediately.

His hand trembled as he dialed the numbers. *Please be there.*

"Hello."

Austin tried to relax his tone, "Kayla, is Hannah home from the hospital yet?" he asked casually.

"No, Mom and Dad went to pick th…her up twenty minutes ago. Why; is something wrong?"

Austin clenched the phone and held his tongue, "No, please have her call me as soon as she returns," he said calmly, and than added, "And Kayla, beware of Enrico…He is malicious." Austin closed his eyes as a new thought drifted into his mind, but he refused to say it aloud. He just felt a brush with reality, realizing history always repeats itself. He was not afraid of Enrico in any way but he refused to take any chances where Hannah was concerned.

Kayla wondered where Austin's final remark came from. She knew, without any shadow of doubt, it was not Enrico harassing Hannah late at night. Kayla fully understood that Hannah ran from another man and chose to conceal that secret from both parties. She began to fear for Hannah's safety and could not fathom her secrecy. *Why won't she confide in anyone?* Hannah had so many people reaching out to her, mainly Enrico and Austin. Kayla shuddered as she recalled her mother's words, *'God helps those who help themselves.'* She became lost in thought. Surely, Hannah must think she can overcome her difficulties alone.

She wished Austin and Enrico could team up to have a better chance of getting through to Hannah, but knew this was not a possibility because they clearly despised one another. She could only stand back and watch as Hannah burned another bridge. This time, Kayla thought Hannah chose to burn the wrong bridge. She immediately hoped Austin would never discover the nature of Hannah's true feelings. Kayla could not deny her womanly intuition. Hannah radiated an out of this world persona in Enrico's presence and he in hers that she never before witnessed in another couple. Clearly, Hannah was destined to be Enrico's Lady Costello. She sighed and left her thoughts wander, determined to find a love that powerful.

Brian and Rebecca picked up Hannah and Enrico in front of the main entrance. Rebecca had no clue they checked out early. They treated their patients to breakfast. Rebecca needed to run some errands afterwards, so Brian dropped the women off at the mall entrance. He crossed his arms and watched them enter.

"Enrico my boy, allow me to buy you a drink; God knows I need one," he remarked grimly. Brian narrowed his eyes as Enrico flinched. He drove across the street to Jack's Bar and Grill. Brian knew it was too early for a drink but he did not care at this particular juncture in time. He imagined wrapping his hand around a cold beer as he stepped out of the car. Enrico followed skeptically. They walked in and sat at a corner booth. "I'd like to have a word with you," Brian said cordially.

Enrico met Brian's gaze, "What's on your mind, Sir?"

The waitress approached, "What can I get you?"

Enrico noticed a beautiful young woman standing before him and all he could see was Hannah staring back at him. Every woman he encountered resembled Hannah and his thoughts trailed off.

The waitress reeled him from his thoughts when she brushed his arm, "Sir, can I get you anything?"

Enrico composed himself and ordered a mescal. Brian ordered the same. The waitress raised her brow and wrote the order down.

"And keep them coming," Brian hollered, as she walked away.

Enrico now raised a brow as Brian stared at him intently. He could not fathom the tension that lingered between them. The waitress returned with their drinks and sat them down. Enrico held the shot glass and swirled the mescal around. He could only imagine what Brian was about to convey.

"How long has it been going on?" Brian asked, as he killed his drink and motioned for another.

Enrico felt uneasy; he tried to penetrate Brian's thoughts with no prevail. He did not like what radiated from Brian's gaze. He could not conceal the truth any longer. He lowered his brow, sighed and then held his head high, "For nearly two years now, but it's not what you think Sir, I love her," he said sincerely, as he held Brian's icy expression. His voice did not waver for he spoke with sincerity and honesty. Enrico watched curiously, as Brian killed another drink.

"I was hoping you'd say that."

Enrico became speechless. He could not fathom what just happened, for Brian completely took him by surprise. Enrico knew the entire conversation held no bearings but it still warranted respect.

Brian's eyes narrowed and darkened as he began to speak. "I believe you are a man of great power Enrico and I fear my daughter needs a man like you. I have an overwhelming feeling that wherever she ventures, you will follow. It made me angry when I first realized your obsession. I thought you had my family fooled, but in the end, I was the fool who didn't notice what was right in front of me."

Enrico's expression remained solemn. He was still unsure where the conversation led. He remained silent, while Brian finished.

Brian killed another drink. "My daughter is here with us now and yet remains a million miles away, just beyond reach." He fought a lump in his throat, as anger and fear flooded his mind. "I fear death follows her. At first, I thought it was your presence I sensed, but then I overheard the phone call the other night. Rebecca remains oblivious to the nature of the calls and I intend to keep it that way. I listened in and nearly dialed 911 after Hannah hung up on that *man*. I dialed the number that appeared on caller ID and the operator informed me that the number never existed. I knew then that the situation was beyond my control. I overheard the two of you talking that night and I heard the concern in your voice. I am well aware that you know more then you let on and I do not expect you to divulge your thoughts on the subject. I humbly ask you to keep Hannah in your good graces and protect her. There must be light at the end of the darkness. She needs you and I need you to help me right now, for my daughter's sake."

Enrico put his head down, "She does need my help and she needs my protection, now more than ever." He felt Brian's random thoughts about finding light at the end of the darkness ironic. He raised his head, "What should I do, Sir?" he asked, not really expecting a reply for he already knew the answer. "I can not do what needs to be done; I can not force her to go away with me when she chooses to be with another," and with that said, Enrico made a fist as he wondered just who the other man was.

Brian nodded and replied, "Austin is a fine young man, but he can't give her the protection she needs."

Enrico's thoughts jumbled, for he just got Brian's permission to take Hannah away with him.

Brian stood up, "It is time to leave, and I know you will do the right thing Enrico. I also know that the two of you did not stay at the hospital last night, *Mr. Smith*," he stated, and then walked away.

Enrico froze as Brian rendered him speechless. Brian made it a special point to know everything about his daughter, especially now. Enrico stood and slowly followed, knowing he stood at the base of the mountain and wondered if he'd ever peak the summit to declare victory.

Rebecca waited patiently at the main entrance as Brian approached.

"Where is Hannah?" Brian asked, trying to mask the concern upon his face.

"Austin called and picked Hannah up shortly afterwards. He seemed overly anxious to hit the road during day light hours. They officially left on their trip. Hannah promised to call before nightfall. Brian, she wanted to say goodbye to you but Austin was overzealous about leaving. Don't be upset with her. This really is an opportunity of a lifetime and I am excited for her."

Brian closed his eyes briefly and then glanced at Enrico. Enrico found a tremendous amount of fear deep within Brian's eyes. He too returned a grave look and nodded.

"Enrico's car is finished and he too will be leaving today," Brian stated, and then asked, "Where is Austin planning to go?"

Rebecca shrugged her shoulders, "Where ever the wind takes them," she replied with a chuckle.

Rebecca did most of the talking the entire way home while Brian and Enrico remained silent. Enrico clenched his fists and cursed Austin privately, as he honed in on their whereabouts.

Chapter 15
An Unexpected Miracle

Austin reached over and laced his fingers between hers, feeling grateful to have her back within his grasp. Her long hair blew in the wind and the sunlight created a radiant glow upon her face—creating the picture of perfection. On one hand, she was sweet and innocent. On the other hand, she was bold and seductive. When the hands came together, they formed an unbreakable bond that made for one hell of a woman. He held on tight and vowed to never let go. He'd love her unconditionally for the rest of his days. She was the alcohol that intoxicated his thoughts, the visions that penetrated his dreams, and the desires that fueled the essence of his existence. Austin suddenly felt warm and feverish. "If you're hot, I can turn on the air-conditioner," he whispered, and then glanced into her eyes, when she remained unresponsive.

Hannah remained distant and guarded her emotions, as she came to terms with the severity of her actions. She left her only safe haven—Enrico. Austin remained oblivious to the turn of events that drastically changed their lives and it frightened her. After an hour of soul searching, Hannah decided to never fear the decision to remain by Austin's side—feeling certain he truly was, her soul mate. Austin is, and will always remain her destiny while Enrico remained an obstacle on the path to self-discovery.

A decent song began to play on the radio and Austin turned up the volume. They sang along to the lyrics as Hannah let go of all inhibitions and gave into new desires. She vowed to put the past behind her and lead an ordinary life. She quietly wondered if she could lead an ordinary life, after experiencing an extraordinary one. She shuddered and glanced down at the emerald ring, "Is it remotely possible?" she sighed under her breath.

Austin drove all day. They watched as farm fields turned into suburbs, suburbs developed into cities and cities became suburbs again. He forced himself to drive most of the night, placing as much distance between Hannah and Enrico as humanly possible. He drove until he could not safely drive any further. His eyelids grew heavy. Austin did not win Hannah merely to lose her due to an accident.

Hannah realized the car came to a halt and sat up. She was not in a deep sleep but still had to wipe the sleep from her eyes, "Where are we?" she asked, and then yawned.

Austin stretched his arms allowing his fingers to brush her cheek, "The outskirts of Rhode Island; I thought we could stay here for the night," he whispered, pointing at an illuminated vacancy sign.

Hannah smiled, "You look tired." She gasped, realizing it was 4:00 AM. They appropriated a room for half price since it was so early. Checkout was at 11:00 AM and Austin desperately needed sleep before then. The room was not the most desirable but it was a place to rest two weary bodies and their ambivalent minds.

Austin dreamt all night, as he tossed and turned. He felt Enrico closing in on them quickly, for Enrico had greater means to narrow the gap between them. Enrico landed his private jet at the nearest airport and pinpointed their exact location. He pointed his fleet of black limousines in their direction and charged. They surrounded the house, blocking every escape route. Enrico entered their home, approaching slowly at first, and then darted ferociously towards Austin. Enrico subdued him effortlessly and claimed his prize.

Enrico then took Hannah into his arms and forced his will upon her. She remained powerless against his strength. Austin watched from a distance as another stole the love of his life. He ultimately sat upright in a cold sweat. Hannah was in grave danger—he could feel it. Austin turned towards Hannah and watched her chest rise and fall as he began to relax. *Thank God, it was only a dream.* He wrapped an arm around his sleeping beauty—offering shelter from all that is evil.

Hannah awoke bright and early. She gently pried Austin's arm from her bodice and did not seem to disturb him. Her eyes widened, remembering she had not called their parents as promised. She found a payphone in the motel lobby and called collect. Hannah reluctantly told her mother where they were and made it clear that their final destination remained undetermined. They said their goodbyes and Hannah promised to call again in a couple of days.

The suns rays warmed her cheeks as she sat outside their room on the small patio and flipped through the bag of maps. She came across a Massachusetts road map and lingered upon *Cape Cod.* Hannah recalled learning about Plymouth Rock in History class. She decided their destiny would take them there. The thought of the ocean made her feel giddy and childlike inside. Austin was about to fulfill her innermost dreams without even realizing it. The excitement remained overwhelming. It was a mini escape from the reality of their trip. Hannah whole-heartedly allowed this trip to revitalize her senses with amazing courage and determination to overcome past events.

Austin joined her and Hannah handed him the map. He tilted his chin to meet her gaze as he towered above her. He noticed how astonishing she looked in the morning sun as he held her gaze. He observed the map and smiled warmly. Austin did not care much for the beach but the look on Hannah's face told him she wished to go. He sighed and smiled. If Hannah wanted to see the ocean, he would take her there. They checked out and grabbed a bite to eat. They drove half the day before reaching the Buzzards Bay parking lot.

Austin's stomach told him it was time to eat lunch but Hannah instantly jumped out of the vehicle, for she was too excited to think about lunch. Tears streamed down her cheeks at the sight of the ocean touching the horizon. She could not determine where the ocean ended and the horizon began. It was a spectacular view. They kicked off their shoes and ran, hand-in-hand, to the waters edge. All doubts and every fear melted away as they stood ankle deep in the ocean.

Life had a beautiful outlook once more. Austin kicked his foot and splashed Hannah. She squealed with delight. He caught a glimpse of a larger wave approaching and pulled Hannah into it along side him. The wave crashed all around them, drenching their clothes. The wave tossed Hannah into the sand and Austin seized the moment. He straddled her and passionately kissed her sweet, yet sultry lips.

Another wave approached and thundered over them. They disappeared from earth for a moment as they rekindled an old flame. Hannah was atop Austin when the wave passed. In that instant, she knew things would be just fine. They spent the remainder of the day sightseeing and glancing at apartments for rent. Hannah saw a quaint little apartment in the town of Cheesequake. She instantly fell in love with the apartment's layout and Austin apprehensively agreed, knowing they would not stay for long.

Hannah called, now-and-then, and spoke with her family. Kayla sometimes called and talked for hours. Hannah spent many days lounging on the beach. The water glistened like diamonds in the afternoon sun, as the white capped crests of each wave remained constant. Consistency is what Hannah desired most. The waves rolled in rhythmically and resided right on queue. Hannah vowed to cherish the past few months.

Austin invaded her private moment today and sat down along side her, looking rather grim. He rested his hands upon her shoulders, "We should leave tomorrow," he whispered.

Hannah felt the inevitable drawing near. She took in the last moments of the surreal splendors of the ocean and squeezed Austin's hand, "It is time to leave," she concurred.

Although neither one discussed it, this is where their hearts felt at peace.

Austin read her thoughts and tilted his chin, luring her gaze away from the ocean. He placed a finger over her lips requesting her silence as he knelt before her in the sand. "I have loved you since we were children. You alone hold my heart in the palm of your hands. I deliberately repeated the fourth grade because I could not bear the thought of advancing without you. Every step I have ever taken has led me to you and I will continue to follow you to the end of time. You are, and will always remain, my destiny. I love you with every beat of my heart and I kneel before you now with no diamond ring, only a promise of my unconditional love. We are soul mates, you and I. Be my wife, Hannah Marie Brockwell, for I promise to love and cherish you forever." Austin began to tremble, anticipating a reply.

He held out a unique wedding band with the word *Forever* and his initials engraved across the side. Hannah gasped; she knew he knelt before her wearing his entire heart on his sleeve. He pledged his undying love and both heart-and-soul fully accepted his proposal. Hannah dropped to her knees and pressed her lips to his, "I want nothing more then to be your wife…Yes!" she whispered.

Hannah noticed that Austin also adorned a unique wedding band on his left hand with the words *and Always* and her initials engraved across the side. Austin had the rings constructed of pure platinum and intricately designed. He slipped the ring on Hannah's ring finger. She made no attempts to withdraw her hand as Austin held it firmly in place. The new ring nestled perfectly along side the existing ring, for Austin customized the band to accommodate that hand. He gazed into her baby blue eyes and found contentment, "I know we are not legally married but I am completely devoted to you and I am bound to these sacred vows. My heart tells me we are destined for one another and I give you this ring as a token of my undying love and devotion; I love you, Forever and Always."

Hannah remained silent and motionless as she took in his words. She wondered if Cape Cod was her wedding present from Austin. She felt as though they were about to embark on their honeymoon, "Are we on our honeymoon now?"

Austin smiled, "This honeymoon can last as long as we like, Baby, for we have all the time in the world," he said, and then drew her full moist lips to his.

Hannah no longer felt distress, only emotional bliss. They agreed to call their folks, announce their decision to elope and then embark on another adventure.

That very evening, Austin and Hannah walked barefoot along the beach. Hannah adorned a simple, but elegant white camisole with a single red rose in her hair. Austin wore Black slacks and a white silk shirt left unbuttoned, revealing his entire chest. They walked hand-in-hand along the beach. They stopped and gazed into one another's eyes as the sun began to set. They silently imagined a pastor standing before them and recited their vows.

Austin slid Hannah's wedding band upon her finger, "I will love you forever," he whispered.

Hannah slid Austin's wedding band upon his finger, "I will love you always," she whispered.

Then simultaneously, they whispered, "Forever and Always!"

Austin opened his mouth to speak, but Hannah placed a finger upon his lips. She opened her heart and shared a special gift with her husband. Austin smiled warmly as his eyes moistened. Hannah entrusted him with her thoughts. They shared a private conversation without ever speaking a word. Austin knew this was a huge leap for Hannah and a small step away from Enrico. His conquest was over, for he won Hannah completely.

Enrico's limo stopped abruptly on the Sagamore Bridge. He felt Savannah's presence just on the other side, as he narrowed the gap. He smiled warmly, but his smile quickly faded. Her presence suddenly felt remote. "So close and yet so far-away," he whispered, as Hannah fully dedicated herself to Austin. His heart sank and his eyes overflowed. Enrico felt a small piece of Savannah die—lost to him forever. He refused to give up hope as he hung-in-the-balance of unfulfilled destinies—Trapped between Heaven and Hell.

He knew nothing lasted forever, all to well. Savannah taught him how to love again and he refused to give up on that love. Each time he held his beloved Savannah, it felt like an eternity. The word *Eternity* has been in Enrico's vocabulary far longer than he can even recall. For once, their love no longer felt eternal. The concept paralyzed his thoughts, as he sensed the inevitable drawing near.

Austin and Hannah left Cheesequake and headed for Ports Mouth, Maine. They stayed there four months and moved on to New Hampshire, then Vermont and New York; they bypassed Pennsylvania and moved on to Virginia. Hannah could not recall all the towns they visited but she'd never forget, Cape Cod. Each move took its toll, but Austin new it was not in vain. They have eluded Enrico for nearly four years now. Hannah never once mentioned his presence. He sensed Enrico was close by in Cape Cod but not anywhere else. They settled into a small apartment in the heart of a small Virginia coalmine community, Hearts Landing. Hannah found the town charming and quaint. When she felt comfortable with the community, they moved again. Austin refused to head any further south, so they headed back up north.

On their four-year wedding anniversary, Hannah went to the doctors to confirm her pregnancy. She was ultimately excited and could not wait to tell Austin the wonderful news. They now resided in a secluded cabin high in the Adirondack Mountains. They felt surrounded in unsurpassed beauty and encompassed by nature. Hannah and Austin truly found their element. Austin rose early to go fishing and came in at lunchtime with the mornings catch. Hannah stood in the kitchen wearing nothing but a little paper sign on her belly that read: *Baby on Board.* Austin's eyes widened and his jaw dropped. They met in the middle of the room and embraced.

"I hope you're as ecstatic as I am."

Austin agreed but his heart shattered. He needed time alone. He hated to admit it, but the child could not possibly be his. Austin's heart suddenly filled with anger and betrayal. "I've been out all morning honey, I need a shower," he said, and then walked towards the bathroom. Austin closed the door and tried to control his emotions. Hannah never left his side these past four years. He knew she was not with another, but the doubt still lingered within his mind.

He flashed back to when he was four. His mother was late for work and rushed to leave on time. She hit an icy patch and slid the vehicle off the highway. The car rolled down an embankment, flipping the vehicle twice. Janice walked away without a scratch as the ambulance rushed Austin to the nearest hospital. The images were so vivid and clear within his mind that he could barely breathe. The doctors did everything they could. He woke, surrounded by lights and voices. He recalled how scared he felt and the way Janice gripped his hand as she sobbed uncontrollably. That was all he remembered about the accident.

Later, when he was old enough, his mother asked if he remembered that dark morning. Austin conveyed his memories and then Janice proceeded to tell him that he could never have biological children. Austin came to grips that he would never have children of his own—at the age of 16. His father passed away when he was three, leaving Austin to carry on the Desmin name. Knowing that he could never produce an offspring was nearly unbearable.

He never had the heart to tell his beloved Hannah his dark and dreary secret. He felt embarrassed and ashamed, as though he was not a man. He stood in the steamy shower, unable to breath, and gasped for air. He hated thinking any ill thoughts of Hannah, but it was not possible that he fathered this child. Austin drew the only plausible conclusion, "Enrico must be the father," he whispered. The thought of another mans offspring alive and growing within Hannah's womb made Austin lose control. Before he would believe such a malicious act, he vowed to get retested. The accident occurred years ago, "Perhaps the doctors were wrong; after all, medical practices have changed since then," he whispered aloud. *Please be wrong.* His heart hoped for the best, while his mind remained skeptical.

Austin turned off the water and dried his copper hair as flashes of a man, he never met, pierced his mind. He fought the images and ultimately prevailed—surrendering his heart to the catacombs of denial. He dressed quickly and retreated to the bedroom with the phonebook. Austin closed the door and killed two Aspirin, for he had a splitting headache now.

He thumbed through the pages of Physicians until he located local fertility doctors. His finger rested on Dr. AnSong in Hauserville. He dialed the number with trembling hands. He was in luck; Dr. AnSong was taking on new patients and had an opening in two hours. "I'll take it," Austin murmured into the receiver. The office was an hour away, which granted him enough time to conjure up a reason for leaving. He thought up a perfect alibi and trudged downstairs, forcing a smile as he approached Hannah.

He found her fully dressed in the kitchen preparing the mornings catch.

"I have the new outdoor cookbook with a great recipe I'm trying," she announced, as Austin entered the room.

He found the strength to meet her gaze. "I have to go into town; I forgot about an appointment. The car needs a tune up, for we've put a lot of miles on it," he managed.

Hannah immediately wrinkled her nose; she hated waiting on vehicles in the garage. "Hurry back," she exclaimed. She leaned in and brushed his lips with hers.

That single touch melted Austin's cold distrusting heart for a brief moment, but it quickly froze again, as he turned and left the cabin.

The drive felt like an eternity. Austin strolled into the doctor's office with his head hung. Normally he was an extremely prideful man, but had no pride left at this particular juncture in time. He sat in the waiting room even longer than the initial drive. He quickly became agitated and cursed the doctor under his breath.

"Austin Desmin," a voice called from behind.

Austin turned his brow and saw a nurse holding a clipboard standing in a doorway. He slowly stood and followed the nurse down the hall to a small examining room. He sat down, as the nurse handed him a clipboard with forms to fill out and a sample cup. She left instructions and pointed towards the restroom. Austin did as instructed.

Thirty minutes later, Dr. AnSong entered and shook Austin's hand. He leafed through the results with a solemn look, tilted his brow and gave Austin grim news. "You are indefinitely 100% sterile," he explained.

Dr. AnSong had no options to give. Austin accepted the cold fact and left the office utterly distraught. He drove home and would pretend all is well—for Hannah's sake. His heart told him she was an innocent in this escapade. He could not fathom Enrico's motives behind this inconceivable and treacherous act. How and when did not bother him as much as *Why*. One thing remained certain; Enrico would never get his hands on the child. Austin vowed this child would be his in every sense. He drew a deep breath, as his heart fully accepted this commitment and made a solemn vow. "Hannah will never know I did not conceive this child," he whispered.

He was now caught in the medium between Heaven and Hell. Having a child with Hannah would be Heaven on earth. Living without Hannah was inconceivable—a daunting Hell. Austin now wondered if they could find a happy medium if fate allowed the child to belong to another—especially if the child was a boy and resembled his *father*. Hannah would certainly know the truth then. He said a silent prayer and returned home, with a heavy heart.

Austin found the next couple of days more difficult then he imagined. He kept an open mind but remained withdrawn and emotionally closed. He sheltered his own emotional state to spare Hannah any grief. Hannah left that afternoon to run errands. Austin felt relieved to have the cabin all to himself. His face appeared worn and ragged, for he had not slept in two days. He felt emotionally and physically exhausted but he kept himself busy and continued to bear the burden alone.

He decided to take a walk down by the lake. It was a beautiful afternoon and the sky was deep blue without a single cloud. Austin squinted his eyes and adjusted them to the suns rays. He needed to clear his mind. His senses felt rejuvenated, as he stood on the back porch. His body became limber and tingled with sensation. He made it to the edge of the yard, turned his brow and listened intently. He heard a faint sound and realized it was the phone.

Austin ran into the house and fumbled to find the phone. His vision blurred and the house appeared dark, but he did not have time to allow his eyes to adjust to the indoor lighting. He stumbled into a kitchen chair as the phone continued to ring amongst the darkness. "I'm coming," he cried. He finally slipped his hand around the receiver and brought it to his ear, "Hello," he managed, but all he heard was a dial tone. He slammed the phone down and stormed away. *All this trouble for nothing.*

He was glad the caller hung up, fearing he might have taken his frustration out on the poor soul—especially if it had been a telemarketer. He cringed at the thought. Austin opened up the back door as the phone rang again. He felt annoyed now and in no mood for conversation but answered the phone anyways. "Hello," he nearly cried. Instantly, the hair upon his arms stood on end as an old familiar voice pierced through his thoughts.

"Good afternoon Austin, it has been awhile," Antonio hissed.

Austin froze, "What do you want Enrico," he snapped.

Antonio chuckled, "I bring you fortunate news…I hope you weren't too distraught these past two days."

Austin interrupted quickly, "Go to Hell," he demanded, as his veins turned to ice.

"Is that any way to speak to the one who blessed you with a child; your child in every way, including the biological sense," he said, and then hung up.

Austin went numb. He scanned his thoughts to make sure he understood correctly. "Why would Enrico bless me with a child to his beloved Savannah?" He wondered if this was remotely possible. Enrico clearly continued to pursue Hannah. Austin could not fathom Enrico's motives to this new twist of fate. Enrico went to great lengths to keep them apart. Austin wondered what new game he played. His gut told him that Enrico spoke the truth about the baby. Austin knew he had to make up for the past two days.

He needlessly gave Hannah the cold shoulder and felt the need to get down upon his knees and beg for forgiveness for doubting her honesty, integrity and most importantly, her love. As he thought about these things, his eyes grew wide. It dawned on him that Enrico knew their whereabouts. At that moment, Austin knew they'd never escape Enrico's immortal soul. He decided it was time to return home and allow Hannah to enjoy her pregnancy surrounded by their family, for Enrico would find them wherever they went. He would surprise Hannah by beginning to pack.

Hannah returned home around suppertime. She sighed and stepped out of the car. Austin has been apprehensive and she wondered if he truly wanted this child. She forced herself to enter the house and demand answers. When Hannah opened the door, she could not believe her eyes. There were boxes and bags scattered about the kitchen. She had to push boxes aside to make room to lay her purse upon the table.

"Austin," she cried out, with skepticism in her voice. She watched Austin enter the kitchen with admiration and tenderness in his eyes. He embraced her and kissed her cheeks until all anger dissolved. She did not understand what brought about this sudden change and she did not care, for she had Austin back. Hannah winced, when she noticed the phone was disconnected from the wall.

Austin caught her lingering and captured her questioning gaze with his. "I didn't want to be disturbed tonight," he whispered, and then led her into the living room. It was in the dead of summer and Austin still lit a fire in the fireplace. In a single touch, they ignited the room ablaze. Deep in the dark of night, while Hannah slept, Austin stole a private moment with the child growing inside its womb. He whispered hopes and dreams he held for the baby after he introduced himself, as *Daddy*. Quietly and motionless, Hannah listened in on his private conversation as his palm caressed her stomach.

That morning, Austin announced his plans to return home during the pregnancy. Hannah felt elated and her eyes moistened. They took their time in packing and made arrangements over the next month. Their families waited impatiently in anticipation of their arrival. The couple had not seen their folks in nearly five years and the reunion was long overdue. Hannah kept her emotions in check. She refused to allow all the unknown fears and concerns interfere with this happy time. At the end of the month, they made their journey back home.

When they arrived in Greenville, they noticed that the town remained unchanged. It was exactly how they left it. They settled into their new apartment before announcing their arrival. They visited Hannah's home first. Austin was unprepared to reveal the pregnancy to his mother, giving his condition. Hannah had begun her second trimester and Rebecca instantly noticed Hannah's newfound glow. Her family was ecstatic. Later that morning, Austin told his mother that he had been misdiagnosed all those years ago. Janice was thrilled, for she never dreamed of having a grandbaby and the thought brought tears to her eyes, as she congratulated him with a long overdue embrace.

Over the next few months, Hannah spent most of her days at her parent's house, often spending the night. It did not take long before the phone calls began in the dead of night. Brian quickly became concerned. He felt his daughter's afflictions, as she endured the additional stress alone. The next time the phone rang, he bolted up in bed thinking, *that bastard is still out there somewhere.* Brian did the only thing he could do to protect his child, who now carried his grandchild, and the decision was not made lightly.

Hannah and Rebecca went baby shopping that afternoon, while Brian made an important call—to Enrico.

He clenched the phone tightly and then relaxed his grip. "Please check on her and make sure she's all right," Brian desperately pleaded.

"It would be my pleasure, Sir."

Brian hung up feeling confident that Enrico would watch over her. He quickly began to feel guilty because Enrico remained completely unaware of the pregnancy. Brian did not have the heart to tell him, knowing how he feels about Hannah. Brian hoped Enrico could come to grasps with reality and accept that Hannah was with Austin now—in every sense.

Enrico hung up the phone with a heavy heart. He knew they'd eventually find one another—It was their destiny. She was truly the only daylight within his blackened world. He longed for her touch. He rushed to her side immediately. Brian told him exactly where to find her. Part of him felt relieved to confront her in a public place, distrusting his heart to be alone with her. He knew his desires would quickly take control and he'd have no choice but to take her into his arms at first sight.

Enrico approached the parking lot as her presence overwhelmed his senses and knocked him back a step. He quickened his pace as his heart beat wildly. He felt like a little kid in a candy store about to sample forbidden sweetness. He quickly honed in on her whereabouts, for his senses were in tune to her every move. He could feel her blood coursing through his veins. Temptation began to fester and the only way to surpass it was to remove the splinter. A few more steps and he would be face-to-face with his beloved Savannah.

He could hear her voice as he narrowed the gap. It was music to his ears. He peered around the aisle as her back faced him. He instantly noticed her hair had grown longer and shimmered like strands of silk. He eyed her up and down; her curves were just as he remembered. He closed his eyes and recalled her standing in his room at the Hacienda. She stood before him as the Lady Costello and left her innocence upon the floor with his robe. Even now, he could not take his eyes off her. He felt like a cat ready to pounce upon its prey.

Hannah turned and Enrico's eyes widened as his jaw dropped. She looked like someone shoved a globe under her shirt. It took him a moment to realize she was with child. The air escaped his lungs, as he fought to breathe. His world grew dim—destined to remain dark throughout the ages—as he lurked in the shadows of his own demise. He was well aware that this child was not Austin's, for he knew about Austin's condition. He could not fathom how she became pregnant. He kept asking himself the same question over-and-over again. *If Austin is not the father... then who is?*

He knew, without any shadow of doubt, she'd never be unfaithful, for she was not the promiscuous type. He pressed his back against the aisle. Then closed his eyes and clenched his fists, fighting off every urge to rush upon her and demand the truth. Not even Enrico himself knew what he was capable of if the child belonged to the mysterious unnamed rogue. The pit of his soul told him it was not true but his mind could think of no other logical explanation. He needed to hear the truth from Savannah. Then, another terrifying thought encircled his mind. He wondered if the rogue used force or if Savannah...

"Enrico...Enrico!"

He opened his eyes, just as Rebecca motioned him to join them.

"Enrico come here; you don't have to hide over there. Please, come and say hi."

Enrico took control of his emotions and slowly narrowed his eyes and focused in on Savannah. He walked with a slow, stiffened stride as he approached them. He came to a halt about four feet away. Enrico refused to meet her gaze, for Savannah's eyes always gave her away and he was still unprepared to accept the truth. She clearly seemed happy and he hoped the child was in fact, Austin's own flesh and blood.

Enrico crossed his arms over his chest as he tilted his chin. He gazed at her belly bulge, then her neck and finally, he met her gaze head on.

"We're so glad to see you again, you must stop by the house," Rebecca said.

Enrico barely heard her. All of his attention remained focused on Savannah. To him, Savannah looked as though she saw a ghost.

Rebecca patted Hannah's stomach, "Isn't it wonderful, Hannah and Austin are expecting," she explained.

Enrico managed to force his stiffened lips in a slight upward direction. The muscles in his cheeks began to throb as he strained to conceal his true emotions. He'd remain motionless and unwavering until she revealed the truth. He knew she'd never cave in and he had to remain firm but gentle, giving her current state.

Hannah felt uneasy and did not enjoy Enrico staring at her for so long, nor did she like the questions that lurked within his eyes. She could not imagine being alone with him at this point. She wanted to crawl into a corner and hide. She chose a path and felt it needed no explanation; yet, his eyes conveyed otherwise. Hannah could feel his turmoil and part of her died, for she never wished to cause Enrico any pain. Part of her wanted to throw herself at his feet and beg for forgiveness. The other part refused to apologize for the wonderful life bestowed upon her.

Rebecca's eyes scanned back and forth between them questionably. She could not fathom the silent hesitation between them. She quickly became uncomfortable, for it did not take a genius to determine that they wished to be alone, for whatever reasons. She glanced at her watch.

"Hannah, I'm sorry, but I have a hair appointment I forgot about. Can Austin pick you up when you're finished browsing?" she asked, and then began to fidget.

Enrico quickly pounced on the opportunity. "I will take Miss Brockwell home," he offered. He knew she was not legally bound to Austin and refused to acknowledge her as being so.

"You mean Mrs. Desmin now," Rebecca returned questionably.

Enrico flashed a twisted smile, "Of course," he murmured. He watched Rebecca hesitantly turn and walk away. He knew her thoughts soared but he did not care. He returned his gaze to Savannah, who appeared paler then before. "Who is the father?" he demanded.

Hannah gasped, for she could not comprehend such a question. His voice was course and full of accusations. "Austin is," she managed after a silent moment. She stared him in the eyes as he read hers. Hannah felt shame radiating from his eyes as though she had done something wrong. She could not take that look anymore and quickly averted her eyes. Suddenly, she felt a sharp pain twisting and knotting within her stomach. It was enough to bring her to her knees, as she panted heavily. The pain caught her off guard and for a moment, she forgot about Enrico and his accusing eyes.

Enrico did not waste a second. He instantly knelt by her side and held her tenderly. "I'll take you to the hospital," he whispered and then scooped her up into his powerful arms as though she were weightless. He tenderly stroked her cheek with his chin. All anger subsided as he rescued her, yet again. She needed him completely and so he attended to her every need. Enrico quickly took her outside to his limo and ordered the driver to take them to the hospital. He watched helplessly as she continued to moan and clutch her stomach.

A nurse rushed Hannah to a delivery room upon arrival. It was not her designated hospital and she was worried about a stranger delivering her child, but the labor pain became overwhelming and those thoughts quickly vanished. The nurse instructed Enrico to remain in the waiting room and he obeyed. Shortly later, the doctor escorted him into the next room. Before Enrico knew what happened, he wore scrubs and the doctor led him into the delivery room. He could not fathom why, but did as instructed.

"It's nearly time for your child to arrive," the doctor told him, and then added, "Your wife will need some comforting and is asking for you." The doctor extended his hand, "I'm Dr. Butler, and I'll be delivering your baby. You are Austin, I presume."

Enrico's eyes widened, as he shook the doctors hand, "Yes, I am", he managed. He could think of no better way to be loving and supportive than to be with her now. He felt responsible for the sudden delivery, for he deemed her guilty before she had a chance to claim her innocence. He rushed to her side and held her hand. She gripped his hand tightly, believing Austin stood by her side. She felt disoriented and was glad he made it in time.

Enrico thought Savannah exhibited true valor, for she showed mounds of courage and strength before his eyes. Never in his life had he ever witnessed anything more beautiful, for men were not allowed in the room with their wives. He wished this child she was about to give life to, was his own flesh-and-blood. He watched in amazement as Savannah bore down, one last time, and took a final breath. The love of his life gave birth to a child that belonged to another and he felt nothing but admiration within his heart.

Dr. Butler held the baby and a moment later, it began to wail. "Congratulations; you have a healthy baby girl," he announced.

They cleaned the baby up and immediately handed her to her father, as they attended to Hannah. Enrico took the crying infant into his arms. The child calmed down when Enrico allowed her to suckle upon his finger. She gazed up at him with bright blue eyes. She had strawberry blonde hair. He thought she looked just like her mother. He saw Savannah reaching for her baby and handed the child to her, "Your daughter, my Lady," he whispered.

Hannah quickly realized that it was Enrico who stood by her side. He was the one who spoke the words of encouragement with sincerity. Hannah did not care, for she was about to hold her baby girl. Her heart filled with love and her eyes overflowed with joy as Enrico cradled the child along her breast. She wrapped her arms around her daughter while Enrico leaned down and kissed her brow. He allowed his lips to linger, giving himself a chance to share in the private moment between mother and child before departing. He knew Savannah would make a wonderful mother, devoting herself completely. He left the room with a heavy heart. His soul told him that the child belonged to Austin. He could not fathom how or why and wondered what new game was afoot.

Austin painted the nursery when he heard the phone ring. He rushed to pick it up, "Hello," he said. He became still when he heard Devlin say, "Hannah is in the Greenville Hospital and she had the baby," and then hung up. It remained uncertain how Devlin knew this, but every instinct told him he had to get there. He fumbled for the car keys and ran down the walkway. His hands trembled as he gripped the wheel. Austin arrived within ten minutes. He parked, ran into the hospital and headed straight to the main desk. "My wife, Hannah Desmin, was brought here in labor," he quickly exclaimed.

The receptionist checked the computer, "Room 304," she said, with a warm smile.

Austin raced down the hall towards the elevator and barely heard her cry, "Congratulations Mr. Desmin." He punched the third floor, but the elevator took forever. He gave up and ran up the three flights of stairs. He ran so quickly that he swore his feet never touched the steps.

Enrico stepped out of the elevator, wondering if Austin was present yet. He felt certain that Austin did not deserve Savannah, but remained uncertain what kind of father he'd make. Today he held the child of an angel. Something or someone blessed Austin with the miracle of life, molded after his own likeness. Enrico did not know what to make of the situation. He knew damn well Austin did not father the child naturally. He could not help becoming fearful for Savannah. He wondered who lied dormant watching and waiting to burst her dreams. He felt certain this child played a dark role in a diabolical scheme. He vowed to protect both mother and child, as he walked through the main entrance.

Austin felt relieved to find Hannah and his child doing just fine. He felt a sense of pride he could not begin to explain as he held his daughter. He instantly began to sense there was something magical in store for her but he could not fathom what.

Hannah touched his hand lightly and looked up at him with sparkling eyes, "We have to name her," she whispered.

Austin smiled at her warmly and placed the baby along her breast. He had never seen anything more beautiful. He watched as she attended to the baby's blanket and made sure their daughter was snug and warm.

Austin immediately thought about the desert rose. According to nature, it should not be there and yet, it still manages to strive and flourish within the desert heat. He thought the name was fitting and well suited for their miracle. "Let's call her Sierra Rose," he exclaimed, without taking his eyes off his daughter.

Hannah agreed without question. "Welcome, Sierra Rose Desmin," she whispered, and then sealed the greeting with a kiss.

The doctor came in to check on Hannah and Austin saw a shadow of puzzlement daunted across his face. He watched, with steadfast eyes, as the doctor took a double take. Without hesitation, he extended his hand out and introduced himself as Hannah's husband, Austin Desmin. He noticed the doctor's eyes flinch as he raised his brow. The doctor cleared his throat and then shook Austin's hand.

"It's a pleasure to meet you Austin, I'm Doctor Butler," he said.

Austin thought he heard Dr. Butler's voice waver. His gut told him something was wrong. Before he could question this rather odd behavior, a nurse stepped into the room and announced they had visitors waiting.

Austin went to the waiting room to find their family waiting anxiously. The room was overwhelmed with mounds of balloons and flowers. Rebecca brought the car seat all decked out with pink bows. She even brought Hannah's overnight bag.

"How did you know?" Austin asked questionably. He knew he did not call and Hannah would not have had time to call. His gut told him she would have called him if she could.

Rebecca threw her arms around him chuckling, "Enrico told us silly; why, he's the one who rushed her here," she exclaimed.

Austin's heart filled with rage but he managed to keep a calm exterior. "Of course," he muttered. He had many questions with little answers. He had taken the last straw and made a silent vow.

Hannah and Sierra spent the night in the hospital. Austin stayed by their side insisting Sierra stay in Hannah's room for the night. He sat wide-awake while they slumbered. He watched them sleep peacefully, for both mother and child had a busy day. He briefly touched Sierra, feeling her heartbeat. In silence, he bowed and thanked Enrico for their miracle, but that was the extent of his gratitude. He hoped and prayed that Enrico would step back and allow them to be the family Sierra deserved.

Enrico stood in the hospital parking lot all night monitoring the main entrance. He refused to allow mother, child or father to be separated. He knew the child held a greater purpose than even he could ascertain. He remained vigilant and mentally prepared for anything, for he no longer had only Savannah to protect; the entire family needed him now. He closed his eyes and felt another piece of Savannah die. He refused to break apart the family, for ties that bind a family are unbreakable. Savannah made Austin her family in a matter of hours and the hands of time could not separate them, for now they shared a child. He knew Savannah would shelter her daughter from the truth. Enrico cursed the rogue as he stood on hallow ground.

Chapter 16
In the Eyes of Temptation

Hannah took one last look in the mirror, pleased with the results of her labors. She adorned a Victorian dress. The dress was low-cut, with a corset bodice that laced up the front. She left the skirt flowing, dyed her hair black for the evening and pulled it up rather fetchingly. She wore nude stockings and black high-heeled pointed boots that laced up the front. Her bodice was black and the skirt was crimson red with a black lace overlay.

Hannah adorned a crimson red velvet chocker with a red rose crested in the front and ruby earrings. She outlined her eyes in black, dabbed scarlet blush high upon her cheekbones and bore crimson lips. The final touch was an eye mask with black sequin. Two small black feathers outlined the edges and truly accentuated the costume. As Hannah checked her costume over in the mirror, she felt eyes upon her. She twirled around to see Austin lounging in the doorway looking rather astonished.

"You make a beautiful Hester Prinn," he remarked, and then added, "Barbara is waiting downstairs." He walked over to his wife and handed her the cell phone, "Call if you need anything," he whispered, as he embraced her, and then added, "Have a great time."

Hannah felt giddy and enjoyed herself already; she took the cell phone and ventured downstairs.

Austin remained in their room and smiled. He had not seen Hannah so excited about something in quite sometime and it warmed his heart. She devoted herself completely to Sierra and Austin felt certain she would enjoy an evening out with her first friend since they initially left Greenville. Barbara worked in the doctor's office and befriended Hannah during her pregnancy. The two women have much in common.

Barbara begged Hannah for months to venture out with her and Hannah declined each invitation—until tonight. Austin could not fathom why. Lately, Hannah did not want to venture anywhere without him and Sierra by her side. He wondered if Hannah did not want to leave him alone with Sierra but quickly dismissed such thoughts, for he too was a devoted father. Austin secretly wondered if Hannah accepted the invitation tonight because it was Hallows Eve and she could slip out undetected, dressed as another.

Barbara waited for Hannah in the foyer. Their eyes widened while complimenting each other's costumes. Barbara dressed as a Victorian Wench. The two women left together, knowing that this would be a memorable Halloween. They had plans to attend the party at the Shady Gap Loft, a local nightclub in town. They arrived at 9:30 PM and the club was nearly packed. Hannah wore a black velvet chain purse tied around her waist and bought the first round, a couple shots of Southern Blue. They managed to find an unoccupied table and staked out claims. Once they sat down, they glanced at one another and simultaneously said, "Let's dance." They jumped up from their seats and made their way to the dance floor. They began dancing and having fun. It was not long until they acquired partners.

Enrico made his way up the steps and paid the cover at the door. He dressed completely in black except for a crimson cloth belt adorned around his waist that flowed to his knees. He had a black mask over his eyes and made a handsomely striking Zorro. He knew Savannah was there, for he could feel her presence. He found an empty table on an upper level where he could overlook the entire club. Enrico instantly honed in on his blazing beauty. She was on the dance floor with a friend and some new gentlemen friends.

The sight of her was breathtaking but he grimaced at the sight of her dancing with another. To him, this was not the proper behavior for a wife and mother—unless the dance was with him. He observed Savannah with animosity when they sauntered to the bar and the gentlemen offered to buy their drinks. Enrico instantly made a fist and clenched it tightly. He let out a sigh of relief when Savannah declined the offer. He watched them kill their drinks and return to the dance floor. He was relieved to see Hannah behaving like the proper Lady Costello. He decided it was time to make his presence known. He made his way downstairs, requested a song and loomed in the corner of the dance floor.

Hannah began to slow dance with her partner. He dipped her and twirled her slowly. On the second twirl, he released her. Hannah loved the way her skirt looked as she twirled. Her partner came up behind her, placed his hands upon her hips and drew her in tight against his thighs. He laced his fingers around hers and crossed his arms, embracing her affectionately. She struggled slightly at first and slowly melted into the cocoon he made for her. She rested her head against his neck as he cradled her brow with his chin. She could feel his hot breath upon her cheek.

They danced slowly, forming a tantalizing web, as the thread of desire grew. Enrico twirled Savannah around quickly. She knew that her partner would attempt to kiss her, so she placed the palms of her hands against his chest to keep an arms length between them. Enrico kept a firm grip on her slender waist as his fingers touched in the back. Hannah panted heavily now, forced her eyes to his chin level and then to his soft and sensual mouth. She then gazed deeply into familiar bright emerald eyes. A wave of exhilaration swept across her face and her eyes burned with a heated desire she could not deny.

Barbara stared at Hannah in disbelief. If she had not known better, she'd insinuate they were hot lovers. She has known Hannah for nearly a year now. The only man Hannah ever talked about was Austin and Barbara knew this man was certainly not Austin. She was not sure what to make of the situation. She watched as her heart began to fill with unwelcome jealously, for she never had a man look at her in such a way to suggest she was the only woman on earth. Barbara could feel the heat radiating from their bodies. Every whimsical movement they made was spellbinding. She could not take her eyes off them and quickly realized nobody else could either, for spectators now encircled them upon the dance floor. Their unified motions were mesmerizing and absolutely jaw dropping.

Enrico and his Lady Costello never unlocked their gaze, as they made passionate and sensual love, right there upon the dance floor within one another's eyes. Every ounce of their souls beckoned for more. His first touch released a longing deep within Hannah not even she could fully explain. Their gaze ignited a fire no amount of water could extinguish. The audience watched in awe as Hester Prinn and Zorro discovered one another. A world and more than a century apart, for no land mass, or even time itself, could have kept these characters from finding one another. Those surrounding them thought there was something magical and mysterious within the irony. When the song ended, everyone began to clap, whoop and holler. They reeled

Enrico and Hannah back from their dreamscape as Enrico engulfed her mouth, thrusting his tongue deep inside. Hannah made no objections and held on for dear life.

Barbara gasped, for she never had the liberties of witnessing such a forbidden escapade before. She was both appalled and intrigued. She clearly did not know Hannah as well as she thought. She watched as Zorro escorted Hester Prinn upstairs to his table. Barbara quickly followed and approached the table as they sat down. Barbara placed the palms of her hands upon the table, "Hannah, who is your friend and does he have a brother?" she asked anxiously, with questioning eyes. Barbara's words penetrated Hannah's heart and clouded her judgment.

"Thank you for the dance sir, but I must depart." Hannah could not bring herself to look Enrico in the eye.

Enrico clasped a hand around her arm tightly and then relaxed it. Hannah felt the power and desire within his touch. She finally gazed into his soft emerald eyes and he said nothing, but his eyes screamed, *Don't go!* Hannah suddenly felt feverish and delirious. She could not think clearly, for every beat of her heart whispered, *Stay*, while her mind screamed, *Leave*. After a long conflicting moment, her heart prevailed and she sat back down, as Barbara joined them.

Enrico presented himself first as Zorro and then extended a hand and introduced himself as Enrico Costello, with a devilish grin. Barbara accepted his hand and revealed her name. Her hand quivered and Enrico realized he made her nervous. He also knew that his encounter with Savannah would be relayed back to Austin and his grin widened, as a sparkle captured his eyes. "I do have a younger brother," he stated, after a brief moment, as an icebreaker. He sensed Barbara's heart flutter and he smiled openly. His smile quickly faded when he felt Savannah's heart grimace. He casually allowed his hand to fall beneath the table, slipped it up Savannah's lacy skirt and relaxed his palm upon her thigh.

He winced, as she remained motionless. He felt her blood become cold as ice and a shiver crept up his spine. A moment ago, her heart was filled with passion and desire but now all he felt were equivocations. Her eyes had been filled with a tantalizing web but now all he saw were lifeless cobwebs. The source was still undetermined. His own emotional state became tangled and complex. They all glanced over their shoulders as the bartender cried, "Last call."

Enrico removed his palm from Savannah's thigh, "How about a drink," he asked, and then stood.

"That would be great," Hannah returned immediately.

"What would you Ladies like?"

Barbara joined the conversation saying, "Why don't you surprise us."

Enrico smiled casually, turned and walked away.

Hannah grabbed Barbara's hand, "We must leave, now," she demanded.

Barbara's face lost all expression, "Hannah, what are you afraid of?" she asked quickly. Before Hannah had a chance to answer, Barbara added, "If you're afraid of Enrico, tell me now and we'll leave, no questions asked."

Hannah watched a flood of concern wash over Barbara's face. Hannah opened her mouth to speak but nothing came out. She did not know how or where to begin. Hannah stood and an echo pierced through her thoughts, "Leaving so soon, my Lady?" She jumped and realized the voice was not inside her head. She stumbled upon a chair, spun around and came face-to-face with a man dressed as a Mexican Bandit. It was not just any man and a shrill of terror nearly escaped her mouth. Hannah quickly covered her mouth with her palm and felt her knees weaken as her head began to spin. Barbara realized something was very wrong.

Barbara managed to slip away unnoticed and made her way down to the bar where Enrico awaited their drinks. "Enrico," she nearly cried out, as she pushed her way through the crowd. Barbara grabbed Enrico's arm, "Enrico, Hannah needs you!"

Enrico turned and faced her with a puzzled expression.

"A man dressed as a bandit, or something, approached Hannah and she nearly panicked. I don't know what's going on here, but she looked terrified."

Enrico immediately looked up at their table.

"I just left them..." Barbara said, as she pointed at their table. She dropped her hand after realizing they were no longer there.

Enrico scrambled to the door and began his descent as a black limo pulled up. He noticed Savannah standing against the building pleading with a man in costume. This rogue had one hand around her waist and one on the back of her head. She pushed her palms against his chest attempting to keep distance between them. Enrico had difficulties pushing his way downstairs, for the steps were jumbled with young men and women three sheets to the wind.

Panic overwhelmed him as he watched the back door open. He glanced at the crowd and then at his lady in distress. Without thinking, he leapt over the railing and landed firmly on the ground. He heard someone in the crowd yelling, "Go Zorro, go." Enrico paid no attention to their antics, for he was on a private mission—Savannah needed him. Before he could reach them, the rogue darted into the limo and left.

Hannah leaned back against the wall in sheer relief. She desperately wanted to go home, for she had enough altercations for one night.

Enrico rushed over and stood before her. He placed his palms on the wall, boxing her in. He caught his breath, "Tell me who this rogue is and I will end his existence," he managed, as his chest heaved in and out.

Hannah remained silent as a tear escaped her eye. She quickly brushed it away with her palm.

Rage began to build within Enrico, "I will find out one way or another, so tell me now," he demanded.

Hannah's eyes moistened once more, as she gave Enrico a pitiful glance. She felt completely exhausted and did not want to fight with him. She could see he was tense and filled with aggression but knew there was nothing she could say or do to ease his mind. Hannah simply ducked under his arm and slowly strolled down the ally.

Enrico leaned his brow against the wall. He could not fathom why she refused to confide in him. Every urge in his being told him to protect her, but it remained unclear whom she needed protection from. Enrico had taken the last straw and refused to play these games. It became clear to him now that this rogue would stop at nothing to entrap her with any means necessary. With a heavy heart, Enrico began to put the facts into a new perspective. His heart and mind collided.

He concluded that Savannah was safer the further apart they remained. For each time he graced her presence, this rogue pursued her. He did the only thing he could think of to protect her. He watched in agony as the love of his life strolled out of his life but not out of his heart. She would forever remain coursing through his veins and continue to fill the empty void within his very soul. The dark day approached rapidly, the day he'd say good-bye and send his Savannah home. However, that would be the coming of another dawn. He kept reminding himself of that but everyday, turned into another day.

Hannah refused to speak of Enrico the entire way home. Each time Barbara brought Enrico's name into their conversation, Hannah quickly changed the subject. Hannah removed her eye mask, stared at it upon her lap and ran her fingers through the feathers. She had much to reconsider and

Antonio's ultimatum only aggravated the situation. Hannah did not even want to admit the consequences to herself if she refused. She felt deeply confused, for this new game of his lacked all the fundamentals of any form of rationale.

Hannah's emotions became obscure. Antonio's words hissed in her ears, his image flickered on-and-off within her mind and she could still feel his hands upon her flesh. Her heart ached in turmoil, uncertain who to run to—Austin or Enrico? It would be easy to give herself to Enrico and embrace him completely; but at the same time, her heart beckoned for Austin. She needed time to reflect upon the entire evening.

Barbara dropped Hannah off and watched Austin open the door for her. Hannah threw her arms around his neck and kissed him tenderly. She heard Sierra crying in the background and Hannah drifted out of sight. Austin turned and waved goodbye but Barbara quickly motioned for him to stay. He closed the front door and strolled over to the car. Barbara opened the passenger side door and Austin climbed in with questioning eyes.

"Austin...I don't wish to upset you or cause Hannah any grief in any way, but I simply must know who Enrico is," she explained carefully.

Austin's face flushed red and Barbara instantly realized she put a foot in her mouth and wished she had not asked.

"Did you see him there tonight?" he demanded.

Barbara refused to lie, "Yes," she replied hesitantly.

Austin put his hands on his brow and mumbled, "So, he still pursues her even after all these years." He shook his head and leaned back. "Tell me everything you know."

Barbara explained most of the details about the night along with the man dressed as a bandit. She explained how Enrico darted for the door when Hannah and the stranger were no longer in sight. "That's all I know Austin, I swear. I'm only telling you this because of how terrified Hannah looked and I thought you should know."

Austin appreciatively thanked Barbara for the information, said good night and then watched her drive away.

Austin turned and glanced up at the nursery window and saw mother and child with sheer delight. His heart told him that he nearly lost his soul mate tonight. He knew Hannah would not want to go anywhere for some time and felt she deserved better, for she lived in the shadows of fear. Austin wanted to calm her childish fears and explain that everything would be all right, but he knew better. Austin cringed knowing it had been months since they heard from Enrico. He needed to remind her of that and not to dwell upon the past. Now, after tonight, he felt old wounds resurface and begin to fester.

He admitted to himself that they were no closer to being out of the woods now than they were five years ago when they decided to leave town. The past slowly caught up with them as though they stood still—just waiting for the sands of time to run out. Austin sighed and shook his head, for he still did not understand who, or what, awaited them. Barbara made Enrico out to be the hero tonight but realized it was a misinterpretation.

Austin realized how manipulative Enrico was by nature. He felt certain that Enrico hired a goon in an attempt to win over *Savannah*—The classic damsel in distress as the hero races in to save the day. His gut told him it had to be true. The entire concept actually amused him because his wife was there at home, with him. "I guess your plan didn't work, Enrico." Austin strolled inside, prepared to hear all about the misadventure.

He felt a little shocked when Hannah was not waiting for him in the living room. He immediately cocked his eyes upstairs and heard faint whimpering sounds. He ventured upstairs, tiptoeing each step, following the sounds. He peeked into the nursery first and found little Sierra sound asleep. He gripped the banister tight and then relaxed his hand and caressed the banister as he forced himself to walk down the hallway towards the bedroom.

His ears honed in on muffled sobs. He knew the bedroom door would be open, for Hannah kept it open every night so she could hear Sierra crying in the middle of the night. It was one of her many motherly instincts. He stood outside and gazed intently around the doorframe. He nearly gasped when he found Hannah crying softly with her hand clenching the phone. He heard her say, "No, you are sadistic," and then dropped the receiver to the floor.

Austin heard a voice cry, "Savannah," before the line fell silent and not just any voice, but a Male voice. She then ripped out the phone cord, took her face into her hands and began to sob uncontrollably. Hannah felt as though she were up against the greatest odds with no hopes of survival. Austin rushed to her side, dropped down upon his knees and took her into his arms. He kissed her brow and then kissed both cheeks tenderly, tasting her bittersweet tears.

"Whatever it is Hannah, we will get through it together," he whispered passionately, and then added, "We will take the good with the bad; but in the end, good always prevails."

Hannah thought about his words for a moment, silent and motionless gazing at a tiny rip in the carpeting. Finally, she raised her brow and, with a twisted partial smile and sharp steady eyes, gazed at him, "Does it always?" she asked, as her soul went aflame.

Hannah felt her blood begin to boil, for her soul knew the truth. The truth was that Antonio had the upper hand and would prevail in the end. She made up her mind at that second that they would not give Antonio the satisfaction of folding out so early in the game. She would make no deal and accept no challenge, not even with the devil himself. She alone evoked the strength and power within her soul to protect her family and loved ones. "We must move, immediately," she insisted, as she continued to hold Austin's gaze.

He tilted his chin and Hannah saw no questions within his eyes, only understanding. "Of course," he whispered, as he wrapped his arm around her. Austin rested his palm upon the small of her back and drew her closer to him. He caressed her luscious lips with his and sparked electricity, neither one expected. They made love, then and there, for the last time in the place they have come to call home.

They went to bed that night and Hannah began to dream. Austin just built a fire and they snuggled up upon the couch together sipping red wine. She felt uneasy and suddenly heard ferocious banging noises all around them. Before they knew what was happening, several men with guns surrounded them. An older gentleman stepped forward a moment later and announced Lord Costello sent him to fetch his prize, his Savannah.

Hannah panicked; certain Antonio sent them. She felt trapped and, for once, Enrico was nowhere in sight. She struggled and fought with her assailants with no prevail. She suddenly bolted upright in bed and glanced around the room as she drew the covers to her chest. Hannah became startled when she noticed a shadowy figure looming at the foot of the bed and nearly screamed. It took her a moment to realize it was Austin.

His gaze held an icy cold undertone, as he remained silent.

"I...I'm sorry if I woke you, but I had a nightmare," she stammered, barely above a whisper.

Austin averted his eyes for a moment and pierced through her gaze with both hands clenched. "Would you like to tell me about it?" he asked coldly.

Hannah quickly read his eyes and did not like what she found. They demanded the truth and warned her to take caution in her response. She knew something was very wrong, "I don't really remember it all, just that it frightened me," she attempted to explain.

Austin never even blinked as he stared at her intently, "Allow me to jog your memory," he returned coldly, and then added, "You cried out for Enrico."

Hannah gasped and clasped a hand over her mouth. She could only imagine what went through his mind. She thought about telling him everything—becoming openly honest with no more burdening secrets. However, in the end, she simply could not. She loved him too much to put him in peril. She kept her sacred vow to keep him out of harms way and conjured up a little white lie. She moistened her dry lips and, once again, met his cold and icy gaze. "Austin…I was running from Enrico and he closed in on me. I felt trapped and that is why I cried out his name." She felt relief when the lines upon his face softened, "Hold me," she whispered, as her eyes longed for his trust and understanding and her body beckoned for his soft sensual touch.

Austin crept up the bed slowly, rested his cheek upon her naval and laced her fingers between his. "I'm so sorry Hannah, I just thought…"

Hannah silenced him before he could finish. She did not want an apology from him nor did she deserve one, for he had every reason to be angry. She realized that Austin also had mixed feelings and concluded that he deserved much more. She wanted so much to un-complicate their situation.

Hannah closed her eyes and wondered how things got so out of control. She fully came to understand the tangled web they weave. Antonio would never stop pursuing her, Enrico would never stop pursuing the truth, Austin would never stop blaming Enrico and she could not stop deceiving the two men who professed their undying love. It was a vicious circle. Since Kindergarten, Hannah learned that a circle has no beginning and no end. Round and round they went, with no way out. The circle would never end, for she became the pursuit of dark and sensual desires as they make another lap within the circle of deception.

Hannah refused to dwell upon the outcome and somewhere deep within her soul, she denied how she even wished the ordeal to end. She kept those private thoughts behind lock and key until the time comes to cross that bridge and open the door to the unspoken truth. Her mind wondered if her heart could accept the truth, for facing Antonio meant facing Enrico in its entirety.

Austin slipped under the covers wearing nothing but his briefs while Hannah was lost in thought. When she opened her eyes, he was lying on his side with his head resting upon his palm, propped up by his elbow, and smiling seductively.

"A penny for your thoughts, my Dear," he whispered with a wink.

Hannah flashed him a wholehearted smile. She threw her arms around his neck rolling him over on his back as she curled her knees around his waist. She felt total exhilaration. He believed her, which meant she managed to keep him safe for one more night. *Round and round we go*, a little voice echoed within her mind, but Hannah silenced it quickly.

Her conscience grew, little by little, with each passing day. Nevertheless, that did not matter because Austin melted away the tension and all her fears subsided as he nibbled upon her ear and pulled her cotton nightgown up beyond her thighs. He rested his hands on her buttocks, squeezing slightly. He tilted his chin and gazed at her beauty. There was no need for word exchange as their eyes and bodies conveyed all thoughts. They paved the way to natural basic instincts and fulfilled intimate desires.

Afterwards, Austin ran a finger down her neck, past her collarbone, and rested it upon her temporary tattoo. She smiled outwardly but felt devastated inside. She knew she was not legally married but the bells of unity rang within her mind and she felt distraught. *Had I committed adultery?* Hannah had no answer, for she had made passionate love to Enrico earlier within her mind. Her heart and mind conflicted. Her mind replied, *Yes*, while her heart screamed, *No*. Hannah concluded that she, mentally, did forsake her vows. Her heart finally concurred and added, *Physically to… due to the sexual nature of the dance.* She could no longer silence the voice of her conscience, for it spoke loud and true.

Then and there, she vowed to never forsake Austin again. Hannah knew she could never allow herself to be in Enrico's presence even if it meant turning her back on him. Hannah also knew that if the three of them ever had an encounter together, her eyes would give her away and Austin would finally discover the truth and she would never allow that to happen.

Chapter 17
The Sanctuary of Home

Enrico went home in utter turmoil. He could not sleep. Jeano offered some comfort but not much. "Jeano," Enrico said with pleading eyes, "Help me discover the truth, this rogue continues…"

"What rogue, Brother," Antonio asked, as he stepped into the room.

Enrico's eyes went cold and became tongue-tied. He did not trust his brother and had no confidence in him. Antonio never followed through with anything; he was a philanderer who fumbled through existence. Antonio cannot be trusted. Enrico knew this all to well. "Brother, if I need your help, I will summon you," Enrico finally managed, "Now leave us, for I have business to attend to." Enrico stood abruptly and locked his gaze upon Antonio. If Antonio would not leave quietly, he was prepared to use force.

"As you wish, my Lord," Antonio hissed, and then left the room.

Antonio closed the door behind him and cringed. That was the last time he'd ever call Enrico, *my Lord.* His bother's rein would abruptly come to an end. He marveled at the sheer thought of it as a wave of exhilaration flooded across his face. It would not be long now and his patience knew no bounds. He was able to put another wedge between Enrico and his sacred Savannah tonight. Savannah had fourteen hours left to respond to his ultimatum. If he got no response, he'd be waiting upon her doorstep. He smiled when he realized his plans came together beautifully. Antonio planned every action perfectly and Enrico played right into his hands. He was the Puppeteer, Enrico his Marionette and Savannah and Austin remained his active audience—Witnesses to Enrico's downfall.

He continued to twist and use them in any manner necessary to pierce more and more daggers within Enrico's heart. Antonio knew he was slowly weakening Enrico, physically and mentally, while he maintained his own clarity and strength. This great battle was long overdue and for once, Antonio had the upper hand. He would not falter and he would not fall before his bother, not again. Once, some time ago, Antonio's plan backfired and Enrico prevailed over all of his deceitful tactics. Antonio had paid dearly for his treacheries and it has taken a lifetime to convince Enrico he had reformed. Now, the realm was within his grasp and it was prime for the taking. His eyes glistened with confidence and he'd show no absolution. Antonio's soul was consumed by greed, power and lust, as total conquest remained his prize—along with his brother's lover. He took drastic measures to ensure Enrico's downfall, even though Savannah had to be the martyr. He would continue to stay on course until they presented themselves to him. Victory was imminent.

Enrico unleashed his innermost thoughts to Jeano. Jeano listened intently and remained nonjudgmental. Jeano realized Enrico was in over his head. The only crime he committed was to fall madly in love with a young woman completely beyond his reach. Jeano knew it slowly cost Enrico his sanity.

"You must remain level headed, my Lord", he exclaimed, and then added, "I sense the truth you seek will only bring more pain to you both."

Enrico closed his eyes and took his brow into his hands. Jeano deserved to know the real reason he has been so conflicted and, with a heavy heart, Enrico bared his soul. "She is the *luz del dia*," he whispered as he rose and began to pace the floor.

Jeano's eyes widened and glazed over. He could not believe his ears, "Is this possible?" he whispered. "When did you discover this revelation?"

Enrico became motionless, unsure he was ready to admit the truth. His mind grew weary as he spoke. "I knew it the first moment she captivated my eyes," he finally confessed. He was certain Jeano would think him foolish and dishonorable.

Finally, everything became clear to Jeano as new perspectives came into view. He was shocked that Enrico could keep such a secret to himself for all these years. He could only imagine the intensity of Enrico's passion for her. Jeano became overwhelmed with mixed emotions, for Enrico has forsaken everything that ever meant anything to him for an unattainable love. Still, Enrico managed to uphold hope and the glimmer of miraculous possibilities. Jeano knew there was no way out for Enrico and was heart-stricken knowing the choice that awaited his friend in the end. Jeano could only imagine how difficult this has been. "Your love for Savannah is far greater than I ever imagined," he whispered, "I'll leave you to your thoughts."

"Are you angry with me?" Enrico asked, before Jeano made it to the door.

Jeano turned and met Enrico's brilliant green eyes, "No my Lord. I began this venture by your side and I will end it by your side, for I want whatever you want. I trust you to uphold your honor and abide by your duties." He hesitated for a moment, and then added, "There is no wrong choice and no wrong intentions, but you must follow your heart…objectively."

With that said, he left the room. Enrico remained uncertain what his chosen duty was and decided to wait until he did.

Austin and Hannah were up before dawn. Both were exhausted but there was much to accomplish. They were no strangers to packing and considered themselves lucky to have rented a fully furnished home, for little was actually theirs. Hannah lingered in the doorway of the nursery and watched little Sierra sleeping in her crib in the only home she has ever known in the short time she has been in this world. Moving now was more emotional than Hannah imagined. She clasped a hand over her mouth and leaned on the doorframe as she closed her eyes. She knew what they were running from, but Sierra did not. Hannah did not feel right uprooting their daughter like this.

Sierra deserved parents she could look up to and an actual home with roots. Hannah wondered if Sierra would ever look up to her. After all, she was an adulterer full of secrets, lies and deceit. Hannah felt trapped, within a dream and a nightmare. Austin and Sierra remained her dream while Antonio became the nightmare. She closed her eyes and still did not fully understand where Enrico fit into the equation. The little voice inside her head echoed once again. *He's the forbidden fantasy.* Hannah gasped at the mere thought and quickly dismissed it without interpreting its meaning. She kept reminding herself where her focus truly lied.

Hannah entered the nursery and started to box up items. She glanced at Sierra, sleeping soundly. Sierra was a special child, for she had seen it in Austin's eyes the day she announced the pregnancy and again in Enrico's eyes when he held her as an infant. Their stunned peculiar eyes still pierced her memories. She still could not fathom Austin's behavior as he acted strangely those first couple of days. She recalled how he spent the next few days alone. In time, she came to believe that he was frightened to become a father and all the responsibilities that came along with the title, especially bringing a child into circumstances such as these. Sierra, however, was not an ordinary baby.

Hannah recalled babysitting for numerous neighbors when she was thirteen. The babies were all fussy and demanded constant attention. There were many nights Hannah swore she'd never have children. Sierra rarely fussed and rarely cried. Hannah felt her daughter was perfect, almost too perfect. She always dismissed such thoughts, convinced she was merely blessed. Hannah cleared all thoughts from her mind and focused on packing, knowing Austin wanted to leave by lunchtime. Sierra sat up in her crib grinning. Hannah changed, fed, and dressed her. When she finished, Hannah sat Sierra upon the floor. Sierra mastered new abilities and attempted to crawl.

Sierra eyed up her ball lying across the floor and reached for it. She gave a little grunt and then, with big blue eyes, looked up at Hannah and pointed to the ball. Hannah smiled warmly as she folded Sierra's clothes. "If you want the ball, you'll have to crawl over to it," she exclaimed. Sierra did not seem deterred; she was bound and determined to get the ball. She lied down and rolled over onto her belly. She pulled her knees forward and propped her arms up.

She swayed back and forth for a moment and then crawled over to the ball. She began to giggle and laugh as she wrapped her tiny hands around it. Hannah watched in awe as Sierra got a twinkle in her eye and pushed the ball aside. She crawled over to the crib and stood up squealing. A tear escaped Hannah's eye as she watched her child pass a milestone. In a matter of minutes, Sierra transformed from being an infant into a toddler. Hannah rushed over and took Sierra into her arms, praising her. She wished to be around for all of Sierra's milestones and vowed to do everything in her power to elude Antonio at any cost. Hannah kissed Sierra's chubby cheek and put her back down to play while she finished packing.

After three hours, the nursery was packed and Austin carried the boxes and the crib downstairs. The only thing left standing was the playpen. Sierra began to yawn so Hannah put her down for a nap. Austin announced that Barry, the next-door neighbor, was on his way over so they could retrieve the moving van. Hannah retired to the kitchen to whip up some sandwiches in an attempt to use up any leftovers. The doorbell rang and Barry walked into the house. Hannah handed them some sandwiches and they left. Hannah walked around the house. Most rooms were empty except for the living room. Boxes were stacked everywhere. She made her way upstairs and gazed upon the vacant bed where Sierra was conceived, lost in thought. She made certain nothing was forgotten as her eyes scanned each room.

She went back downstairs and shuffled through some boxes. She sighed with relief as she removed some stationary and a pen. She sat down quietly at the kitchen table and glanced at the telephone. It was time to give Antonio the message. She refused to call him, as instructed, and decided to leave him a note instead. She cleared her mind and allowed all emotions and frustrations to pour out of the pen unto the paper. When she finished, she folded the note with trembling hands and sealed it an envelope. She wrote Antonio's name on the front and placed the envelope into her back pocket, pulling her sweatshirt down so it was concealed. All loose ends had been tied up and she was ready to leave and begin a new life somewhere else.

Shortly later, Austin pulled into the driveway with the moving van. Austin loaded the van while Hannah prepared Sierra for the long trip ahead. Austin would drive the van and Hannah would follow in their SUV. They headed four hours east to Honey Grove; it was a mutual decision. Both vehicles were packed and Austin finished fastening Sierra's car seat in the backseat. He closed the door, "Ready?" he asked, with an unsteady smile.

Hannah remembered the note in her back pocket, "I promised the landlord I'd leave the house keys on the kitchen table," she returned, and then darted into the house. She left the envelope upon the table and walked out quickly, glancing at her watch. They would be halfway to Honey Grove before Antonio arrived. She smiled at Austin as she climbed in and fastened her seatbelt. The time had come to leave this part of their lives behind them. She shuddered, realizing this was the last place they'd call home.

Antonio did not even bother to wait by the phone. He sensed that Savannah had no intentions to call. He left the hotel suite and ventured downstairs. Valet called for his limo and brought the vehicle around front. Antonio sported blue jeans, Ebony boots and a midnight blue silk shirt. His swarthy hair glistened in the sunlight as he adorned a pair of mirrored shades. He immediately lit a cigarette to help ease the tension, for his adrenalin ran full throttle. The limo pulled up and his door was opened for him. He got in and motioned the driver to proceed.

Thirty minutes later, they pulled into Savannah's driveway. Antonio immediately stepped out, before the driver had the chance to open his door. He strolled up the front walk to the door and did not bother to knock as he entered the house. He knew damn well she was not there, for her SUV was nowhere in sight. He immediately noticed that the house was nearly empty. He made his way to the kitchen and stopped mid-stride when he sized up the envelope—addressed to himself. He smiled as he clutched the envelope. He tore it open and began to read.

Antonio,

I'm sure this note must come as a shock, for I take you as a man who doesn't get many rejections. I must decline your offer. Hell will freeze over first before I make a deal with the devil. Last night will be the last time you ever place your hands upon me. Your actions are incomprehensible and I question your motives. You'll never be half the man Enrico is. For years, I have remained silent. My silence is growing thin. Do not attempt to contact me again. I don't think you'd enjoy the outcome. I have nothing more to say. Adios.

    Antonio folded the note and placed it within his pocket. He nearly threw the envelope upon the floor, but remembered it was addressed to him. He decided to take it with him just in case Enrico showed up. Antonio left the house emotionally pleased with the outcome, for Savannah played right into his hands. All he needed was a little more patience—and time.
    Austin and Hannah drove into Honey Grove right on schedule, around 4:00 PM. Honey Grove was a small country town. They did not wish to stay long so they did not bother to find out everything about the town. Their plan was to move every four months. Halfway through town, Austin eyed up a sign that read: *Fully furnished two-bedroom apartment. Available immediately.* He pulled along the curb, reached for his cell phone and dialed the number. A woman answered the phone and confirmed that the apartment was still available but only for the next few months. Without hesitation, Austin said, "We'll take it." They parked in the driveway and awaited the landlord. She arrived twenty minutes later and gave them their keys. She thought it strange that the couple never asked for a tour; but in her experience, any tenant was better than no tenant at all. They immediately ventured inside for observations. The apartment was bigger than they expected.
    They only unpacked necessities and tried not to get too comfortable. Austin went out of his way to stay clear of the neighbors. At this point, he trusted no one. Three months passed by quickly and Austin already chose

their next destination; Pennsville was another small town two hours north. Sierra was walking and beginning to talk. Today was her first birthday. Hannah bundled her up and took her outside to play in the snow while Austin decorated the cake and prepared the kitchen. He had blown up the last balloon and put the candle upon the cake when the phone rang. Austin quickly answered it, for he was expecting their parents to call and wish Sierra a Happy Birthday.

Austin cringed when he heard an old familiar voice.

"Austin, so nice to talk to you again," the voice hissed.

"What do you want?" Austin demanded.

The voice fell silent for a moment, "I've called to give little Sierra her birthday present," the voice exclaimed.

Austin shook his head in disgust, "We don't want anything from you," he replied.

The voice chuckled, "Sierra will get a new baby sister for her Birthday, for my mind is made up," the voice said, and then hung up.

Austin became dumfounded. Enrico was going to bless them with another daughter. Austin was delighted and leery at the same time. He could not fathom Enrico's motives. He had much to think about, for Enrico *was* a man of his word.

Antonio hung up the phone with a devious smile upon his face. He knew it would become more and more difficult for them to move with two children. It was all part of his perfect scheme. They, and Enrico, would soon grovel at his feet and they'd present all of his greatest desires upon a silver platter. *Patience*, he reminded himself, *Patience*.

Austin and Hannah gave Sierra the best birthday party possible. Austin had to work especially hard to give Sierra his undying attention, for many other things weighed upon his mind. That night, he charmed the pants off Hannah and they made love in a heated frenzy as though there were no tomorrow. Afterwards, Hannah gazed into his eyes, still wrapped in his embrace.

"Where did that come from," she whispered.

"From my heart," he whispered back, and then kissed her brow tenderly. "I love you completely, Mrs. Hannah Marie Desmin."

Hannah knew she would never grow tired of Austin's charm, "I love you too, Austin." *More than words can express...for actions speak louder than words.*

A month later, they moved to Waynesboro and found a similar apartment. For weeks, Austin kept asking Hannah if she was okay. Hannah would answer the same each time, "Austin, I'm fine, stop worrying." In his heart, he knew that a precious life slowly began to grow within her. Two weeks later, Hannah announced the pregnancy. They shared a happy tearful embrace. Austin still could not fathom why Enrico would grant them such happiness after years of torment but he told himself he would never take for granite the two miracles that were bestowed upon him. Hannah's first trimester went by quickly. Again, she never got morning sickness.

They left Waynesboro and moved to Glendale, an hour and a half northeast so Hannah could continue to see the OBGYN she became familiar with. Hannah continued to glow throughout her second trimester. Her hair grew longer and shined with radiance. Her heart felt complete and became so full she thought it would burst.

"What should we name her?" Austin asked, and then realized the slip of tongue.

"Who says this child is going to be a girl?"

"Wishful thinking! I want many daughters with your generous spirit and flawless beauty."

He desperately desired a son but knew he could never, on his own accord, produce one. That longing would always be a void within his heart. Nevertheless, he was grateful to have another precious gift of life, in some magical twist that was his own flesh-and-blood. He did not understand how it was possible and frankly, he did not care how or why. Hannah went into labor two weeks before her due date. Austin rushed Sierra to her sitter and raced Hannah to the hospital.

Six hours later, as Hannah took one last deep breath, she gave birth to a beautiful healthy baby girl. Both parents were ecstatic. One of the nurses commented about Austin being a very proud Daddy. They all could see the love radiating from him immediately as he was handed the child. He gazed into his daughter's eyes and swore it was love at first sight. Hannah was very pleased with the family they made. She looked into Austin's eyes.

"Go ahead and name her," she whispered.

They counted each finger and each toe as Austin smiled widely.

"Let's name her Elaina," he exclaimed.

Hannah thought for a moment, "That is a beautiful name, Austin." She took her daughter into her arms and with adorning eyes whispered, "Welcome, my darling Elaina."

The doctor told Austin that mother and child were doing just fine and would be released the next day. Austin went home to prepare and explained to Sierra that she has a new baby sister. Austin and Sierra went to the hospital the next morning. Hannah introduced Sierra to Elaina. Sierra thought Elaina was a doll baby and both parents laughed. Austin took his family home and grimaced to himself when he realized it was not much of a home. He quickly dismissed all negative thoughts, for today was a wonderful day. They stayed in Glendale long enough for Hannah to have her six-week checkup and then they moved, again.

This time they moved six hours south to Stone Gap. They were able to find a vacant small townhouse. Austin hated residing in town, for Sierra did not even have a back yard to play in. They celebrated Sierra's second birthday. Two months later, they moved to Stormstown. After that, they found themselves in Schnecksville, Smithsburg and then Foxdale. They celebrated Elaina's first birthday and shortly later Sierra turned three. The constant moving began to play its toll upon the family. Both Hannah and Austin felt exhausted. Before they knew it, Sierra was four and Elaina was two. Austin desperately wanted to settle down in one place, preferably near their hometown but knew that was not a possibility. Hannah made it very clear that their families remained safer this way. They had moved so many times that Austin could no longer keep track of all the places they lived. He kept reminding himself, just one more time. He thought about their ten-year anniversary quickly approaching next year.

Austin moved his family to Fowls Mills, a very small-secluded town up north. He found a large farmhouse for rent. He knew it was perfect the moment he drove by it. Hannah quickly became fascinated with its history. The home was comprised of stone and was constructed in the mid 1800's. She felt they had their own mini castle. The home was sturdy and strong; Austin felt it could withstand anything, even Enrico. Austin sent for Bandit as a housewarming present for Hannah.

"Welcome home," he announced, and then presented Hannah with Bandit.

Immense joy overwhelmed Hannah. Her eyes became moist, as she watched her children run around their vast yard with Bandit. The dog instantly became smitten with them. She took Austin's hand and held it tightly, "This is both wonderful and thoughtful, Austin," she exclaimed, and then turned to face him.

The wind began to blow, so Austin tucked her long glistening hair behind her ear as they gazed at one another. They became lost in one another's eyes, radiating full of love. Hannah relaxed her grip as she let her thoughts slip away. She went to explain why they should not get too comfortable but could not bring herself to utter a word. She wanted nothing more than to be caught up in the unsurpassed serenity of their newfound home. The word *Home* has not been a part of their vocabulary for some time. She wondered what Austin meant by his initial announcement.

The family settled in nicely. Their moderate means of living with two children slowly began to diminish Austin's inheritance and he refused to spend another cent. Austin wished to leave the rest to his daughters. He hoped they would find true happiness someday with an actual home and firm roots. Austin arranged to work as a farm hand whenever necessary to reduce the monthly rent by half, but it was not going to be enough. He hated the thought of Hannah working, but there was no other way.

He was sure that they could get by if she picked up a part time job. He felt vulnerable with his back against the wall. He could not protect her if she was not within his sight. He knew Hannah was a resourceful woman, but he could not stand the thought of her out there all alone. He decided not to give it a second thought. There was no other choice and he would think optimistically, for it has been five years since Enrico jaded them with his presence. His heart wanted to believe they have seen the last of Enrico but the ring was a constant reminder of his ever-lasting presence.

Hannah interviewed for a part time job in an accounting office at a local retail company. A week later, the company offered her the position. She accepted it immediately and felt relieved to be behind the scenes, out of sight. Four months came and went and then another four months. Elaina celebrated her third birthday and Sierra was about to turn five. Hannah felt the inevitable close in around them. She woke up on the morning of their tenth anniversary in sheer panic. She had the familiar nightmare of being presented to Antonio with no way out. She felt tense and wanted out of the house for a while. Therefore, Hannah picked up an extra shift at work, where she could sit alone to consider all possible alternatives.

Austin heard Hannah struggling in her sleep and wondered if she was all right, but Hannah left before he had a chance to ask. He decided to use his time wisely. He straightened up the house and put a bottle of Champaign on ice. He cleaned out the fireplace in the living room and got it ready for a quiet evening. He placed various candles around the room. He made a mental note to have the girls fed, bathed and ready for bed. He did not expect Hannah home until six o'clock. While straightening up, he came across Hannah's cell phone. Normally he would never pry but their marriage has been anything but normal—giving the circumstances. He checked Hannah's messages and discovered one saved message. A cold tingle crept down his spine after listening to it.

Mrs. Thompson, from Aspen Reality, called to confirm the home in Crescentville was still available for rent. Austin cupped the palm of his hand over his lips and shook his head slightly. Clearly, Hannah felt the need to move. He closed his eyes in dismay. He knew her actions were inevitable, but he hoped part of him could make her feel safe and secure enough to stay. He wanted so much to make tonight special. Suddenly, he felt guilty not having any money to buy her an anniversary present but he'd present her with the best present possible and it would truly come from the heart.

With a heavy heart, he removed an old piece of scrap paper from his wallet. He instantly felt weary, unsure if he could follow through. He decided to find the strength and courage to give Hannah the two things she deserved most, closure and retribution. He walked upstairs, heavy footed, nearly forcing himself to enter their bedroom and wrap his fingers around the receiver. He hesitated and then picked it up. He stared at the numbers, trying to reassure himself he was doing the right thing. With a slow and trembling finger, he dialed 1-800-555-6706. Austin felt relieved when a familiar voice said, "Hello, Austin."

Devlin clutched the phone with all his might. "Devlin, I need your help," he heard Austin say. Devlin heard concern in Austin's voice and closed his eyes, "I'm listening," he replied. There was a brief pause and Devlin hung his head as he guessed what Austin was about to say.

"The time has come to end this," Austin murmured.

Devlin barely heard him, "I know," he replied.

"Under one condition."

"What's that?"

"That Enrico doesn't lay one hand upon her!"

Devlin fell silent. Finally, he said the only thing left to say, "The man that Hannah fears, will not touch her."

"Do I have your word?"

"On my mother's grave…you have my word."

"Make it happen…and Devlin…I fully hold you responsible for any misgivings."

"I'll send for you at midnight, and I assure you…no harm will come to either of you." With that said, Devlin hung up. He immediately called his most trusted colleague, spoke briefly and hung up.

* * *

Austin hung up the phone uncertain if Enrico would arrive at midnight. If so, he could end it tonight, for they were not going anywhere. He had much to do. He hoped, one day, Hannah would forgive him for this charade. Austin had no fears, for he felt certain his plan would not fail. Enrico would finally pay for his actions. Austin paused with a sense of complexity. *Can I destroy the man that gave me so much only to take away so much?* His thoughts lied with his daughters now. He felt despise, loathing and gratification all at the same time. He took caution to the wind as he waited for Hannah to return home.

Chapter 18
A New Battle Begins

Hannah returned home to find the house absolutely spotless and the girls ready for bed. They greeted her at the door as she entered, while Austin stood in the living room doorway concealing the true nature of her surprise.

"The girls haven't napped all day and will be in bed shortly," he explained.

Hannah instantly showed her gratification, with a sparkle in her eye and a seductive smile. He prepared a nice supper for her, knowing she would need all her strength for the final battle. His gut turned with hostility and a little anticipation combined. Hannah's gut also turned, knowing she'd break his heart with pending news. They have all come to call this house their home but an old familiar presence overpowered her rationale. In time, she hoped he would understand.

Enrico made up his mind. He could not withstand questioning and worrying about her any longer, so he summoned for Jeano. He knew the time had come, time for revelations, retribution, and revenge. He closed his eyes for, even after five years of separation, he was truly unprepared for what lied ahead. Savannah no longer shared his bed, but she'd live within his heart forever and he within hers. That was enough to keep her in his life, until now. It would be hard to relive those two weeks, for both of them. Enrico also knew that it was finally time to meet Austin. He needed to know if Austin was truly worthy of her love before releasing her to him—once and for all.

Jeano knocked upon the door and Enrico cried, "Enter."

"You summoned for me, my lord." Jeano announced, as he entered the room.

Enrico stood and looked him square in the eye, "I have summoned you…not as a servant…not as a colleague…but as a friend."

Jeano quickly read his eyes and knew that the time had come. He saw both anticipation and uncertainty cascading from Enrico's gaze.

"I want you to bring Lady Costello and Austin to me, as quickly as possible."

Jeano needed no further explanation. "It shall be done as you command, my Lord." Jeano started to exit the room.

"And Jeano," Enrico said, rendering Jeano immobile. "Lady Costello is not to be man handled in any way. Do I make my self clear?"

Jeano turned about face and nodded, fully understanding Enrico's request, and he was gone.

Enrico had a lot of work to do before their arrival. He had to prepare separate rooms, for he could not allow himself to be alone with Savannah for fear of letting his desires, which loomed over him the past five years, consume him. He told himself he'd remain a gentleman during the inquisition. Just the mention of her name brought an ache to his loins that only she could fulfill. There had not been another woman these past five years and he feared he would pounce, given the first opportunity.

Enrico quickly made rounds from one room to another. He instructed most of the staff to leave and promised to send word upon their return. He made up a room for Austin in the adjacent bedchamber next to his. Enrico knew it would be difficult to have the other *man* under his roof, for them both. He would not underestimate Austin's capabilities or rationale. Austin may be a problem and he would take all necessary precautions. Enrico came to grasps with the fact at hand; if he hurt or allowed anyone else to hurt Austin, Savannah would never forgive him. Enrico became tired as the setting sun approached and felt the need to get a few hours of sleep before their arrival, but there was no rest for the weary. He attempted to lie down with no prevail, for all he could do was wait and patience had never been his strong suit.

Jeano prepared the jet, taking six of his most trusted colleagues along. He felt six was too many, but refused to take any chances. He was well aware that neither Lady Costello nor Austin would come willingly. Jeano arranged everything. He considered all possible scenarios and doubled preventative measures. Jeano's men armed themselves with stun guns, only to be used if necessary. He felt they were ready and gave the order to leave. It would be seven hours until they arrive in Pittsburgh, Pennsylvania. Then it would be a four-hour car ride from there. He already had two cars and a limo waiting for them at Pittsburgh. It would be a long day for everyone.

Austin and Hannah read to Sierra and Elaina and tucked them into bed, as bandit nestled at the foot of Sierra's bed. They walked downstairs, hand-in-hand.

"I need to talk to you," Austin whispered.

"I have something to tell you too," Hannah replied, and then retreated to the den.

Austin lit a fire and they nestled upon the couch together. Austin took her hand into his and gazed at the Ring of Eternity.

She caught him lingering and in a soothing voice asked, "What's on your mind, Honey?"

Austin gathered his thoughts and replied, "You first."

Hannah picked up the newspaper lying upon the coffee table and let out a sigh, "I think we should move. I found a great house for rent six towns away in Crescentville."

Austin closed his eyes, for he could not bear the thought of moving again. They have been happy here this past year and their daughters adjusted well. He briefly glanced at her ring and felt there was no end in sight to this nightmare.

This was not the life he dreamed of, but they promised to love each other for better or for worse. Austin knew he no longer had just Hannah to worry about, for they had two precious daughters who remained innocent victims in all of this. He often wondered how fair it was to bring children into the picture but he could not imagine life without them. He loved those girls. Hannah reached out and touched his arm.

"What do you think, Austin?" she asked carefully, knowing he was lost in thought.

Austin began to pale and asked, "Did you have another nightmare last night, Sweetheart?"

Hannah immediately dodged the question. "I have already put my two weeks notice in at work and we have an appointment to tour the house tomorrow at three o'clock." Hannah paused and then stated, "It should make for a nice day trip with the girls." Crescentville was a prosperous community with vast opportunities; she knew they should have no problem finding work there.

"Please open up to me and tell me how you feel. We are in this together!" They both sat there in silence and then she began.

"I can feel his presence closing in and we have to act soon," she whispered with a shudder, "I fear what will happen if he finds us."

Austin poured her a glass of champagne. "Hannah it's been nearly five years," he stated softly, as he handed her the glass. "I can't run anymore. We must face our fears, together."

Austin grimaced as Hannah stared into the flames. She nodded and reluctantly agreed. "He's on his way right now."

Austin reached for the phone lying upon the coffee table and handed it to her. She knew he wanted her to make arrangements with the baby sitter. "We can run or we can make a stand and fight for the life our family deserves," he whispered.

Hannah made the call, still uncertain of their decision. She hated to lie and began to fear it was a part of her soul now. She told the sitter that her grandfather in Oklahoma passed away and they must leave immediately. The sitter told her to bring the girls over and to take all the time they needed. Hannah hung up the phone as Austin gazed into her moist blue eyes.

"We're doing the right thing, Hannah."

Hannah closed her eyes, "Are we?" she managed to whisper.

Hannah gathered up the girls' clothes, diapers and some groceries. Hannah noticed they did not have much milk left and informed Austin to stop at the store. They carried the girls to the car and buckled them in the back seat. Austin ran into the gas station for a gallon of milk and some juice. They arrived at the sitter's house and Hannah felt like her legs would not move. She felt no need to hide her emotions; after all, her grandfather had just passed away. Angela already had beds made up for the girls and laid them down. Hannah and Austin hugged and kissed them both.

"We really appreciate this, Angela," Hannah whispered.

Angela waved her hand aside and said, "It'll be a pleasure to have them." Angela noticed how sad Hannah looked and she completely understood, for her own grandmother passed away earlier that year and Hannah and Austin watched her children for a week.

Hannah caught Angela reading her eyes. *If she only knew the truth.* She held a lot of respect for Angela and the two have become close friends this past year.

"We have to get going, Hannah," Austin whispered.

As they got back into their car, Angela hollered, "Take your time…really…and don't worry, they'll be fine."

As Austin backed out of the driveway, Hannah placed her hand upon his leg and her hand trembled. "I have a bad feeling we're never going to see them again. Please tell me I'm wrong."

Austin flinched and reached for her hand, "I promise you, we will see our girls again." Hannah's mind felt some ease, for Austin sounded so certain.

"You are my rock," she whispered.

After arriving home, Austin darted upstairs.

This may have been planned, but he refused to take any chances. He went to the bureau on his side of the bed and picked up his Ruger P95.9 MM semi automatic handgun. He slept with it loaded every night, anticipating the worst. He grabbed his shoulder holster and stripped off his T-shirt. He put the holster on and picked out a long sleeved shirt, slightly baggy, and buttoned it up over his firm chest. It was perfect. If Enrico showed up, he refused to go without a fight. He needed to make Enrico see that they did not want him in their lives.

Jeano picked up three vehicles and departed Pittsburgh. Jeano sat in the back of the limo, which traveled between the sedans. They looked like a black freight train upon the highway, as they followed closely. Jeano knew it would not be much longer. He opened a bottle of Château De'Grand and placed it on ice. He took out three glasses and set them aside. As they parked in front of Hannah's house, he poured the wine. Jeano took out 50mg of Amitriptyl and sprinkled it into the glass closest to him, for 50mg of Amitriptylin is enough to knock out a man for twelve hours.

"This should be enough to subdue Austin until we reach Costa Rico," Jeano whispered. Amitriptylin is colorless, odorless and tasteless. *Austin shouldn't suspect a thing.* When Jeano was pleased with his work, he stepped out of the limo and assessed the situation. The stone domicile was dark, except for a single light. His Colleagues already surrounded each entrance point and stood alert. They patiently awaited his orders.

Hannah sat motionless upon the couch. She instantly felt eyes upon them. *Do not fight me*, echoed throughout her mind. She flashed Austin a somber expression, "They're here."

He returned a grave nod and peered through the blinds, saw several figures and instantly realized he could not end it here. There would be no showdown, not yet. Austin immediately stood in front of Hannah. Simultaneously they heard the front door, back door and basement door breaking. With in seconds, five men encircled them with guns. The house grew silent except for the sounds of footsteps upon the basement stairs.

Jeano reached the top step and heard, "All clear." He entered the room and met Hannah's gaze. Hannah jumped up and the men quickly closed in.

"Place your hands where we can see them," they shouted fiercely.

Austin barely had time to react but managed to throw a hand towards them and one towards Hannah, distancing both parties. He had no idea what went through Hannah's mind or what she was capable of when backed into a corner.

Jeano gave the men a gesture to keep their distance and they each took a step back. "Austin, I can see you are a reasonable man, for you know you are out numbered. We can do this the hard way or the easy way," Jeano asserted, knowing they were at a disadvantage.

"Who sent you?" Hannah demanded.

Jeano simply answered, "Lord Costello, my Lady."

"Which one?"

Jeano flinched, as he stared into her hateful eyes. He found pain and fear deep within her soul and quickly replied, "Enrico, my Lady."

Hannah immediately eased up as Jeano noticed her facial expression soften. "Then I suppose we shouldn't keep him waiting then, should we?" she commented flatly.

Jeano removed one set of arm restraints from his coat.

"That really isn't necessary," Hannah stated sharply.

Jeano, however, now focused on Austin.

Austin held both hands out and Jeano restrained him. Hannah wrapped her arms around Austin and explored new limitations. Two men immediately seized her, while another forced Austin outside. Jeano read their eyes and found a glimmer of disloyalty hidden deep beneath the exterior. Without hesitation, he shot both men. Hannah gasped and retreated to the corner.

"Does anyone else wish to defy Lord Enrico Costello? If so, come forwards and prepare to die dishonorably."

Each man lowered their weapons, without hesitation, and remained steadfast. Jeano still distrusted each man that remained loyal and realized the rogue had access to Enrico's men. *Only Enrico has the power to persevere and eradicate the Mystical Realm and Sacred Vows that surround us.* He shook his head and turned towards Hannah. "Do not fear me my Lady. On my Father's Honor...you will arrive safely." Jeano offered a helping hand.

Hannah accepted his hand and stood. She glanced at the floor, but the traitorous men no longer lied there. Her mind recalled similar events and yet, had no answers. She now wished to embark on this journey—The Journey of Reckoning. As this battle ceased, a new battle began.

Jeano motioned her to the front door and soothingly whispered, "After you, my Lady."

Hannah now led, as Jeano and the remaining men followed. She stepped into the limo and embraced Austin warmly, while the men took their positions.

"Are you alright...what happened in there?" Austin questioned with furious eyes, feeling cast aside.

"Would you like a drink?"

Austin immediately stretched his arm out as Jeano handed him the closest glass. He quickly drank the entire glass in one gulp. It tasted refreshing, almost too refreshing. Jeano appeared relaxed and Austin now questioned his contentment.

Twenty minutes, Jeano thought. "And you, my Lady?"

Hannah said nothing and Jeano took her silence as a no.

Austin's eyes began to feel heavy. Before anyone realized it, he fell asleep.

"Now we can speak freely," Jeano whispered, and then pointed to Austin.

"What did you give him?"

"Simply a sedative." Jeano narrowed his eyes, "Why did you ask which Lord Costello sent for you, my Lady?"

Hannah merely shook her head, "Forget about it...it doesn't matter now."

"My name is Jeano Martinez, my Lady. I am Enrico's most trusted servant...and friend."

Hannah managed to say, "Hi," for she hardly felt the need to be formal under these circumstances. She desperately wanted to ask if Antonio would be present in Costa Rico, but simply could not. Enrico does not yet know about their encounter and she intended to keep it that way.

Jeano watched her closely and made a mental note that she wished to ask something. "Is there a question weighing on your mind, my Lady?"

Hannah stared at him now, for she was amazed at how clairvoyant he was and it frightened her. She began to foreshadow where the conversation led. "Do you have any more of that sedative?"

Jeano gazed into her eyes and attempted to read her thoughts with no prevail. He took out the bottle, sprinkled it in the remaining glass and handed it to her. She quickly drank the entire glass. Within ten minutes, she was sound asleep. Jeano watched her in astonishment. She did not sleep peacefully, for there were demons deep within her soul, begging for freedom. Jeano promised to release those demons and help Enrico overcome ultimate, yet unconfirmed, betrayal.

At Pittsburgh International, they made the transfer to the jet. Jeano personally carried Hannah onto the plane and lied her down upon the bed. She looked like an angel to his fragile eyes. Austin slumbered on the couch. The men kept their watchful eyes upon Austin, while Jeano watched over Hannah. Hannah slept for 8 hours and then awakened. Jeano did not give her as strong of a dose and knew she would regain consciousness shortly.

"How much further Jeano?" Hannah asked, as she wiped the sleep from her eyes.

"About three and a half hours."

Instantly realizing Austin was nowhere in sight she yelled, "Where is Austin?"

"He's asleep upon the couch, my Lady. Do not distress." Jeano saw a window of opportunity and he seized the moment. "I spoke to Enrico awhile ago and he is thinking about sending for his brother, for he wishes the two of you to meet."

Hannah felt the entire world cave in around her and attempted to choose her words carefully. "I have no interest in meeting Antonio!"

Jeano's eyes widened, for he never mentioned Antonio's name. Hannah remained unaware of her falter as Jeano attempted to press further. "Why not, my Lady?"

Hannah refused to answer and remained silent the rest of the journey.

Jeano was lost in his own thoughts now, for there was much to reveal. He handed Hannah a plate of breakfast and she reached for it in acceptance. Jeano did not know what to expect upon arrival, for this was the darkest revelation since The Great Tragedy. He kept his thoughts to himself as they ate in silence.

The jet landed at the San Jose International Airport around noon. Austin was still out cold. As Hannah departed the plane, she noticed Enrico standing beside a black limo. Hannah closed her eyes, for most people dream about riding in limos their entire lives and now, Hannah began to dread it. *Enough is enough.*

Jeano attempted to reveal the immanent news with no prevail. He lacked the courage and the strength to shatter what was left of Enrico's immortal soul. He decided to let the secret unravel itself and merely help it along, as Enrico ran to Hannah and embraced her.

Enrico quickly noticed that she did not return his embrace and escorted her to the limo with a heavy heart.

"What about Austin?" she whispered.

"He'll follow," Enrico stated, as kindly as possible. He noticed she looked tired. It had been five years and they were still comfortable with one another. "We have much to discuss," he said soothingly.

"I have nothing to say, Enrico." Hannah took Enrico by surprise when she sat beside him and reached for his hand. She wanted to ask why he sent for her but already knew the answer and gazed into his emerald eyes instead, "No good can come from my being here. I will only bring you turmoil." With that said, she embraced him with body, mind, heart and soul. Hannah knew it was the last time he'd hold her as his beloved Savannah and part of her died.

His body ached for her touch. She was just as beautiful as ever, even more so now. He'd soon find out if Austin truly deserved such a woman. If Enrico held any reservations about Austin's love, he'd never let Savannah go. They stole a private moment and held one another all the way to the *Castillo de Maldito*. The limo stopped in front of a huge castle that made the Castillo de Isla look like a summer cottage. Enrico took her hand as they walked inside. The remaining servants instantly became aware of her presence.

"Lady Costello," they continued to whisper, all beside themselves.

"Enrico, may I freshen up before dinner?"

"You will find suitable attire upstairs, the second door to the right."

Hannah quickly blushed, as an old memory flooded her mind. Even after all these years, he could still evoke the silent spirits lying dormant in the depth of her soul, with a single glance.

Noticing, he leaned into her and whispered, "May I join you, my Lady?"

Hannah's eyes widened and she slowly shook her head and walked upstairs as Jeano approached.

"Did you uncover anything?" Enrico asked quickly, as he watched Savannah ascend the stairs.

"No, my Lord!"

"Where is Austin?"

"He's in his room...and is demanding an audience with you, my Lord."

"Open the cantina," Enrico ordered, "And then bring our guest down."

Jeano opened the cantina and made sure it was fully stocked. Jeano himself would be the bartender, for he entrusted no other man with Enrico's well being. Not after learning Enrico's own flesh and blood betrayed him.

Chapter 19
Dark Revelations

Two guards brought Austin into the cantina, sat him upon a chair and restrained his right wrist to the table. Austin was well aware that he still concealed his 9 mm Ruger. *It ends right here... right now.* He flashed a cold loathing smile. Then, a tall, dark haired man entered the room moving slowly. Austin leapt to his feet.

"Are you Enrico?" he demanded.

Jeano did not take his eyes off Austin now. Austin noticed the man's eyes darken and become frigid.

"No, I am Devlin."

"Devlin," Austin whispered coldly. He clenched his fists, "You promised Enrico would not touch her!"

Devlin grinned, "No...I promised he would not touch her, referring to the man who wronged her."

Austin finally came face-to-face with the voice on the phone, the man who divulged much information for one purpose and one purpose only—Hannah's safety. Nevertheless, that did not change the circumstances at hand. "Where is Enrico? I was expecting Enrico."

"Enrico is in disposed; I can answer any questions you may have."

Austin sat back down and relaxed a bit. Both men stared at one another, trying to read one another's eyes.

"Lord Costello will meet with you later. Until then, he sent me to make sure you don't need anything."

Austin scanned his memory for any shred of information that could be used to his advantage. He wished to learn more from Devlin.

Devlin reeled Austin from his thoughts, "Would you like a drink?"

Austin looked up, realizing he was staring at the table. "I could use one."
Devlin watched him curiously now and motioned for Jeano.

Jeano approached and poured two shots of mescal. Austin picked up the shot glass and hesitantly drew it to his lips, but quickly sat it back down. Devlin questioned his behavior. Jeano calmly retrieved two new glasses and a fresh bottle. Austin opened the bottle and poured the glasses. Devlin glanced at Jeano. Jeano simply closed his eyes and waved his hand aside and Devlin needed no further explanation.

Their expressions softened, for there was much to learn from one another. They sat there, at first, drinking and making small talk. Soon they were talking and laughing like old friends.

"How long have you worked for Enrico?"

Devlin grinned, "More years than I can recall."

Austin told his side of the story, while Devlin listened intently. "I know Hannah fears Enrico. I sensed it the day she ran from him at the Pittsburgh airport and I vowed revenge."

Devlin noticed the anger and confusion in Austin's eyes and answered intuitively, "I was also present that confusing day; she did run from Enrico in fear of what we have yet to uncover."

Devlin realized that her fears and secrets were far greater then he imagined, for her own *husband* remained clueless.

Could it be possible? Could the enemy be someone other than Enrico? Austin felt uncertain if he could even trust Devlin at this point, but there was something so trusting and honest about his demeanor. "How will I recognize Enrico when I see him?"

Devlin smiled, somewhat coldly, "You will know when he enters a room, for everyone will rise and become silent." Devlin stood, "I must depart now, for I have matters to attend to."

Austin stretched his right hand across the table as far as he could and shook Devlin's hand, "You are a good man, Devlin. I only hope that you stand in my corner."

Devlin smiled, "I'll remember you said that," he said, as he shook Austin's hand and then walked out of the room.

Austin was not the man Devlin expected. Savannah did not tell him what she runs from. "He thinks it's me," Enrico said aloud. This makes Austin dangerous and he knew he must take caution for, if he allowed Austin to be hurt, Savannah would never forgive him. He'd soon discover the truth and Enrico nearly felt sorry for him. Austin was truly worthy of her love, but realizing that did not make it any easier. Austin, however, was the least of his worries. He quickly returned his thoughts to Savannah, for she still loved him after all these years. Enrico felt unbearable torment, unable to touch her and feel her heart beat against his. It made his loins ache. He walked upstairs and tapped upon her door. "Savannah, time for dinner." He knew the time had come for truth and honesty.

Two guards led Austin into the dining hall. Austin never saw a table so large before. It seated at least twenty-six. Twelve up each side and one on each end. Jeano's colleagues, from earlier, already seated themselves around the table, as Jeano assumed the far head of the table. Austin situated to Jeano's left. Other men came and took their seats until there were two reaming chairs—Reserved for Lord and Lady Costello. Austin unbuttoned a couple of buttons on his shirt, appearing to become more comfortable. He had a vengeance and justice would prevail. Then, it was announced.

"Lord and Lady Costello," the door attendant cried.

Everyone seated at the table rose and remained silent.

Simultaneously, Enrico and Hannah stepped into the room through separate doors. Austin leapt to his feet, for the man standing in the doorway was Devlin. Austin felt enraged, for Enrico had deceived him. He no longer concealed his 9mm Ruger now and pointed it directly at Enrico.

"No," Hannah cried, as she ran and stood between them.

Austin could not fathom why she protected Enrico like this and felt his heart skip a beat. Enrico grasped her arms and pushed her aside. Enrico and Austin stared one another down.

"Hannah, what is the meaning of this?" Austin demanded.

Hannah tried to think of something, anything to say, but no words came to her lips. She felt dizzy with a whirlwind of emotions that have been suppressed for far too long as her knees gave out and her vision grew dark. Hannah collapsed right where she stood. Austin lowered his weapon and six men instantly subdued him, seizing the gun.

Enrico ordered them to release him and the guards complied. Enrico looked at Austin and sympathetically said, "I am not the enemy here, surely you realize that now." Austin remained silent as Enrico gently picked up Hannah and said, "I am just a man in search of answers…like you." Enrico left the room, "Come, we will determine the underlying factors…together."

Austin and Jeano followed him upstairs. Enrico knelt by the bed, laid Savannah down, and gently slid his arms out from beneath her. He attended to the pillow and then brushed his fingers along her check. Austin seized his arm and forced Enrico to face him.

"You love her...don't you?" Austin demanded, truly not expecting an answer.

"I do...God help me, I do. I love her with all of my being," Enrico replied, with sincere honesty, but then added, "Alas, our souls are not destined; I know this now. All I can do is correct the past. That is why I brought you here, to help unleash her demons and then send you both home...together. This will all be but a distant dream."

Austin was not sure what to think but something in his gut believed Enrico's words.

Enrico seized Austin's arm, "We must draw our strength, for she will need us both."

Austin simply nodded.

Jeano knew it was time to come forward, but could not. Instead, he convened and devised a plan to help them uncover the truth on their own. He stepped forward and glanced back and fourth between them, "I've been doing some thinking. Savannah runs from you," he explained and looked directly at Enrico. Enrico made no comment but the look in his eyes told Jeano that he agreed. "I wonder where Savannah will run, now that she is here, if you needed to go away unexpectedly," Jeano said, hoping his words were understood.

Enrico connected the dots within his mind. "Brilliant."

Austin nodded. Neither lover wanted to deceive her like this; but there was no other choice, for they desired answers.

Hannah awoke to an empty room. Startled at first, but then relieved that all eyes were not upon her now. She needed to know what happened so she ran downstairs and found everyone in the great room. Austin sat upon the couch, next to Jeano, and Enrico stood by the door.

"I'm glad you decided to join us," Enrico exclaimed.

She glanced around the room with confused eyes.

"I fear I have some dire news, my Lady," Enrico stated, looking rather anguished, but the question she found lurking within his gaze was 'How are you feeling?'

Austin suddenly realized how much he hated Enrico calling Hannah, 'My Lady,' but if that was the extent of their relationship, he supposed he could overlook the little things.

"What dire news?"

Enrico nearly averted his eyes, for he hated to back her into a corner with nowhere to run. "I have business to attend over the next couple of days at the Castillo De Isla," he managed.

Hannah gasped.

Enrico nearly smiled as another lie came to his lips, "Don't worry, my Lady, for I have sent for my brother to watch over and protect you while I am away. He was more than happy to oblige."

"What," she cried, and then demanded, "When do you leave?"

"Within the hour."

"When is Antonio due in?" Hannah's mind became cluttered as she faltered.

Enrico stepped forward, fully aware that he never mentioned Antonio's name. He chose his words carefully, for it remained uncertain what that entailed and he could not push to far to quickly. Enrico wanted to embrace her and tell her he was not really leaving. "I have to leave now, my Lady," he whispered instead. He turned towards the front door.

"No, don't go!" she screamed, and ran into his arms and began kissing him.

Everyone gasped in surprise, including Enrico. Austin sat there in disbelief, as his world collapsed and the love of his life fondled another, merely out of force. *I would rather be tortured.* He hoped Enrico would remain a gentleman.

Enrico gently seized her arms and pushed her back a step, as tears streamed down her cheeks. "Where is this coming from, Savannah?" he demanded gently.

"Stay with me Enrico; please stay with me tonight," she hesitantly said, and then adding with a pretentious smile, "I'll make it worth your wile, My Lord." Enrico stared at her with confusion, love, and anger. He never knew he could feel so many different emotions all at once. He was well aware of Austin's presence in the room and yet, she seemed not to notice—or care. Enrico wiped a tear away as he embraced her affectionately. He stole a glance at Jeano and saw the truth deep within his eyes. Jeano knew more than he revealed. Enrico whispered, "Come my Lady, let's retreat to the Clover room," as they disembarked.

Jeano, understanding Enrico's intention, quickly left the great room to prepare. Enrico led Hannah out of the room, as she trembled in his arms. He motioned for Austin to follow. They walked down the hall, up a flight of stairs and down another hall. Hannah imagined how Austin must have felt, but his safety was far more important to her than his emotional state. She hoped, when this was all over, that he would understand and forgive her.

They walked into the Clover room. The carpet, walls, and ceiling were emerald green. It was completely empty, all but a single chair sat in the center of the room. Jeano already stood in the rear of the room. He stood with his back to them. Hannah noticed he carefully concealed what he was working on. He walked past Hannah and met Austin in the doorway. Jeano grabbed Austin's arm and instructed him to stay in the hallway for a few moments.

"I will motion for you when we are ready but you must, at any cost, remain silent."

Austin remained clueless as to the nature of the request but obeyed. He kept a watchful, yet distant, eye from the doorway.

Enrico now stood behind Hannah with his powerful hands upon her shoulders and forced her forwards. Hannah struggled, for it was too familiar and it frightened her. Enrico remained firm, even when she started screaming for him to release her. His eyes grew black with intent and he barely heard her.

"This is for your own good," he whispered, "Do not fight me."

That was the last straw. Hannah panicked and managed to break free from his grasp.

"No one here will hurt you, Savannah; please sit down. We just want to talk," Enrico nearly cried, remaining firm. He crossed his arms coldly over his broad chest, "We can do this the easy way or the hard way."

Hannah gasped. "You're no better than he is." She shouted fiercely.

Enrico stiffened as though she had struck him, for her accusing words stabbed at his heart. Enrico darted across the room. Startled distress turned into white-hot anger, for he was nothing like the man in question.

Austin watched in confusion, undecided whether or not to help Hannah or Enrico. Hannah managed to elude Enrico once more. She eyed up the doorway and bolted but, before she made it to safety, Austin blocked her escape. Hannah froze in her tracks; the shock of betrayal rendered her immobile. Enrico crept up behind her and picked her up, kicking and screaming, as he carried her to the chair. Jeano quickly restrained her legs with leg cuffs, while Enrico cuffed her left arm. She resisted with every ounce of her being but they finally subdued her.

Hannah stared at Enrico with jaded blue eyes, "I will never forgive you for this…you promised," she cried, as a glazed look of desperation swept across her face in an overwhelming attempt to attain freedom. Hannah felt betrayed, for Enrico broke a sacred vow.

Enrico wanted to apologize and comfort her, but he could not and felt his heart shatter. Jeano took out a syringe as Enrico rolled up her sleeve and kissed her hand. Jeano placed a band around her arm, as Hannah glared at

Enrico with contempt. Enrico suddenly felt guilt and shame in her presence and quickly joined Austin in the hallway.

Jeano looked into Hannah's eyes. "This will burn if you don't relax your arm."

Hannah immediately quit struggling and tried to relax. "Why?" she whispered, as Jeano inserted the needle into her arm.

"Just relax," he whispered, "It will all be over soon."

"Don't do this Jeano."

He saw how fragile and vulnerable she looked as she pleaded to him with those big blue eyes. He tilted his brow, looked at her suspiciously and whispered, "Hannah, I know the truth about Antonio; Enrico can handle it."

Hannah stared at Jeano and dampened her lips. "There's more to it than that." She instantly relaxed and began to feel weary.

Jeano knew it was now time to begin. He motioned Enrico to stand by. Jeano began to speak to Hannah in a slow and soothing tone. His words spoke to her soul and his voice lured her into a deeper disposition. Jeano possessed a special gift. One passed down from generation upon generation. Jeano inherited this gift from his father, Devlin Martinez, and he from his father. Jeano had no son, and so, the gift would die with him. This knowledge remained a secret anguish Jeano carried alone. He tried to teach Enrico once, with no prevail.

"Hannah, listen to my voice. No one else is present. It's just you and I and the sound of my voice is all that you hear. Clear your mind of all thoughts and visions. You and I are completely alone. As I count to ten, you will close your eyes."

Jeano counted to ten and Hannah closed her eyes. She felt herself drifting away and no longer felt at the mercy of another. She finally felt serenity.

"Imagine that you are seated on a front porch swing overlooking the ocean, watching the waves approaching the shoreline, one after another. The cool sultry breeze blows through your hair. Life is peaceful, calm and tranquil." Jeano motioned for Enrico.

Enrico quietly entered the room and stood directly behind her.

"When you feel my hands upon your shoulders you will remain calm and silent. The touch of my hands will break into the deepest pit of your soul and eliminate all mental barriers."

Enrico reached down and rested his hands upon her shoulders. She remained still and silent. Jeano's soothing voice probed deeper into her soul.

"I am going to ask you a series of questions and I want you to answer in single words only. Let us begin. Hannah, I want you to picture Enrico in your mind. What two words come to mind?"

Hannah remained silent for a few moments and then replied, "Love and Betrayal."

Jeano knew he could show no emotions in his voice no matter what. He met Enrico's gaze and found it wide with intent and continued, "Love from whom?"

"Myself."

"Betrayal from whom?"

Hannah remained silent. Enrico felt her tremble beneath his powerful, yet gentle, hands. He flashed Jeano an insipid look and shook his head. Hannah was clearly not ready to answer this question, yet.

Jeano moved on, "I want you to picture Austin in your mind. What two words come to mind?"

"Love and Death."

"Love from whom?"

"Myself."

"Death from whom?"

Again, Hannah remained silent.

"I want you to think about Enrico leaving you in the company of another. What two words come to mind?"

Hannah remained silent as this question invoked anguish. "Pain and Fear," she managed, with a cold undertone.

Enrico felt her discomfort as she spoke and briefly tightened his grip to offer reassurance.

"Pain for whom?"

"Myself."

"Fear from whom?" he asked slowly, unsure she was capable of answering the question.

She made a fist with both hands and Enrico felt her body tense. "Antonio," she whispered.

That was all Enrico needed to know and he removed his hands to release her but as soon as he no longer had contact, Hannah slipped into a deep sleep. Enrico was enraged by this dark revelation. He now had a vendetta against Antonio as he carried Savannah to his room. Enrico needed to be alone with her, but he would not deny Austin the right to know the truth either. Jeano led Austin to the next room and removed the curtains from a large mirror. Austin could see and hear into Enrico's room but they could not see or hear him.

Enrico laid Hannah down and dimmed the lights. He loomed in the darkness and waited for her to regain consciousness.

His mind scrambled with bits and pieces of information. "Why did you run from me, I possess the power to end this nightmare," he whispered. Then the answer came rushing into his mind. *Antonio threatened the people she loves...including her family, Austin and even myself.* "Damn Antonio to hell," Enrico cursed tersely. He had been betrayed in the gravest way by his own flesh-and-blood. Enrico remained in the shadows, thinking of calculating ways to make Antonio pay dearly, and refused to allow history to repeat itself.

Antonio's life hung in the balance, out weighed by honor and duty. Enrico reeled from his thoughts when Savannah began to toss and turn. "A nightmare," he whispered, and then clenched his fists in anger. *What did he do to you during those two weeks?* He recalled back to when he spent Christmas day at the Brockwell home and how Kayla remarked that it was so chaotic that she did not see Hannah those two weeks. Enrico felt trapped in his worst nightmare and somehow it managed to get worse. He knew that Savannah no longer belonged to him, for she would never see past Antonio in his eyes. He knew that he and his brother shared similar features and grimaced at the thought.

Hannah dreamt that Antonio hunted her like a wild animal. He merely wanted to display his trophy for all to see. She ran as fast as she could. He managed to cut her off and continued to pounce in front of her. He grabbed her and she could not escape his grasp. Her mind echoed, 'We can do this the easy way or the hard way.' She started to scream within her mind and realized she was sitting on a bed, in a dark room, screaming for her life.

Enrico raced to her side and embraced her, but she began to fight him.

"Get away, don't touch me!" she screamed, as tears trickled down her pale cheeks.

Enrico felt helpless when she became hysterical. He embraced her and repeatedly whispered, "It's me Savannah...it's Enrico."

She calmed down, returned his embrace and whispered, "Thank God."

They held each other for what felt like an eternity. Neither one wanted to see disappointment and regret in the others eyes, for Hannah concealed the truth and Enrico was blindsided by Antonio's tactics.

"I will make this right," Enrico managed.

"He'll kill you both if he finds out about the confession."

"I will never fear my brother."

"NO," she screamed, as she released him, and then added, "He must never find out!"

"I can handle my *Brother*," he quickly returned.

"Can you assure the safety of my husband and my innocent daughters," she demanded.

He closed his eyes, for he could not.

She read his facial expression, placed a hand upon his arm and said, "Then he will never know about this Enrico. Promise me!"

Enrico could not promise her, for Antonio would pay dearly for his betrayal.

Austin watched in dismay. All these years he thought it had been Enrico. She protected her loved ones by carrying this pain and fear alone.

Austin bowed his head. *That must be why she never wanted to be spontaneous, for fear that Antonio lurked around every corner.* He felt her pain and sorrow but most of all, he felt helpless and alone. He knew there was nothing he could say or do to calm her fears. He wanted to help her get revenge, retribution, and closure so they could continue with their lives—a life without Antonio and Enrico lurking in the shadows. He wondered now, as he watched Enrico give attention to her every need, if he would ever stop pressuring her. Austin would never step aside, nor did he condone Enrico's constant habit of stepping in to be the hero. Austin wanted to be that hero, just once. He knew his time was coming but for now, Hannah needed Enrico's love, sympathy, and most of all, his protection. He watched as the love of his life embraced another.

Enrico looked into Savannah's eyes. Hannah turned away and closed her eyes, for she did not like the questions that lurked behind his emerald gaze. He leaned towards her, gently clasped his strong fingers over her trembling chin and forced her to meet his gaze. "Savannah," he whispered, "I must know everything."

Hannah reluctantly nodded as Enrico held her gaze.

"I will ask you a question and simply nod if the answer is yes." Enrico began to speak slowly and clearly, as his emerald eyes never left her baby blue eyes for a single moment. "Did Antonio orchestrate the photo shoot?"

Hannah nodded in dismay.

"Did he recognize the Ring of Eternity?"
She nodded gloomily.
"Did he identify himself?"
She nodded again, as unspoken fear grew and festered within his eyes.
"Did he cause you physical pain?"
Again, she nodded.

A cold shadow dimmed his facial expression now. Enrico raged like a mighty torrent as his blood reached its boiling point when he asked the final question. "Did Antonio take you to his bed, more than once?"

Hannah closed her eyes and the last nod rendered him speechless.

Enrico leapt to his feet and paced the floor quickly with unresponsive eyes. He needed to think, but all that came to mind was Antonio thrusting into her soul. The image cut through his heart and nearly collapsed him to his knees. He looked at Hannah and noticed she was sound asleep. He needed to discuss his plan of action with Austin. Enrico illuminated the room so she would not awaken in fear again. He then covered her up gently and kissed her brow, as he whispered, "I love you, Savannah." He left the room and locked the door. He alone held the key.

Enrico raced into the next room and met Austin's blackened gaze. "Antonio must die!" Austin stated with clenched fists.

Enrico agreed but, out of respect for Hannah's fears, they needed to seek revenge without Antonio discovering the truth about her confessions. Austin stared at Hannah through the mirror now. He spoke to Enrico in a low tone.

"Send for Antonio and the truth will reveal itself, with all of us under the same roof. We will see that she isn't out of our sights for a second."

"Never," Enrico returned, and then added, "I will not put her through that. You saw her...she became hysterical with the thought of his arrival."

Austin shook his head, "I don't like it any more than you do, but she needs to confront her fears," he said, and then added coldly, "Antonio had all the power, so let's turn the tables! My Hannah is a strong and resourceful woman."

Enrico contemplated, "Let it be so...against my better judgment." Enrico looked at Austin, "If she needs me, I will not hesitate," he stated honestly.

"I'm counting on that!"

Enrico and Austin made all the arrangements. Jeano remained skeptical telling Enrico to send them home now before more harm can be done and then seek revenge against Antonio. Enrico could not do it, for he knew Savannah needed closure—Austin was right about that. Their dream, which turned into a nightmare, was not over yet. Jeano abided and Enrico reluctantly unlocked Savannah's door.

Chapter 20
Unforeseen Deception

Hannah became restless but she did not dream about Antonio this time. She now felt conflicted between two men. One loved her for who she has always been while the other loved her for the person she always dreamt of becoming and her heart ached. She loved them both but felt a special connection to one—The once-in-a-lifetime connection many seek but rarely find. In her heart, Hannah knew which man she wanted to be with and he'd love her forever. She made her choice and both heart and mind fully accepted the truth. Hannah drifted awake to a knock upon the door. It was one of the servants, Maria.

"Breakfast will be served in an hour, my Lady."

Hannah showered and dressed casual. She walked downstairs, unsure if she could eat anything. She walked into the dinning hall and found Austin and Enrico already seated with their breakfast. She sat down as Maria served her. Hannah thanked Maria politely. "It looks wonderful, thank you."

Maria smiled warmly and then walked away.

Enrico's heart pounded fiercely, for it would not be long now. He hoped that she had enough time to finish her meal. Enrico realized how little Savannah ate since her arrival and knew she would need her strength. Then, without warning, Antonio walked into the room and stood directly behind Hannah.

"Enrico, what a pleasant surprise; I am so glad you sent for me but why the urgency?"

Hannah stared directly ahead refusing to turn around, for she recognized the voice.

Enrico did his best to speak pleasantly and said, "Dear brother, I am in a predicament. I must go out of town tomorrow and as you can see, I am entertaining guests."

Antonio waved his hand aside, "I would be glad to entertain in your absence." He spoke openly to the room but gazed in Austin's direction.

Hannah could not believe her ears and now wondered if she dreamt the entire confession.

"Please, sit down and join us for breakfast," Enrico managed.

Antonio sat down and Maria immediately brought another plate. Antonio glanced at Austin as curiosity invoked his thoughts.

"Where are your manners Enrico? Introduce me to our guests."

Enrico flashed a twisted smile. "This is my new colleague Austin Desmin and this is the beautiful Lady Savannah Costello."

Hannah had to force her brow and managed a tremulous smile. Antonio was in total shock and yet, seemed pleased.

"It is a pleasure to finally meet you, my Lady," he murmured, with a conflicted smile. Antonio was pleased, for it had been ten years and she still invoked a rise within his loins. It was all Enrico and Austin could do to control their emotions. Hannah also masked her inner turmoil with a deceptive calmness.

Hannah vowed to show no fear and reveal no true emotions. She drew in a deep breath and forbade herself to panic. After seeing him, she felt like the weight of the world lifted from her shoulders. All her fears nearly vanished. She now had a new agenda. She wished to make Antonio squirm like the serpent he is. Suddenly, an icy contempt sparkled within her eyes that spoke defiance. "Antonio, you look oddly familiar to me. Have we met?" she asked boldly, with a cold loathing grin.

Antonio's smile, as he averted his eyes, quickly faded. "No, my Lady!"

Extreme satisfaction rushed through her when he danced around her words and briefly averted his darkened gaze.

Enrico watched and listened as Savannah became audacious while Antonio squirmed with each question. He leaned back in his chair dumbfounded by her newfound inner strength. He had no idea what transpired the sudden change, but marveled at it.

Hannah now had the upper hand and she dished out more. She seized the opportunity at hand. Hannah rose, as if by a force, and walked behind Enrico as she wrapped her arms around his neck. Every rhythmic move of her body spoke defiance. She nestled tightly against Enrico and tilted her chin, "Baby,

I need a moment alone with our new host. I have a surprise in store for you and I need Antonio's help," she ordered, with the voice of authority.

Enrico's eyes darkened dangerously with disapproval as he hesitantly stood and walked towards the door. He stopped suddenly and slowly turned in a half circle luring her in with a finger jester, and said, "A kiss before I depart, my Lady."

Hannah walked over and Enrico took her face into his protective hands and drew her close, sheltering her from Antonio's gaze, as he whispered, "I'll be in the hallway if you need me." He then kissed her cheek and motioned for Austin. The two men left the room hesitantly as Hannah closed the door behind them, offering them no choice in the matter.

Hannah turned to find Antonio directly in front of her. This would have startled the old Hannah, but she embraced this new transformation and held no fears. Hannah remained stoical in the face of danger. She moved closer until she left him no room at all. "You ever touch me again and I will kill you!"

Antonio twisted his lips cynically and smiled. "I love a good challenge...you run and I'll chase!"

Hannah's glare turned cold as ice. "I'm through running and I'm done hiding. It's ends here and now," she demanded, and then turned to walk away.

Antonio grabbed her delicate wrist, pulled her close against his chest and restrained her. To her, he was still just as strong and powerful as ever. He caressed her long slender neck with his moist lips and whispered, "When my brother leaves, you will be mine once again. I promise you that."

She detected a trace of warning in his demeanor. With that said, he released her. His words sounded tense and meaningless, like those used by superficial men. "When Enrico leaves, I will be forced to kill you then," she remarked forcefully.

"So, what is this surprise you're planning?"

"I don't know. I'm sure you will think of something," she stated, and then walked out of the room.

Enrico brushed her arm as she passed through the door. "I'll be with Austin," she whispered. Hannah left feeling the need to be alone.

She wandered down a long corridor and ascended the stairwell. It was smaller then previous ones she encountered and assumed it was the servant stairwell. Hannah's mind raced frantically. *Had I just threatened Antonio?* She smiled deviously, for she was no longer afraid of the man that inflicted so much oppression unto her. She felt strength and courage as she took the matters into her own hands. Hannah finally realized that she did not need the protection of a man, for she actually remained their protector. Hannah felt her senses awaken, but secretly wondered if she were being naive. She quickly dismissed that thought for, once if her life, she laughed at the face of danger and embraced self-deliverance.

The ring upon her finger slipped to the side. The emerald now rested against her little finger. Hannah gasped. She could not fathom the meaning. She quickly went to investigate, but hesitated. Hannah was not ready to say goodbye to Enrico, for there was still unfinished business to attend to. She could not grasp how or why she felt this way, but a voice deep within her soul told her that Enrico needed her. Hannah continued walking with a heavy heart, for there were still so many unanswered questions.

Antonio contemplated her idle threats. *Had she just asked me... informally...to play the childish game of tag?* He never cared much for the game as a child. Enrico always won and if Antonio did win, it was due to cheating. The game always bored him but then, there was never a beautiful woman awaiting him in the end. He smiled to himself. "Let the games begin." Antonio suddenly, unexpectedly, felt eyes upon him and reeled around. Enrico loomed in the doorway with crossed arms.

"What game would that be?" Enrico questioned. Enrico knew Antonio made the phone calls to Savannah all those years ago. Moreover, it was Antonio who tormented him with false visions, attempted to abduct Savannah the night they stayed in the hotel, and dressed as the thief in the night on Hallows Eve—attempting to steal his prize possession. His thoughts were in disarray.

"Just your surprise from the beautiful Lady Costello," Antonio replied.

Enrico's gaze became transparent. Antonio thought he could see straight through him.

"What troubles you brother?" Antonio asked, searching for answers.

"What do you think of my lovely Savannah?"

Antonio thought for a moment and answered, "I think her a great prize to be won. I can see why you wish to keep her around."

"And all to myself," Enrico added quickly.

The longer Enrico spoke to Antonio, the more enraged he became. His own flesh-and-blood had betrayed him and showed no remorse. *He actually has the audacity to say, 'I think her a great prize to be won.'* Enrico knew Antonio already helped himself to his prize possession, his Savannah. His skin began to crawl. He could not think of anything but vengeance. It completely consumed him now. He wished Antonio to suffer, as Savannah has suffered.

"When do you leave?"

"Midnight."

Antonio studied Enrico carefully. In his mind, he questioned Enrico's mood, actions and tone. *Perhaps Enrico is putting two-and-two together.* He'd have to plan his surprise now to have it ready by midnight. "Always a pleasure brother, but I must attend to some unfinished business," Antonio stated, and then left the room.

Enrico slammed the door after a few moments. He needed to know what Savannah and Antonio discussed alone in private and what unfinished business Antonio had to attend to. Jeano opened the door just as Enrico slammed his fist against the wall.

"My Lord!" Jeano cried.

Enrico flashed him an annoyed look and said, "I wish to be alone." Jeano immediately went to leave the room but Enrico stopped him abruptly, for there was much to discuss.

Antonio ventured upstairs, dialed a colleague and made arrangements of his own. He needed to remove Austin from the picture. An idea emerged, as he hung up the phone. He refused to underestimate Austin, for Enrico introduced him as a colleague and Antonio could not fathom why. Antonio felt certain his plan worked effectively. "Surely Austin thought those phone calls were from Enrico." He pondered over the idea for a while when the sound of footsteps echoed in the hallway. He quickly stood to investigate. It was Savannah and she appeared lost. Antonio grabbed a wooden box from his bureau, for he had a gift for the Lady Costello. He silently crept into the hall and stood with his back to the wall, waiting for her to turn the corner.

Hannah became completely agitated. She never did have a good sense of direction and could not fathom where the servant stairs were. Hannah suddenly wished she did not tell Enrico she'd be with Austin. *Perhaps it's on the other end of the corridor.* She began to walk and made the right turn. Hannah instantly felt hands upon her arms and around her waist. Then, before she knew what was happening, Antonio clasped two gold bracelets, outlined with tiny red roses, around her wrists. Hannah gasped, understanding their meaning.

"Some insurance, My Lady."

"Remove these now!"

Antonio forced her into his bedchamber and closed the door. He backed her up against the wall until they were chest-to-chest. His hips thrust against hers as he placed a knee between her thighs and laced his fingers around hers, forcing her hands high above her head.

Hannah felt completely vulnerable within his hands. Antonio had her right where he wanted her, in every sense. He explained what he expected from her, how she should act and what she should say. Hannah became infuriated.

"Never! I will never submit to you ever again."

"You adorn my bracelets upon your wrists, my Dear." Antonio reminded her that she wore his bracelets and explained that he also sent one to each of her daughters and if he had to activate hers, it would activate theirs as well.

Hannah gasped at this. "How can you be so cruel?"

"My Lady, only you have the power to protect them."

Hannah was in disbelief, for she had no choice. Without hesitation, she agreed and felt his mouth over hers. He gave her explicit directions that she must follow to the letter, or let her children face Antonio's wrath. Just like that, he released her.

Hannah left the room rather emotional. She knew she must keep it together. This ploy would crush all those involved. Hannah loved no other person more than the two little lives she gave birth to, and her heart ached. Her daughters meant the world to her. Hannah would sacrifice Austin and Enrico's feelings and even her own body for her children. She looked down at the shackles upon her wrists and the one on her finger and now knew what a cunning fox feels like caught in a foot trap.

Regardless of how sly the fox, it still manages to fall prey to the trapper. She felt vulnerable, trapped and alone. Like the fox, she could not even fight back and felt like giving up. Fox were trapped for their pelts and Hannah could not think of a single reason why she had been entrapped. Neither man forced her into marriage, but both claimed her for his own.

None of this made sense to her. If it were merely a power struggle between brothers, she hoped it would end soon. She was not something that could be toyed with whenever a man felt the urge. Hannah hated the situation at hand. She thought back and wondered why she was so taken by the stranger in the black Corvette. *If I had remained coy than no one would be here now...twelve years later.*

Their encounter still haunted her dreams. Enrico intrigued her, but Hannah felt like she overlooked something but could not place her finger upon it. She reeled herself back to reality saying, "Snap out of it Hannah, none of that matters now…what's done is done." Hannah refused to give it another thought, for she needed to focus on the present. She felt determined to get her family out of this mess and permanently remove Antonio from the picture.

Antonio was quite pleased with himself, still in his room. He made plans and arrangements. He could not wait to place his mouth on her warm firm breast and suckle her nipple, once again. He was going to take her to his bed and, this time, he would hold nothing back. She had transformed from a young, beautiful and naive girl, into a gorgeous, exquisite and seductive woman.

He would shock the palace with his rebellious antics and eliminate Enrico and Austin once-and-for-all. He would take the Lady Costello to his bed, while Enrico watched. Antonio has mastered patience and the art of pleasuring a woman. He knew exactly where to caress a woman's bodice and how to entice her soul. He ventures slow, feeling everywhere and lingering in certain places, but not to long.

He drove the women of his world delirious, most belonging to other men, lords and commoners. No woman has ever been off limits to Antonio—especially the unattainable Lady Costello. No woman has ever resisted his savory charm, his handsome appearance and his sweet seductions. "No one, except for Savannah, that is," Antonio whispered and then grimaced. He vowed to win her over completely and she was already under his control. The rest would come at midnight. He ordered the servants to fully stock the cantina and have it ready by eight o'clock. The rest was up to him.

Enrico had a horribly strange feeling in his gut all afternoon, for Savannah behaved strangely. She did not fear Antonio as she had before his arrival. He commended her courage but did not understand it. He knew Austin was just as confused as he was. *Antonio is up to something, but what?* Just then, Savannah entered the room.

"You called for me, my Lord."

Enrico saw beyond her eyes and felt that something troubled her. He walked over, took her hands and stood dead in his tracks. He noticed the gold bracelets that now adorned her wrists. "Where did you get those?"

Hannah thought for a moment and knew she had no other choice than to lie. "Austin gave them to me as a Christmas present a few years back," she replied.

Enrico accepted her explanation, led her to the sofa and sat her down.

"I'm glad you called for me Enrico. I have something to discuss with you."

Enrico remained silent and listened curiously, as Hannah explained they would have some drinks in the cantina.

"I sure could go for a drink right about now," she whispered.

He stared at her attentively, as though he were reading the cover of a book he was about to open, and remained silent. His silence sent a chill down her spine.

"Enrico, please say something," she finally managed.

Enrico said nothing for a moment and then rather grotesquely said, "You wish for me to sit down and have a drink with my *Brother*."

Hannah, knowing this was not going well, snapped back, "You expected me to have breakfast with him this morning."

Enrico closed his eyes. "I had no choice," he whispered.

"Well, I have no choice either," she cried.

He immediately stood and dropped to his knees and placed his hands upon her waist. "What do you mean by that?" he asked, growing concerned.

She put her hands on his shoulders, "It's nothing."

"This is clearly not nothing," he whispered, trying hard to control his anger.

She knew he was in turmoil and could not fathom why she wanted them to drink and have a good time. *Oh God; if he is this upset now…how will he react tonight?* She now dreaded the evening even more than before. She hated to see Enrico this way and her body trembled.

Enrico felt her tremble in his hands. "Tell me what is going on? Did Antonio force you into this? I swear to God, if he put his hands on you in any way today. Savannah, you must tell me…now!" he said, with dangerously darkened eyes.

Hannah looked down at the floor. Enrico knew what that meant, for she did not wish to answer. Her eyes always gave her away. "I want you and Austin to leave me. I'll be fine… just leave it at that," she nearly demanded.

Enrico closed his eyes and shook his head. "I can not and will not abandon you."

"Please Enrico," she pleaded, "I can't put you through this; I've caused you enough pain."

For a moment, he was at a loss for words, "Antonio caused that, not you," he managed. Hannah stood to leave, knowing she could say nothing more. He blocked the doorway, "I don't think you should be alone," he stated.

She gazed into his eyes, "Know this; if I need you, I will come to you," she whispered, in an attempt to reassure him.

There was no doubt about it; tonight was going to be hell on them both.

"Then I shall stay with you until you ask and, Savannah, I will not hesitate," he whispered. He took her hands and slid a finger over one of the bracelets, "Austin has good taste."

If only Enrico knew the truth. Her biggest fear was that Enrico would think less of her when he learns the truth, and wonder why she did not confide in him. Hannah leaned in and kissed his lips; they felt warm and soft. For the first time in a long time, she longed for his touch. She no longer trusted herself alone in her presence, "I do not trust myself with you Enrico; please let me leave, for Austin's sake."

Hannah departed as Enrico watched helplessly.

Hannah retreated to her room, hoping Enrico and Austin would not question her further about the bracelets. Her mind-sought solitude, while her heart desired company but uncertain from whom. She wondered why love had to be so complicated. A knock upon the door reeled her from her thoughts, "Enter," she cried, without thinking. Hannah quickly sized up the door as Enrico entered. She let out a sigh of relief.

Hannah met his emerald gaze, "I'm glad you came, for I have something to tell you," she whispered, realizing she could not take Antonio's blackmail any longer. Hannah finally realized she needed help. Enrico crossed the room and sat down beside her. He continued to hold her gaze with sympathetic eyes. Random thoughts cluttered her mind and she did not know where to begin. Enrico took her into his massive arms and caressed her cheek with his chin. Hannah could feel his warm breath upon her. She realized he did not wish to discuss the matters at hand. She let out a whimper and nearly caved before his unspoken proposal.

"Enrico, we can't," she whispered.

He tightened his grip upon her, forcing her to stand. Enrico held her face in his hands, "You would not deny your lordship this simple pleasure... would you?"

Hannah closed her eyes as Enrico unbuttoned her blouse and exposed her bare shoulders. He spun her around, pressed her back against his bare firm chest, rested her head upon his shoulder and began to kiss her neck. "We mustn't," she continued to whisper. Hannah sensed a difference within him. She could not begin to describe the intense emotions that overwhelmed her. Her heart beat wildly as she wriggled free from his embrace. Hannah took a step back and gazed at him questionably, for Enrico did not intend to take no for an answer. She could not fathom his behavior and she wanted him to leave.

Enrico saw confusion within her gaze, for she clearly did not trust him. He wondered how she could possibly sense the deception. Rage instantly coursed through his veins. She saw through his manipulative tactics and he suddenly felt defeated. Enrico removed a small black box from his pouch and opened it quickly. He motioned for her, but Hannah held her stance. Enrico lunged forwards as Hannah attempted to bolt, with no prevail. He picked her up, tossed her upon the bed and quickly straddled her. He restrained her wrists high above her head. Hannah attempted to release herself vigilantly.

"What has come over you?" she screamed.

Enrico did not answer as he removed a syringe and inserted the needle into her thigh. She cried out, but it was too late. Within seconds, she began to feel drowsy.

"What did you do?" she managed to ask before closing her eyes.

Enrico smiled, completely pleased with himself. He knew it was only a matter of time before his plan was complete. He quickly disrobed her and positioned her upon the bed.

Enrico now had a million thoughts running through is head. He departed to seek out Austin. He found Austin downstairs in the cantina having a beer. "Need a drink?" he asked questionably.

Austin looked up over his bottle and said, "Yeah."

"Mind if I join you?"

Austin shrugged and Enrico sat down. The bartender immediately brought Enrico a mescal, for he knew this was Enrico's preferred drink. They sat in silence for some time, before Enrico broke the silence.

"Where did you get those bracelets, they truly are unique?"

"What bracelets?"

Enrico's eyes widened, "The ones that Savannah...I mean Hannah wears," he stated.

Austin stared at Enrico; "Hannah told me that you gave them to her this morning." Austin read Enrico's eyes and knew that Hannah fabricated her statements. Both men took another drink and exchanged a look. Simultaneously, they stood and said, "We must find her—now." They left the room together and ran towards Hannah's bedchamber. Enrico stood outside the door, knocked twice and shouted her name. "Savannah…Unlock the door!"

Enrico charged through the door when she did not respond. Enrico and Austin stood motionless just inside the room. They stared at her with blackened eyes. Hannah sat up, wiped the sleep from her eyes and focused on Enrico standing before her. Hannah's head pounded with an unexplainable pain. Her eyes widened and she leapt from the bed, wrapping a sheet around her bodice. Antonio smiled at her disturbingly.

"You are full of surprises, my Lady."

"No," Hannah screamed and wondered how she could be so blind. Antonio deceived her in the worst imaginable way and she felt incapable of proving her innocence.

Enrico and Austin cursed Antonio as Hannah stole all the attention. Austin could not move. A million questions coursed through his mind but he found no answers. Austin opened his mouth to speak, but no words came to his quivering lips. Nothing made sense to him now. He needed a stiff drink. Austin wanted to drown his sorrows. Never in a million years did he imagine their love would end like this. He stumbled back downstairs knowing Savannah deceived him, for Hannah would never betray their love like this. He found refuge in the cantina.

Enrico stared at her intently with piercing eyes. Hannah attempted to run into his arms, but Enrico pushed her away as tears streamed down her cheeks.

"Enrico let me explain."

He closed his eyes as vivid images of Hannah giving herself to Antonio filled his mind. He recalled the dreadful night at the cemetery. He now witnessed, with his own eyes, the callous truth behind the visions—the same visions that haunted the depths of his soul all these years. He managed to shelter his heart from those visions and Hannah's photos. *Oh God, the photos!* He now believed that Hannah peered at Antonio seductively. *Pictures do not lie!* Nevertheless, the photos did not explain the bruises upon her. He wondered if it were the classic love-went-bad scenario and his heart shattered.

"There is nothing left to explain," he demanded. His tone became violently harsh. "Perhaps you should clothe yourself, my Lady, for I will deal with you later." Enrico quickly returned his attention to Antonio. He'd pay for seducing her like this. Enrico knew in his heart that Hannah deceived him, for his Savannah would never follow through with such a malicious act—she would never betray him like this. He searched the room, but Antonio was nowhere in sight.

"Nothing is as it seems, Enrico...Please don't leave!" Hannah grasped his arm in one last attempt to make him understand.

Enrico shook free from her embrace. "Antonio is a coward," he whispered, as he walked away and never glanced back.

Hannah remained in the room—alone. Little-by-little, she put the pieces of the puzzle together as her world turned upside down. Hannah knew, without a shadow of doubt, she did nothing wrong. *How can I convince them?* Neither Austin nor Enrico would ever forgive her. Every ounce of her soul told her that Antonio did not make love to her. She dressed quickly feeling unsheltered from new horror.

"Looks can be deceiving, my Lady."

Hannah jumped and reeled around to meet Antonio's pleased expression. He grasped her arm.

"Come my Lady; my plan is in motion and now let us finish this...once-and-for-all."

Hannah followed as Antonio led. She went peacefully hoping true love would prevail and uncover the truth.

Enrico searched the palace with no prevail, for Antonio was nowhere to be found. He ventured into the cantina and unexpectedly found Austin there. Austin handed him a mescal. They exchanged a glance, but neither lover uttered a word. They both felt that she deceived them in the worst imaginable way. Both wondered where they would go from here. Savannah was not the woman Enrico thought she was. They stood and listened to the sound of approaching footsteps. Enrico was a bit surprised to see Antonio enter with Savannah by his side. Neither lover raced to her rescue, for she appeared to follow in her own free will.

"The great Lady Costello would like a drink," Antonio announced, as he coaxed Hannah into the room. A sensual beat began in play in the background and everyone reluctantly sat back down.

Enrico immediately jumped back to his feet and announced, "I will retire to my room for the rest of the night." He extended his hand to Savannah, "I expect you to join me, My Lady," he demanded.

Hannah watched helplessly as Antonio reached for his watch and quickly replied, "No, I wish to remain here."

Enrico stood in front of her with disgust upon his face and sat back down. Antonio lit a cigarette and laid the pack upon the table. Hannah instantly seized the pack and lit one. She hated cigarettes, but this was a way to let Enrico know that she needed him. She attempted to speak to his soul, but he quickly slammed the door in her face and despair filled her heart.

Their private conversations ceased to exist. Hannah felt another piece of Savannah die at that very moment. Hannah wondered why Enrico could not see past the deception and wondered where his heart truly lied.

"Hannah, you don't smoke," Austin questioned.

"Looks can be deceiving," she whispered, in a condescending collective tone. Hannah attempted to speak to Austin's heart and found the door wide open. "I'm innocent," she conveyed, without ever saying a word. Austin's facial expression conveyed that he understood and Hannah felt a shred of hope.

Antonio stood up, extended his hand to Hannah and whispered, "Dance with me, My Lady!"

Hannah took his hand and felt another piece of herself die. Antonio smiled coldly as she rose and followed him to the dance floor.

Enrico jumped to his feet, "Lady Costello will dance with no man other then myself!"

Antonio gripped her wrists, spun her back to his chest and placed a hand upon her neck. Enrico lunged forwards as two of Antonio's colleagues entered the room. Enrico hesitated, for he did not recognize them.

"Careful Brother," Antonio hissed, as he revealed a small dagger. The dagger bore an engraving of a serpent upon the ivory handle and Enrico recognized it instantly. "Shall we go for two and two, Brother," Antonio threatened, as the dagger blade rested upon Hannah's neck.

Enrico read Antonio's eyes, saw this was not a random threat and stood down immediately. Austin stood as Antonio nodded, giving his colleagues a direct order. Hannah attempted to free herself from Antonio's grip, but it was useless. Austin and Enrico were subdued, shackled and chained to the wall like animals.

"The more you resist, the more Savannah will endure," Antonio informed them.

Enrico ran the end of his chains and screamed, "This is an outrage Antonio. Release me and let us finish this like men."

"All in due time, Brother." Antonio smiled, quite pleased with himself and directed his gaze to Savannah. "I have a proposal for you, my Lady." Antonio then removed her bracelets and released her altogether.

Hannah immediately backed away from him.

"Let us play a game of chance, my Lady."

Hannah stumbled to the table and fumbled for a cigarette, for her nerves could not bear any further stress. She wondered what game Antonio proposed but refused to ask, for she feared his reply. Enrico remained silent searching for a means to escape. He watched helplessly as Savannah searched the table for a lighter and found none. Antonio came up behind her and held out a flame. Hannah threw the cigarette down, for she refused to give him the satisfaction.

Enrico remained silent and watched their every move, feeling certain something critical escaped his keen eyes. His anger softened and every urge to protect her returned to him now, for he still loved her. His Savannah did not behave like Antonio's lover. Enrico instantly realized that he overlooked Antonio's diabolical scheme. All qualms he reserved against Savannah instantly vanished, for every single action reminded him that she feared Antonio in every way. He wondered if he helped seal her fate.

Antonio smiled and crossed his arms, for his patience knew no bounds. He wanted and needed her to ask, so he remained silent until she did. As he stood there starring upon her seductively, all she heard in her mind was, 'We can do this the easy way or the hard way,' and she shuddered. She could not bear to look at Enrico or Austin now. She knew they stared at her because she felt their eyes upon her. Hannah thought to be clever now and looked at Antonio, relaxed her body and chose a stance that spoke defiance, "What's the alternative?" Hannah thought about racing into Enrico's arms but she did not wish to invoke Antonio any further and cause Austin undue pain.

Antonio smiled even harder, "Do you really want to know the alternative, my Lady, because I prefer it?"

Hannah gasped, expecting a different response.

She could not take it any longer, "What's the challenge?" she cried.

Antonio could not have been more pleased, "The game, my Lady, is simple. If you can elude me for one hour, I will release your lovers and renounce victory."

"And if I can't?"

"Do you have to ask, my Lady? I'm offering you a sporting chance."

Hannah suddenly felt like the fox again, only a pelt was not to be had, for Antonio desired her flesh. She felt dizzy and weak now. If she refused, he would have her now; but if she played, it would buy her another hour. "And if I refuse?" she asked hesitantly.

Antonio merely shook his head.

"What are the rules?"

"The entire palace is fair play and the game is over when you can no longer run. I will pull no punches with you, Savannah...I need you and my body desires you in everyway." He moved towards her as she backed away. "To make it fair I will give you a twenty minute head start...beginning now." Antonio set the timer on his watch. Hannah glanced at Enrico and raced out of the room, as she became the hunted and Antonio the hunter.

Antonio felt amused. He pressed more buttons on his watch and a series of panels slid across the wall, revealing several televisions. A couple more buttons and they powered up. Antonio could see nearly every room in the palace. He watched as Hannah ran down the main corridor. Antonio turned his back to Enrico and prepared to show the full extent of his true powers. "This is the last thing Elissa saw before I slit her throat." Antonio turned slowly and met Enrico's gaze.

Enrico's eyes widened as he came face-to-face with his mirror image. He quickly put two-and-two together and knew damn well that Savannah did not betray him.

"We both have our powers, Brother. As you can see, I have mastered the art of deception. You are a fool, for even your beloved Savannah saw through my disguise. Had your love truly been unconditional, you too would have seen the truth."

Enrico's blood boiled. *Elissa thought...* but Enrico was incapable of finishing his own thoughts. Even Savannah thought he was out to harm her. Enrico felt unimaginable pain, sorrow and hatred he could not begin to explain. If there was ever a time that heaven and hell collided, it was now. Enrico desperately wished he took the time to listen to her silent plea. Enrico shook his head violently as Antonio tormented him with the bitter truth. This was no time for regrets and Enrico needed to focus on the situation at hand. He needed to be Savannah's savoir now more then ever.

"Antonio, if you place one hand upon her, I will see you executed...Medieval Style! As God as my witness...before your death...you will kneel before me and beg for mercy."

Antonio smiled and replied, "And if I lay both hands upon her fresh, sweet naked flesh and press my mouth to an exposed breast, what then?"

Enrico cringed. He used his entire strength fighting against his chains. Chains of bondage have always been his weakness. Chains bound him to his beloved Savannah and chains bound her to him. She was his only weakness and Antonio knew this. "If you wish to make me suffer then do so, but do not harm Savannah; do not inflict any more pain upon her," Enrico pleaded.

"No more than you brother," Antonio harped.

"It's not the same and you know it," Enrico insisted.

"Enlighten me," Antonio coaxed, with a sly grin.

"You forced her into your life and into your bed; I did not," Enrico replied condescendingly.

"Just a mere technicality, dear Brother." Antonio taunted Enrico now with vivid images of his intentions. "You located her and tracked her, while I tamed her.

Enrico refused to dignify Antonio's reply with a response.

Chapter 21
Blood Is Not Thicker Than Water

Enrico suddenly realized that Austin had not spoken a word in Savannah's defense. He turned and found Austin lying upon the floor. Everything happened so quickly; he never realized Austin became unconscious. He knelt down to check on his newfound comrade and felt relieved to find he was not dead.

"I thought some privacy was in order, Brother-to-Brother."

Enrico glanced at the screens as Antonio's timer went off. Her twenty minutes were up. Hannah appeared to be frantically searching for a place to hide—upstairs. Enrico felt certain Antonio would run and pounce, for they both knew Savannah did not stand a cold chance in hell. Antonio remained calm and watched her every move. The cameras were on motion sensors. When Hannah walked out of the view of one, another turned on.

"I shall wait until she comes to me," Antonio hissed.

Enrico thought Antonio to be a serpent awaiting his prey, waiting for the perfect time to strike. "What makes you think she will come to you?"

"Two reasons, Brother. One, because you are here, and two, she believes I left in search of her. Savannah will back track to her safety zone...which is right here...and I will be waiting for her as she re-enters the room." Antonio removed a hand carved wooden box from behind the bar. He opened it up, removed two metal bracelets and used his watch to activate them.

"What do you intend to do with those?"

"It's quite a simple device," Antonio said, as he explained his intentions.

"You Bastard!" Enrico screamed, for it was beyond his comprehension. Enrico thought his brother to be weak and cowardly. "Place them upon me," he demanded.

"I do not wish to man handle the Great Lady Costello; I merely want her obedience and wish to pleasure her like no man, or you, has ever pleasured her before." Antonio felt pleased with himself for enraging Enrico like this. They both looked at the screens as Hannah ventured closer and closer to them. Antonio summoned his guards to take Lord Costello to the dungeon and they did so, obediently. Enrico did not go without a fight, but he could not attain freedom.

Hannah knew her plan was fool proof, for Antonio had to be somewhere else in the palace by now. She chose to hide in the cantina with Austin and Enrico and await their freedom. Hannah stood just outside the doorway and could hardly wait to embrace her one true love. She closed her eyes and pictured his face. It was now time to announce her profound love for him—once-and-for-all. She listened intently just outside the room and heard silence. She ventured in to meet her destiny. Instantly, Hannah felt eyes upon her.

She turned around and gazed at Antonio. She screamed as he grabbed her and placed the bracelets upon her wrists. Hannah tried to fight as if it would be her last breath, but he was too strong and overpowered her. Antonio embraced her warmly, whispered soothing words into her ear and kissed her neck.

"I do not wish to hurt you. I merely wish to pleasure you like no man has before."

For a moment, she forgot who he was and nearly gave in. Hannah quickly refocused, for *it was* Antonio and fear overwhelmed her.

"Let's retreat downstairs, my Lady; someone awaits patiently for you."

Hannah immediately noticed Austin lying upon the floor. "Austin!" she screamed. Hannah boldly met Antonio's cold gaze, "What did you do to him?"

"He is merely sleeping, my Lady," he whispered, as he led her out of the room.

"I can walk on my own accord."

Antonio released her as she led and he followed. She played right into his trap and did not even know it. He whispered directions, "Past the main stairwell, down to the first intersection, make a right down the hallway and pass through the last door on the right."

Antonio opened the door as Hannah walked inside. The room was enormous and there was a fireplace on the far side, which appeared to tower over them. Hannah thought it could engulf them, as she gazed at it intently. Antonio walked across the room and pulled on the flue chain. The stone slab beneath his feet creaked and moved to the side. A hidden stairwell now became visible. They descended down and, as they reached the bottom step, Hannah heard Enrico's voice and saw him entrapped within a steel cage. She raced over to him and he embraced her through the bars. Enrico appeared ragged and Hannah knew he attempted to free himself.

"I love you so much Savannah. We will never be parted, not even in death," he whispered. He took her face into his hands and kissed her passionately. He then grabbed her hand and reached for the Ring of Eternity.

Antonio seized her arm and ripped her from his brother's embrace. Enrico started shaking the bars ferociously.

"It's useless brother, the bars are constructed of titanium but it amuses me to watch you…so please…do continue," Antonio beckoned, as he watched with luring amusement.

Enrico's eyes turned black as midnight.

Antonio turned a few lights on and then the stereo. There was a bed on the backside of the room. Hannah thought it looked like two king size beds and began to tremble. Antonio opened a bottle of 1789 Château Late, a rare red wine. "I've been saving this for a special occasion."

Enrico immediately raised his brow, for he recognized the bottle. It was a gift to Antonio from Enrico when they reconciled their differences after their mother passed away.

Antonio held up the bottle, "I hope it pleases you, My Lady."

Hannah glanced at Enrico and noticed that he had not taken his malevolent eyes off Antonio. She loved Enrico and it pained her greatly to see him suffer like this.

"If you are thinking about running back into my brother's arms, think again…my Lady. Your bracelets are activated and there are two beacons on each wall; if cross that line, you will regret it."

Hannah did not care, for she had to reassure Enrico that everything would be all right. She ran to him as he grabbed her arm and forced her back.

"Get back Savannah, now!" he cried, when he heard a beeping sound.

Hannah persevered forward and kissed him one more time. She quickly turned to run back and it hit her like a brick. The pain she felt in her wrists was overwhelming. She managed to cross the line as tears streamed down her face. Both men gazed at her sympathetically. Enrico felt helpless to help and Antonio felt relieved, for now he would not have to inflict the pain himself. Antonio swept her into his arms and kissed her cheeks until her tears subsided.

"You see my Lady, you must listen to me and no harm will come to you…not by my hand; I promise," he whispered softly, and then handed her a glass and said, "Drink this, it will help calm your nerves."

Hannah accepted the glass and drank it quickly. All Enrico could do was stare, as the love of his immortal life fell to the mercy of another. Antonio's death now grew imminent.

Jeano remained trapped in the clover room but he was clever and had many tricks left up his sleeve. The clover room was his and he secretly installed a second keyhole on the opposite side of the door—he alone held the key. He waited until the coast was clear and slipped out undetected. Jeano grew fearful and needed to find Enrico. The last he knew, they were having drinks in the cantina. He ran downstairs and quickly traversed the corridor. He no longer ran as well as he did in his younger days, for he had taken a bullet in the leg for Enrico once. It now felt like a lifetime ago. Jeano would gladly offer his own life, for Enrico was the son he never had. Jeano sensed Enrico's conflict between rage and fear, as he waited outside the cantina. Silence lingered in the air, so he stepped inside.

Austin stood motionless eyeing up the doorframe as faint sounds of footsteps approached. His eyes darkened when a dark figure entered the room. Austin wrapped his chains around Jeano's neck. "Where is she?" he demanded.

Jeano gasped for air and was no match against Austin's strength. "I do not know where they are!"

Austin immediately let go when he realized it was Jeano.

Jeano continued to gasp for air after his release. Austin became furious. Jeano looked at his shackles carefully. "I can pick this," he said, as he crossed the room to the bar and grabbed an ice pick. He ran back over, tossing a chair out of his way. Jeano released all qualms as he picked the locks and, one-by-one, they fell upon the floor.

"How do we find them?"

"We must arm ourselves first," Jeano replied, and then strolled back over to the bar. He personally kept a couple of handguns behind the mescal. He looked but they were no longer there. "Damn it!" he cried, "Come Austin, we can get more," he said, and then left the room.

Austin quickly followed and took caution. "We must be careful; Antonio has collogues crawling everywhere."

They checked the hall, as two guards passed, and slipped down the corridor. Austin followed Jeano, uncertain where the corridors led. They made so many turns that Austin no longer knew where he was. Jeano led the way to Enrico's room and they slipped in undetected. Enrico kept a stash of weapons in the bottom bureau. Jeano handed Austin his 9 ml Ruger.

Austin seized the gun with pure pleasure, for he brought it to kill the man that wronged Hannah. Jeano handed him another and Austin gladly accepted it. Jeano also handed him a knife and Austin quickly attached it to his belt. Jeano felt more comfortable now, as they proceeded. Jeano instructed Austin to sit down upon the bed. Austin obeyed, but reluctantly. Jeano placed his hands upon Austin's shoulders and closed his eyes, focusing all internal energies towards Austin.

"Close your eyes, clear all thoughts and picture Hannah within your mind."

Austin did so, knowing Jeano attempted to locate her. *Hannah, come back to me!* Hannah consumed his heart, mind and soul now. Every thought, every moment—good or bad—rested upon their relationship, which felt stronger than ever. All the trials and tribulations throughout the years strengthened their relationship and intricately bound their souls to form one hope, one dream and one spirit. Austin opened his eyes, feeling enlightened. He still held Hannah's heart and always would. Somehow—Someway, this all seemed trivial and nonexistent. He could not shake this newfound outlook as he broke mental contact.

Jeano relaxed and tried hard, but her presence felt cloudy and he knew that Enrico no longer possessed control. "This isn't going to work," he explained, and then released Austin. "I will try to locate Enrico!" Jeano walked to the wardrobe and picked up one of Enrico's shirts, closed his eyes and sensed Enrico's presence. Austin watched in amazement, for Jeano upheld a gift beyond mortal comprehension.

Antonio continued to play on Hannah's emotional state downstairs. He lured her closer, using any means necessary. He removed his shirt, revealing his rippled chest. He poured another glass of wine, drank it and sat upon the bed. Antonio removed his ebony boots slowly and carefully in an attempt not to alarm her. Hannah watched him as sheer panic crept into her soul. He patted the vacant space along side him and whispered, "Come and sit my Lady…you look fatigued."

Hannah just stood there motionless.

Antonio reached for his watch and turned the setting down. He did not wish to push the button but he prepared to use force—if necessary. He stood and walked toward her slowly, with open arms. "Come," he murmured softly.

Hannah took a few steps backward and heard the beeping sound again. She reeled around to see the glowing red lights upon the wall and instantly ran backwards. Before she knew it, she ran into Antonio's arms. Hannah fought for a few moments and accepted the fact that it was a hopeless battle. She became compliant and succumbed to Antonio's tyranny. She fell limp in his arms as he tried to calm her fears.

"Isn't that better?" he whispered.

Hannah could not bring herself to look at either Antonio or Enrico now, so she buried her face into Antonio's massive chest as her entire body began to tremble. Antonio slid her sweater off her shoulders and down her arms until it fell upon the floor. A majestic love ballade began playing on the stereo, for Antonio had every detail planned.

"Dance with me."

Antonio coaxed her arms around his neck and slid his hands around her waist. They started moving slowly at first. The wine went to Hannah's head now and she felt the music within her soul. Antonio rocked her back-and-fourth. Hannah closed her eyes and suddenly imagined that she was dancing with Enrico at the hacienda, all those years ago. She allowed Enrico to lead her, as they danced passionately and erotically. He dipped her backwards until her head nearly touched the floor. As Enrico brought her up, he leaned down and kissed her, beginning at her navel and ending at her neck. This would be considered a distasteful and sinful ritual condemned by the small church going community, which hence she came.

When he reached her mouth, she kissed him deeply and engulfed his entire mouth, as she thrust her tongue deep inside. She felt Enrico's face with her hands and then ravaged his chest. Hannah never opened her eyes, for she saw Enrico within her mind and felt his presence within her heart. They danced rhythmically and poetically. Every move felt like the graceful stroke of a paintbrush, as an artist created one beautiful masterpiece by combining many hues and textures.

Two bodies slowly merged into one. Antonio carefully unbuttoned a few buttons upon her blouse and Hannah felt his hands slip to her thighs. Her senses were in tune to his every move and his every touch. He picked her up and drew her close, as her thighs hugged his hips. He buried his head into her chest and suckled upon her breasts. Hannah let out a gasp as they rocked to-and-fro to the sensual beat of the music. Antonio carried her to his bed before the song ended.

Enrico watched their movements in horror. He knew Savannah drifted away in her mind. He presumed back to the dance they shared at the Hacienda. He felt nothing but solicitude, given the circumstances. He could not believe how arrogant and selfish Antonio behaved, for Savannah did not wish to be taken to his bed and Antonio knew this. However, their appearance now would suggest otherwise. Enrico did not blame her for becoming lost in her thoughts, for it was a way of protecting and sheltering herself. His thoughts embraced the visions that haunted his mind all these years and realized the terrible accusations that overshadowed his heart and clouded his judgment.

Savannah imagined herself in his arms right now, not Antonio's cowardly embrace. Enrico wondered how his brother would react to the truth when she comes back to her senses, as the song ends. Enrico prayed Antonio would not strike with his entire wrath, for he knew Antonio could not live with the stigma of being second best. He waited and watched as his heart pounded uncontrollably. Enrico kept a mental track of each time Antonio touched her in appropriately, for this would be the number of times Antonio would suffer for his betrayals.

Antonio could not believe the transformation within Savannah. He had never been kissed like that before. He longed for her, as he desired no other woman before. She danced with him in the most passionate and sensual way. Savannah showed no fears and held nothing back. She even had her hands upon his hips and he knew at that moment that he was in total control. Antonio felt certain she desired him in every way and he'd give her everything—and so much more. Antonio knew the song was nearly over, as he sat her down upon his bed. He felt her body beckon for more as her hands ravaged his chest and her mouth caressed his lips.

Jeano and Austin made their way through the palace to a room with an enormous fireplace. Austin now felt like a mouse stuck in a maze in search of a piece of cheese. He held his 9mm Ruger in his hands caressing it and stroking it as he would Hannah. His father's handgun would be her salvation and his retribution. He could taste revenge, as it consumed his soul. Jeano gazed at Austin intently and wondered which hero would walk away fully satisfied. He shook his mind free of all thoughts, for predetermined destinies held no mysteries.

"We're close," he stated, and then glanced around the room.

"Not close enough," Austin gravely corrected.

They searched every nook and cranny but remained clueless. Jeano instructed Austin to start pulling and pushing on everything in sight. Austin walked over to the fireplace, was in awe by its magnitude and froze in his tracks, as he heard music coming from somewhere down below. Austin did not recognize the music but an eerie feeling came over him, as the music ended. He frantically pulled on everything. Jeano glanced over at him, also fearing the worst.

Antonio straddled Savannah and gave her the benefit of the doubt, as he removed her bracelets. "What would you like, My Lady."

Hannah pulled him close and whispered into his ear. His eyes widened and he rolled them over so she could be on top. Antonio noticed her eyes were still closed. Hannah straddled him, ran her fingers through her long blonde hair and slowly unbuttoned the remainder of her blouse. Antonio felt the extension of his body tingle with sensation, for he filled with anticipation now. Enrico stood and gripped the bars in disbelief. Hannah unbuttoned the last button and removed her blouse. She was on her knees wearing nothing but her brazier. She tossed the blouse at Antonio. He caught it and drew it to his face. The aroma smelled like her, sweet and sensual. Hannah opened her eyes and met his gaze. She came to her senses—and like a jackrabbit—leapt from the bed.

Antonio expected this, for he knew this was too good to be true. While she unbuttoned her blouse, he separated the room with steel bars. Silently it came down when she removed her blouse. Antonio took no chances, for he was afraid she would run to Enrico and he would remove the Ring of Eternity. He already had one narrow attempt at escape.

Hannah ran smack into the bars. She screamed in terror, as sheer panic overfilled her heart, and stood their screaming Enrico's name while shaking the bars. Antonio grabbed her and forced her back onto the bed.

"My Lady, we've just begun!"

"Release her from your unholy grasp," Enrico shouted.

Antonio did not hear him. All his focus and attention lied with Savannah now. He forced her down upon the bed and straddled her once more. He did not intend to hurt her but he clasped his hands over her dainty wrists, holding her steadfast. He held both wrists with one hand, unbuttoned her pants with the other and slipped his hand inside. For the first time in his life, he knew no patience. Antonio needed her now and he lost total control.

Austin panicked when he heard Hannah screaming. "Damn this palace," he cried. He looked up and noticed the flue chain. Austin yanked on it and instantly felt the floor creek from beneath his feet and jumped aside. Jeano stood beside him now. Once the stairs were visible, Austin raced down. He noticed Enrico encaged like a wild animal and then saw Hannah behind bars as well—on a bed—with Antonio hovering over her. Austin drew his Ruger, walked to bars and fired five shots. Everything happened so quickly that Jeano never even reached the bottom step.

Antonio immediately fell over. Hannah rolled off the bed, jumped to her feet, buttoned her pants and grabbed her blouse. She ran over to Austin and held him in her arms the best she could. Tears streamed down her cheeks, tears of joy and relief. The whole ordeal was finally over and they were free. Austin kissed her brow through the bars. "Let's get you out of here," he whispered, beginning to choke up.

Jeano released Enrico from his prison. Enrico stood back and allowed Austin to have this moment. For now, he remained vigilant and kept his eyes upon Antonio. He knew this was not over and he watched skeptically as Jeano tried to reverse the sensors in the panel box. Enrico needed in there and he needed in there now. He saw no reason to alarm Savannah, for she and Austin were having a rather touching reunion.

Enrico knew his brother could only die from his hand. Enrico thought death was too good for Antonio now. He wondered if this is what Antonio desired the entire time. *Death* had not been a word in their vocabulary for quite some time. Enrico had been condemned to many lifetimes of servitude without death. If Antonio desired death, it was a wish not to be granted.

He'd make Antonio suffer as no immortal has ever suffered before. Enrico felt a devilish smile overwhelm his lips at the mere thought of it. Blood is not thicker than water, for this man was no longer his brother. His smile quickly faded as Antonio knelt upon the bed. Antonio shook his head a couple times as if to regain his bearings. Jeano glanced at Antonio and went into double time, for he was out of time. Antonio stood as the bars rose.

Austin saw Antonio and forced Hannah out of the way. Both he and Enrico stood in front of her.

"How can this be?" Austin gasped. He still had another round left in the chamber and drew his gun.

Enrico placed his palm upon the weapon and lowered it gently, "I will handle this," he demanded and stepped under the gate and motioned Jeano to lower the bars.

"So, it has finally come to this," Antonio hissed. Antonio knew that he had no chance against Enrico, for he was a natural born fighter and prevailed in every battle. "I have been waiting endlessly for this moment, Brother!"

"Jeano, take Savannah and Austin upstairs immediately and then come back down."

Jeano did not hesitate, but Hannah refused to leave.

"I won't leave you Enrico, not with this monster."

"It will be all right…I promise," Enrico replied, never taking his eyes off Antonio.

"Now Jeano!"

Austin took hold of Hannah's arm, "We must go upstairs…now," he spoke cordially. Austin and Jeano led her upstairs.

"Wait here," Jeano commanded, and then descended the staircase.

Hannah and Austin found themselves alone upstairs in silence. Austin embraced her warmly, "Are you alright?" he asked tenderly.

Hannah returned his embrace. "Thanks to you Austin; I love you so much."

He too professed his love towards her. To Hannah, the moment felt awkward. She desperately needed to know what that meant. She came to the conclusion that is was merely stress, for being in Antonio's presence nearly made her have a nervous breakdown and recovery would take awhile. Hannah was glad that Austin was with her. She lunged into his arms and embraced him. All awkwardness melted away with her tears. He held her tight and swore never to let her go.

"It's over," he whispered and kissed her lips tenderly.

She returned his kiss and asked, "Why do I feel like the worst is yet to come?"

He gazed into her big blue eyes and whispered, "I feel that too."

They stood and waited for the worst—unable to run any longer.

It felt like an eternity passed when they finally heard footsteps approaching on the stairs. Austin forced Hannah back and drew his weapon—expecting the worst. Jeano and Enrico emerged from the stairs.

"You no longer have to worry about Antonio ever again," Enrico proclaimed. That was all he felt needed to be spoken about the situation downstairs. "Savannah, come here," Enrico said with disappointment in his voice as Jeano left the room. Jeano could only imagine how hard this must be for him. Hannah walked over to Enrico as he extended his hand to her. She grasped it. He looked at Austin and said, "Austin, it was a pleasure meeting you…take care of her and I'm sorry," as he placed his fingers around the Ring of Eternity.

Before Austin could think twice about Enrico's remark, the ring had been removed from Hannah's finger. Enrico took special care not to let go of Savannah's hand as he took the ring into his. As soon as the ring was removed, Austin felt cold and collapsed to the floor. Hannah screamed in horror.

Never letting go of her, Enrico silenced her, "I know you do not understand but in time you will…Austin went home."

Hannah stared into his emerald eyes. Enrico found many questions within her gaze.

"I need to ask you a question, Savannah," he said, holding the ring in his hand.

"Alright," she replied.

"I am asking you to spend one last night with me; I know in your heart you still love me. Will you stay with me?"

Hannah thought she heard, *'Forever,'* at the end of his question. She put a hand upon his cheek, "I will stay with you tonight," she whispered.

With that said, he placed the ring back upon her finger. She glanced down at Austin and winced, for he no longer lied upon the floor. Enrico's words echoed within her mind, over-and-over again, *'Austin went home.' What does that mean?* She simply could not fathom the meaning. Somewhere within her mind and heart, she did not want to understand. She felt that he was just fine and she'd see him soon. Right now, all she could think about was one last night with Enrico.

Jeano entered the room and looked around solemnly. Enrico motioned and Jeano approached slowly. "I must have a word with you Enrico," he said gravely.

"In the main house," Enrico replied.

They meandered through the corridors until they made it back to the main house. Hannah and Enrico held hands the entire way.

"I will return in a moment," he whispered, as he let go of her hand. The two men quickly exited the room.

Jeano looked at Enrico with questioning eyes and searched for the appropriate words. "My Lord…Why is she still with us?" He held no reservations about Austin, for he knew Austin was rightfully where he belonged.

Enrico waved his hand aside and shook his head. "Do not worry, my dear old friend…I will send her home in the morning. You have my word."

Jeano's worries quickly vanished. "And the children?"

"They are safe and sound with their father awaiting their mother," Enrico replied softly and then added, "I have taken care of everything."

Jeano stared into Enrico's bright green eyes, "They deserve to be a happy family," he said, reassuring Enrico that it was the right thing to do.

Enrico's heart became heavy as he felt the truth in Jeano's words and came to believe it as well. "Jeano, I do not wish to be disturbed tonight…for any reason."

Jeano nodded grimly, as he understood the request.

Hannah was alone in the great room but did not feel alone. She felt at peace, for it had been a long time since she felt safe and secure. She did not yet understand the complexities of Enrico and Antonio's rivalry and refused to ask. Her thoughts lied elsewhere. Part of her felt she betrayed Austin's love by staying one more night. The last thing she wanted to do was hurt him. Nevertheless, she found strength knowing that Enrico became her first throughout the whole ordeal and she wanted him to be the last.

As this chapter of her life ended with Enrico, a new page would begin a new chapter of her life with Austin. She had only spent two nights with Enrico a decade earlier. She wanted just one more moment with him. Something in her soul told her she would never see, hear or feel him ever again. This reality overwhelmed her. She was on an emotional roller coaster. They shared but only two nights together, but she knew that he would live within her heart forever, for she would never let him escape.

Hannah glanced around the room. She noticed every little detail, as though she was seeing the palace for the last time. Her mind kept reminding her of all the unknowns and unanswered questions. She released all ill thoughts, for nothing mattered to her now and all she could focus on was one last night with Enrico—another memory to last a lifetime. She watched as Enrico entered the room. His come-hither-us gesture with his index finger sent tingles up and down her spine. She immediately ventured to his side. Hand-in-hand, they walked upstairs to his bedchamber. As usual, he led and she followed. When they reached the door, he swept her into his strong arms, carried her in and placed her down upon the couch. He walked back to the door and locked it.

He turned around and stared at her. Savannah was very much alive within Hannah's soul now. Enrico penetrated her thoughts and recalled every moment they ever shared. Hannah closed her eyes and recalled their first encounter, the hacienda, the hotel, Hallows Eve and everything in between. They embraced their past along with the present. Enrico did not dwell upon their future, for they had none. Hannah suddenly realized this is what Enrico dreaded all these years. Her eyes moistened as her heart accepted his sweet honesty. There were no longer any secrets between them. Hannah nodded and Enrico closed his eyes, knowing she fully understood his legacy and her own destiny.

Enrico wondered what he had done to deserve another night with his angel, his Lady Savannah Costello. For whatever it was, he swore to do it over-and-over again. She remained the Beacon of Light—unsuspectingly leading the course of destiny to those lost at sea, unable to find their way home. Enrico wanted that light to shine forever. He knew that a large piece of himself would surely die, as the light grew dim but that would come later. Now, his focus was on her and every thought was with her at this very moment in time. He knew that he would remember this night as the greatest night of his existence. His body beckoned for her, his heart longed for her and his soul desired her. Enrico nearly lost her tonight without the chance to reveal his true feelings and he refused to jeopardize another opportunity. For the first time in his life, Enrico felt nervous and speechless and did not know where or how to begin.

They could finally be together, after all these years, and he wanted it to be perfect. He wanted something magical that she could take home, something that would always remind her of him. Just like that, an idea emerged from his thoughts. He walked over to the bureau and opened two cabinet doors, displaying state-of-the-art stereo equipment. A smile overwhelmed his face as he marveled at the thought of modern technology. He sifted through CD's until he found a perfect melody. He thumbed down and saw track 7. He put the CD in, dimmed the lights and pressed play. It was the same Spanish ballade they danced to at the hacienda and they rekindled an old memory. To Enrico, the song had always had an erotic and sensual beat. Every word in the song rang true. He approached his Savannah slowly—as if for the first time.

Hannah watched as he took great care in selecting a song. She knew the lyrics would come from his heart. He extended his hand to her and drew her close. She felt for his chest and felt his heartbeat within her hand. Enrico slowly removed her blouse revealing her white lacey brazier. The music began and so did he. He pressed her chest against his and gently picked her up and carried her to *his* bed. Every word in the song did ring true, for she felt as if he were singing to her heart. Every inch of her body longed for his touch. He straddled her, no longer taking caution, as he gazed into her big blue eyes. He'd remember her lying there beneath him forever—the way she looked, her clothes and this song.

"Savannah, I love you, body, mind, heart, and soul. We belong together, you and I; it is our destiny." He wanted to tell her that Austin was a lucky man, but he knew better. He wondered how guilty she would feel later.

Hannah gazed up at him. She read his mind and stroked his powerful arms. "I'm sorry it took me this long to realize how much I love you Enrico, nothing we do can ever be wrong. I can't tell you enough how right this feels." She took his face into her hands. His face was rough and she realized he had not slept in days. She pulled herself up to him and kissed him passionately as she engulfed his mouth. He thrust his tongue deep inside.

"There's more where that came from, my Lady."

She smiled seductively, "Show me more, my Lord."

Enrico laid his hands upon her thighs, "I think you should lose these," he whispered, referring to her pants. He unbuttoned them and she wriggled them off. The rapture of the night enticed their souls. Hannah ravaged at his trousers until they slipped upon the floor, for she lost all control now.

They stared at one another in awe. He never saw anything so beautiful and she had never seen anything more handsome. They reached for one another and touched each other's soul at the deepest level. She stroked the extension of him as he spread her thighs.

"I must enter your soul now," he whispered. He pounced and thrust deep within her soul, as Hannah whimpered beneath him. Enrico rolled over and now she straddled him. She leaned forward, kissed his lips, arched her back and moved her hips back and forth rapidly. To him, Savannah looked like a goddess and he moaned with pleasure, "Oh, my Lady."

Hannah unleashed years of denied desires and she began to slow down, for the night was still young. Enrico rolled her once again and embraced the warmth that radiated from her bodice. Hannah was now on the verge of sensual bliss. He withdrew his extension and ripped off her brazier.

"Do not stop," she whispered.

"Patience is a virtue, my Lady," he whispered, and then engulfed her breast. He lingered on one and then moved on to the other. She felt them tingle as his tongue rolled around her nipples. He caressed her naval, met her gaze, and smiled. He moved lower until she found sensual bliss. She whimpered as she ran her fingers through his swarthy black hair. He moved up slowly, lingering everywhere. He briefly kissed each nipple, and engulfed her mouth. He entered her soul once more. It was raw passion unleashed after many years. She felt him explode as they each found sensual bliss. The motion became slow and tender.

Enrico rolled over next to her as they caught their breaths. She slipped into his arms and he stroked the small of her back.

"You are full of surprises, my Lord," Hannah said and kissed him tenderly.

They gazed at one another.

"I must ask you a question Enrico," she whispered, as her smile faded.

Enrico felt some concern. "You may ask anything."

"I do not wish to leave you, my Lord."

His smile also faded, "As much as I long for you to stay with me, I cannot and I will not do that to you!"

"I do not understand Enrico, we belong to each other." A tear escaped her eye, "I will not leave you."

Her plea deeply touched him, but it made his decision even more difficult. "In time you will understand Savannah...I promise." Enrico wiped away a tear, as he silently fought every urge to keep her. "You belong to me...tonight, but your heart forever belongs with Austin. I hope someday you can forgive me."

"You are already forgiven...whatever that entails."

They remained in silence for a moment, constantly touching and caressing. "Enrico," she whispered, as she looked into his green eyes. "I can't help but wonder how differently things could have turned out between us. Running from you felt safe when in actuality, running to you turned out to be my salvation. Antonio robbed us from all those years together." Hannah trembled in his arms.

"Do not think about the past, for we are together now…in the present," he whispered, and then straddled her once again.

"Ready for round two, my Lord?" she asked smiling.

He grinned and engulfed her mouth as they began again.

Chapter 22
Awakening of the Senses

Austin emerged from sleep with the undeniable urge to stretch. He felt like he slept for an eternity, for he never felt so rested. He thought he was still asleep, but swore he heard his mother yelling at someone. He opened his eyes and glanced around the room unaware of his surroundings. The room was white and he was lying in a bed. The lights were bright enough to hurt his eyes. Janice ran into the room and embraced him firmly. Austin realized she was crying when he felt warm tears against his cheek.

"My dear sweet Austin, you've come back to me." Janice stepped back noticing that he did not respond and realized his vision had not fully returned to him yet.

"This is to be expected; it will take some time for your son to regain verbal and motor skills...if at all," a man's voice explained.

Austin did not understand, for his mind was in a chaotic frenzy. He suddenly felt hands all over him, poking and prodding. He felt tubes coming out of him everywhere. Almost instantly, his vision returned. He could now see, hear and think clearly once again. Austin instantly realized that he was in a hospital bed surrounded by nurses and doctors with clipboards. He sat up and all eyes were upon him. His throat felt dry and he saw a glass of ice chips beside the bed. Austin reached for the cup and brought it to his lips, as whispers surrounded him. Everyone began to write relentlessly. The only thing going through his head right now was Hannah.

"Hannah...where is Hannah," he whispered with a raspy voice.

A nurse seized his arm, "Lie down and try to relax," she insisted.

"I do not wish to lie down and I demand to see Hannah...Now!"

Janice stepped in front of Austin, and the medical personnel, sheltering him from prying eyes. "I would like to have a moment in private with my son, if you don't mind."

The nurses and doctors reluctantly left the room. Janice knew the girl he spoke of and she stared at him intently.

"What do you remember of Hannah, Austin?"

"Everything," he responded, "Please take me to her."

Janice winced, "I don't believe you are strong enough, son."

Austin loved his mother but he grew tired of her idle chitchat. He ripped the IV's from of his arms, stood and frantically searched for clothes.

Janice stared at him in disbelief. "Austin, what year is it?" she asked earnestly. Austin looked at her oddly and could not fathom such a question.

"It's 2004; why?"

She gasped and wondered how this was possible.

"Mom, I need clothes; if you won't take me to see Hannah, I'll find her on my own."

Janice walked to the closet, removed a duffle bag and handed it to him. She turned her back while he dressed. Austin recognized the clothes, for they were from high school. He thought it odd but did not question it.

The doctor walked back into the room and stood dead in his tracks. He did a double take, "Austin, you should not be up," he cried.

Austin read the word *Johnson* across his nametag. "Dr. Johnson, I am officially checking out...now!"

Dr. Johnson glared at Janice but she simply waved her hand aside and made no attempts to persuade Austin into staying.

Austin strolled past the doctor, "Come mother," he said cordially, as he flashed the doctor a resentful look.

Dr. Johnson immediately called for two orderlies to restrain Austin. They grabbed his arms and Austin became enraged.

"No one will keep me from my family," he shouted fiercely.

Austin slammed the orderlies up against the wall and they immediately stood down. Dr. Johnson was mesmerized, for all medical theorizes and all of his medical training told him that this young man should have no physical strength whatsoever. He watched Austin walk down the hallway in awe. Austin had verbal and cognitive skills along with physical strength and Dr. Johnson simply could not fathom how this was possible.

Janice stood in the doorway, "Dr. Johnson, we will be in touch," she said flatly, and then followed her son.

Janice walked more slowly than Austin did, for she thought of calculating ways to break the grim news to him gently. The bitter truth would surely crush Austin and Janice wished to make it as painless as possible. She approached her new SUV and felt shocked to see Austin standing at the passenger side door. He had never seen this vehicle before, for she had just leased it six months earlier. She stood motionless for a moment and then removed her keys and pressed the unlock button. Austin opened the door and climbed in. He appeared anxious and she felt dreadful; clearly, there was a lot neither one of them fully understood. She climbed in, but did not start the vehicle. She gazed at him instead.

"There is no easy way to tell you this, so I'm just going to say it. You and I have always had a good relationship; I've never pulled any punches with you and I hope you know that I would never lie to you...not ever." She placed her hand upon his, "Austin...Honey, you've been in a coma for the past twelve years."

Austin remained silent for some time, scanning his memory for evidence of her claim. He sighed, for it must be true. Enrico spoke numerous times about sending them home.

This is what Enrico meant when he said, 'You will understand in time.' A thought crept into his mind. *Did I dream the whole thing?* Austin quickly dismissed it. His face grew solemn as he thought about his precious daughters and wondered where they fit into the equation. New fears began to grow and fester. "Where is Hannah?" he managed to whisper, and then added, "She will need me."

Janice watched him carefully and attempted to read his eyes before answering. "She has also been in a coma for twelve years. Austin, do you remember the accident?" she asked compassionately.

"What accident?"

She desperately searched for the right words. "You and Colby were returning from an overnight stay in his black Corvette. Colby struck Hannah that morning, while she walked her dog, and then struck a tree. You and Hannah instantly went into shock and then lapsed into your comas."

Austin grew silent and recalled past events. He and Colby did skip school that Friday and were racing home. Those images were now vivid.

"This car can go 0-60 in 5.2 and I had it up to 110 already!" Colby stated, prepared to prove what the vehicle was capable of.

"Easy Colby...I have a date tonight."

"Where's your sense of adventure? You used to be fearless." Colby's eyes left the road for a second as he grinned at Austin and floored the accelerator.

They cruised around 90 as they crested the hill.

Austin saw a figure along the road and reached for the steering wheel. "Colby Look Out!" His reflexes forced the wheel left but the vehicle-veered right instead. Austin felt a thud and then the vehicle rolled several times.

The vehicle rested upon its roof. Austin was ejected and now lolled alongside the car. He attempted to assess the situation, as his vision grew dim. He did, however, notice a young listless woman next to the tree line. Long blonde hair flowed around her and Austin began to scream, as an older man knelt before him.

"Calm down Son...Everything's going to be just fine."

Austin stared into the man's eyes when numbness overtook his body and he drifted away to the sound of approaching sirens.

Austin escaped his thoughts and recalled the episode he encountered on Cold Springs Road. *My mind attempted to recall those events and I dismissed them.* He agonized over his thoughts and glanced at his mother. "What happened to Colby?"

Janice reached for his hand and closed her eyes. "He died upon impact." She hoped knowing the truth would offer some comfort.

"What hospital is Hannah staying at?"

"St. Luke's."

"Why all the way over there?"

Once again, Janice found herself searching for the right words, "Honey," she whispered and then looked deep into his eyes. "Hannah became pregnant while in a coma here at this hospital and her family transferred her to St. Luke's and there she became pregnant again...do you understand?" She hoped that he did.

"What happened to the children?" Austin's heart became heavy as he prepared for the worst.

"The doctors advised for an abortion each time..."

Austin screamed, "NO," and felt his heart shatter.

Janice quickly finished, as she gazed at him with sincere curiosity. "But, her family is very religious and refused."

Austin quickly refocused, "Thank God for that," he whispered, as the tears began to swell. He fought back the lump in his throat. "Where are the girls now?" he whispered, and then closed his eyes.

Janice winced, for she did not say they were both girls, "At St. Luke's with Hannah, for they were also born in a coma state and have remained in comas since birth."

"Take me there immediately," he demanded and then added, "They are my daughters."

Her eyes widened with many questions but she did not ask, for she did not want to upset or disappoint him any further. Janice knew they could not possibly be his daughters, but continued to drive towards St. Luke's.

"We have to make one stop," he stated softly.

Hannah and Enrico became lost in one another's eyes, cherishing their last morning together. They spent the entire night making love. Enrico wanted desperately for her to stay and to raise her children with him. He refused to give into these desires, for he respected Austin tremendously. Hannah would soon return home to her chosen family but for now, she was all his.

"Will you take a walk with me this morning; I have something to show you?" he whispered, as they showered.

She turned around to face him, "I'd like that very much."

Hannah stepped out of the shower and dressed. She met Enrico at the door and he took her hand. He led her outside and down a boardwalk, which led to the ocean. Hannah wondered why she never smelled the sultry air until now. The sun was bright, the water was blue and the sand was white. She wondered if she had ever seen anything more beautiful before and quickly recalled Cape Cod. They removed their shoes and walked along the waters edge. She paused for a moment, placed her hand upon his bare chest and kissed him with every ounce of her being, as Savannah quickly faded within her soul.

Austin and Janice arrived at St. Luke's an hour later. They remained silent the entire way. Janice knew this was going to be a shock to Hannah's family, for she knew Hannah's mother was there most every morning. Janice parked the vehicle and took Austin's hand, "Austin, let me speak with Rebecca before you barge in," she insisted.

Austin nodded.

Janice approached Hannah's room as Rebecca stepped out. She called out to Rebecca and Rebecca welcomed her warmly. The two women had become close over the years since their children were involved in the same accident and shared the same prognosis.

Janice started at the beginning when Austin emerged from his coma. Rebecca remained silent and skeptical as Janice explained everything she knew.

"I think my son is delusional from the coma but yet he knew things that I never told him," she whispered, as tears filled her eyes.

Rebecca hugged her, "We shall humor him then and allow a DNA test; it may offer him some perspective then," Rebecca said, with a warm smile.

"Thank you for understanding," Janice managed.

A short time later Austin had his mouth swabbed and then his daughters. He visited with the girls and hit his knees. He thanked the good Lord above for their safety. Austin closed his eyes; uncertain which Lord deserved the honors, as his daughters rested motionless, fragile and alive. He held their little hands and kissed their cheeks, "You and Mommy must return to me," he whispered. The paternity test results would take two hours but Austin had all the time in the world, for he refused to leave his family's side.

Austin ventured into Hannah's room and silently vowed to remain by her side until she returned to him. Rebecca watched helplessly from the hallway, for this poor young man believes Hannah to be his wife and the girls to be his own children. Rebecca knew this was not a possibility and wondered if the truth would counteract with his miraculous recovery. He truly was a walking miracle. Everything she had read about long-term coma patients told her to expect her daughter to be in a vegetative state with severe brain deficiencies.

Yet, Austin had the same prognosis as Hannah and there he was. To look at him, you could never tell he was in a coma. She prayed to God to let Hannah return to them with mild complications, but she was willing to welcome her daughter back in any form God chose. Austin was an inspiration to her. She then thought about how difficult it would be for Hannah to see her children, for she would have no recollection of their birth or worse yet, their conception.

Rebecca shuddered at the last thought. She felt responsible, for if she had been around more it may never have happened. The thought of someone taking advantage of her daughter's vulnerable state has been unbearable throughout the years. Children are a precious gift form God and she could never, knowingly, inflict harm on one. Many nights she spent in the nursery rocking the girls. She had not named them, for she let that up to Hannah. She knew there was a long road ahead and this young man, who had so much hope and optimism, inspired her.

Austin felt his mother-in-law's thoughts and turned around, "Would you like to wait with me," he asked enthusiastically, and then added, "She will be waking up any time now; I feel it."

Rebecca flashed a pretentious smile, for she did admire his enthusiasm but she did not wish to encourage him. She stood slowly, walked into the room and positioned herself in a corner chair.

Austin knew that Rebecca did not know what to say, so he started the conversation. "Hannah will be delighted to see you," he whispered, trying to coax a genuine smile from her.

Rebecca merely stared at him with a heavy heart. Austin wanted to explain where they were the past twelve years but he did not know where to begin.

"Can you tell me what's in your head and heart...I mean right now? Austin, please tell me what you believe!"

Austin gazed into her sympathetic eyes, "I will tell you all you need to know," he said, as he began the story. "Hannah and I were...have been married for ten years and we have two beautiful daughters together."

Rebecca interrupted him for a moment, "What are their names?"

"The oldest was born December 26, 1998 and we named her Sierra Rose. Our youngest daughter was born May 12, 2002 and her name is Elaina Marie," he replied.

Rebecca gasped, startled and amazed that he knew their birth dates. She wondered how this was possible, "Continue," she whispered softly.

"I have vivid memories of the accident. We were not awake in this world nor were we in Heaven. We were trapped somewhere in between. There was a man, named Enrico, who kept saying he would send us home but neither of us knew what that meant, for the world appeared so real. Only now...that I've been sent home...do I understand."

"Is she with this man now," Rebecca asked, completely intrigued now.

"Yes, she is and he is a complete gentleman. I know he will send her home to us; they merely have to say goodbye and I feel it will not be long now," Austin closed his eyes, for he could only assume why it took so long.

Rebecca stood, approached Austin, and took his hands. "I don't know why, but I believe you Austin. I must call Hannah's father to join us." Rebecca flashed a warm genuine smile and then left the room.

Austin brushed Hannah's cheek and gazed at her with nothing but love and admiration in his eyes, for his love truly remained unconditional.

Hannah felt a brush along her cheek and then Austin's presence. She stopped Enrico dead in his tracks, as Savannah completely slipped away. Hannah took one last look around at the unsurpassed beauty that surrounded them and the one standing in front of her. She met his gaze, "I must return now," she whispered, as a vision of Austin sitting beside a bed became more vivid.

Enrico closed his eyes and whispered, "I know," and then added, "The time has finally come." Enrico kissed her one last time as the cool sultry air blew through her hair. The sun made her hair shimmer like diamonds and made her eyes sparkle, and he could not resist. "I make one last promise to you, my Lady; I will be with you during your final moments." Enrico removed an unruly strand of hair from her eyes, took her hand into his and slowly grasped the Ring of Eternity. "I love you Savannah, with all my heart and soul. Never forget that," he whispered, and then removed the ring from her finger.

Hannah instantly felt a cold chill come over her when he no longer had contact with her. She felt weak and her legs gave out from beneath her, as she collapsed in the sand. Enrico knelt down and held her limp body in his arms. He kissed her brow and before he knew it, she vanished before his eyes. Although Enrico denied his heart and abided by his duty, Savannah banished from his world forever. He felt empty inside. He no longer held the woman that took two lifetimes to find. He was condemned to spend eternity trapped forever, somewhere between Heaven and Hell. He often found himself wondering if he were in purgatory. They call him the Savior of Lost Souls, for he finds those who become lost and sends them back home. Enrico now wondered who would save him. He felt uncertain if anything could save his immortal soul. Selfishly, he kept Savannah with him all these years but she came with strings attached, for Austin followed. In two lifetimes of saving lost souls, no two people have ever entered his realm together before.

Enrico knew what that meant, for there was no doubt about it. Hannah and Austin were genuine soul mates. Not even Heaven itself could separate them, nothing could. Enrico knew this to be true, because he himself had tried with no prevail. In the end, her heart belonged to Austin. Enrico managed to smile, for he knew that he would live forever within her heart and the far reaches of her soul. He held no regrets. She taught him how to love again and single handedly brought redemption to his immortal soul. Knowing this made his sacrifice a little more bearable. He picked up the pieces left of his heart and headed back to his empty life, forced again to focus on another day—and another lost soul.

One thing remained certain; his Savannah will have a guardian angel forever. He would check in on her from time to time. He made a promise to her and vowed to keep it. He would be the one to hold her hand upon her deathbed. In due time, he will see his Savannah again. Until then, Enrico decided then that he had many more lifetimes to make Antonio pay for his betrayals. This was the only light at the end of his tunnel, for he had no other motivation left and decided to reveal the full extent of his revenge but he had other matters to attend to first.

Both Hannah's parents walked into the room. It did not take long for her father to arrive. He had taken a new job in town, to be closer to Hannah.

"Kayla, Jenna and Jacob are in route with their families," Rebecca announced.

"It won't be long now," Austin told them as he felt Hannah's finger twitch in the palm of his hand, and smiled warmly.

Hannah's parents watched in awe, for Austin seemed so confident. He, single handedly, raised their spirits and expectations.

Enrico also stood by her side now, though no one could see him. He wished to see the happiness upon her face as she awakened. Hannah did not awaken immediately as expected.

"Something is wrong," Enrico whispered, though no one else heard him. Enrico knew she should have returned by now. He could not sense her whereabouts and became nervous.

Hannah found herself in a tranquil place. There was a shape in front of her; neither man nor woman, but she had no fears.

"Why have you sought me out Hannah Marie Brockwell?" a voice echoed from the light.

"How do you know my name," Hannah asked.

The voice remained calm, "I know everything about you Hannah. Why have you come here instead of returning home to your family?"

Hannah remained silent for a few moments, for her mind was lucid but she searched for courage. "I have come to beg your forgiveness of his Lordship, Enrico Costello." Hannah's voice did not waver, as she whispered, "He is a good man."

The voice also remained silent for a moment. "I know all too well who and what Enrico Costello has become. Allow me to fill in the gaps. Enrico is the Savior of Lost Souls. He seeks out those who are lost and confused, like yourself, and sends them back to their families. He did not return you right away, in the beginning, because he stayed true to his duty and his conscious. He selfishly kept you against my best wishes; he disobeyed me, Hannah, and wronged you. Now…how do you feel?"

Hannah needed no time to think, as she fully understood everything, for she remembered the car accident, "My feelings do not change, and I have no regrets about the past twelve years. I have found my soul mate and we share two beautiful children together. Enrico made all of this possible and I am truly honored to call him an acquaintance."

"Sweet child, so young and so innocent, Enrico disobeyed me and in doing so, he wronged you and in the end…"

"Forsaken his own feelings and upheld the utmost honorable intentions."

The voice remained silent. "You make an interesting point," the voice finally conveyed, and then added, "So you plead for Enrico's soul, do you?"

"Yes I do," Hannah replied.

"I chose Enrico to be the Savoir of Lost Souls because he is a kind and passionate man. In many ways, Enrico is too passionate. Perhaps I will rethink his position. Enrico has served his duties well in the past, but he has disobeyed me and sinfully wronged you. I cannot simply dismiss these charges."

Hannah fell to her knees, for this would be her final plea. "If you need a new Savior of Lost Souls, take me in Enrico's place. I too am kind and passionate. I am willing to sacrifice my family for Enrico's happiness, for it is the right thing to do. I too have sinned and I ask you now for my judgment day."

The voice drew closer and the figure placed a hand upon Hannah's forehead. Hannah felt inner peace and strength she never came close to feeling before. She could not comprehend it and knew she would never be able to explain it. She finally felt what unconditional love means. The figures hand remained upon her forehead.

"Rise my child."

Hannah stood.

"Your judgment day will come, but not today. I am touched by your plea; allow me to explain."

The figure emerged from the light and stood before Hannah. "Hannah Brockwell, both Enrico and yourself have overcome the challenges presented before you. You were Enrico's one and only *luz del dia*. You remain his *daylight*. Enrico knew this the first moment he saw you. I alone gave Enrico the task to search for you, for I have created the world that entraps him. I too seek answers."

Hannah stared into the most beautiful emerald eyes ever bestowed upon her. They were more vivid than Enrico's and Hannah knew Enrico's mother stood before her.

"My name is Angelina Costello," the woman said, as she read Hannah's thoughts. "The Ring of Eternity could have perished along with my body, but I chose to link it to my son's immortal soul instead. I was well aware that one son deceived me, but did not learn of Antonio's treacheries until last night. Enrico denied Antonio death, bringing the nature of his redemption full circle. You have a pure soul Hannah, for you are willing to risk your mortal soul to free Enrico's immortal soul. Enrico embraced his immortal soul by sending you home. Austin is your soul mate. Enrico, though angry at first, came to understand this. He refused to send you home without Austin. That is why Enrico did not send for you in the beginning. Enrico lost his own soul mate more than two centuries ago. He refused to bestow the same fate unto you. You have brought redemption to Enrico's soul and for that, I am forever grateful."

Angelina reached out and placed her other hand upon Hannah's shoulder. "Austin Desmin is an honorable man, for he upheld unconditional love in the face of deception and has proven himself worthy of the task at hand. I will grant you one last miracle before I send you home and release Enrico from his immortal soul. I will bestow a child upon you, and not just any child, my grandson. My grandson secretly perished along with Enrico's one true love."

Hannah quickly became confused, "What child?" she asked compassionately.

Angelina smiled warmly, "Austin can explain," she stated.

Hannah searched for answers, but found none. She wondered if this was all a dream. A man now emerged before her.

"Tell Austin his ball cap is tucked away in his closet," the man stated.

Before Hannah could ask any further questions, Angelina handed her a trinket.

"See that our grandson receives this on his twenty-first birthday; now, it is time for you to return home."

Hannah awoke with Austin by her side the moment Angelina's hand left her shoulder.

* * *

Hannah felt disoriented, but she was not afraid. Austin leaned down and kissed her cheek.

"Your vision and clarity will return to you in a few moments," he whispered.

Hannah tried to focus on his face and could not, but she recognized his voice. She also heard her mother and father crying.

"Welcome back Hannah," they cried, as they rushed to her side.

Familiar loved ones now surrounded Hannah. Her vision returned to her as she stretched. She smiled warmly. Hannah gazed at Austin, "It's over, all of it," she whispered, as they embraced. Her parents started to explain things to her and she waved her hand aside, "It's all in the past," she declared. Hannah felt the trinket in her hand and secretly tucked it under the pillow, for she did not need to see it to know it was a priceless family heirloom.

Enrico watched with astonishment, for she was as beautiful as ever. Hannah felt Enrico's presence and gazed at him. Enrico wondered how this was possible. He watched closely—yet from afar—at the tearful reunion. Enrico saw a light and heard a familiar voice behind him.

"Come my Son, for it is time for you to return home."

Enrico stood dead in his tracks. He had been waiting for this day, since Hannah first came into his life, "Will I be her guardian angel?" he asked sympathetically.

"No," the voice echoed.

Enrico's heart felt despair, "Will I hold her hand upon her death bed? I made a solemn vow." Enrico dropped to his knees, as he begged for forgiveness. The voice remained silent, but Enrico heard the answer within his heart and he wept as no man had ever wept before. He stood, stole one last glance at his salvation and entered the light, gone from her world forever.

Hannah felt his presence fade and knew he too returned home. She felt complete and at peace. A nurse ran into the room.

"The children are awake," she declared and stared at Hannah who was also alert. "They want their Mommy and Daddy," she exclaimed.

Everyone heard a commotion in the hallway. All eyes were at the doorway as Sierra ran into the room, "Mommy...Daddy...Nanny and Pappy," she screamed, as little Elaina trailed shortly behind, "Mama, Dada." The girls rushed into the arms of their parents and then into their grandparents.

Rebecca and Brian were overwhelmed with joy. "How is this possible," Rebecca whispered, and then added, "The girls can walk and talk but yet have been in comas since birth." She could barely comprehend it and she did not wish to.

All the medical personnel had gathered at the doorway in disbelief. They have never seen anything like it. This was truly a miracle from a force far greater then themselves. A doctor pushed his way through the crowd.

"I have the paternity results," he announced, "Austin is 100% the father of both girls."

The family smiled at the doctor, for they had no doubts the moment the girls ran into the room.

The doctor looked around the room in shock and total amazement. Hannah's physician walked in and asked all sorts of questions. He was dumfounded when she answered each and every question with amazing clarity.

"Can you walk?" he whispered.

Hannah stretched one last time, jumped out of bed, picked up her daughters, "I could run a marathon," she cried, hugging and kissing her girls until the whole family began laughing with delight.

The doctor left the room, shaking his head, "I must consult colleagues," he whispered. He had no explanation or answers for what he just witnessed.

Janice entered the room. "Grandma," the girls screamed. Janice hit her knees and embraced her grandchildren for the first time that she knew.

"Grandma, are you sad?" Sierra asked as she wiped away a tear.

Janice gazed at her granddaughter, "No baby…I'm extremely happy," she whispered.

Hannah glanced around the room, "This place is nice, bet can we please go home now," she said jokingly. She glanced at Austin and it dawned on her, "Where is home for us," she asked.

"Anywhere you want it to be, sweetheart," he replied, and then smiled. Austin knelt down, took her hand into his and was pleased to see her ring finger bare, "I love you Hannah Marie Brockwell and I'd follow you to Hell and back; I will love you forever and always. Will you be my wife?" he asked sincerely, as tears streamed down his cheeks.

"Yes; we have waited far too long." Hannah's heart overflowed, for they were officially engaged after all these years as man and wife.

It was very emotional for them both. A nurse reluctantly removed all Hannah's IV's. The room cleared as Hannah dressed and placed the trinket in her pocket. Hannah left the room and the entire staff, even those from other floors, for the word spread quickly about their miraculous recovery, watched the family walk out to begin a new life.

Austin held her hand; he knew that someday he would ask her about the delay in her return, but not today. As they walked out the main entrance and into the sunlight, there was a beautiful rainbow stretched out far across the sky.

Rebecca was the first to comment, "But it didn't rain today."

Hannah squeezed Austin's hand; she alone knew what it meant. Her heart told her that Enrico gave them his blessings. *He too, is home at last.* The world suddenly took on a new meaning for Hannah, for it filled with love, praise, and inspiration. She felt as if she could accomplish anything and she felt like a brand new woman.

Chapter 23
Confessions of the Heart

They went home to start their lives over again. Hannah sat upon her bed and turned when Jacob entered the room. Hannah gazed at him in astonishment, for he was a welcome sight. Her heart already revealed he was not dead, but seeing made a believer out of her. She immediately raced to his side and embraced him. He returned her embrace and sat her down.

"Hannah, I am so sorry to put you through that," he whispered, and then added, "I knew Enrico was a man of his word."

Hannah's eyes widened. He took her hand and then he began.

"I was on maneuvers when Enrico wandered on to the base and explained that my Sunshine wished for my presence at her Graduation Ceremony. I thought he was crazy, but I boarded his jet anyways, and hoped for a miracle. I did not understand and did not want to understand, for there you were standing before me upon that stage. I thought my eyes had deceived me. Enrico led me outside and reluctantly explained everything. I sat in disbelief for a moment when he explained that I must return home in the morning. I begged him to send you along with me. He explained that you had unfinished business to attend to and vowed to send you home when the time was right. I stared into his eyes and found both truth and honesty deep within. I fully understood when I awoke in the hospital. The navy issued me an honorable discharge and I immediately raced to your side. I attempted to speak to your soul as I ran my fingers along your cheek while you slept in a coma."

Hannah gasped, "Jacob, I felt that and knew that I would see you again."

Jacob's eyes moistened, "Enrico kept his promise and returned you to me...to all of us.

They embraced one another. Hannah wept for joy, for someone else truly understood and she could not deny what her heart recalled.

Hannah and Austin became the center of everyone's attention. They were even on several talk shows. Medical professionals and psychiatrists paid them by the hour just to talk to them about their experiences. The family stayed with Austin's mom for a while. In no time at all, they saved up enough money to buy their own home. They purchased the ranch home where love first found them. They renovated the home, while they planned their wedding. It seemed silly to them to make it such a big affair, for in their hearts they have been married for ten years.

Nevertheless, it warmed their family's hearts. Rebecca was having a great time with it, while Hannah tried on wedding gowns.

"Oh Hannah, your wedding will be a fairytale just like your enchanting life," Rebecca exclaimed.

Hannah smiled, knowing she knew she did not deserve the love of two worthy deserving men. In many ways, it was far from a fairytale. Austin and Hannah left out certain aspects of their adventure, as so many have come to call it. She pushed the thoughts aside for it felt like a lifetime ago and all she wanted to do now was focus on the present and what lies ahead.

When Hannah returned home, she retired to the bedroom. Austin sat upon the bed waiting for her.

"Did you have a good day with your Mom?"

"Yes I did, thank you for asking," she replied, and then took his hand and whispered, "Austin, I think we shall need to add another addition onto the house."

He gazed into her eyes, "Why is that?" he asked curiously.

She smiled, "We are going to have another baby." She sat down beside him upon their bed and asked, "Who is Angelina?"

Austin perked his head up, but did not answer. He walked across the room and removed a manila folder from the dresser. He returned to the bed and handed it to Hannah. Austin re-found the same information on the Internet in hopes of offering Hannah some insight regarding their misadventure. Hannah opened the folder and read each article carefully. She closed the folder and fully understood the magnitude of their journey. Hannah asked the final question that lingered within her mind.

"Why did Angelina choose me?" Hannah recalled the man standing before her and walked slowly to Austin's closet. She thumbed around while Austin watched her curiously. Hannah retrieved an old dusty ball cap and handed it to Austin. "Were you looking for this?" she asked slowly.

Austin jumped up and seized the cap. "I thought I lost it forever in the accident." He met Hannah's astonished gaze, "It belonged to my father," he explained, and then added, "How did you know where to find it?"

Hannah closed her eyes and remained silent, for she felt it was time to be open and honest with one another. Austin read her thoughts and finally confessed the inability to have biological children. "Antonio blessed us with our daughters, Hannah. We have much to talk about." Hannah nodded as they discussed every aspect of their journey for the first time since their return.

They began from the beginning. The truth was emotional on them both. They bared their souls to one another. In the end, they agreed Sierra and Elaina remained the light that emerged from the darkness.

Austin closed his eyes, "Is this child Enrico's?" he asked calmly.

Hannah smiled, for she fully understood. She took Austin's hand, "Yes, but it isn't my child. This child is a gift from Angelina and your father. He's the one who told me where to find your ball cap."

Austin's eyes widened, as many questions entered his mind. He collected his thoughts and asked one at a time. "Who is the mother?"

"Angelina told me her grandson secretly perished along with Enrico's true love, his soul mate. According to these articles, I would have to say this child inside me is Elissa and Enrico's son, now entrusted to us."

Austin leapt from the bed, "We are going to have a son," he exclaimed. Joy overfilled his heart, "I always dreamed about having a son to carry on the family name!"

Hannah smiled warmly, "I wondered why Angelina chose me to be Enrico's *luz del dia*, his daylight. I finally understand the reasoning. Austin, I believe your father watched over you and Angelina watched over Enrico. I also believe that their paths crossed and they decided to help one another. Since I am your soul mate, I became the savoir. True love prevailed and here we are today."

Austin thought about her words. If Hannah understood correctly, he knew she was an innocent bystander trapped in the middle of two parents seeking guidance for their children. He held mixed feelings about the situation now, for Angelina and his father preplanned Hannah's destiny for the greater good of their children.

Hannah read Austin's thoughts. She tilted her chin and gazed into his deep brown eyes, "I have no regrets Austin. You saved me without ever realizing it. I left town subconsciously aware that I wanted another life. I did not only run from Antonio, I also ran from myself. Since I was a child, I longed to leave Greenville and seek adventure only to yearn for our return. This is where I truly belong and this is where we belong. I wish to raise our children here. I chose you Austin. My heart longed for the man who loved me, Hannah Marie Brockwell."

Austin could hardly contain himself, as he threw his arms around her, "You complete me in every way Hannah and make me so happy; I love you," he said softly, as he kissed her passionately. He backed up from her, grinning from ear to ear, "We should up the wedding to next month, for the house is nearly finished and the contractor can add another room in no time at all."

Hannah instantly agreed. They married two months later in the fall. They chose November 5th, the anniversary of the tragic accident that united two soul mates. Hannah and Austin's wedding was an emotional day for everyone. They kept it small and simple. Hannah looked lovely in Austin's eyes. Sierra and Elaina were flower girls, and Kayla's son was the ring bearer. Both Austin and Hannah felt choked up when Austin slipped the ring upon her finger, as he recited his vows. That night, they spent their honeymoon in their new home. They continued to make public appearances and became an inspiration to other families coping with coma victims. Hannah gave birth to a baby boy on March 6, 2005.

Hannah cried when she held their son for the first time. She looked deep into his tiny emerald eyes and then glanced at his wavy black hair. Austin gazed at the child with astonishment, as he took the baby into his arms and drew him to his chest.

"My son," he declared. His mind told him that this was not his child, but his heart conveyed otherwise. He'd love and cherish the son of the man who returned Hannah to him, as his very own. This was his child in every sense. This child was the greatest gift, and Austin vowed to treasure him forever. He vowed to teach the boy to be honorable, like his father before him. This was a silent promise Austin made to the infant. They named their son Ricardo Colton Desmin, and nicknamed him Rico, after his father. Their family finally felt complete.

On their first official anniversary, Austin visited Colby's grave sight. He finally said goodbye to his best friend. Austin became emotional and revealed his thoughts about that fateful morning. Colby's decisions that morning sparked the chain of events that led to where he stood. Austin wondered what might have happened if he drove that fateful morning and the accident never occurred. He and Hannah still would have fallen in love; Austin's heart told him so. A tear escaped his eye, as he realized they would not have their three wonderful children, whom he deeply treasured. "Your death was not in vain; goodbye, my friend." Austin walked away with a heavy heart.

Austin left Colby's gravesite as a gust of wind passed through him. His ball cap blew across the cemetery. He did not find his prize possession merely to have it taken from him again. He ran after it. Each time he got close, the wind blew it ever further. The cap finally rested beneath the shadows of an enormous Great Oak. He bent down to retrieve his cap and noticed a tombstone nestled at the base of the tree. Austin instantly recognized the tree, for he planted it with his mother the day his father rested beneath the ground. He recalled her words *'This tree will have your father's strength and will grow out of our love and devotion for him.'* Austin did not understand then.

He fell to his knees and read:

In Loving Memory of
Colton Byron Desmin-Consuelo
Devoted Son, Husband and Father

He continued to hold the cap and stared at the words compellingly.

Austin was three when he last visited his father's grave and could not read the words. Throughout the years, he had questioned his mother why they never visited the grave sight but she always changed the subject. Austin needed answers so he left quietly to ask the one person who could offer answers.

He found his mother baking in the kitchen. Janice instantly noticed how pale he looked and met his gaze, for the time had come for new revelations.

"Mom, who was my father?" he managed to ask, after a brief moment in silence.

Janice turned and walked into her bedroom. She returned with a shoebox and handed it to him, "Your father did not want you to have this until you were ready," she whispered.

Austin sat down in the living room and opened the box. It contained old worn photographs, letters from his grandmother and the certificates containing his birthright. "I don't understand."

Janice knew it was time to fill in the gaps, so she began. "Your father's mother spent four years in a coma and when she awoke from deep sleep, she discovered a month later she was pregnant. She spoke of a wonderful life those four years as though she continued to live, similar to your adventure. She claimed the father of her son, your father, was a man named Count Byron Consuelo. Her family ridiculed her and claimed she was delusional until she legally changed your father's name to her maiden name, Desmin. Your father always believed your grandmothers claims, but he did not want the stigma of being a bastard's child. He believed, in his heart, he was a Consuelo. He carried the notion throughout his life."

Austin stood, "I'd like to be alone," he whispered. He gathered up his new belongings and retreated to the cemetery. He sat at is fathers grave. He recalled reading about Count Byron Consuelo, the father of Angelina Consuelo. Austin realized that Angelina was his father's half sister. He finally understood the role his father played in his own adventure. It dawned on him that Enrico is technically his cousin and that they were pawns in something much greater than they could have imagined. He could not help wondering what great destiny was in store for his son. "Time will only tell," he whispered.

He stood, placed his cap upon his head and turned, as a gust of wind blew the cap off his head yet again. It fell to his feet. Austin bent down and grasped the cap. He fell to his knees when a distant familiar presence fell over his hand. He closed his eyes, as his father began to speak to him. Austin's mind filled with thoughts and words as his heart overflowed with emotions. He carefully listened to each-and-every word. When his mind fell silent, he opened his eyes and they began to moisten. Austin looked beyond the distant shadows and found his daylight, for it shined down upon him brightly. He finally came to know and understand the man that gave him life. He sat in silence for a while and left with an enlightened heart.

Ricardo grew into a fine young man and towered over Elaina. They continued to keep a special bond throughout their childhood. Ricardo earned a black belt in Karate and worked side-by-side with Elaina. Elaina opened up a shelter for abused women and estranged wives. Any woman could use the facility without judgment. Elaina dedicated herself completely to the cause. Ricardo taught self-defense along side her. They focused on unfulfilled dreams and helped all women to discover new dreams. Their motto became, *Overpower and Overcome.* Hannah and Austin were very proud of them. Hannah visited the shelter from time to time. Each time, she wondered what happened to Antonio. Part of her feared he watched and waited for the perfect opportunity to strike—Dormant in the Shadows. Ricardo observed her deeply lost in thought one day and embraced her. This took Hannah by surprise. She stepped back and felt his concern. She instantly flashed a warm smile and never thought twice about Antonio again.

Ricardo asked Hannah, on his sixteenth birthday, which family member he inherited his tan complexion. She smiled and simply said, "Your Great Grandfather." Hannah knew he was not ready to accept the truth nor was she ready to give it. Hannah sat down and wrote the entire story for her children to read upon Ricardo's twenty-first birthday. She knew in time he would understand everything. Austin wanted to leave his birthright to Ricardo and acquired the same safety deposit box that his own Grandmother set aside for him. He placed the documents, a small box and their memoirs inside for safekeeping.

Hannah stared into the mirror at her reflection. She no longer saw a scared naïve young woman staring back at her. Hannah is now fifty-one and they will celebrate Ricardo's twenty-first birthday tomorrow. She examined the lines upon her face and wondered if Enrico would recognize her now if he saw her. Hannah smiled warmly as her heart conveyed all thoughts on the subject. She and Austin have led an amazing life these past twenty-one years and Hannah would not trade them for anything in the world. But at times like this, she still wonders, *Why me?* She was not the first woman to climb Mount Everest or the first woman astronaut to the moon. She was simply Hannah Marie Brockwell who desired another life. Hannah wondered if Angelina too wanted a different life and chose a woman who walked in her shoes. Hannah sighed, for there was no way to know.

The family celebrated Ricardo's twenty-first birthday. Austin wrapped a key, along with an address, and presented Ricardo with his gift. He desperately wished nothing would change in their relationship, for Ricardo was his son in every way. Austin has loved the boy as his very own since day one. Austin watched Ricardo grow throughout the years and felt proud of the man that now stood before him. Austin and Ricardo embraced as father and son.

"You're a chip off of the old block," Austin whispered, and truly meant every word. Austin recalled reaching across the table to Enrico's hand. His eyes moistened, for now he shook the spitting image of the man who returned his soul mate to him, nearly twenty-two years earlier. Enrico's blood may course through Ricardo's veins, but Austin instilled his integrity and values within Ricardo's very soul. Ricardo stared at his father with questioning eyes. Austin smiled warmly, understanding that his son could not fathom his emotional behavior. "You will understand soon," he whispered. Austin finished the celebration as he and his son enjoyed a private moment with a couple shots of mescal. Hannah and Austin left the children before Ricardo opened his final present. Hannah and Austin watched with heavy hearts as their children departed to seek out their own adventure.

Ricardo drove all night wondering what secrets the key unlocks. He retrieved his belongings and drove to the nearest hotel. All three sat around their parent's memoirs and took turns reading the pages aloud. Ricardo clenched his fists several times and secretly vowed revenge against Antonio. Somehow—Someway, victory would be his. He turned to the final page and found a ring tied with a single black ribbon. His eyes widened as he gazed at the Ring of Eternity. He knew time would unleash its powers once again, and he would be waiting. Rico took Elaina's hand and embraced his future, for nothing stood in his way now.

Hannah and Austin continued to grow old together and continue to possess their special gift. They continued to hold conversations without ever speaking a word. Sierra Rose now had a family of her own. Hannah and Austin enjoyed their grandchildren since the day of their birth. Austin left Hannah one cold winter night at the young age of 88. She felt like the biggest part of her died that night. She held his hand as he slipped further away from her, "I'll meet you on the other side," she whispered.

He smiled warmly, and then he was gone.

Austin had lived a good long life and Hannah knew that her frail fragile body would not hold on much longer, not without her soul mate. Hannah managed to hang on an additional five years. She was determined that Austin would live on in her memories and within her dreams. Each night she imagined him by her side holding her. Hannah awakened one night when she felt a brush against her cheek. She opened her eyes as Enrico knelt by her bedside.

"It is time to come home now," he whispered. He gazed at her, not as a frail old woman, but as the young vibrant woman, he could not live without. He extended his arms, "Come Savannah, it is time."

She thought it was a dream. *Can he really be here now?* He released her from her thoughts.

"Someone is waiting for you," he whispered.

She accepted his hand. He helped her out of bed and they walked into the light. As soon as they passed through, Hannah realized she was young again. She no longer felt agony over her broken heart, and her frail body functioned normally again as he led her up a grand staircase. Hannah saw Austin waiting for her on the other side, as she crested the final step.

Enrico stopped and brought Hannah to a halt. He gazed into her heavenly blue eyes, "My Sacred Vows prevail as your journey comes to an end, fulfilling final destinies…you are home," he whispered, and tenderly kissed her hand. He then placed her hand into Austin's and faded into the light.

Hannah and Austin had yet another joyous reunion. Enrico kept his promise and once again returned Hannah to Austin—for the last time. The pair would never separate again, for their souls in life, coma and even in death reunited with one another.

Printed in the United States
66567LVS00005B/121